PRAISE FOR

THE FIRST RULE OF TEN

"Awareness and adventure go hand-in-hand in this wow of a whodunnit. It's got plenty of surprising plot twists, but even better, it's rich with insight into the complexity of human relationships and being alive in this modern-day world. What could be better?"

— **Geneen Roth,** author of *Women, Food and God*

*"Talk about a 'perfect Ten!' Savvy, sharp, and spiritual, Tenzing Norbu is one of the most compelling detectives I've encountered on the page. And **The First Rule of Ten** is a great introduction—a complicated, involving story that combines cults, crime, and Buddhist teachings to great effect."*

— **Alison Gaylin,** Edgar-nominated author of *Hide Your Eyes, Heartless,* and *You Kill Me*

*"Now this is a detective for the 21st century! Who could resist a former Buddhist monk who lives by the dharma, drives a vintage yellow Mustang, eats five-star vegan PB&J's, and enjoys a close relationship with a sentient being named Tank—a blue Persian of a certain size? On the other hand, his relationships with beings of the human persuasion aren't nearly so smooth. Which is great for a P.I.—no one messes with Ten—but lousy for romance. Tenzing Norbu is wholly original and very, very real—a great addition to detective fiction. **The First Rule of Ten** has really got me hooked!"*

— **Julie Smith,** author of the Skip Langdon series

THE
FIRST RULE
OF

THE
FIRST RULE
OF

TEN

A TENZING NORBU MYSTERY

GAY HENDRICKS
AND
TINKER LINDSAY

VISIONS
HAY HOUSE, INC.
Carlsbad, California • New York City
London • Sydney • Johannesburg
Vancouver • Hong Kong • New Delhi

Published and distributed in the United States by: Hay House, Inc.:
www.hayhouse.com® • **Published and distributed in Australia by:**
Hay House Australia Pty. Ltd.: www.hayhouse.com.au • **Published
and distributed in the United Kingdom by:** Hay House UK, Ltd.:
www.hayhouse.co.uk • **Published and distributed in the Republic
of South Africa by:** Hay House SA (Pty), Ltd.: www.hayhouse.co.za
• **Distributed in Canada by:** Raincoast: www.raincoast.com • **Published in India by:** Hay House Publishers India: www.hayhouse.co.in

Cover design: Charles McStravick • *Interior design:* Pam Homan
Photo of Gay Hendricks: Mikki Willis
Photo of Tinker Lindsay: Cameron Keys

This is a work of fiction. The use of actual events or locales, and
persons living or deceased, is strictly for artistic/literary reasons only.

Library of Congress Cataloging-in-Publication Data

Hendricks, Gay.
  The first rule of ten / Gay Hendricks and Tinker Lindsay. -- 1st ed.
    p. cm.
  "A Tenzing Norbu Mystery."
  ISBN 978-1-4019-3776-8 (tradepaper : alk. paper)
  I. Lindsay, Tinker. II. Title.
  PS3608.E5296F57 2012
  813'.6--dc23

                                   2011039773

Tradepaper ISBN: 978-1-4019-3776-8
Digital ISBN: 978-1-4019-3777-5

15 14 13 12   5 4 3 2
1st edition, January 2012
2nd edition, March 2012

Printed in the United States of America

Lama Yeshe and Lama Lobsang
Dorje Yidam Monastery
Dharamshala, India

Venerable Brothers,

Last Friday night, I tasted one of life's
sweet little experiences.

Saturday, I got shot.

It makes me wonder if I have a low
tolerance for things going well in my world.

Or maybe I just need to be more mindful of
what's going on, both outside and in.

This may come as a surprise to you, but
I've decided to put some rules back into my
life—just not the scriptural kind I was so
good at rebelling against back when I lived
in the monastery. These are life-rules, drawn
from my own experience, regardless of whether
it's humbling, exhilarating, or painful.
Rule Number One is this: If you're open to
learning, you get your life-lessons delivered
as gently as the tickle of a feather. But if
you're defensive, if you stubbornly persist
in being right instead of learning the lesson
at hand, if you stop paying attention to
the tickles, the nudges, the clues—*boom!*
Sledgehammer. Or in this case, the mangled
slug of a .45 automatic.

The truth is, the pain caused by the bullet-
graze was insignificant compared to the deep
ache of uncertainty provoked by my brush with
death. I felt lost, swarmed by questions to
which I had no easy answers. But once I could

see a way forward, I actually started feeling grateful to Leon—the poor, misguided being who pulled the trigger.

I do regret how much I scared Bill. I'd never seen him look like that—drawn and pale, his eyes dark with fear. He told me when he heard the shot, found me on the floor, he thought I was done.

Turns out I was, just not in the way Bill meant.

You two know me best, so you know this is true: From the time I was a teenager, reading all those contraband detective novels by candlelight in our sleeping quarters, I never wanted to be anything but a modern incarnation of Sherlock Holmes. So when I made Detective five years ago, I thought I had my life all wrapped up, with a nice, pretty bow on top. But lately, the realities of working for the LAPD have been closing in on me. I can hardly breathe anymore.

Some cops are happy to spend the bulk of their time shuffling papers and testifying in court. They'd rather pass their days getting hammered by defense attorneys than roam around out in the big world, messing with actual criminals. Not me. I like the action. I spent enough years sitting cross-legged in confined spaces, eyes closed, sheltered from anything that might challenge reality. Or nonreality, for that matter.

No offense.

It's just that every minute in court, or chained to my desk, is a minute I'm not out putting bad people away, which last I heard was the whole point. The number of hours I spend on real police work has been declining steadily over the past couple of years, until these days when I'm lucky if I pull 15 hours a week outside.

Poor Bill's no stranger to my discontent. My partner's been putting up with a swelling stream of complaints about the paperwork, the politics, the endless bureaucratic hassles and mandatory regulations that are taking all the joy out of the job. I mean, monks deal with endless rules, too, but at least where you are, the goal is freedom from suffering. Not piling on more and more of it.

Once again in my life, something had to give. Once again, something has.

It's over. I'm no longer a cop.

Well, time to go. Tank is eyeing his empty food bowl with impressive concentration. I send my prayers and good wishes to you both, as always. Please give Kino my heartfelt congratulations on becoming Abbot. Tell him I am well. You can also tell my father. Should he ever ask.

Until next time,

9O

Ten

CHAPTER 1

I was just sitting down to a cold beer and hot corn soup, at the end of a long week, when my phone rang. I glanced at the number.

Great. *Her.* My stomach contracted, arming me for whatever barbs my ex-girlfriend Charlotte had in store this time. I tried to breathe a little flex into my gut. Good luck with that.

"Hello?" I said. "Charlotte?" I braced myself for the onslaught.

Then she surprised me.

"Ten? I'm getting married. I thought you'd want to know."

Charlotte, married. To someone else. A hot streak of jealousy sliced through me, which made no sense at all, considering I was the one who broke things off.

"Tenzing? Aren't you going to congratulate me? You owe me that, at least."

And there it was; the familiar "you owe me" card. It loosened up an avalanche of bad memories—the many ways I constantly infuriated her, the times she, in turn, disappointed me. Our last fight bloomed inside my brain like a bad seed. Prompted by her insistence that I had bought the wrong kind of lentil (I hadn't), the small spat quickly escalated, culminating in my yelling at Charlotte, in one of my finer expressions of loving-kindness, that I'd never liked the way she smelled. Since the day I met her.

She responded by swatting me with a dish towel, a sharp snap to the side of the head.

Honestly? I admired her for it. It woke me up to the hard truth that we were never going to be right in each other's eyes. And that it didn't have a thing to do with either of us. Not her. Not me. We were just a couple of warm bodies stepping into old, familiar roles, long established in the past, and sure to run us well into the future if we didn't do something to change the wiring. Two con artists conning each other, with the occasional great sex thrown in just to keep us good and confused.

That fight was the last time we saw each other.

I could sense Charlotte's edginess growing on the other end of the line as she geared up for one last dramatic blowout. The familiar tension bounced back and forth between us, looking for an ally.

My eyes drifted across the room to the big plate glass window framing the far wall. It was dark outside, but beyond that darkness lay the ocean, wide and expansive, mutable yet constant. I felt its spaciousness waiting out there. Just waiting for me to acknowledge it. I took a deep breath.

"Congratulations, Charlotte." I said. "I wish you both well."

I hung up gently. Then I just stood there, phone in hand, trying to digest this new chunk of information. I waited. After a moment, my insides shifted. The heaviness inside—that cold iron ball that had hardened around all the times we'd disappointed each other, pissed each other off—actually started to soften, to melt a little. Well, what do you know?

"Hey, Tank," I called out to my favorite feline, curled up on his cushion. He opened one eye. "Guess what? She-who-hates-cats is getting married."

Tank's tail flicked once. He was pleased. So was I. Relief and something bordering on glee flooded through me. Now and forever, there would always be a buffer, somebody else she could blame for everything being wrong with her life, before she got around to blaming me.

I strutted around my house for the rest of the evening, feeling pretty good about my existence on this fine planet.

The next day I got shot.

Here's how it went down. My partner Bill Bohannon and I were finishing up a quick lunch, steaming bowls of Pho at a Vietnamese place we like in Echo Park, before heading back to Robbery/Homicide. As I opened my fortune cookie—don't ask me why, but Angelenos demand fortune cookies from any Asian establishment, Chinese or not—the radio crackled to life: "Code three, four-one-five. Possible DV in progress." Headquarters was calling for any available patrol cars to investigate a Domestic Violence incident. The address was only a couple of blocks from the restaurant. I glanced down at my tiny strip of future: "Destino está pidiendo," it said. A Vietnamese fortune, written in Spanish. Only in Los Angeles. I turned it over.

"'Destiny is calling,'" I read to Bill. As if on cue, the radio crackled out a repeat of its call to action. "Let's go," I said.

Within minutes we skidded into the driveway of a dismal-looking little bungalow near Rampart, first on the scene. Ramshackle front steps led to a splintered porch boasting a couple of metal folding chairs so battered they were safe to leave outside, even in this neighborhood.

A siren wailed in the distance. I had a fleeting notion that we should wait for backup, but Bill was reaching for his door. That's all it took. I rolled out of mine and hit the ground without missing a stride.

I was sprinting toward the porch, Bill somewhere behind me, when he yelped out in pain. I glanced back. My partner was hopping up and down on one foot, swearing a blue streak. Bad time to twist an ankle.

Here's where things started heading south. And from there they careened even further, about as far south as things can go.

Loud shouts erupted from the house. I was caught between Bill's gimpy ankle and the fracas inside. My gut begged me to pause, but the adrenaline screamed, "Go!" The split second of indecision ended with the unmistakable report of gunshot, followed by a wailing female scream. I drew my revolver and ran to the screen door.

"Hot shot! Hot shot!" I heard Bill yell into the radio behind me. "Code ninety-nine."

I pressed my face against the thin mesh and peered inside. A man slouched on a sofa to my left, cradling a .45-caliber semiautomatic. He was around my age, maybe 30, lanky, Caucasian, with a scraggly beard and long, greasy hair. Pretty calm, considering. I followed his gaze across the room, where a second man was sprawled on his back on the floor, a ragged hole in his chest.

Not good.

A woman in her 20s, also lanky, also Caucasian, huddled in the corner, hand to her mouth. Her screams had subsided into a series of strangled, high-pitched yelps. I looked closer. One of her eyes was swollen shut, a purple and black protrusion under her brow.

Apparently I wasn't the only one with relationship issues.

Bill called out, "What's happening?"

"Stay put for a minute," I called back. "We've got a situation here."

"Ten, don't you dare even think about going ins—"

I stepped inside, vaguely aware that the swelling volume of siren wails indicated at least two squad cars en route, and getting close. Not much time to try to resolve this peaceably before it turned into a goat rodeo.

"What's your name?" I asked the guy, keeping my voice calm and friendly. He was lazily twirling the heavy automatic in his hand, like he was used to handling it. I saw it was a Springfield, an M1911. He wasn't pointing it at me, though, so I kept my Glock at my side. "Leon," he answered dreamily.

He canted his head in my direction. I checked out his pupils. Fully dilated. He was seriously stoned on something.

"What's yours?" he asked.

"Ten," I said.

"Say, what?" Leon said.

I inched over to the body. The guy wasn't moving, and his skin was the leached gray-green that signals zero life force. But I had to be sure. I squatted beside him and lightly pressed his neck, where there should have been the steady rhythm of pumping blood.

Nothing. He wasn't even circling the drain. Whoever he was, he appeared to be gone.

I sent off a quick, silent blessing: *Om mani padme hum. May you enjoy peace and joy in the afterlife and in all your future lives.* Reciting the mantra would hopefully plant the seed of liberation in him, sinner or saint.

I straightened up. "My name is Ten," I told Leon. "Like the number."

"Ten," Leon said. "Never heard that one before."

"Short for Tenzing."

"Never heard of that, either."

"There are lots of Tenzings where I come from," I said.

"Oh, yeah? Where's that?"

"Tibet, by way of India," I said.

"No shit," he said. Then, "I been to Iraq."

It was like I'd landed on some television talk show, only this show had a real live killer-host, who was playing with a loaded hand cannon.

I started moving closer to Leon, careful to keep my weapon at my side. I didn't want to turn this into a pissing contest. Or maybe I did. Tiny tingles of adrenaline started to dance in my bloodstream, the precursors to a full-on flood. My heart bumped faster against my ribcage. My senses sharpened. Delicious. A small voice inside whispered a warning—*Careful, Ten. You're playing with fire here. Disarm him, and wait for the others.*

I ignored it.

"Did you get that hardware in the military, Leon?"

He hefted the big pistol in his hand and looked at it with fondness. "Yeah. First time I've shot it since Fallujah."

"Nice piece," I said. "Right now, how about putting it down and let's talk some more?"

This got a hard laugh out of him.

"No disrespect," he said, "but I don't want to talk to you that bad, Mr. Ten. Tell you what I'm gonna do instead. I'm gonna make your job a little easier by confessing to this crime here."

He waved the muzzle toward the body on the floor. "See that piece of crap over there with the hole in his chest?"

I nodded. Took another baby step toward him.

"I shot him."

"You did, hunh?" Another step, nice and slow.

"Yep. . . . Should've done it years ago. Should've done it the first time he beat the living hell out of my little sister."

This provoked a fresh wail out of the woman in the corner.

"Shut the fuck up, Sis! I did you a favor," Leon snarled. She slid down the wall and wrapped her arms around herself. Leon fixed his reddened eyes back on me.

"So I, Leon Monroe Taylor, hereby confess to shooting that asshole over there, Jeremy Pitts. And let the record show I wish I'd offed him a long time ago." He blinked. "You got all that?"

"Yes, I got it, Leon. Now, how about putting the gun down?"

I was close now, maybe a yard away.

His face split into a wide grin. "Here's where I really save you some trouble."

He jammed the .45 up under his chin.

"Leon, no!" I lunged. The air exploded with a deafening roar, and what was left of Leon Monroe Taylor slumped sideways.

I felt a sharp sting on the left side of my head. Blood patterned the walls and floor. Leon's sister let out a muffled scream and kept screaming as the door crashed open. Two uniforms burst inside, Bill limping along behind them.

My ears were ringing hard from the explosion. My hands were shaking. I moved to the body to check for a pulse, but there was no carotid artery left to check. I bowed my head, and mentally sent off a second invocation on behalf of a second victim in as many minutes. Leon had just killed a man and then taken his own life. He would need all the help he could get negotiating his way through the *bardo*.

Bill pulled me away from the body. He pointed at my head and mouthed something.

"What?" I said. "I can't hear you." He flinched. I must have been yelling.

"You're bleeding," he threw back at me, though it came out gargled, like he was shouting underwater. He gestured to my head. "You. Were. Hit."

Roger that. I touched the side of my face. Sure enough, a thick rope of blood was streaming down my cheek and neck. I inched my fingers up and found the source, an inch-long, narrow wound traversing my left temple. That's the problem with scalp wounds. They're bleeders, shallow or deep. One of the cops pressed a wad of paper towels to the side of my head as a compress. The other one got on his radio and called for an ambulance. Bill took Leon's sister aside, both to comfort and to question.

All I could think was: *What a complete and utter cock-up. Two bodies, three victims, and a world of explaining to do to the higher-ups. Way to protect and serve, Tenzing.*

The side of my head began to throb. The adrenaline was already wearing off. Bill nudged me.

He jabbed at the floor with his finger, his expression grim. "Your lucky day."

I looked down. Bill called it right, as usual. A single spent slug was imbedded in the wood. It must have traveled through Leon and ricocheted off a metal joist, grazing my temple. A half inch closer and I'd be getting my oatmeal spoon-fed by a nurse for the next 40 years.

As it was, I got a ride to the ER, four stitches, and a tube of ointment.

I emerged from the hospital an hour or so later. I inhaled deeply. The outside air smelled piercingly sweet. Bill rolled up in his new minivan and I climbed in and buckled up, like a good boy. We sat in silence for a moment.

"So," I said.

"So," he replied. "I sprained my ankle and you got shot. Not our best day."

"I'm sorry, Bill," I said. "I messed up, didn't I?" Bill glanced over at me. After a moment, he clapped me on the knee.

"Nothing a cold draft beer won't fix," he said.

I know I'm supposed to practice nonattachment, but there are times the pull of an ice-cold pint of beer trumps the promise of a lifetime, maybe even two, of equanimity. I can attest that one of those times is right after somebody skins you with a speeding bullet. I've been shot at before, by people actually trying to kill me, but thankfully, they all missed. So it's ironic that my one actual bullet wound in the line of duty came from a guy who was only trying to shoot *himself.* Never mind, though. Never mind that it was only a ricochet bullet and a four-stitch flesh wound. I'd been hit—come *this* close to losing my "precious human form." My hands had stopped shaking, but my inner being hadn't, and while a long meditation might calm me down, right now a beer sounded better.

We parked at the nearest watering hole and walked, or limped, in Bill's case, into the cool of the semi-deserted bar. The barkeep set us up with two frosty glasses of ale on tap, and we paused for the Holy Moment of the First Sip. We took our swigs and sighed in unison as the spirit-reviving beverage gushed over our parched taste buds.

"Homework time," I said. "Anything we can learn from all that?"

"Here we go." Bill rolled his eyes, but the corners of his mouth twitched in amusement. After any kind of heat goes down, I like to think out loud, ask myself if there's anything useful I can learn from the situation. Call it an old habit from my monastery days. The goal is not to assign blame, but to glean any learning that will help me handle it better next time.

Bill humors me, especially when I'm buying.

"Here's one," he said. "How about, 'Wait for backup'?"

"*Touché.*" We each took another swallow. Bill said nothing as I sorted through the mix of reactions, giving them time to settle.

"There's nothing like getting shot to make you start asking the big questions," I finally said. "Even more so when you're sitting in the ER as someone stitches up your temple—which is, by the way, the most fragile portal to your brain. You tend to wonder, 'Why? What's the point? What's the real message here?'"

"And did you come up with anything?"

I focused on my glass, staring at the amber liquid.

"Yeah, I think I did. The way I see it, certain incidents are like cosmic alarm clocks, you know? They jolt us into awareness. 'Wake up!' they scream. 'The time is ripe for your job karma to change!' We ignore such moments at our peril."

Bill was silent.

"The truth is," I continued, "I've been ignoring too many mornings where I wake up filled with dread at the idea of going in to work. Wishing I had a cold, so I could call in sick. Taking unnecessary risks, once I got there. I've been pushing my luck, Bill, just like I used to do at the monastery. And today my luck almost ran out."

"I don't love where this conversation is heading," Bill said.

I met Bill's eyes.

"It's time for me to move on. Like the cookie says, destiny is calling."

"I don't get it, Ten. It makes no sense. You're already the best detective we've got and you're barely thirty years old."

"It's not about that, Bill. It's about the job moving in one direction and me moving in another."

Bill dropped his head. A wave of sadness passed between us. After a moment, he looked up.

"Okay, then, partner. Okay. Better to get out now before this work starts killing off your brain cells."

Regret laced his voice, and I realized it wasn't just about me leaving. It was about me leaving and him staying. Bill's put in almost 20 years on the job. A couple more years and his pension will kick in, big time. That's important, especially since the twins came along six months ago. Twenty years of trying, and he and Martha finally got lucky with the *in vitro*. Enter Maude and Lola. Enter crazy babyland and over-the-moon parents. Bill, a lifelong Dodgers fan, immediately outfitted the tiny newborns in blue Dodgers caps with MAUDE and LOLA emblazoned across the fronts. I'm surprised he didn't get them mitts.

My heart always twinges at the thought of those babies. The idea of parenthood does that to me, part longing, part terror. Mostly the latter.

Anyway, their family joy came with a price tag, just like everything else in this world. With each day that passed, I'd sensed the growing split in my partner between Bill-the-detective and Bill-the-dad. For months now, halfway through every shift, he'd started checking his wristwatch, as if already counting the minutes until he could get home. I don't blame him for wanting to be with his beautiful family. But I also can't help but notice he's never the first guy through the door into the field anymore, and always the first to volunteer for assignments that keep him around the office. Bill's heading for a desk job, and he knows it. He knows I know it, too, and it has cast a light pall over our partnership.

The truth is, I'd already lost my partner. My message came courtesy of a stray bullet, but maybe Bill's twisted ankle carried a message of its own.

I set down my beer and turned to face him. "I'm putting in my papers first thing next week. I'm done."

Bill held out his hand. I shook it.

"Congratulations," he said. "I still don't like it, but I think it's the right move."

"Thanks. I appreciate that," I said, and meant it. "Anyway, rumor has it they'll be promoting you to Detective Three before too long."

"Yeah. But you and I both know what that means. . . ." He trailed off, gloomily contemplating his desk-bound future.

I touched the bandage on my temple.

"Change is hard," I said. "But inevitable." I held up my glass. "To change."

"To change."

We clinked.

CHAPTER 2

"No way," the Captain said. He'd paged through my reports, finally reaching my letter of resignation.

"So you effed up, Norbu. Don't eff it up more by having a full-blown tantrum here."

I shifted awkwardly, trying not to look down at him. He hadn't asked me to take a seat yet, part of my reprimand.

"I just can't hack the other stuff anymore, sir."

The Captain snorted.

"Not good enough, Norbu. What are you, three years old?"

He pitched forward and glared hard at me across the mountain of files on his desk.

"You cannot quit, Ten," he said. "Not now. Oh, Christ, take a seat, will you? You're doing that monk-stare. Gives me the creeps."

I sat down and softened my eyes—I guess I'd been focusing so intently I was forgetting to blink.

"You could run this place someday. You could be sitting right here. You know that, right?"

I felt the walls press closer and my heart rate accelerate, which was unfortunate. Panic does not lend itself to tactful responses.

"That's exactly what I'm afraid of," I said.

The Captain's skin acquired the hue of red brick. Oops. Looks like I pushed the wrong button on someone's emotional dashboard. I scrambled to recover, pointing to the mound of paper on his desk.

"Look, sir, you've obviously found a way to handle the administrative part of this job. I just haven't."

His eyes flared hot with rage. *Not helping, Ten.*

"Goddamn it," he bellowed, banging his fist on a tee-tering pile of files. "You think I like this crap? Hell, no, I don't like it. But that's what it takes to keep the show run-ning, so I just by God deal with it."

I held up my hands in a vain attempt to slow his rant, but he'd already built up a major head of steam. Soon, he was unloading a familiar litany of protest: his victim-hood in the face of the demands of the mayor's office; the idiotic requests from the Police Commission; the fact that he can't even effing drop an effing eff-bomb any-more without somebody putting it on effing YouTube; the impossible budget constraints; the growing demands for personal and financial disclosure. All of us in the squad had heard variations on this particular theme dozens of times, another reason I wanted out. I sure as hell didn't aspire to be this guy in 20 years, sitting at my desk, bray-ing a daily aria to self-pity and resentment.

I relaxed, took a nice deep inhale and exhale, and tried to listen for any cracks in the wall of bombast, any clues to help my cause.

His complaint veered onto a slightly different track.

"And with this boneheaded governor's new auster-ity budget and his chickenshit solution to kick all the inmates back down to us, which means overcrowding, which means earlier releases, I'm looking at higher crime rates, escalating costs, and no effing fat to trim."

He paused to take a breath, and in that pause, I met his eyes briefly. Bored in. He squinted back: *What?* Then I saw him rewind a few lines. Actually hear himself. Start to do the math. I decided it was safe to help a little with the calculating. I moved my gaze to the window, to keep it casual.

"IA reviews. They're not cheap, are they?" I ventured.

He grunted. I took that as a sign to keep going.

"And I'd be on paid leave until they were done inves-tigating me? What's the average? I'm betting six months, at least?"

Another grunt.

"At the end of which, you and I both know you'd be reinstating a detective who is starting to hate his job, and is getting sloppy because of it. Taking unnecessary personal risks . . ."

I stopped there. Waited. Gave him all the space he needed. The Captain may be volatile, but he's also wily like a fox.

He took off his glasses and polished the lenses with his tie. Straightened a few stacks of papers. Leafed through my reports one more time. Then he picked up my letter of resignation and tore it into precise halves, then quarters. He dropped the pieces into the circular file under his desk. He stood up.

"Congratulations, Norbu. You are hereby officially laid off, due to the fact that we're probably looking at adding a minimum ten percent to our costs this year, and due to the other fact that your salary alone will keep at least two eager, fully committed patrol officers on the street where they're needed. It's a tough decision, but that's why I'm here."

I met his gaze. His eyes were steely. But his mouth allowed the ghost of a smile.

"I guess that means the state will have to pay me unemployment for a year, sir," I said.

His smile broadened.

"Bet your sweet monastic ass it does."

I cleared my cubicle, turned in my badge, gun, and security key card, and picked up my final paycheck. I took the elevator to the first floor, crossed the spacious lobby, and walked down the narrow hallway to exit my workplace one last time. I wanted to get out of there fast, to avoid all the explanations, all the prolonged good-byes. I checked my gut for any regrets.

I couldn't drum up much nostalgia for the police headquarters itself, impressive though it was. It had only been open for business 16 months. The windows gleamed, the helipad worked, and the tenth-floor rooftop patio, dubbed the stogie stage, was a boon to all the smokers. I found it ironic that smoking occurred right next to the memorial to our fallen brothers. I also found the whole place a bit sterile.

Unlike its predecessor, the Parker Center, the new headquarters had so far eluded an official moniker. Apparently in this era of political correctness, no one past or present passed muster as a namesake anymore. Despite that, the building quickly acquired the nickname "Death Star"—a nod to its monolithic mass, its angled, glassy face, and the sense that at any moment it might open its maw and zap you with a super-laser.

I stepped into the afternoon sunshine, letting my eyes adjust. I noticed the public "lawn" finally had some grass poking through. The entire site was originally earmarked to be a neighborhood park, but the powers-that-be decided it was a much more civic idea to spend over $400 million on a fancy new home for the brass. They did thoughtfully reserve one lone acre of sod for the public, but promptly tented it over for their annual fundraiser two months in, killing off any and all vegetation.

Late last month, I showed up at Second and Main to help local volunteers clear weeds, trim overgrown feather grass, and bag up heaps of the usual municipal flotsam and jetsam, from Starbucks cups to discarded needles. Personally, I thought it was pretty ballsy of my superiors to take over land that was designated as a downtown community park, build their new headquarters, then ask that same community to landscape the remaining meager patch of neglected soil—you know, now that the LAPD couldn't afford the upkeep.

No, I wouldn't miss the Death Star.

I would miss the people, though. I'm an isolator by nature, so the structure of a job, with its enforced social interaction, helped keep me a part of the human race. I'd miss my fellow detectives. Most of all, I'd miss working with Bill.

On cue, my hip pocket buzzed. I didn't even have to check the screen of my cell phone. This kind of thing happens to me all the time.

"Hey, Bill."

"Hey, Ten. The Edison. Seventeen hundred hours. We're holding a happy hour wake."

"Who's it for?"

"You."

I was flattered. The Edison was our high-end after-hours haunt, saved for special occasions. Then again, it was Wednesday, meaning payday, so everyone was feeling flush. I decided to leave my Mustang in the lot and walk. I'd come back for it later. Save on parking, now that I was unemployed.

Tucked in an alley halfway between the Death Star and Disney Hall, the Edison was an easy stroll. I enjoyed stretching my legs. We'd had a lot of rain and the air felt prewashed, and crisper than usual. I ducked into the little corridor off Second Street, between Main and Spring, and was waved right inside. In a few hours, the line would stretch around the block.

I headed down the steep flight of stairs, enjoying the sensation of stepping back in time. A century ago, the Edison was a glorified boiler room, a municipal power plant buried in the bowels of downtown. Now, reincarnated as a blend of art deco, speakeasy elegance, and exposed industrial pipes and girders, it generated a different kind of power, the power of "it," of the place to be. Detectives love coming here. It's close, and it's classy. The dress code—no flip-flops, torn jeans, or muscle tees—means no riffraff. And the 35¢ charge for the first happy hour cocktail, a prohibition drink at prohibition prices, makes it seem like a bargain.

The trick, of course, is to stop at one.

I headed for the Generator Lounge. Cops tend to congregate there because it has its own exit and is wedged into a back corner, flanked by two walls facing outward. We love to face out. We're like the Mafia, that way.

As my eyes adjusted, I found Bill and six or seven fellow detectives from Robbery/Homicide, most of them lifers, already digging into a platter of hot-and-sour shoestring fries. Bill handed me a stein of ale.

"This one's on me," he said. "Now you owe me big time."

"Right. Now I owe you thirty-five cents."

Sipping, I tasted honey, apricots, and a kiss of hops. Chimay White, one of my favorites.

"Bless you," I said to Bill. "And bless those industrious Belgian Trappist monks."

Marty, who came up with me at the Academy, clinked on his glass with a knife to get everyone's attention.

"To Hizzoner Tenzing Norbu," he said. "First to get in, first to get out." His face was a little ruddy. He was already into the $12 second drink.

He gave an exaggerated bow.

"Damn, Ten, when you showed up for training, bald as a cue ball and shyer than spit, I thought, 'Hallelujah, this weirdo's going to anchor the curve, he's going to make me look goo-ood.'"

He turned to the group.

"For the life of me, I couldn't figure out how he kept kicking my butt so bad, mine and everyone else's. He was a Buddhist monk, for Chrissake. I actually considered taking a break from the horizontal mambo myself, just to level the playing field."

"Celibacy is overrated," I said.

A volley of bad bedroom jokes and raunchy stories followed, all of which I'd heard a thousand times. My mind drifted to those early days, the intensive six months of training, cruising the streets as a newbie patrol officer, then moving up the ranks until I achieved Detective I, then II. I could still recall the heady sense of anticipation back then, the excitement that propelled me into each morning. Like being in love.

A shout of welcome interrupted my reverie. A long-limbed redhead, wearing a diaphanous gown, sparkling green wings, and not much else, rolled a wooden cart into our midst. It held a glittering array of neon elixirs in individual glass bottles.

When Prince Siddhartha, the Buddha-to-be, sat in deep meditation under the Bodhi Tree, the demonic shape-shifter Mara appeared in the form of seductive women to test his mettle. Here at the Edison, temptation came in the form of the Absinthe Fairy.

"Libations, anyone?" she crooned. "You get to keep the bottle."

Marty was all over her like a rash. He pulled out a roll of bills, happy to pay top dollar for his next round of distilled relief.

I looked over at my ex-partner. Bill caught me catching him peeking at his watch. He looked a little sheepish, but I tipped my chin toward the exit. I'd already reached my limit of small talk. We said our good-byes and aimed for the door.

"Hey, Ten!"

I turned. Marty again. His cheeks were flushed from the absinthe. "So what's next?"

"Not sure," I said, playing for time. I was afraid actually voicing my lifelong aspiration, inspired by long, late nights with Arthur Conan Doyle, might cause it to evaporate into thin air. "But I'm thinking, maybe, private investigation"

With that, one of the older detectives launched into some sort of musical chant, a series of *Dunh, dunh, dunh, dunh*'s. The others joined in. I looked at Bill helplessly.

"It's the theme song from an old television series, *Magnum, P.I.,*" he said. "Don't worry about it."

"Grow a mustache," I heard Marty shout after me as we headed out the door, followed by hoots of laughter.

Bill walked me to my car.

"So," he said.

"So."

"I got you something."

Bill fished around his pockets and pulled out a small evidence bag. He opened it and tipped the contents into the palm of my hand.

"Think of it as a little reminder to look before you leap."

I stared down at the misshapen slug. My lucky charm.

"Thanks," I said. "Now I owe you another ten cents."

"Watch your back out there," Bill said.

I put the bullet in my pocket. I was certainly planning to try.

CHAPTER 3

Home. Free.

I skated the dry mop across my floor, enjoying the light grip of fingers on handle, of bare feet on smooth, hard wood. The back-and-forth, back-and-forth rhythm transported me to predawn in Dharamshala, performing my morning job of sweeping the meditation hall before the swarm of lamas descended on it. It was my favorite time of day, a few moments to be alone with my thoughts before the mandatory schedule kicked in, the prayers, the practices, the painstaking rituals and endless dry debates. The constant worry that I was breaking yet another obscure rule by, say, scratching my nose before noon, or tying my robe under the wrong armpit when a woman was passing by on the road.

People assume life in a monastery is filled with blissful, solitary contemplation. People assume wrong.

I paused, breathed in the morning air, the slight tang of eucalyptus and ocean salt I have come to know as the smell of contentment. Somehow, this little getaway in Topanga Canyon has become my place of refuge.

Up until a few years ago, the concept of "home" eluded me. It conjured up a jumble of pictures and feelings, a contradictory collage of resistance and longing—the monastery in Dharamshala; the small, dark house in Paris where I'd lived with my mother, Valerie (as she insisted I call her), until her untimely death; and some nameless, unsettled craving for a place just out of reach. Nowhere felt right.

Maybe that's a good thing. Now that I am here, I know enough to really savor and appreciate it.

I ran the mop under my floor-to-ceiling bookcase, over-flowing with all the books I'd devoured since I moved here—I'd had a lot of catching up to do: European and American history; Eastern and Western philosophy; William Shakespeare; Stephen Hawking; illustrated guides to local plants and trees; how-to books on subjects ranging from vintage cars to long-term relationships (much more mysterious); even an obscure but fascinating political tome by Kautilya, ancient adviser to a King of India. The top two shelves were stuffed with detective novels, and the first book, on the first row, presiding over all like a wise elder, stood my beloved, tattered *Complete Works of Arthur Conan Doyle*.

I set my mop aside and scanned the rest of my little cottage—the simple, elegant Japanese lines; the clean white walls and dark burnished hardwood floors; the big deck I added, overlooking the ocean; the tiny kitchen bathed in morning sunlight. Each piece evoked a fresh swell of gratitude, of *Yes, I belong here.* My place was small, about 1,200 square feet, but the interior space was designed so cleverly that I never really had the sense of being cramped. I sent a silent thank-you to my former landlord Zimmy, his wife, Haruka, and even the rock-star lifestyle that led him into rehab and me into renting, and eventually buying, this house.

Poor Zimmy. He built this place made-to-order for his bride, and then the hits stopped coming and the wife started roaming. She soon left him for greener pastures, a bass player no less, the ultimate low blow. Zimmy moved out for a long stint in a recovery facility, and I moved in. A year later Zimmy was a little cleaner, and I was a little wealthier.

I added Valerie to my gratitude list, for gifting me enough inheritance to use as a down payment. Zimmy had no desire to come back to Topanga Canyon, and I never wanted to leave. He took the money and moved to a pear farm in Oregon. Last I heard he was clean, sober, and happy, living a new life with a new woman.

Like the Buddha says, the presence of change is the only constant. Understand that, and you've got a shot at serenity. I was glad the cycle of change had brought me to this particular place.

Might as well thank the Buddha, too.

A warm mass of fur started doing circle-eights between my legs.

"Hey, Tank. You like having me home, don't you?"

I reached down to tickle him under his chin, and he stalked away, tail high. Like all cats, Tank prefers affection on his own terms. Like someone else I know.

I watched him settle happily on the hearth to contemplate his feline existence. The ultimate seal of approval for this place came from Tank. The first time I set him down inside, 18 pounds of Persian Blue rolled onto its back and stuck all four paws in the air. His way of saying, "This is it. This is the one." And what Tank wants, Tank gets.

That was right after Tank landed on my doorstep, or deck, to be more accurate, about five years ago. I had just made Detective I. My new partner, Bill, and I were sitting outside, watching the sky darken from pale blue to azure, when a loud *thunk!* announced the arrival of a heavy animal right behind my chair. I jumped to my feet, expecting a raccoon. Instead, I found a big, make that huge, cat, his blue-gray fur matted, his green eyes glowing.

"It's a cat!" I crouched down.

"That's not a cat. That's a tank," Bill said.

"Hey, there, Tank." I wriggled my fingers. He walked right over and leaned into me, rubbing his head against my knee as he emitted a deep drone of contentment.

The next day, I posted fliers all over the canyon. I even placed a notice in the *Topanga Messenger*, but nobody surfaced to claim Tank, once he'd claimed me. You've probably heard the old joke: dogs have owners, cats have staff. I took pleasure in being Tank's butler, chef, and valet. His main job was to hang out near me and purr. It was a good deal all around.

I replenished his water bowl and padded into my meditation room, a tiny alcove screened off from the living area, for a little contemplation time of my own.

I set out my meditation cushion and moved to the low makeshift table at one end. The base was a small, beat-up suitcase, the same one I was clutching as I departed the monastery over ten years ago, released from my monastic life, heading to Los Angeles to work at the dharma center. Excited. Scared. Feeling as if I no longer had a place to stand, like I had no roots anywhere.

On top of the suitcase I had placed two reclaimed redwood planks, leftovers from the deck construction. Then I draped the whole thing with the maroon robe that had marked my time as a lama.

Old and new. Past and present. Before and after. Monk and cop.

And now?

I eyed the small stone Buddha, the centerpiece of my table, for answers. He was silent, as always. He prefers to make me work for my own insights. Above him hung my painted silk *thangka*—a parting gift from Yeshe and Lobsang. It depicts *Samsara*, the "Wheel of Life," or as my tradition prefers to remind us, the "Wheel of Deluded Existence." Lobsang's smile was wry as he handed me the portable scroll; "Think of this as your mirror, my friend." I knew what he was saying. I might be entering an exciting new world full of personal freedom, but freedom always comes wrapped in its own set of challenges. As long as my actions remained dominated by anger, ignorance, or pride, I'd stay trapped in illusion, spinning in an endless cycle of suffering.

I let my eyes rest on the *thangka*. The jewel-colored images were rich and complex, a bold mix of insight and ignorance—animals, deities, fanged demons, compassionate Buddhas, and even two skeletons, tucked in a corner, distracting themselves from the inevitability of death with a merry dance. In all, a perfect visual rendition of what goes on between my ears most of the time.

I lightly touched the smattering of objects scattered like accidental offerings around my stone Buddha. A feather from a red-tailed hawk . . . a bright piece of coral . . . a dried sprig of wild lavender—small souvenirs from past adventures.

I placed the slug, a darker talisman, next to them.

I began my sitting meditation.

Before I settled into an awareness of my body, I sent out a wish for safety and happiness to Yeshe and Lobsang. Perhaps they, too, were sitting, far across the world in India. More likely, they were already in bed. I smiled, picturing their reactions when they read my latest letter, the one I wrote last night. I'd started this pen pal tradition when I was just a boy, shuttling back and forth between father and mother, Dharamshala and Paris, my first notes scarcely more than the word *hello*. They were my link between worlds, a way of touching my only consistent emotional anchors. Something about the act of writing Yeshe and Lobsang steadied me, and I'd never broken the habit.

Reading my latest news, Lobsang would no doubt scowl a little, sure that I was once again displaying too much obedience to my flighty mind. "Always unsettled, like a hummingbird," he used to scold. Yeshe? His only wish would be that this change continue to deepen my understanding of the Dharma, of the way things are.

I closed my eyes and let the different parts of my body relax. My eyelids, jaw, neck, and shoulders. I let my attention circle the faint throb of pain in my temple. Moved past my chest and belly, to my thighs, feet, hands. Peace and spaciousness spread through my limbs like thick honey.

I winced, stabbed by a familiar anxiety. *What if I fail? What if I am making a huge mistake? What if my father is right about me, that I am too lazy and unfocused to ever amount to anything?*

I surrounded the thoughts with affection and let them float away.

Brought my attention back to the rise and fall of my breath.

I gave myself six months. A lot can happen in six months, right?

As it turned out, a lot can happen in 24 hours.

CHAPTER 4

"Hey, boss. Any luck?" I heard from outside my kitchen window, where Mike was fiddling with my newly installed data line.

I clicked the connection icon on my computer screen, one more time. Nothing.

"Nothing!" I called.

"Well, scroty-balls to that!"

As usual, Mike was an endless source of new expressions.

He was soon at my side. His fingers flew across my keyboard. Waves of incomprehensible numbers and symbols appeared and dissolved on the screen. He surfed through the data, nodding to himself and mumbling. He sat back. I could see him mentally dialing down the level of difficulty, so a primitive IQ like mine could understand his explanation.

"Your computer's too old," he said. "I could wave a dead chicken over it, but it will never, ever hold a high-speed connection."

"So what do I do?"

"I suggest you send this up north. Silicon Valley."

"Silicon Valley?"

"Yeah. They're opening a computer museum up there. They can put yours on display, next to the abacus."

I elbowed him, right in his bony rib cage.

Mike Koenigs was only 6 years younger than me, but it might as well have been 60. He was raised on data like I was on chants. When he was a little kid, he used to breathe on the school bus window and then trace algorithms on the foggy glass.

Mike was skinny as a rail, with a thatch of black curly hair and a Van Dyke beard of which he was overly proud. His workday, like a vampire's, started at sundown, and he had the chalky complexion to prove it. He pedal-buzzed around on his eROCKIT, an imported electric hybrid motorbike, knees jutting from both sides. He was gangly, awkward, and tongue-tied around most people, but a flat-out genius when it came to computers.

Mike and I got acquainted the hard way, when I arrested him on a cyber-hacking beef. He'd compromised the database of his own bank, and the Glendale branch of the Bank of America was not happy about it. He said his intent was not malicious, unless you call exacting revenge for bad customer service malicious—some might call it instant karma. In any case, he was so ticked off at their inability to correct a computing error that left his balance several hundred dollars short, and their insistence that it was his own miscalculation, that he hacked into the bank's system and transferred the exact amount in dispute from the bank manager's account to his own. The cyber-prank resulted in a major panic for the bank, and an arrest for Mike. I was the one who persuaded the DA not to try him as an adult.

Mike was 17 at the time, just an overgrown adolescent wiseass, but I could see he was a burgeoning genius. He had the talent. He was still looking for the right stage on which to perform. I kept an eye on him in Juvenile Hall and encouraged him to use the time to get a degree in programming. On the day of his release, I took him out for a cup of coffee.

"You've got two doors in front of you," I said. "Behind one is a pot of gold. Behind the other, a permanent bed at the Gray Bar Motel. Anybody as smart as you is going to either get very rich or spend the rest of his life dodging the law. Pick one."

Fortunately, he chose right. He was now earning over $150,000 a year as a security consultant—way more than me, by the way—making sure bank systems were hack-proof against guys like him. He was also able to make my life as a detective much easier.

When Sherlock Holmes plied his trade, he and Watson often ventured out into the "thick, choking" London fog, as Conan Doyle described the dank atmosphere caused by the soft, bituminous coal burned during that time. I was filled with longing as I devoured those dog-eared paper-backs night after night, in my room at the monastery in Dharamshala, tracing their patient footwork through the cobbled London streets. Even the smoky miasma they inhaled seemed romantic. I prayed for the chance to rattle around an acrid city myself one day, collecting evidence.

Okay, so cruising in a black-and-white during 78-degree sunny winter days isn't exactly the same thing, but that's the point; nothing ever stays the same. Much has altered since Sherlock's time, and the biggest transfor-mation is in how we do our detective work.

Exit cobblestones. Enter the Internet.

Sherlock might well have scorned such an instanta-neous tool, dismissed it as lazy, but smart detectives now-adays, even the ones who work for the LAPD, make sure they're on good terms with at least one computer jockey. In my case, whenever I needed my e-mail fixed, or Inter-net access installed, or a little discreet hacking of my own done, I had Mike on my speed dial.

I guess you could say he was my own private Dr. Watson.

"Earth to Ten. Earth to Ten. Come in, please."

I left Sherlock's world and reentered the technical challenges of my own.

I said, "So what you're saying is, that fat, expensive data line I just installed is useless unless I upgrade."

"Maybe not. Toss me your text buggy."

"My . . . ?"

"Your cell phone, boss."

I handed it over.

He looked at it in disbelief. Handed it back.

"Pleistocene-era, my man. And fugly to boot."

As I opened my mouth to protest, I heard the unmistakable choppy stutter of an old Volkswagen wheezing up the gravel hill that leads to my driveway.

Two visitors in one day. Unheard of.

Mike and I moved to the kitchen window. A rusted Volkswagen Beetle—the original model, the one you could fix at home, blindfolded—surged into my driveway, coughed once, and died. After a moment, the door creaked open and long, California-girl legs unfolded a lean body from the driver's seat. She rolled her shoulders a few times, and stretched. As she turned to look at the house, her face was illuminated in the afternoon light. She was older than I'd first thought, already in her 40s. Her thick blond hair, threaded here and there with silver, was plaited into a long braid down her back. Her face and arms were tanned—the tawny color of sage honey.

"Time warp. What a trip. She's straight off of Yasgur's Farm," Mike said.

"Who's Yasgur?"

Mike shot me one of his "Are you joking?" looks.

"Yasgur's Farm. Woodstock? 1969? Peace, love, and acid? Boss, you have some serious gaps in your cultural literacy."

Woodstock I had heard of. Missing that event was one of Valerie's deepest regrets, or so she'd often informed me after several glasses of wine. It sat at the top of a long list of resentments she'd held against her estranged parents until the day she died.

This lady did appear to have a strong vintage-hippie thing going on. Her yellow and brown paisley dress was long, loose, and flowing. She had a crocheted shawl around her shoulders, and her handbag was of Indian cotton embroidered with tiny mirrors that winked in the late afternoon sun.

"Man," Mike said. "That lady's so outdated she's back in."

She spotted us watching from the window, and waved.

"I'm going to let you handle this one," Mike said. "I'll keep examining the entrails here." He went back to work on my computer.

I stepped outside and waved back. She walked right over and offered her hand. I caught a faint whiff of stale incense.

"My name's Barbara Maxey," she said, her voice pleasant. Her palm was rough and dry, like she did a lot of outside work.

"Tenzing, Tenzing Norbu."

"You're a long way from Tibet."

That was interesting. Most people I met had no idea that Tenzing was a common Tibetan name.

She gestured toward the house. "I'm guessing Zimmy Backus doesn't live here anymore."

"Not for a couple of years," I said.

"Is he . . .?" Her face creased with anxiety.

"No, no, he's fine, as far as I know."

She looked relieved.

"I used to be married to Zimmy," she said, "but I was part of the living-out-of-a-van era. B.S., we called it back then. Before Success."

"No kidding, you were married to Zimmy?"

"Wife number one. The one before the Japanese wife. I never lived up here." She took in the view, and a wisp of regret passed over her features. "It's beautiful. A beautiful place to be."

I waited. After a moment, she half smiled at me. I was oddly touched.

"They still together?" she asked.

I told her about the bass player, and she winced at the indignity of it.

"Zimmy and I hooked up as drug buddies first, before we made it official. We never had much of a marriage. We went through a major mountain of cocaine before we split up. Four years of haze and hell is what it was, and I was the one keeping the engine stoked with coke."

I'd only known this woman for 30 seconds and we were already deep into her marital and pharmacological history. Usually that kind of instant confession turns me off, but there was something endearing about Barbara's candor, an underlying sadness that kept her confession from seeming in any way self-serving, a ploy to arouse sympathy. I found myself wanting to protect her.

I told her I'd bought the house from Zimmy, and gave her a quick synopsis of Zimmy's life since.

"Pear farm?" She shook her head. "That must be some different version of Zimmy than the one I knew."

"I think rehab really worked for him."

"I'm glad to hear it," she said. "I had to join a cult to get clean. And then the cult ended up being worse than the dope. I mean, it only took six weeks to get off coke, but ten years to escape that freaking place."

"How long have you been out?"

She gave me a wide, full smile, and I saw the stunning young woman she must have been before drugs and disappointment had their way with her.

"Since yesterday."

How bizarre was that? Today was my first real day of freedom, and hers, too. I was intrigued. Why had the universe arranged for us to meet on such a hopeful day for both of us? It seemed auspicious, and my heart perked up at the possibilities.

Barbara gestured at my house. "That's why I came here. This house is the only place I thought I might find somebody I know. I have nowhere else to go. The group I was in, they didn't allow any communication with anybody from our past. No phones, no letters, nothing."

Nowhere to go. That feeling, I understood.

"What about your family?"

She shrugged. "No family. Just me."

I understood that, too.

"Where did you get the car?" I asked.

She ducked her head. "Stole it," she said. "It belonged to them."

"The cult?"

She nodded sheepishly. "But I figured I had something coming to me, with all the crap I put up with from them."

She scuffed at the dirt. She was wearing old work boots under her dress, an oddly attractive combination of masculine and feminine. It occurred to me she might like to come inside. Have a cup of tea.

"When's the last time you talked to Zimmy?" she asked.

"Maybe a year and a half ago," I said.

"Did he say anything about his royalties?"

A sour gorge of disappointment rose in my throat. She was angling for something after all. My heart snapped shut.

"Zimmy and I never talked about that kind of thing," I said, my voice cool. I glanced at the house. "Listen, I need to get back to work. Is there anything else I can do for you?"

"I think something bad may be going on. I need to warn Zimmy. I want to make sure he stays safe. I still care about him."

I didn't believe a word of it.

"Tenzing, do you have a phone number for him?"

"I'm sorry, but I haven't talked to Zimmy for almost two years. The last number I had is from rehab days. All I know is he lives on a pear farm, like I said. With his *new* family."

She finally caught the change in tone. She looked at me curiously, but said nothing.

"Sorry. I can't help you," I said. "Have you tried his old record label?"

Her eyes flashed with anger. "That's part of the problem," she muttered, crossing her arms protectively. She didn't elaborate.

I said nothing.

Then her whole body sagged, as if the past 24 hours had finally caught up to her. Forlorn, is how she looked. Forlorn, and far away. I tried to summon up some compassion for her, but I had nothing tangible to offer—I was feeling kind of forlorn myself. Empty, and not in the good Buddhist sense of open and spacious, but devoid of feeling. So I told myself she'd figure it out on her own.

She straightened up and met my eyes. "Thanks for your time. Listen, the starter on the car is shot. Can you help me give it a shove down the hill?"

I got Mike. With Barbara at the wheel, we leaned our shoulders into it and soon the Beetle was out the gravel driveway and rolling downhill. Barbara popped the clutch, and the engine clattered to life. Her hand fluttered one small wave out the window of the battered old car. Mike and I watched her chuff away, until she disappeared.

"What was that about?" he said.

"Nothing. She's looking to get rich off her ex—my former landlord Zimmy Backus. I'd love to call Zimmy and warn him, but I have no idea where he is anymore."

We walked inside.

"So here's the deal," Mike said. He pulled out his phone and his fingers started dancing. Postage-stamp-sized web pages swelled and shrank until he found the one he wanted. "Setting up a home office that actually functions will cost you at least three grand in new equipment. But you also have at least three cell-phone upgrades coming to you, so I'll start working on that right away. Meanwhile, you're going to have to do your gumshoe footwork the hard way. By foot."

"Or I can call you."

"Or you can call me." Mike mounted his electronic pedal-bike, a flamingo perched on a two-wheeler. Got to love the guy.

"Mike?"

He turned.

"Thanks."

"*No problema.* Hey, you want me to find this Backus dude's whereabouts? I do love me a challenge."

"Be my guest," I said.

I walked back in the house and fixed myself a pot of green tea. I sat on the deck and sipped. The day darkened into night. Barbara Maxey, she of the blond braid, callused hands, and wide sunflower smile, floated up. I dismissed her. Nothing auspicious about it. Just another ship, passing in the night.

When I'm wrong, I am so wrong.

Chapter 5

"No way," I said into the phone.

"Come on, Ten. Just a nice, relaxed dinner with the family."

"I know Martha almost as well as you do, Bill. There is no such thing as relaxed where I'm involved. Who's she got lined up this time?"

Bill said nothing. I returned the favor. When it comes to playing silent chicken, I have much more patience.

I didn't have long to wait.

"Fine," Bill snapped. "Her younger sister Julie's in town. Half-sister, technically. She's an amazing cook, Tenzing. The real deal. A professional chef. Good-looking, too."

"I don't care if she's the radiant goddess Tara incarnate. I'm not interested."

For the past six months, since she quit her job to have and raise the twins, Martha has been on a one-woman tear to fix me up with a new girlfriend. I finally caught on after the third "accidental" drop-in of an available female right around the first course of yet another supposedly relaxed family dinner.

Bill sighed.

"I'll be sure Martha makes it clear you aren't looking for a mate. Anyway, Julie's almost as gun-shy as you. She's coming off a disastrous breakup with a crazy sommelier. You don't want to know."

"No, I don't."

"Come for dinner, Ten. Martha misses you. Hell, another day or two, and I may even start to miss you. Anyway, you haven't seen the girls in months."

I heard the crunch of tires turning into my driveway. This hideaway home of mine was becoming a regular Greyhound bus station.

"I'll call you back," I said.

I crossed to the window. A black-and-white pulled up, followed by a dusty sedan so nondescript I immediately made it as an unmarked police vehicle.

I recognized the local cop the minute he clambered out of the car and hitched up his pants. He was middle-aged, built like a cement wall, with a permanent look of disappointment etched into his features. I'd seen him around. His main beat seemed to be traffic citations, handing out greenies to entitled yuppies making illegal U-turns around town.

Hey, I'd be disappointed, too. A traffic beat isn't exactly the pinnacle of police work.

I didn't recognize the plainclothes detective. He was bone-thin, with a hawk face. His suit was in serious need of a visit to the dry cleaners.

They ambled toward my back door.

I tucked my T-shirt into my jeans. Pulled it out again. Smoothed my hair. Noted the flicker of nerves in my chest.

Remarkable. I'd only been a civilian for a few days, but apparently that's all it took to cross the invisible boundary separating the rest of the world from law enforcement. I was no longer a member of that exclusive club. I wasn't sure I liked the feeling.

They clomped up the back steps and rapped on the door. I opened it and extended my hand.

"Ten Norbu."

Hawk Face gripped hard. "Detective Terry Tatum," he said. "This is Officer Morris."

Morris's handshake was damp and halfhearted. I refrained from wiping my palm on my jeans.

"I've seen you around town," I said to Morris. "What's up?"

Tatum stepped in before Morris could reply. Interesting. Must be two jurisdictions.

"We're hoping you can help us with an investigation," Tatum said. "But first, I guess congratulations are in order. I hear you just put in your papers."

"Word gets around fast. What division are you in?"

"Sheriff's Department. Fifteen years on the job."

"My sympathies," I said, which elicited a tiny, tight smile from him. There's no love lost between the LAPD and County.

I gestured toward the kitchen table. They sat.

"Want a cup of coffee?" Dumb question. They were cops. Of course they wanted coffee.

I busied myself setting out two mugs, filling them with the strong Arabian brew left over from breakfast and stored in a carafe. I tend to make a lot of coffee. I don't always drink it all, but I like knowing it's there. As I set down the mugs, I mentally ran through my cold cases, trying to work out what brought them to my house.

I came up blank.

"So, what's the investigation?"

Tatum and Morris exchanged glances.

Tatum again spoke first. "There was a woman in a beat-up Volkswagen seen coming up your road yesterday. One of your neighbors thought she might have turned into your driveway."

"Barbara Maxey," I said. "She was looking for her ex-husband, Zimmy Backus."

I gave them the quick sketch of my brief interaction with her, leaving out my little *frisson* of attraction.

Morris scribbled in a small notebook. His writing was spiky and crabbed. It looked disappointed, too.

"This about the car?" I asked. Stealing a rusted VW didn't usually warrant a house call by two cops from two different departments, but you never know.

Detective Tatum's face narrowed. "What about the car?"

"It's hot. She stole it. From the cult, she said."

"That explains the expired plates," Morris put in, and made another note.

Tatum just shook his head. "No. We're definitely not here about the car."

"What did she do, then?" Car theft aside, she didn't strike me as felon material.

"She didn't do anything," Tatum said. "She got it done to her."

A thin spear of dread drilled downward from my heart to my belly. I swiveled in my chair to look out the window. *I think something bad may be going on.* I took a deep breath. Turned back to Tatum. He was eyeing me closely.

"What happened?" I asked.

Tatum opened his mouth. Then closed it. One more silent exchange with Morris. I knew this look too well—Bill and I had shared it many a time when questioned by a well-intentioned citizen. I was the civilian now. Kicked out of the tribe, maybe for good.

Well, I would have to create my own tribe, then.

"We've got her on a slab downtown," Morris said. "We need somebody to I.D. the body. She's got no next-of-kin as far as we can tell, so that leaves you."

I have nowhere else to go.

I stood up.

"I'll meet you there."

I headed south down Topanga Canyon, pulling a left on Pacific Coast Highway. Usually I loved to take the Mustang through her paces, but I was too distracted to enjoy the drive. I hugged the coast, glancing once or twice at the ocean to my right. It was dark and choppy today, like my mood. I wondered about Barbara's connection to Zimmy, her concern about his royalties. I had been so quick to dismiss her fears. Too quick by far.

I continued onto the 10. It was smooth sailing for about nine miles, until I ran into the inevitable clog of cars that meant downtown was close. I zigged onto the 110 toward Pasadena, zagged onto the 5 South, merged onto the 101, and took the Mission Road exit. Driving in L.A. was like negotiating a labyrinth. It took me years to learn my way around.

I entered Boyle Heights, land of the gang, home of the disenfranchised. Last count, it was over 90 percent Latino, and who could blame them? Their forefathers were victims of restrictive covenants that limited land ownership throughout

L.A. to only the whitest of lily-whites. South Central and Boyle Heights were the exceptions. Now these two neighborhoods marked their territories with spray cans and bullets.

I pulled into the County Coroner's entrance and parked in an open slot in front of the emphatic "Visitors Only!" sign. That was me, now. A visitor only.

Ahead of me loomed an ornate confection of brick and cement that seemed better suited to an art academy than its singular, grim purpose. Eight hundred bodies passed through the County Coroner's building every month—anyone whose death was sudden, unnatural, or suspicious in any way. Anyone not under the care of a doctor. Anyone who had fallen off the map. *I have nowhere else to go.*

I slowly ascended the stone steps, dreading the job ahead. The last time I came here, it was to buy a beach towel—among other distinguishing features, this was the only Coroner's office in the country with its own gift shop. Skeletons in the Closet stocked an array of morbid but amusing knickknacks, from skull business-card holders to numerous items decorated with the ominous traced outline of a fallen homicide victim. Some of the proceeds raised money to educate kids about drunk driving; though it seemed to me a tour of the morgue after a bad pile-up might serve just as well. Whatever. At the time, I'd been invited to a retirement party for a fellow cop who was taking his pension and hightailing it to Hawaii. The Body Outline Beach Towel seemed like just the thing.

I entered the lobby. Passed a small cluster of people surrounding a young woman racked with sobs. Passed an elderly man, sitting, staring blankly ahead, at nothing. Took a deep breath in, then out. Mortality is hard to face, but impossible to avoid. Me? I'd been trained to view the inevitability of death as a goad to living a more meaningful life—by showing compassion to others, for example. I only wish it were that easy.

I headed for the morgue.

CHAPTER 6

Death wears many masks, and I've seen more than my share: from the smiling visage of an esteemed lama who, after a lifetime of compassion for all sentient beings, passed peacefully while seated in an advanced state of meditative luminosity, to the gaping stare of a young gangbanger, cut down in his neighborhood war zone by a blunt act of violence. I was at that scene within moments, and his dark spirit still circled his place of death like an angry raven.

Then there's my first. The death that marked me for life. When I found my mother, she was lying in a heap on the floor, her once-beautiful face mottled and puffy, misshapen from the toxic mix of prescription drugs washed down with a liter of Bordeaux. The stink of stale vomit and alcohol clung to her like a stain. I am still haunted by it. *The cologne of death.*

"Ready?" Tatum asked.

I nodded.

The attendant tugged the sheet to just below the chin. Barbara Maxey's features were pale, yet somehow defiant as well. Death had robbed her of her ruddy complexion but not of her fine bone structure. I shivered in the chill, antiseptic air of the morgue as I scanned her face. No visible signs of trauma, at least that I could see. I wanted to ask the morgue attendant to pull the sheet lower, but something told me to wait.

I turned to Tatum and nodded again.

"That's her, then? Barbara Maxey?"

"Yes. That's the name she gave me, anyway."

Morris passed over a long-expired California driver's license. Barbara smiled back at me, many years younger, glowing with the bliss of the newly clean and converted. She must have just joined the cult.

"That's the only I.D. she was carrying," Morris said.

"What was the cause of death?"

They said nothing. I waited.

"You want me to show him?" the attendant said, glancing at the cops.

They were silent.

"Guys," I said, "I've only been a civilian for forty-eight hours. Give me a break."

So Tatum did. He nodded to the attendant, who drew the sheet down below her collarbone.

The bruising was massive, and unmistakable; clear hand marks encircled Barbara's slender throat. The larynx area was especially discolored, a violent contusion of purple and black. Whoever did this had been brutal about it. I took a few breaths to quell the surge of nausea in my gut.

"Finished?" the attendant asked. The cops nodded, and he draped the sheet over her face. He took a moment to smooth out the wrinkles. I appreciated that he did that.

I still held her license in my hand. I met Tatum's eyes.

"Can I have this?"

He frowned. Government-issued identification of any decedents was usually returned to the issuing agency for disposal.

"I'll destroy it within the day. I promise."

Tatum glanced at Morris. Morris shrugged a halfhearted consent.

"Thanks."

I pocketed the license.

Tatum walked me out. He was through with me, but I still had a few questions.

"Where did you find her?" I asked.

"Topanga State Park. A couple of early-morning joggers spotted her. She was in a sleeping bag, set back a ways, near the creek. Looked like she'd spent the night up there. Or I should say part of the night. The ME says time of death was probably around 3 A.M. this morning."

We had reached my car. Tatum's eyebrows arched. I could see him trying to figure out how the hell a guy like me had a car like that. It happens a lot—'65 Shelby Mustangs in mint condition are pretty rare. Then his cell phone beeped, pulling him back to reality. He'd have to leave this particular mystery unsolved. He turned to go.

"Detective Tatum."

He glanced back.

"Did he say anything about the manner of death? Did you do a tox screening to see if any drugs were involved?"

"Let it go," Tatum said. "You're off the clock. You don't need that kind of garbage floating around in your head."

"Was she clean?"

"Let it go," he said again, and walked off.

I crawled home through early rush-hour traffic, but I was grateful for the time to think. To remember. To plan. I had Barbara's license. It should be enough.

Tank greeted me at the door with the throaty, indignant complaint of a domestic quadruped that hasn't eaten all day. I made up for it with his favorite: a squeeze of tuna juice, straight from the can, drizzled over his bowl of food like a benediction.

I grabbed a handful of satsuma tangerines and moved to the deck to clear my head. I sat for some time, peeling the loose, leathery skins, popping tart sections of citrus into my mouth. Thinking. *What did I miss? What would I have done differently, had I known I was meeting Barbara Maxey on her last day on earth?*

Tank wandered out and climbed into my lap. He burrowed close. Soon he was purring, his big body vibrating against my belly. I pocketed the peels. The citrus oil on my fingertips smelled tart, and bittersweet.

I knew what was bothering me. I had sensed a couple of things during my brief time with Barbara. Sensed them, and dismissed them. Made wrong assumptions, because of old ideas that still ran me. I'd picked up an impression of weary despair she carried with her, as if she knew time was running out. Despair and a deep loneliness. And yet, and yet. That final set of her shoulders, that last, light wave from her as she headed down the road, pointed to a woman with a renewed sense of purpose. She had been at a crossroads, where hope and despair intersected. Perhaps if I had invited her inside for a cup of tea she might have unburdened herself. Gone in a different direction. She might have locked in on the hope-beam and ridden it to a pear farm in Oregon, rather than ending her days in an old sleeping bag in a park.

As for me, I'd broken my First Rule, already. Ignored the nudge to know more. Rejected the light tickle of attraction. Because to embrace our similarities might lead to intimacy, and there was nothing more dangerous than that. She'd been honest with me. I hadn't, with her. She'd taken a huge chance. I'd played it safer than safe. She'd followed a hunch. I'd ignored my own.

And now she was dead.

"There's no such thing, Tank," I said, stroking his back. His spine rippled and rolled beneath my palm. "There's no such thing as a minor lapse of awareness. You're either present with what is—right here, right now—or you're someplace else."

A swell of regret washed over me. Tank lifted his head, then nestled closer. Well, I couldn't change the past. But I could address the present.

"Sorry, old boy," I said, spilling Tank onto the deck. "Duty calls." I walked into the kitchen, reviewing what I needed. I put the kettle on to boil. I checked the fridge. Sure enough, I had some leftover brown rice from the other night, so that was okay. The cakes might be a problem. Then I remembered the tin of home-baked cookies, delivered by Martha on Christmas Eve. I opened it. Nope. Empty, except for a few sugar cookie fragments, remnants of edible snowmen, dotted with green and red sprinkles.

I stood for a moment, frustrated. And realized the solution was right in front of me, in the form of half a loaf of moist, spicy pumpkin bread. Every few months, I make a special trip to Carmen Avenue in Hollywood to visit the Monastery of the Angels: a cloistered nunnery, incongruously located a mile south of the famous sign. Set apart from the neighboring world of tinsel and greed, two dozen good sisters prayed year-round for the lost souls of the City of Angels, and baked year-round to support themselves by selling pumpkin bread that rivaled the nectar of immortality.

I cut three dense slices. I smiled. Not so different, in fact, from my own monastery's *torma*, the sacrificial barley flour cakes used in every ritual.

I divided the rice equally between three bowls. Grabbed a slightly used candle from my dump-everything-in-here drawer, and also a spare stick of incense. I was a little rusty on the details, but incense never hurts.

A shrill squeal announced boiling water. I filled the pot and let the green tea steep. I laid out the three bowls of rice, three slices of pumpkin bread, and two shallow saucers, one empty, one filled with water. I went into my meditation room and returned with my Buddha statue, hawk feather, and mangled bullet. Set them down as well. I lit the candle and melted enough wax on a small plate to set the taper upright. Propping up the incense presented a bigger challenge. Finally I moved the tiny potted impatiens I was coaxing to life on my windowsill to the table, and pressed the smoldering stick into its soil. Then I set two cups on the kitchen table and filled each one with the steaming, fragrant brew. I stood still for a moment, surveying my work. What was I forgetting?

Of course. Barbara Maxey. *She who has left life.*

I reached into my pocket for the driver's license. I carefully leaned it against one teacup, so she was facing me.

A little makeshift, but my intentions were pure. I was ready. I hoped she was as well.

First I invited Barbara to unburden herself, as I wished I'd done the day before. I sipped my tea as hers cooled in her cup, opening my heart and mind to her, wherever she might be. I let the whisper of connection I'd sensed grow, and deepen.

I felt her despair. I felt her hope. I felt something else that saddened me—the deep anguish of an addict who had traded one self-medication for another. She hadn't escaped the monster; she'd sidestepped it for ten years. She'd locked herself up in a society where giving up personal freedom in exchange for staying clean seemed like a fair trade. She'd had to stay vigilant, obsessive about her abstinence. But she knew the monster was still out there, waiting for her to become vulnerable again. I bowed my head to her valor, and I acknowledged her courage at daring to leave her self-imposed prison, to make a new beginning for herself, to seek another path.

I sensed her terror, to be back out in the world. To be helpless and unprotected, where monsters could find her. Where at least one did.

I lightly touched her photograph. "I'm sorry," I said.

I couldn't change the past. But I could address the present. Time to begin the bardo ritual.

I dipped the hawk feather in water and sprinkled it over her smiling image. Mentally reciting what I could remember of the prescribed texts, ritual invocations to the deities of the spirit worlds, I alternated offerings: rice to the Buddha statue, who symbolized the higher realms, and cake to the smashed fragment of lead, representing shadow worlds peopled with dark forces. Rice, then cake, light, then shadow. Six realms. Six gifts. With each offering, I asked that she be allowed to pass through safely, released from peril, invited into joy.

I recited the final blessing out loud, the closing words flowing from my heart to hers: "When the time has come to go alone and without friends, may the compassionate ones provide refuge to Barbara, who has no refuge. Protect her, defend her, be a sanctuary from the great darkness of the bardo. Turn her away from the great storms of karma. Provide comfort from the great fear and terror of the Lord of Death, and deliver her from the long and perilous pathway, into the light."

My eyes pricked with tears. I picked up Barbara's smiling image, and carried it outside, with the candle. I swapped candle and license on the plate, and held the flickering flame to one corner of the plastic. Black smoke curled into the dusk. I had to reignite the image again and again, and it took a long time to reach critical mass, so it would burn on its own.

Certainly longer than it took to strangle a woman to death.

I tried to be patient. I owed that to Barbara. The laminated plastic bubbled, scalloped, and blackened. Small flecks of grit floated up with the smoke. Finally, all that remained were a few curled, incinerated bits of ash.

The sky was growing dark. The air was still, though I could hear the faint hum of traffic below. I turned toward the ocean, where only yesterday Barbara had gazed with longing. I lifted the plate of ash to my mouth. I blew.

When the time has come to go alone and without friends . . .

I went inside and called Bill. Told him I'd be honored to share a meal with him and his family.

CHAPTER 7

"So, let me get this straight," Bill said. "Your very first client as a private detective is a woman who didn't hire you, and can't pay you. Because she's dead."

I was enjoying a predinner beer on the patio with him and Martha. Maude and Lola were just inside the screen door, sound asleep in their matching, battery-operated cradle-swings. They rocked back and forth in a steady rhythm, like infant metronomes. They were swaddled tight, tucked deep in their carriers. With their round faces and tufts of red hair, they resembled a pair of chubby leprechauns.

The last time I saw them, they were tiny and bald. Barely hatched. Now they had hair, and two chins. Each.

"I hadn't thought of it in those terms," I said, "but I guess that just about sums it up."

Martha said, "Bill, honey, be a little more encouraging. Everybody's got to start somewhere."

"Good point," he said. "And who knows? Maybe dead clients are the best kind to have. I can see real advantages to working for someone who can't talk." He took a swig of beer. "Too bad she didn't have a pot to piss in."

Martha patted my knee. "Don't take it personally— Bill worries about everything. He's already figured out the safest route for the girls to walk to school, and they're not even crawling."

"Don't remind me," Bill said glumly. "Next thing, they'll have boyfriends with Harleys."

I pulled out my final paycheck and waved it at Bill. "Don't worry. I'm still on the payroll one more week. Then I get unemployment, if I decide to register."

"What do you mean, *if?*"

I shifted in my chair. "I don't know," I said. "It just doesn't feel right to me somehow."

Bill shook his head. "You and your feelings, Ten. You've earned unemployment, and then some."

"But I haven't. I got paid for the work I did. This is getting paid for work I'm *not* doing. I know it sounds crazy, but I feel like as long as I'm on the dole, I'll be right back where I was. Not moving. Not changing. You know, stuck."

Now it was Martha's turn to look concerned. "But how will you support yourself?'

"I've got some money saved up. Anyway, I think I've figured out a new way to make money."

"I'm not buying lip gloss from you, buddy. I have a lifetime supply," Bill said.

Martha snorted. Her love of Avon products was legendary.

Maude/Lola let out a little squeal and rustled around in her swinging cocoon. Then Lola/Maude caught the vibe and started to wail. Martha stood up and walked inside, unbuttoning her blouse.

"So what's the problem?" Bill asked.

I tried to put the niggle into words. "I'm starting to think maybe money, I don't know, carries its own weight with it. Like karma. If I'm really going to make this leap into supporting myself through my own talent, I have to trust that the money will come. Either I believe I'm of value, or I don't. My entire life, I've been supported by one institution or another. I want . . . no, I *need* to see if I can go it alone."

"Sounds like wishful thinking," Bill said.

"That's right," I said. "But sometimes wishing works."

Bill glanced inside at his nursing daughters, medical miracles tucked close like footballs, one on either side of his contented wife. He smiled.

"I guess sometimes it does," he said.

The doorbell rang; both babies startled and broke into wails, and blissful calm became chaos in an instant.

Bill grabbed one beet-faced daughter, and Martha held the other to her shoulder and patted her on the back. I opened the door to a laughing brunette, loaded down with groceries.

"Ten, I'd like you to meet my sister, Julie Forsythe," Martha called over the cacophony.

I stuck out my hand. The sister gave me a look over her bulging shopping bags, then twisted and lightly elbow-bumped my palm. *Suave start, Tenzing.* I relieved her of the two bulky bags. Her dark eyes were flecked with gold. A mass of soft brunette curls fell to below her shoulders. She was quite beautiful. Almost exactly my height, that is to say on the tall side for a woman, on the not-so-tall side for a man. Her arms were toned, her skin lightly freckled. She was strong, but her curves were full and feminine. I was very glad I'd changed into clean Levi's and the dark brown T-shirt that Charlotte used to say matched my eyes.

I wasn't looking. This wasn't a date.

Julie said, "I don't know if Martha told you, Ten, but I'm fixing dinner tonight. Want to give me a hand?"

I followed her into the kitchen like a meek puppy. Bill and Martha headed to the bathroom to give the twins their bedtime bath.

Soon Julie was briskly chopping carrots. I couldn't help noticing the large butcher knife she was wielding expertly. Her hand was almost a blur. She was wielding her hips, too. Fascinating. She chopped with her whole body.

I blurted out the first thing that came to mind.

"How did you learn to chop like that?"

"Culinary Academy," she said, without looking up from her task. She organized a neat pile of carrots, and moved on to the celery.

"It's the first thing you learn in C-school—how to dice quickly without tiring your arms or hacking off your fingers." She put down her knife and waggled her hands.

"See? I've been a chef for close to ten years and I've still got all ten of my fingers."

"And here you are with a guy named Ten," I said. "Must be your lucky number."

I winced. What had gotten into me? I was babbling like an idiot.

Julie played it just right. "Ten years, ten fingers, guy named Ten. Coincidence or . . . ?" She let the sentence trail off dramatically. "Here." She tossed me a Persian cucumber. "Show me what you got."

She quickly illustrated the secrets to slicing and dicing while keeping fingers attached to hands. (Secret One: Tuck your fingertips under and push the vegetables toward the knife with your middle knuckles. Secret Two: Pay attention.) I even started to relax. Julie seemed about as far away from needy as any woman I'd met in a long time.

"So how long are you visiting for?" I asked.

"Don't know. I may move here. I'm in town to audition for a job as sous-chef at the new W."

She was moving here? I grabbed another cucumber and hacked intently.

"All righty then, here we are," Julie said, picking up on my anxiety. "Two eligible, nervous urban professionals channeling their tension into chopping."

I concentrated harder on the cuke.

"I don't know about you," she added, "but I'm getting worn out deflecting all Martha's matchmaking candidates."

"Tell me about it," I answered. "The last two dates Martha engineered for me had all the forward trajectory of a set of dropped car keys."

Julie threw back her head and belly-laughed. I found myself liking her a little more, especially the way she'd named our nerves out loud. Internal memo to self: next time I'm feeling anxious with someone, just express it. Possible exception: when I'm with a criminal brandishing a weapon at me: "I'm feeling a little anxious." "Oh, you're anxious? Let me take care of that–*BLAM!*"

Bill and Martha came in with the twins, so we could say good night. They were clean and pajama'd, their hair standing up in damp red spikes. One of the babies caught my eye and she grinned, her mouth dropping open like a hinge.

"Hey, Lola," I said, pleased with myself for identifying her. Lola was a grinner practically from day one, while Maude always gave you a flat-eyed stare, as if to say, "Prove it."

"Ummm, that would be Maude," Julie said.

So much for my investigative abilities.

Thirty minutes later, we were serving up a cashew-and-vegetable stir-fry with basmati rice. Expertly chopped cucumber salad on the side.

Bill was soon regaling Julie with my new theory of moneymaking. He'd had a few more beers and was now into the red wine.

"He claims the money will just fall out of some tree. *Poof!* Like magic! So, Ten, where's it going to come from?"

"From wherever it is now," I said.

"How much wine has this knucklehead had, Martha?" Bill chuckled. "He's beginning to lose the plot."

He picked up the bottle and started to pour himself another glass.

Martha gently moved Bill's goblet away. "Honey, I think that's enough. Your skills as a career counselor are going downhill rapidly."

A slight twist of irritation crossed Bill's face. Then he sighed. "You're right, love. Sorry. I'm just jealous, is all."

The table fell silent. Sometimes it takes three beers and two glasses of red wine to unlock a cop's tongue. *In vino veritas.*

"You and I aren't so different, Ten," he said. "The day after I got out of the army, I joined the LAPD. I've never had any other kind of job. Now I see you heading out on this big adventure into the unknown . . ."

Some friends might choose to placate, to say reassuring things like "You're a great cop and you have an even greater life." I'm not one of them. I like it when people try to talk me *into* my feelings, not out of them. So that's what I did with Bill.

"What about my new life looks attractive to you?" I asked. That got a smile from Julie.

Bill's reply was instant.

"Freedom," he said. "Freedom to be your own man."

"Anything else?"

Martha stood and started to stack our plates.

"Picking what you want to work on rather than, oh let's see, getting handed a stack of files every Monday morning, getting grilled by morons in court, putting up with dingbat administrators downtown, being hauled in front of a committee every time your weapon discharges. Stop me if there's any you haven't heard."

"I get the picture," I said. "Those are all the reasons I bailed out."

"Well, maybe that's what I should do, too." Bill yawned, and stretched his back until it gave a satisfying set of pops.

"How about you bailing into bed?" Martha said. "You're talking like a man who needs a good night's sleep."

Bill didn't argue with that. He stood up and gave my shoulder a squeeze. "Keep me in the loop," he said. "Don't leave me behind."

I stood and gave him an awkward man-hug.

"You are the loop," I said.

Bill headed to bed, his gait unsteady.

Martha waved me off dishwashing duty.

"It's my only alone time," she said. "Julie, why don't you walk Ten to his car?"

"Subtle," Julie said.

We strolled up the sidewalk to where I'd parked my prized possession. I found myself wanting her to say something.

She didn't disappoint.

"Wow," she said. "I'm not a car person, but wow. What is this?"

"A '65 Shelby Mustang," I said. "I bought it back when I was a lowly patrolman. Not like this, of course. It was totaled. I spent three years restoring it. Helped me get my mind off cop stuff for a couple of hours every evening. Some genius mechanics over in Santa Monica did most of the heavy lifting, like rebuilding the engine."

"I like the color, too," Julie said, running her hand along the vivid yellow contours of the hood.

Charlotte had hated that color.

"How about I give you a ride in it sometime?" I said. "You could even drive it if you like."

I regretted the words the moment they slipped out.

"Deal," Julie said. "How about I reciprocate by cooking you dinner?"

"Uh, deal," I said.

"I'm here at least through the weekend," she said.

We stood there a little awkwardly.

"It's just a dinner, Ten," Julie said. "Don't worry. I won't let Martha order the wedding invitations quite yet."

She walked away, laughing quietly.

CHAPTER 8

Ding!

I jarred awake, heart pounding. Something had invaded my dreams. An alien sound. Was it from outside?

My phone dinged a second time from the bedside table. I groaned. A text message, at one in the morning. Mike, being Mike. Why couldn't he keep daylight hours like the rest of us humans?

I rolled over and closed my eyes. Gently invited my breath to deepen and slow down, my hammering heart to return to . . .

Who am I trying to kid?

Rather than spend the next hour doing battle with my curiosity, I sat up, turned on the light, and grabbed my cell phone. I squinted at the glowing screen.

The first text read, ZB's #, followed by a 503 number, which I assumed was Oregon. XPECTING YR CALL.

I moved to the second message.

NOW.

I glanced at the clock. Now? Really? I pictured Mike snickering, his goateed features rendered ghoulish by multiple light-emitting diodes emanating from all the electrical apparatuses in his office-cave. He loves to yank my chain.

Ding!

REALLY, I read.

Apparently retired musicians and computer wonks keep similar hours. (Also reluctant lamas on long retreats, but that's another story.)

I used my landline. Cell reception can be sketchy at best up in my canyon. Sure enough, one ring later, I heard

Zimmy Backus's distinctive drawl, graveled by long nights of nicotine and howling into mikes.

"Tenzing Norbu, as I live and breathe. Your man said you were looking for me. What's the word?" He sounded the same—hoarse, but openhearted. I remembered how much I liked him.

"Good to hear your voice, Zimmy. You doing okay up there?"

"More than okay, my friend. Jilly and I, we have a baby now. Named him Burroughs, after the Beat writer, may his subversive soul rest in peace. My life today? It's better than my wildest dope-induced dreams. I should be long dead. Instead, I got me a wife, a kid, a dog—the whole enchilada."

"Plus a pear farm, right?"

"Yeah, well, I don't actually grow those suckers myself. I just own the land they're on. Somebody else does the growing. I do think good thoughts about them a lot, though."

"That counts."

We both chuckled. If we lived closer, we'd probably be friends.

A shadow passed over my heart.

"Did Mike tell you why I wanted to talk to you?"

"Nope. Just that you did. What's up?"

I explained that I was no longer with the LAPD, that as of this week I was a private detective.

"Cool," Zimmy said. "How's that working out for you, then?" If he was impatient for me to get to my reason for calling, he didn't show it.

The truth is, I was stalling.

I took a deep breath.

"Zimmy, you had a visitor here a few days ago. She didn't know you'd moved. Barbara Maxey."

Zimmy barked with laughter.

"Barb? I don't believe it. I was just thinking about her the other day, swear to God. I've been trying to track her

down. I owe her an apology, you know, amends. Barbara
Maxey. Talk about a flash from the past. How the hell is
she? How can I reach her?"

This was getting harder, not easier.

"You can't . . . She's not . . . I'm so sorry, Zimmy. She's
dead."

The silence was heavy and dark. Then I heard soft sobs.
I waited. Said nothing as he tried to pull himself together.

"What happened? Did she OD?"

I guess that's the first place fellow addicts go, recovering or not.

"No. At least I don't think so," I said.

For the third time in as many days, I relayed the story
of Barbara Maxey: her visit to me, and all that followed.

"It's just too weird. I don't think about her for years,
then I do, and now this?" His voice broke. "Ah, Jesus."

He put down the phone. Blew his nose. When he came
back on, his voice was firmer.

"Thanks for calling to tell me," he said. "Is there anything I can do to help?"

That's Zimmy for you, in a nutshell.

"Maybe," I said. "Barbara wasn't just looking you up
for old time's sake. She wanted to warn you. Something to
do with your royalties. Any idea what she meant?"

He went silent. Finally he said, "I might. I had a situation recently, a run-in with somebody over royalties. But I
don't see how Barbara could possibly fit into the picture."

"She said it was heavy. 'Something bad' were her exact
words. Was your situation bad enough to kill for?"

"Jesus, Ten, I don't think so, but . . ."

"But what?"

"I sort of got threatened myself the other day. I
thought I took care of it."

"Sort of? What happened?"

"Some guy came by the ranch. That was strange all by
itself. I'm way off the grid up here."

"So I noticed."

"Hey, that's the way I like it. I spent close to thirty years on the road, twenty of them grinding it—I must have sung in every dingy dive in every Podunk town in America. God, those places were depressing. No wonder I self-medicated. Then I had a hit or two, and it was the same thing, only bigger—bigger stages, bigger tours, bigger excuses to do bigger drugs. Different venues, same ol' same ol'."

He drifted off for a moment. I waited.

"Yeah, so these days I try to stay in one place as much as I can. Today it's all about Jilly and Burroughs. Keeping it simple, you know? So when this asshole in fancy slip-ons showed up at my front gate, he was dragging some bad memories along with him."

"Who was he?"

"Wasn't so much who as what. Sharp suit. Ostrich loafers that set him back at least a thousand. He was straight out of the old music-business days, Ten. Godfather time. You know, the Mob."

I knew next to nothing about the music business. I certainly didn't know there was a Mob connection.

"How'd he find you?"

"Good question. I'm guessing the Internet. Can't hardly hide anywhere, anymore. Anyway, my foreman left him cooling his designer heels on the dirt road outside the entrance. Came and got me."

"So you talked to him?"

"Yeah, I figured I'd better. I never unlocked the gate for him, though. I took one look at the punk and knew whatever he was selling, I wasn't buying."

Fascinating as all this was, I couldn't see what it had to do with Barbara. I glanced at the clock. It was nearing two in the morning. I swallowed a yawn. Maybe Zimmy heard, because he picked up the pace.

"Long story short, he said his name was Tommy Florio, and he wanted to talk comeback tours. Another bullshit artist is what I thought. I told him I wasn't interested in any comeback tour, because I wasn't interested in coming back. Then he handed over some papers, along with a fancy basket of gourmet foods. Said did I know I was owed a bunch of royalties? That my record company had scammed me? He claimed he knew how to make it right."

My ears perked up.

"So, is that true? About the royalties?"

"Well, yeah. Probably. I mean, record companies skimmed from just about everybody in the early days. We all bitched about it. Still do. But back then if you bitched too much, you found yourself without a contract."

"Did you take him up on his offer?"

"Hell, no. I like money as much as the next guy, but no way was I going to have some goon 'make things right' for me. I refused his offer and told him where he could shove his bribe. And that's when things got heavy, like you said."

I grabbed a notebook. Wrote down: *Tommy Florio. Royalty scam. Heavy.*

"Florio tells me I'm making a big mistake. Pissed me off even more. How is he supposed to know whether something I do is a mistake or not? Then he says, 'You don't want to end up like Buster.' That got my attention, because Buster and I go way back. We hit *Billboard*'s Top Ten around the same time, me for Rock, him for R&B."

"I'm sorry, Buster . . . ?"

"Buster Redman. 'Shake It Out'? 'Come Runnin'?"

I said nothing.

"Jesus, Ten, he's one of the greats!"

"I spent my formative years in the monastery, remember?"

"Right. Sorry," Zimmy said. "Buster's a touchy subject. He passed away last year. The man was a flat-out genius, and he never got the money or attention he deserved. His death was pretty sudden. Beulah—that's his old lady—insisted something fishy was going on, but there was never any proof. I thought she was blowing smoke. Now I'm not so sure."

"You think this guy Florio was threatening you?"

"You're the cop. What do you think?"

"Ex-cop. Did you keep the papers?"

"Yeah, they basically authorize his company to go after any unpaid royalties due me."

I asked him to fax me the contract. Gave him all my numbers and told him to call if anything else came up. I also jotted down Buster's widow's number. I was just about to hang up when he stopped me.

"One last thing," he said. "Speaking of numbers, the guy had mine. It scared me."

"I don't think you need to—"

"My home phone, Ten. Not my cell. Nobody knows it except my neighbor, my wife, and me. The little weasel has my home number. I asked him how he got hold of it and all he said was 'Give my regards to Jilly and . . . little Burroughs, is it?' So I ask you again. Does that constitute a threat? What do you think?"

I need to warn Zimmy.

"I think it's good we're talking."

After the call, I couldn't settle down. I rolled to the right, then the left. Punched my pillows. Tank leapt onto the bed and started to knead the covers. I reached over and buried my fingers in his fur, just at the scruff of his neck. I thought about Zimmy, escaping his old life, building a new one in his own personal Garden of Eden. Thought about a guy in a sharp suit. Thought about where Barbara was headed. What she'd left behind.

I sat up. Thumbed a text to Mike. Pressed SEND. It went through easily in the clear night air. I flopped under the covers one more time as my query sped through the ether.

Time to locate Barbara's religious retreat. Maybe stir up a serpent or two.

CHAPTER 9

I felt my four-legged alarm clock before I saw him. Tank's loofah tongue was doing its best to exfoliate my left cheek.

"Okay. Okay. I'm up!" I said, pushing him off my chest.

Sheets of light streamed in the kitchen window. It was midmorning already, and nobody but my Persian knew or cared if I was upright. I stepped onto the deck in my boxers and tipped my face toward the warmth. I could learn to love this self-employment gig, maybe a little too much.

To counter the self-congratulating sluggard in me, I spent the next several hours on maintenance. Barbara's fear was one thing, Zimmy's story another. But invite the two together, and the situation resonated with threat, radiating warnings outward like the overtones of a struck gong. I had better be prepared.

I began with my body. Four days off was three days too many. I stayed on the deck for a 20-minute routine of standing and sitting postures—a yogic version of the LAPD-recommended light aerobics and stretching. I went back inside and pulled on sweats and running shoes. I paused to dump a can of cat food in Tank's bowl before I left. He gave me a look, the one that says: *This is the best you can do?* Then he lowered his head, barely deigning to eat.

I stepped into the dappled driveway and started with an easy jog down Topanga Canyon Drive. I veered left onto Entrada Road and picked up the pace, running the mile or so to the Trippet Ranch entrance into the park. I was nowhere near Barbara's campsite, but I felt a prick of sadness nonetheless.

I did a weave and sprint up Musch Trail until I had a good sweat going. Then I stepped off the trail and did 30 reps each of push-ups, curls, leg lifts, and lunges. Used a tree branch for another 30 pull-ups. There weren't any wooden horses to vault, or chain-link fences to climb, so I turned around and ran home. I calculated time and distance as I jogged into my driveway. Seven-minute miles. Good. I might not be a cop anymore, but I still more than met the physical requirements to qualify. I planned to keep it that way.

I addressed my inner health with 20 minutes of mindful awareness on the meditation cushion. Mostly I was aware of endorphins. Fine by me. Sometimes running works better than sitting.

Food next—an avocado, mesclun, and sprouts salad with cherry tomatoes and toasted pine nuts. Iced green tea. I was Mr. Virtuous today.

I had one more job to do. I went to the bedroom closet, unlocked my gun safe, and pulled out three cases, one wooden, one aluminum, one of sturdy gray nylon. I took all three outside and set them on the deck. I opened the wooden case first—my gun-cleaning kit—and set up my station with the care of a field surgeon. I pulled out the gun mat and spread it out on the deck like a tablecloth. Then I lined up oil, solvent, cotton swabs, rags, toothbrush, and a polymer pick with a hex-shaped shaft. I added two chamber-cleaning bores, one for my duty gun, a standard 9-mm Glock, and the other for my passion piece, a custom-made Wilson Combat .38 Super. Supergrade. Super reliable. Super cool.

I was glad my brothers in Dharamshala couldn't see me. They'd find it hard to understand my fascination with guns. I find it hard enough to understand myself.

Three things in my life present an ongoing challenge to the practice of nonattachment: my cat, my car, and my classic Supergrade .38. I live in fear of losing them, even as I know that someday, one way or another, I will. But it's like my body—I may not control the expiration date, but I can certainly influence the quality of the shelf life.

To that end, I set about cleaning the two guns patiently and with intention, another meditation of sorts. The urban warrior's, maybe.

I started with the Wilson. I hadn't had an opportunity to dry-fire the little beauty, much less take it to the range, for over a month. I ejected the magazine and emptied the chamber, double-checking that the magazine well was clear. As I fieldstripped the weapon, I paused to feather my thumb across the checkered mainspring housing and slide. As always, I marveled at the precision and sheer beauty of each component, from the cocobolo wood grip to the throated and polished five-inch barrel.

There are eight elite master gunsmiths in the United States. Four of them work at Wilson Combat. Superior craftsmanship is what drew me to their custom-built firearms—that, and the fact that they are family owned and operated. When you don't have family to speak of yourself, mom-and-pop organizations hold a special draw. No pun intended.

I wiped, scrubbed, picked, bored, lubricated, and swabbed, until the reassembled piece glowed inside and out. I stood up. Racked the slide and pulled the trigger. There was a satisfying *click*. Everything was back where it should be. The Super .38 serves me perfectly, like a trusted comrade. I'm not a tall man, but I'm solid. Same thing with my hands. My standard-issue service Glock was more than adequate—a big improvement, in fact, over the pre-Bratton-era Beretta. I figured I was set, weapon-wise. Then I borrowed a buddy's Wilson .38 at the practice range. Hit a four-inch grouping at 25 yards. Twice. I was in lust. I had to have a Wilson for myself. Within the year, I did. Mind you, if I ever go back to Dorje Yidam for a visit, my love of guns is yet another thing I won't discuss with my father.

Tank slalomed between my legs, then pawed at my ankle. I looked down. Something was trapped between his jaws, something he'd caught and wanted to show off to me. I squatted on my haunches to take a closer look.

It was a hummingbird, and it was still alive. Tiny wings fluttered furiously, but that bird was going nowhere.

"Let her go, Tank!" Instinctively, I tried to pry open Tank's jaws, but his own instincts kicked in, and he tightened his toothy clench.

Wrong strategy, Tenzing.

I looked around to assess the situation. Nobody was here, nobody but me, my cat, and his struggling prey. So I changed course, moving onto our little secret superpower, Tank's and mine. The one I would take to my grave. I looked my pet straight in his chartreuse eyes.

"I honor you as a hunter, but as a favor to me, would you please let the bird go?" I said. Tank blinked once. *Not good enough pal.* So I pulled out the big guns, psychically speaking, and sent Tank a clear mental image, a picture of him gently opening his jaws, allowing his prize to fly away.

A split second later, he did it. He opened his jaws. The hummingbird dropped, wet and stunned. Maybe already dead. Tank and I waited. Then the little bird rose straight up like a helicopter, darted left, and hovered nearby, no doubt giving thanks to whatever hummingbird-deity they call on in such situations.

Tank was pretty smug about the whole incident. I tried to reinforce this by praising him vociferously for allowing a fellow sentient being to live.

As I zipped my Wilson inside its nylon pistol rug and retrieved the Glock from its aluminum case, I took note of the irony. Here I couldn't bear for a hummingbird to die, but I was making sure my handguns stayed good and lethal for fellow bipeds.

On the other hand, as far as I know, hummingbirds don't turn homicidal.

I repeated the entire cleaning process with my service gun. Then I tidied up and locked both weapons and the cleaning kit back in the safe. I paused for a moment by the closet, sensing the weight of my feet pressing against the floor, enjoying the flow of air expanding and contracting my lungs. . . . For the first time in days, I felt centered, ready for my new life.

My ancient fax machine emitted a strangled squawk from the other room and beeped haltingly before spitting out pages. A quick glance told me it was Zimmy's legal document, as promised. I made myself a fresh pot of coffee and sat at the kitchen table to read.

Florio's contract was a simple two-page agreement, granting permission for the law firm TFJ & Associates to seek unpaid royalties owed to Zimmy by several record companies. Benign, at first reading.

I reread, slowly, pausing to underline any passages that confused me. A couple of dubious clauses earned that privilege.

The first: *If royalties are recovered, TFJ & Associates shall be entitled to 35 percent of said moneys.* The number seemed high to me, but what do I know? I made a note to check on similar contingency-type legal efforts.

A second passage also caught my eye: *TFJ & Associates shall be entitled to reimbursement for legal fees and expenses incurred during the recovery effort, said reimbursement to precede division of royalties.* No mention of a cap on the fees and expenses. I'm not a lawyer, but this seemed to me an open invitation to skim off the top, big time, leaving Florio and Company licking cream off their whiskers, and Zimmy no better off.

But the capper, the red flag flapping wildly in the breeze, was the final section, stating that TFJ & Associates would purchase a "Key man" term life insurance policy in the name of Zimmy Backus. If Zimmy should die before royalties were recovered, guess who was named as sole beneficiary? Hint: it wasn't baby Burroughs.

I called Mike, waking him up.

"Key man policies, " I said. "What are they?"

Mike groaned, but he knew the faster I got an answer, the faster he could go back to sleep.

"Logging on," he muttered. "Searching ... Searching ... and ... here we go. Okay: a company will sometimes take out a Key man, or Key *person* policy on a corporate executive when his or her death would cause significant financial strain to the business."

"Interesting," I said.

"Yeah, I'm guessing like an Oprah, say, or an Ely Broad. Someone irreplaceable. Going back to sleep now, boss."

I applied my new knowledge to the contract before me. From what Mike said, corporate beneficiaries usually came into play in situations where huge money was at stake, not the relatively minor unclaimed residuals of a retired rocker name of Zimmy Backus. Why was this clause in there, making TFJ & Associates the beneficiary? Why would they exclude Zimmy's surviving family from participating?

I knew the answer, of course. Greed. They wanted the "filthy lucre" for themselves, to borrow a phrase from Dr. Watson. I moved to the phone. Time to check in on Buster's widow, Beulah. It took about eight rings before a paper-thin voice quavered hello. I introduced myself.

"Who?" she said.

"Tenzing, Mrs. Redman. Tenzing Norbu. I'm a friend of Zimmy Backus."

"Louder, dear," she said.

This might take a while.

I raised my voice and upped my enunciation, and soon we were getting along famously. Beulah may have been hard of hearing, but her humor was sharp and her mind lucid.

"Yes, young man. Buster signed the contract. He was a trusting man, my husband. Me, I thought Mr. Florio was slippery as sin. Any man takes that much time with his clothes, got to be compensating for something. Plus, he had a short upper lip. My daddy was a salesman. He taught me, never trust a man with a short upper lip."

I couldn't help it. I pressed my fingertip against my upper lip, measuring. It seemed okay. Trouble is, I had no idea what constituted short.

"Do you know the total amount of the royalties Mr. Florio was hoping to recover for your husband?"

"Let's see. I believe it was somewhere around two hundred thousand dollars. Or so he claimed. Seemed high to me."

I did a quick calculation.

"So, after Mr. Florio's cut, Buster would have ended up with maybe a hundred and thirty?"

"If you say so. And Lord knows, we could have used it. We were having some money troubles. Buster thought Mr. Florio had been sent straight from heaven. I was thinking he was more likely from that other place, the one full of brimstone." Beulah sighed. "Anyway, thank Jesus we got the insurance money. At least now I'm getting by."

I was pleasantly surprised. "Florio paid out on the life insurance policy?"

"Mr. Florio? Come again?"

I gave her a quick explanation of the Key man clause.

She said, "I don't know anything about that. I'm talking about the policy Buster had. Fifty thousand dollars. We've been paying on it for years. How much was the other one for?"

"I don't know," I said, "but I plan to find out." I chose my next words with care. "Mrs. Redman, I understand you had your . . . suspicions about Buster's death." I needn't have worried. Beulah was all too happy to let loose a fresh diatribe, well-rehearsed, against the ageism, racism, and flat stupidity of the medical establishment when it came to the death of an old black man.

"He was doing fine. Then he wilted almost overnight, like a daisy in an empty glass. He was fine, and then he was gone. What's natural about that, I ask you? I'm sorry. I have to go. I'm getting all worked up." And she hung up.

I jotted down a recap of our conversation. I mulled over Beulah's suspicions, which led me back to Barbara's. I called Mike.

He answered with the forced alertness of a man who's still dead asleep.

"Where are you with Maxey?" I said.

"What? No good-morning?"

"Good morning," I said. "Where are you with Maxey?"

"Jesus, Ten. Who died and made you captain of the go-getter's club?"

I waited. Heard Mike pop a can of caffeine. Got my pen ready.

"So. She's a strange one. It's like she fell off the face of the earth for ten years while she was in the cult. I did hunt down a couple of mug shots before she found God, while she was still with Zimmy B. They got busted for possession. Neither did any time for it, though. Things were a little looser then."

"Find out anything about the cult?"

"Does Humpty Dumpty have balance issues?"

"Who?"

He chuckled. "Brush up on your nursery rhymes, Ten."

"Oh. Okay." With an ex-patriot alcoholic for a mother, and a Tibetan monk for a father, my upbringing was pretty lean on traditional bedtime verse. Maybe having Bill's twins in my life would help fill in the gaps.

"So, the cult's called Children of Paradise. No relation to the movie. Forty members, give or take. Their slogan is 'God Will Provide.' Inventive, no?"

"Okay, so originality is not their strong suit. What else?"

"What else is, they're camped on land out in the boonies, past Lancaster. They're like those uncontacted tribes, living in a collection of yurts on a buttload of undeveloped acreage. Which they own, by the way. Jointly. I checked. Forty-two members. Every one of them is on the deed."

Forty-two, minus one.

"Google Earth doesn't work up there, but I found a picture of the place in an old *Sacramento Bee* article. I'll send you the link. Sorry, I mean, I'll print it out and fax a copy to you. Or should I use pony express?"

"I'm working on the new computer, Mike. First I have to earn some money."

"I hear you. So, and this is refreshingly different, Children of Paradise got busted a few years back for stealing electricity from the power lines that connect to a hog farm up the road."

"God doesn't provide electricity?"

"Apparently not."

"Anything else?"

"You're a greedy little sucker, for a monk. That's about it for now. I'll keep looking."

"Good work, Mike. In the meantime, I need your help with another matter."

"Ten, I do have an actual job that pays me," Mike said.

I gave him a moment to remember how he got that job.

"Never mind," he sighed. "Shoot."

"Is there any way you can find out how much life insurance money was paid to a company called TFJ and Associates, on behalf of a musician they insured?"

"What's the musician's name?"

"I doubt you've heard of him. Buster Redman."

"You're joking, right?"

"Excuse me?"

"Ten, if you'd bothered to join Facebook, you'd know I posted a remix edit of Buster Redman's '77 track 'Tender Is Rough' just last week. I've been sampling the dude for years, along with every other digital deejay I know. He's like the poor man's Isaac Hayes, only more badass. So, yes, I will definitely run this down. Which insurance company?"

"I don't know."

"You're killing me, man," he said. "There are like a trillion insurance companies, and most of them are locked up pretty tight. Could be a mother to crack."

I waited.

"Give me an hour." Mike sighed. "First I have to break into the Royal Bank of Scotland's security system. For a metric load of pounds, I might add."

"In that case, hurry up," I said. "Bankers are just thieves. I've got a killer to catch."

CHAPTER 10

It was close to dusk when my cell phone buzzed. I was in the garage, polishing the Mustang with an old T-shirt. Tank was hiding underneath the chassis. By now he'd figured out I was on some kind of major sanitizing tear, and he feared for his furry life. Free time was not his friend.

I stepped outside, making my way to a cellular sweet spot next to the eucalyptus.

"Hey, Mike," I said.

"No time," he answered, "so I'll make it quick."

He sounded tired and wired. I wondered how much rocket-fuel he'd consumed today.

"Item Number One: Children of Paradise was founded by a guy who called himself Master Paul—real name Paul Alan Scruggs. He died three years ago. A legitimate nut, if there is such a thing. He used all his savings to buy this property and start his own church. Made everyone who came with him a part owner."

"Paul Alan Scruggs. Got it." I said.

"Item Two: I got lucky on the insurance thing. I found a policy assigned to TFJ by a smaller company, National Life."

"Excellent!"

"Well . . . maybe. The thing is, it wasn't on Redman—it was for a woman named Freda Wilson. Ever heard of her?"

"No."

"Neither had I, but I did a search. Guess what line of work she's in?"

"She's an old-time rock-and-roller."

"Close," he said. "She had a couple hits on the country charts back in the late seventies. She was a teenage phenomenon, a real looker, blond and built, with the pipes of an angel, but her success was short-lived."

Two-hit wonders in R&B, Rock, and now Country. An eclectic bunch of has-been musicians, comprising their own uncontacted tribe. Until Tommy Florio unearthed them.

"Did you find out how much the policy is for?"

"Sure did. Two million bucks."

This was getting interesting.

Mike said, "I bet I can guess what your next question is going to be."

"How's Freda's health?"

He laughed. "Smart man. Good news on that front. She's alive and kicking in the San Fernando Valley. Her home's a one-bedroom in Van Nuys, so she's definitely not living large. I'll text you her address. Then I'm done for the day. Which brings me to Three: I'm deejaying tonight at the Ecco. I'll stake you the cover charge. Interested?"

I declined politely. I was about as interested as I was in getting a root canal, but I wasn't going to tell Mike that. Anyway, I had my own tracks to lay.

I opened my Thomas Brothers and worked out my route—old school, but with no Internet, I had to make do. I'd start with a visit to Van Nuys, which was less than a half hour away. I could look in on Freda Wilson before it got too late. Then I'd head toward Antelope Valley to scope out the cult.

I fed Tank, rewarding him for his earlier show of mercy with a shot of chunk light tuna juice, straight, no rocks. I slapped together my own go-to favorite dinner, a peanut butter, Nutella, and banana sandwich on sprouted wheat, with a cold milk chaser.

I gave it five stars.

I changed into dark jeans, a navy T-shirt, and a black windbreaker. Grabbed my Jackass Rig shoulder holster and the Wilson out of the closet. Good thing I cleaned my

Supergrade this morning—the tritium night sights might come in handy. My pulse quickened at the thought.

I took my beater car, rather than putting unnecessary rattles through the Mustang's 40-year-old suspension. The ancient Toyota had proved virtually indestructible, and was my preferred set of wheels for harsh terrain. I figured Antelope Valley qualified.

By the time I got to Van Nuys it was closing in on darkness. Freda Wilson's house was tucked in a cul-de-sac of one-story bungalows, front lawns studded with "For Sale" signs. People were hit hard here. I felt for them. When things are going well in the economy, it's easy to justify paying half a million for a two-bedroom box on a quarter acre of dirt. You can sell it in a year or two and make enough to maybe buy yourself an SUV. But when things stop going well, and stay stopped until you can't remember a time you weren't worried, you wake up one day and wonder, *What the hell was I thinking?*

I looked around. How many of these sellers would become walkaways next? Laid off. Mortgages under water. Only one choice left, to disappear into the night. I shook off the thought. Getting a little too close to my own situation, as of last week.

A battered pickup truck lay askew in the Wilsons' driveway. A skateboard leaned against the front porch. I sat outside for a couple of minutes, to get myself in the right frame of mind. I've found I can learn a lot from uncoached responses to an unexpected visitor. Some people are pissed. Others, curious. They may flare with suspicion or shrink with fear. The possibilities are infinite— just the kind of situation I like. I took a few deep inhales; then headed up the concrete walkway to the front door.

No bell. I knocked on the peeling wood.

After a few minutes, a lanky, gaunt-faced man opened the door. He was wearing a stained white undershirt, polyester track pants, and the dejected look of the long-term unemployed.

"Yes?" he said.

I introduced myself and volunteered my hand, which he stared at for a moment before giving it a perfunctory shake. I don't claim to be able to see auras, but this poor guy was emitting waves of depression like smoke.

"Wesley Harris," he said.

A husky voice came from behind him. "Who is it, honey?"

I peered over his shoulder and saw a middle-aged woman wiping her hands with a dish towel. She wore a shapeless tunic over leggings. Her face was still lovely, but there was little else of the "looker" left. Dark smudges of fatigue underlined her eyes. Her hair, dyed fuchsia, spiked upward in a jagged butch-cut.

"Freda?" I asked. "Freda Wilson?"

"Freda Harris, now," she answered and moved to Wesley's side. They both stared at me.

They weren't scared. They weren't suspicious. They were ... absent. Like optimism had long since left the premises.

"May I come in for a moment?"

Wesley roused himself enough to shake his head. "We can talk here."

A teenager with a stringy ponytail and a face pocked with acne slouched into the foyer to suss out the situation. One look at the three of us and he rolled his eyes and wheelied out of there as if we were contaminated. And Martha wonders why I don't want kids.

Freda and Wesley listened as I explained that I was a private detective looking into an issue with royalties. The moment the word *royalty* came out of my mouth, I saw anticipation surge in Wesley's face.

"You found something? You have money for us?" he said. He put his arm around Freda and squeezed. "Well, hallelujah. It's about time."

I felt a stab of anger at TFJ & Associates, for putting me in this position. Once again, I was bearing bad news.

"I'm not representing TFJ and Associates. I'm investigating them. For possible fraud."

"I don't understand," Freda said. "We haven't heard a peep about the royalties in a long time. Now you show up talking about fraud? I'm confused."

Wesley's shoulders slumped. "Maybe you're confused," he said. "Not me. Nothing's changed." He walked back into the house. From behind, he looked like an old man.

Freda's eyes followed him, darkened with sorrow. She fingered a gold cross hanging around her neck as she turned back to me. She coughed the deep, hacking cough that told me she was, or had been, a heavy smoker. "Don't mind him," she said. "Now, what's this fraud business about?"

I told her my suspicions concerning Florio's dealings with Zimmy Backus and Buster Redman. She smiled slightly when she heard the two names.

"I never met Zimmy, but me and Buster, we did a few shows together." The look in her eyes told me she was drifting off into memory-land.

"Did you get a visit from a Tommy Florio?" I asked, reeling her back.

"Sure did. We signed a contract with him last year. He was supposed to go after some money he claimed the record company had stolen. Since then, nothing."

"If you don't mind my asking," I said, "how much was he talking about?"

"Well, he said it could be a hundred thousand dollars. I found that pretty hard to believe. I never had but two songs you could call hits." She coughed again. "Sorry. Last of the flu. I'm not contagious."

Freda glanced back at the house. "I've got to go," she said. "I still have to put supper on the table."

I thanked her for her time. Wesley had long since disappeared inside, and I didn't think he'd mind if I left without saying good-bye to him.

I ruminated in my car for a minute or two. My conversation with Freda led me to one inescapable conclusion, and it was the same conclusion I'd reached after talking to Beulah Redman: Buster and Freda were worth a lot more dead than alive. Mike hadn't yet found an insurance payout to TFJ from Buster's death, but I was reasonably sure one would turn up. On the good-news side, Freda's policy had been in effect for a year and she was still very much alive, and Buster's death was uncontested.

What if there wasn't any foul play involved? What if Florio took out the policies because Buster was old, Freda was a smoker, and Zimmy was a recovering addict? It made payouts a pretty good bet. Maybe what they were doing was shady, but not actually illegal. I needed to know more before I could make a realistic assessment of everything, especially whether Freda was in any immediate danger.

As I reached for the ignition, doubt flickered a warning in my gut and my hand paused.

Why threaten Zimmy, then? Follow the First Rule, Tenzing. Don't let the tickle come back as a gut-punch. Here's a perfect opportunity.

I climbed out of the car, hurried to the front door, and knocked before I could talk myself out of it. As I waited, I scribbled my cell phone number on the back of an envelope. I was going to need business cards soon.

Wesley opened the door, his eyes lifeless. I handed him the envelope.

"Call me if Tommy Florio gets in touch," I said, "or for any other reason. You both take good care, okay? I mean it." Wesley's eyes met mine, and for a moment his face brightened, as if remembering what mattering to another human being felt like.

It was nearly 11:00 when I finally turned off the highway onto the gravel road I hoped would lead to the Children of Paradise headquarters. I'd arrived here without a hitch; now I just had to figure out what the heck I was hoping to accomplish.

If I were back at the monastery, I'd already be asleep at this time of night—we were in bed by nine and up at four. But the Children of Paradise were not exactly a conventional religious community. What would *they* be doing at this hour? This being Southern California, they might not even be climbing out of their hot tubs yet.

I rolled along the gravel past acres of trees planted in rows. Fruit trees, maybe. It was hard to tell. The branches were bare, and the withered trunks, washed by moonlight, looked forlorn and ghostly. I wondered if this was their normal state, or if they had been attacked by some disease. Maybe they had simply succumbed to the recession like everything else.

My tires crunched down the road for a little over three miles when I spotted a broken-down building to one side. It was divided into stalls that looked like they had once stabled horses. A quarter mile farther along, a driveway was blocked by a padlocked gate. A hand-lettered wooden sign nailed over the entrance announced:

CHILDREN OF PARADISE SANCTUARY
Visitors by Appointment Only
661-555-9040

I punched the digits into my cell phone. I had no intention of calling them tonight, but who knows what Mike could do with a phone number?

I decided to drive past the sign, in hopes of discovering another point of entry. Sure enough, within half a mile I spotted a little dirt road on the right. I turned onto it, killing the headlights, and bumped my way along deep ruts, finally steering my way up a small incline. I parked at the summit and was treated to my first view of Paradise.

I took off my windbreaker. Slipped my holster over my left shoulder and nested the Wilson safely under my arm. Put my windbreaker back on. I pulled a Maglite XL100 out of the glove compartment, fed it fresh batteries, and stashed it in my pocket. Added my Microtech H.A.L.O.—a knife favored by film crews as much as cops—for good measure. I didn't necessarily expect any trouble, but when you're nosing around other people's property in the dark, there's a certain comfort in having a mini-arsenal within reach. I turned my car around, aiming its nose for the exit, stepped outside, locked it, and moved closer to get a better look.

This particular Eden was definitely a down-market version, the rustic model where angels occupied canvas yurts. Beyond the waist-high fence, set at the base of the hill, I counted eight of the domed tents, each about 20 feet in diameter. The structures were dark and quiet. Toward the rear of the compound loomed a larger yurt, nearly twice the size of the others. Light glowed from its windows.

I patted the comforting contours of my underarm cannon and vaulted the waist-high fence. It felt good to be back in action. I hadn't realized how much I missed the hum and buzz of adrenaline in my bloodstream. This particular high was even better than the standard cop-speed, because what I was doing was not, shall we say, strictly legal. In my mind I heard Bill's voice chiding me: "Not strictly legal? Try one hundred percent illegal." I thanked him and proceeded down the hill toward the yurts.

My phone vibrated in my pocket. I grabbed it and flipped it open next to my mouth. Mike's timing couldn't have been worse.

"Not now!" I hissed.

There was a pause.

"All righty, then," I heard Julie say. "Guess I'll catch you later." *Click*.

Great.

I called right back, but her voice mail picked up.

"Sorry about that," I said after the tone, keeping my voice low. "I thought you were someone else. . . . I mean someone I work with. A guy, a guy I work with . . ." Why did I call back?

Holy crap but I got goofy around this woman. "Anyway, I'm right in the middle of . . . this thing. I'll call you later."

I turned off my cell and stowed it in my pocket. Sighed. My buzz was killed. It wasn't her fault, but as I picked my way down the hill to Paradise, I found myself blaming Julie anyway.

CHAPTER 11

The night was cloudless. The full, fat moon spread a blanket of silvery light over the dirt pathway, so my Maglite stayed in my pocket as I worked my way downhill. Crickets sawing a concerto filled the night air with a peaceful rhythm—until I neared the illuminated yurt and heard two angry male voices coming from inside.

I approached from the rear, edging around the perimeter until I reached a window, more of a tent flap, really, with netting to keep the bugs outside. There was no shortage of them here: the mosquitoes dive-bombing my face and arms were intent on a midnight snack.

I sidled up to the flap and peered in. Two men were conversing on the opposite side of the yurt. I couldn't hear the particulars, but their tone was contentious, the volume rising and falling in tandem with the vacillating tension. The man on the left slouched back in his chair, beefy arms crossed behind his head. Even sprawled, he managed to be imposing. He was in his early 50s, sporting a long white robe of thin cotton, and none too clean. His shaved head gleamed with menace, and his jutting auburn beard moved when he talked.

Crude swords decorated with some sort of scrollwork covered both forearms—primitive blue-inked symbols that shouted time behind bars. A geometric, X-shaped structure composed of small rectangles, like some sort of molecular compound, straddled the nape of his neck. I had never seen a tattoo quite like it. His hands were huge, big as mitts, with flat, spatulate thumbs. Squat toes, wiry with red knuckle hairs, poked out of a pair of leather sandals. His ruddy face looked calm enough under the steady torrent of words from his companion, but I sensed that inside, a suppressed fury was ticking away like a time bomb.

As cult members go, he was a lousy poster boy.

The second man, spidery-thin but with a small paunch, was at least two decades younger. He also had on the white robe and sandals, but he had accessorized his outfit in a unique, attention-getting way: a double-barreled shotgun slung loosely over the crook of one arm. His elder didn't look worried, though, and the acolyte seemed more clueless than threatening.

I was dying to know what they were saying. I spotted a second window-flap across the way, so I ducked out of sight and inched my way around the structure, doing my best to mimic Tank's stealth when stalking a lizard. They were right by the opening, too close to risk taking a peek. I hunkered underneath to eavesdrop.

Shotgun was talking. "You keep saying it's not time yet, but when's the time ever gonna come?" He had a high, raspy, three-pack-a-day voice.

"You and I both know that God's in charge of that," said Thumbs. His low rumble betrayed no trace of the irritation I'd sensed—apparently he was used to dealing with impatient disciples. The cadence suggested some sort of foreign accent, but I couldn't identify the origin.

"That's what's got me wondering," Shotgun whined.

"What's got you wondering, Roach?" His voice darkened.

"Oh, so now I'm back to being Roach, hunh?" The whine tightened. "Just because I'm the only one with enough balls to come to you and ask you to your face—"

A low growl made the hairs stand up on my arms. "Stop bumpin' your gums and get to the point," Thumbs snarled. His patience was proving paper-thin, as I'd suspected, but hapless Roach plowed on ahead.

"The point is, I'm wondering—well, not just me, a bunch of us are wondering whether you're getting kinda confused about where God leaves off and Eldon Monroe begins?"

Oh, boy. This Roach needed to brush up on his survival skills. There was a moment of silence, then the creak of a chair, followed by the unmistakable *slap* of an open-handed blow across the face. With those paws, it probably felt like getting broadsided by a cast iron skillet. Roach's yelp brought to my mind a whipped dog. Eldon Monroe thought so as well.

"You little cur," he snarled, the words a hostile burr, "don't you dare talk shit to me like that."

Roach was breathing heavily through clenched teeth. I could hear the frantic hiss from outside.

"Don't call me that," he whimpered.

"I'll call you a cur because that's what you were when you came to me, a stupid lop, a chump nobody but me was willing to school. Is that what you want to go back to? The shoe?"

It sounded like they had served time together. But where? What did 'shoe' refer to?

"No." Roach choked back a sob.

"I'm trying to make you a man and you want to be someone else's bitch? That's your goal in life?"

"No!" he moaned, louder this time.

"I can't hear you, Brother."

"NO!"

"If you're not Roach, who are you?"

More heavy breathing. Finally, "I am Nehemiah."

"That's right. And *what* are you, Nehemiah?" Calm again. Almost seductive.

"A night watchman."

"A night watchman? Is that all you are?"

"No." As Nehemiah, this guy seemed to recover his confidence. "I'm a night watchman for God, Brother Eldon. I serve God. And I serve you."

At times like this, I am grateful I somehow learned to value self-discovery over blind obedience to authority. The Buddha himself said we shouldn't believe *his* words without question—we must discover the truth for ourselves. "Be a lamp unto yourself," he counseled his disciples. "Find your own way to liberation."

Brother Eldon saw things a little differently.

"Obey your God, Nehemiah. Obey me. Go! Guard God's Paradise!"

I got a sudden urge to "find my own way" out of there, and quick. I scooted around the yurt and hoofed it back up the hill, moving as fast as I could without making any racket. I sprinted toward my wheels, only to slam to a halt, as if collared by the grip of dread. A man stood by my car, his rifle aimed directly at my head.

There was no question of reaching for the Wilson, so I settled for a rapid risk assessment. My opponent was elderly, but built like a barrel. His hunting rifle was an old Marlin, probably from the 1940s. An excellent option for bringing down venison.

Or an unwelcome trespasser.

My eyes further noted the worn jeans and work boots, and my mind tilted, seeking to reconcile his calm demeanor and choice of apparel with the other two members of the cult. The facts didn't compute.

"Who are you?" I said, finally. It was the best I could come up with on such short notice.

He squinted at me, slowly lowering the rifle.

"You a cop?" he asked, his accent a rough Western twang.

"LAPD," I said. I figured we could work out the finer distinctions later.

"Thought so," he said. "Only a cop'd meet a pointing gun with a question. What are you doing way the hell up here, anyway? Them crazy hippies done something wrong?"

He proffered his right hand. "John D. Murphy. Most people call me John D."

"Tenzing Norbu," I said, returning his shake. "Most people call me Ten."

John D worked his brain around my name a few times, then gave up and jutted his chin toward the fields beyond my car. "That's my farm, across the way."

"Okay," I said. "I hope I'm not trespassing."

"Naw. It's just I don't see many folks on the road this late, so I like to take a look."

"Sorry. I didn't mean to alarm you. Have you lived out here a long time, John D?"

"Yep, my whole life," he said. "Made my living off ahmens, till the blight came."

For a brief, terrifying moment, I thought I had made a bad mistake and John D was a crazy cult member after all, one of those types who believed they were going to survive some cosmic disaster by rising up into the air, leaving the rest of us sinners behind. Then I realized he was saying the word *almonds*—his odd, nasal pronunciation a half-sigh, half-benediction—and by *blight* he meant an actual tree fungus.

"My daddy worked these fields, too," he went on, "but my kids? They never wanted much to do with raising almonds, and I'm beginning to see their point."

I opened my mouth to commiserate when a raspy voice rang out through the night air. We both reached for our weapons.

"That you up there, John D?" God's favorite night watchman, Nehemiah, strolled up the hill, bathed in moonlight, shotgun at the ready.

"Hey there, Brother," John D called down to him. "Sorry, but I can't quite recall your name." John D leaned his rifle against the side of my car, and I removed my hand from under my windbreaker.

"Name's Nehemiah," Roach called back. He swung his legs over the fence and sauntered toward us. His eyes darted in my direction. They were narrow and beady, like a ferret's.

"Who's this?" he asked, in a none-too-friendly voice.

John D didn't miss a beat. "This here's my son, Charlie," he said. "My older son. You've prolly met my other son, Norman, that works for the county water department."

"Don't look much alike, do you?"

John D laughed that one off. "Charlie here, he comes from my first marriage, to my Chinese wife."

Mild irritation spider-walked my spine. If you want to rankle a Tibetan, tell somebody he's Chinese. I mentally exhaled—this wasn't the time or place for petty sensitivities. There was a bad man with a gun involved.

Nehemiah strafed my features with his lifeless prison-eyes. He said, "What brings you here in the middle of the night?"

John D clapped me on the back and said, "Charlie here is thinking about coming home, getting back into the family business." He could lie like a champ.

I played along. "It's a fact. People are eating a lot more almonds these days."

Nehemiah wiggled his jaw around. "I wouldn't know. I got teeth problems. Ain't crazy about real crunchy things."

"Well, I guess we oughta get on home," John D said. "Charlie just got back. Couldn't wait to see the lay of the land again."

"Where you been?" Shotgun asked me.

Yes, where had I been?

"Navy Reserve," John D said. I straightened my shoulders. I was tempted to try out a salute, but that might be pushing things.

Shotgun shook his head. "That wouldn't work for me. I get seasick."

I could think of other problems that might interfere with Brother Nehemiah's navy career as well, but I didn't want to go there.

We turned to leave.

"John D," Nehemiah said, "how come you ain't never joined us for a service? We must've invited you a dozen times. It's where the Real Word is being spoken."

"You mean to tell me the rest of those words I've been hearing my whole life ain't even been real?" John D's eyes twinkled.

THE FIRST RULE OF TEN

"Yes sir, that's right." Nehemiah's voice grew fervent. Apparently, irony is no match for a brain washed clean by the Real Word.

John D smiled. "Well, Brother Nehemiah, you are a man of conviction. I respect that." Nehemiah preened a little at that.

"You take care now," Nehemiah said. He strolled back to the fence and walked off whistling.

John D looked over at me and grinned. "What do you think, son?"

"I'm impressed," I said. "Where did you learn to fib like that?"

"I used to be in law enforcement, just like you," he said. Which explained his quick draw.

"I worked for the Sheriff's department for a few years when I was just out of high school. Till I was old enough to take over for my daddy." John D waved his arms at the dead and dying trees around us. "Good thing Nehemiah there don't know squat about almonds. He woulda realized nobody's gonna grow nothing on these trees." The lines in his face deepened as he surveyed the ghostly grove. "Well, I'd best be off."

"Want a lift back to your place?"

"I wouldn't say no," he said. "My knee's tore up something awful."

We got in my car and lurched our way back to the gravel. He directed me onto a second dirt road, just off to the left.

"Let me ask you something," I said as we bumped up the drive. "What kind of interactions have you had with the Children of Paradise?"

"They never give me trouble," John D replied. "'Bout the only time I see them is when I'm out walking my land. They'll be down there singing or doing some ritual or other. I wave to them. They wave back. End of story."

"Have they been your neighbors long?"

"They moved in maybe a dozen years ago. This other guy was their leader then—don't recollect his name either—but he died a few years back. The new guy, I've just met him the one time, when they were having problems with the hog farm."

"They were stealing power, right?" I said.

"Yeah, but they've always got some kind of fight going with the hog farmers. The Children of Paradise don't eat meat, and when the wind blows the wrong direction, they get a face full of hog stink." John D punched my arm lightly. "Hey, I'm not exactly a fan myself. When the wind blows southeast, I smell it all the way over here. Some L.A. outfit owns it, prolly the Mob, and like most business owners, they don't have to deal directly with the stench they create."

The Mob again.

He caught my look. "Don't you know a lot of the big pig farms are owned by the Mafia?"

What I didn't know about the Mob was clearly a trough-load. "Tell me more."

"Oh, yeah," he said. "The Eye-talians got into garbage collection a hundred years back. Nobody else wanted to haul waste. They saw the need, so they took it over. If you're in the garbage-hauling business, why not pig farming, too? One hand feeds the other, you know? Pretty dang smart, you ask me."

I didn't know whether this was true or just the ramblings of an old man's imagination.

An image flickered through my mind: *Ostrich loafers mincing up a dirt road with a basket of gourmet goodies, and a contract that stunk as bad as this hog farm apparently did.*

I tucked the vision away for future reference. The correlation seemed far-fetched, but at this stage I was still just gathering dots—I'd start connecting them later.

The dirt road ended in the front yard of an ancient wooden one-story ranch structure set within a small cluster of trees. A dim light glowed on the porch. The rest of the house was steeped in shadows. It looked like a very lonely place.

"Care to come in?" His voice was casual, but I knew better.

"Sure."

I followed him inside. His house was clean and sparsely decorated; a big recliner and a flat-screen television dominated the main room. A few family photographs decorated the mantel. John D gestured me to sit on a small leather sofa pushed against the wall, and disappeared into the kitchen.

He came back with two icy-cold beers. I knew I liked this guy. He sank into his recliner with a contented grunt. We sipped in silence.

The room seemed to darken a little.

I glanced over at John D.

He was deep in thought, and that thought was making him sad. I just waited. None of my business. He turned to me.

"I wasn't lying," he said.

"Excuse me?"

"I wasn't lying, not completely. I did have a son called Charlie, and he was in the Navy Reserves." I wasn't sure how to respond, so I said nothing.

"Little bits of him are all over some godforsaken road in Al Asad," John D continued. "The rest is buried at Arlington National Cemetery. He got blowed up, making the world safe, at least that's what I used to think. Now I don't know what to believe."

I felt the ache of his loss, resonating deep in my own chest. "I'm sorry," I said.

"So am I, son. So am I." Then John D folded the grief tight and tucked it back in, wherever it was he stored it.

"So, Ten, you never did tell me what our robe-wearing friends did to get you to come all the way out here. Anything I oughta be worried about?"

I told him my Barbara Maxey bedtime story, taking my time. I was curious to see what he thought. He mulled it over, frowning as he drew the same conclusions I had.

"You're thinking they might have sent someone after her," he said. "Maybe kilt her because she broke away?"

"I don't know," I answered. "I don't have any evidence to support that scenario."

For the second time tonight, a vivid image invaded my cerebrum.

Flat, spatulate thumbs, pressing, squeezing, crushing the life out of Barbara's fragile neck as she stared up in horror at a hirsute face and crazy, leering eyes.

I shuddered. Maybe my brain didn't know enough yet, but my gut sure did.

"You figure something out?" John D was watching me.

"No. Maybe. I don't know."

We lapsed into a second silence, lost in thought.

"You ever see things?" I asked John D. "You know, with your mind's eye?"

He thought about it. "Sometimes I see these streaks of light, like ghosts. Floaties, I call 'em. That what you mean?"

"More like actual visions," I said.

"Can't say that I do. Why? Do you?"

I was too far down the road to turn back. Anyway, for some reason I already trusted this man.

"Before I was a cop, I spent a lot of time in a monastery."

"No fooling. You were a priest?"

"Not that kind of monastery. A Buddhist one. In India. My father's a practicing monk over there. Anyway, my teachers encouraged me and my fellow novices to notice any pictures that sprang to mind—you know, visualizations that arose without even trying. The more I noticed them, the more they seemed to happen."

"You talking about ESP?"

"It's more like staying attuned to what's happening beneath the surface, and somehow picking it up in visual form."

"Like dowsing for water," John D said. "Only it's your mind that's bent like a branch."

"Exactly. One time, I was maybe seventeen, I was called to the bedside of an old monk. My father thought it would be instructive. The monk was somewhere around eighty—he didn't know exactly when he was born—and deep in his final passage."

"You mean dying?"

"Yes. Dying. He was lying in bed, with his eyes closed. I was only allowed the briefest of visits. I sat cross-legged on the floor next to him. I started chanting from one of our traditional liturgies for the dying. All of a sudden, the clear image of a snowball fight flashed across my mental screen; you know, just a bunch of little Tibetan boys, lobbing snow at each other. It was like I was there. The monk must have sensed a change in my concentration. His eyes flickered open, and he turned to look at me. 'Describe,' he said."

"No kidding. You tell him what you saw?"

"Yes. I told him. After a minute, he smiled. 'That was the day I became a monk,' he said."

"No kidding," John D said again.

"He described how a lama showed up at their little village that snowy afternoon and invited the boy to come live with him in the monastery."

"And his parents agreed?"

"Well, it's a great honor, to have a monk in the family. And they were very poor, so it was one less mouth to feed."

"Hunh."

"Anyway, then he started to weep. I was astonished. I had never seen a grown man cry, much less one of the monastery elders. He said, 'I've always wondered what my life would have been if I hadn't left my friends that day.'"

"What did you say?"

"I . . . I told him that his life had been full of merit, one I could only hope to emulate. After a moment, he just motioned at me to continue with the prayers, and closed his eyes. He crossed over later that night, sitting upright, surrounded by the senior lamas."

John D cleared his throat. "You ask me, sounds like that's a fine way to go."

I was flooded with sharp longing for my own friends, Yeshe and Lobsang, so very far away. They knew me like no others, sensed my every mood. They loved me, without judgment. They nourished my being.

John D seemed to register the press of grief in my chest. He walked over to the mantel and returned with a faded photograph.

I looked down at the photo. A young man and two strapping boys posed side by side, grinning amid a thick grove of blooming almond trees. The older boy sported a cowboy hat and a carefree grin. The younger was looking up at his big brother, his mouth serious, his eyes ablaze with admiration. The trees were mostly swathed with snowy white blossoms, though here and there one boasted a frothy explosion of pink.

"That's me with Charlie, and my other son, Norman. Back when their mother was still alive. Back when we were all full of hope." John D rubbed his callused thumb across the picture. "Things don't always work out the way we want them to, Ten. Don't mean they're not working out the way they're supposed to."

I handed the picture back. I touched his arm lightly.

"Thanks. I'd better get going."

"Hang on, hang on, young fella." He bustled back into the kitchen and returned with a small paper bag, which he pressed into my hands. "Take some of my almonds with you. Case you get hungry on the way home."

Visions are well and good, but sometimes the simplest deed will warm the cold places in our heart when we least expect it. As I drove away, I vowed to someday return John D's act of kindness.

CHAPTER 12

As I cycled through my morning maintenance rituals, I was all too aware of the conflicting jumble of feelings inside. Each one vied for my attention, like siblings at a dinner table: excitement over the many tasks ahead; anxiety at the possibility of failure; concern for John D. Woven through all of these was a thin but familiar thread of dread—the sense that I was about to volunteer to be berated, yet again, by a woman I liked. I had to call Julie back, deal with the disastrous call of the night before, but I kept putting it off. This uncharacteristic procrastination told me I'd already assigned my heart in some way to this woman. After one dinner. How had this happened?

I picked up the phone, looking over to Tank, asleep in a patch of sun.

"She probably won't pick up anyway, right?" Tank didn't answer.

She did, on the third ring.

"It's Ten. Is this a good time? Can you talk?"

She snorted. "Gee, thanks. Rub it in, why don't you?"

I swallowed. "Julie, I'm sorry I snapped at you before."

"A girl steps outside after a long night of work, sees the full moon, gets up her nerve to call a boy about it, and *bam!* You put me off my feed, Tenzing, and I'm not happy about it. Nothing puts me off my feed."

"Look, I owe you an explanation. I also owe you a ride, and you owe me a meal. How does tonight sound?"

She thought about it. I waited, wondering which way she would tip. Which way I wanted her to.

"As it happens, I'm off this evening," Julie said. "Come to my place. We can take the Mustang for a spin, and then you can fill me in while I fill you up."

I got directions—she was renting one of those temporary furnished apartments at the Oakwood in Burbank—and hung up feeling a little better about things.

A FedEx truck scraped over the gravel into my driveway. Now what?

Moments later, I was looking down at Mike's face, displaying an uncharacteristic ear-to-ear grin, filling the screen of a brand-new, very fancy cell phone. I spent one second wondering what Mike was so happy about, before I started to mess around with my new toy, tapping and stroking the little stamp-sized images the way I remembered Mike doing.

At first, it was like trying to control little balls of mercury. Icons kept skittering away, disappearing and reappearing willy-nilly. Once I got the hang of it, though, I discovered that I not only had access to the Internet and my e-mails, I could also check on the weather, the stock market, Facebook, and YouTube. People could track me wherever I was, and I could get directions to anywhere, and listen to music by anyone. Now if it would only open cans of cat food, life would be perfect.

I called Mike. The reception was clear as crystal. Man, I hate it when he's so right. I left a message.

"Okay. You win. I did need this gizmo to tide me over before I can afford the whole home office upgrade. Thanks." I went to press END, then changed my mind. "Question: who took that picture of you? Why the goofy grin?"

It was time to hit the road. I grabbed an old pair of binoculars and fed my beast. The new, 21st-century me downloaded door-to-door directions to today's destination, and added Julie's address and number to my address book. I was pretty pleased with myself. On a whim, I also Googled "Hog Farms." We were strict vegetarians in the monastery, avoiding the consumption of any other sentient beings. In Paris, my mother was whatever suited her at any given moment. One week, she would eat nothing but fruit and nuts. Another week, only meat would do. Raw, cooked, gourmet or junk food, whatever she ate, I ate, or I didn't eat at all. Since I've been on my own, I've tried to listen to what my body needs, while holding some awareness of the source of my nourishment. Mostly, I eat fresh fruit, vegetables and legumes, with the occasional cheese, egg, or fish product when there are no vegetarian alternatives. No red meat, though. The closest I've come to pork is bacon bits at a salad bar, which I've so far avoided. Anyway, what I knew about pig farming wouldn't fill a thimble.

What I learned about pig farming made me wish I owned a gas mask. Among other unsettling facts, apparently pilots are encouraged to avoid flying over hog farms at altitudes lower than 3,000 feet, due to instances of fainting in the cockpit from catching piggy updrafts. In other swine-related news, entire hog farms occasionally spontaneously burst into flames from the various gases produced by the active little fellows.

"We're talking some potent emissions, my friend," I told Tank.

My phone produced a cascade of syrupy harp arpeggios, Mike's tongue-in-cheek choice of ringtone for a meditating ex-cop.

It was Julie.

"About dinner," she said. "I forgot to ask, anything you don't eat?"

I didn't hesitate.

"Pork," I said.

CHAPTER 13

My neck was killing me. I lowered my binoculars, rotated my shoulders and head, and steeled myself for stage two of my observation plan. It was already midafternoon. Except for a handful of raw almonds, I hadn't eaten since breakfast. I'd already spent several hours standing on a hill, studying from afar the outfit that caused such olfactory distress for the Children of Paradise. Fortunately, the wind was blowing east, so I was spared the full effect of nastiness.

Here's what I'd learned so far. This wasn't much of an operation. By my count, there were about 20 employees, mostly Hispanic, mostly just hanging around. Occasionally, someone would be doing the things you'd expect workers on a hog farm to be doing: feeding hogs; dealing with the inevitable aftermath of feeding hogs; waiting around to feed them again. Some of the men wore surgical masks. Others, mostly the older workers, went without. Maybe you got used to the smell after a few years. I found that a scary thought.

The moment had come. I had to drive closer to glean anything further.

Even safely sealed inside my car, it was bad. When I reached the entrance, I braced myself and rolled down the window. I instantly experienced two things—a burning sensation in my eyes, and a gust of empathy for the neighboring cult. The powerful blend of foul-smelling excrement and pungent garbage, topped by a nostril-stinging high-note of urine, was almost unbearable.

I caught myself: Here I was complaining about a strong smell, without giving any thought to the suffering of the poor animals inside. Their rebirth into the animal realm was already a form of slavery, and their present living conditions were horrific. I tried to balance my revulsion with an equal amount of compassion for these highly intelligent animals.

Window raised again, I took shallow, acrid gulps of oxygen through my mouth as I steered the Toyota up the entry road to the farm. The main building was set well apart from the actual operation. No surprise there. The far side of a parking lot held a dozen or so cars and pickup trucks. One car stood out—a shiny black Mercedes, an E550, top of the line. A classic midlife-crisis car. The sexy two-door convertible hardtop still sported dealer plates—a Pasadena dealership.

At least one person here was bringing home a lot of bacon.

I parked. I stretched. I strolled to the front door, as if I hadn't a care in the world, which is hard to do when your gullet is spasming in protest at the stench. I entered, and was hit by a blast of cold air. They must keep the air purification and cooling system cranked up high to keep the pig smells out. Everybody in the office was wearing a sweater.

I took a tentative sniff. Not bad.

A dazzling bottle-blond young woman in a tight, low-cut pullover manned the front desk, so to speak. Her head was lowered as she tapped away at her computer keyboard. Behind her, a couple of young men and women sat at their own desks, staring at screens, talking quietly into headsets. At the far end of the room was the only closed door.

Low-Cut flashed a bright smile at me. "May I help you?"

I decided to aim for humble and disarming. "I sincerely hope so, ma'am. I'm a private investigator, looking into the Children of Paradise community next door."

A sour little look rippled across her face. She caught herself, and quickly snapped the smile back into place.

"Yes? And?"

"And, I know that your company had some problems with them a while back. I was wondering if I could talk to your boss about it."

She shook her head. "Mr. Barsotti is unavailable right now."

Good. A name.

"I'm guessing Mr. Barsotti will want to know about this," I said. "When do you think he'll be available?"

"I'm not sure," she said. "It could be a while."

"No worries. I can wait." I looked around in vain for a place to sit down.

"We don't get a lot of visitors." Her voice was clipped.

"I can't imagine why," I said, testing for signs of humor.

No response, except that immovable smile.

I moved to the corner. Just stood there, waiting. She eyed me for a minute or two, nibbling on a hot-pink finger-talon, then went back to clacking away on the computer.

I turned my back to her and stepped close to some old framed photographs of what looked like prize-winning hogs on the wall, as if I were admiring their girth and blue ribbons. Actually, I was adopting the time-honored but effective secret-agent trick of using the reflection off the glass to spy on her. She glanced at my turned back, picked up her phone and had a short, whispered conversation punctuated by a couple of more quick peeks in my direction.

Fortunately, I was also half-facing the window into the parking lot. Within moments, a man exited the back of the building and hustled toward the new Mercedes, shrugging a sport coat over his dark lavender shirt and matching tie as he trotted. He looked to be in his mid-40s. His longish hair was uniformly dark, except for suspiciously perfect little flags of silver at the temples. Prominent nose. Fairly fit body, though his somewhat loose jowls hinted at a recent weight loss. I was too far away to see, but I was betting on manicured fingernails. All in all he wasn't bad-looking, in that "I'm determined to look younger than I am" way.

It had to be Barsotti, in a rush to get out of there. I wondered why he was so anxious to leave.

My gut twanged. *A man in a hurry is a man with a secret. Follow him.*

I turned to Low-Cut. "Sorry. Just remembered something I should take care of. I'll have to come back another time."

"Okay," she chirped, without looking up from her work.

I decided to double-check I had the right guy, just in case. "By the way, how does Mr. Barsotti like his Mercedes?"

"Oh, he just got it, and he *loves* it." She wasn't too bright. I suspected Barsotti hired her for what was below her neck, not above it.

I popped out of the door just as Barsotti was smoothly reversing out of his parking place. Engine purring, the sleek machine glided toward the exit.

I sprinted across the lot and jumped into my jalopy. I reached the main road just as he was accelerating, maybe a quarter-mile ahead. I goosed my hard-working engine, willing it to catch up. I felt like a mutt chasing a greyhound. Soon Barsotti reached the freeway entrance.

He turned onto the ramp heading south on the 14 toward Los Angeles. Thank goodness. I didn't want to restart things with Julie by canceling our dinner.

For once, heavy traffic was my friend. If both the 14 and the 5 hadn't been jammed with stop-and-go traffic, his wheels would have left mine in the dust. As it was, we surged and slowed our parallel ways back into town.

Just north of where the 5 and the 170 meet, the lanes inexplicably cleared, and I almost lost him. I floored my Toyota, pushing the tachometer to redline as I merged onto the 170. Every nut, bolt, and belt in the car rattled and howled in protest, but I managed to just keep him in sight as he suddenly zipped off the freeway at Roscoe. I felt a niggle of recognition. I'd been in this part of North Hollywood before, but I couldn't say why. Then Barsotti again turned, this time onto Coldwater Canyon Boulevard.

I was confused. Coldwater Canyon serves as a back way into Beverly Hills, that famous playground of the rich, where shiny new luxury sports coupes feel most at home. But if that was his destination, he should have taken the later Coldwater exit, made a left at the bottom of the ramp, and climbed over the hill to the high-rent side of town. We were a far cry from there.

As I turned onto Coldwater myself, I realized why this area seemed so familiar. I was a stone's throw away from Wat Thai, the ornate Theravada Buddhist temple located, incongruously, right off the freeway. Two turns and you think you're in Bangkok.

A pair of looming demons guarded the gates of this classic Thai temple, with its red roof and ornamental eaves outside, and a plump, gilded Buddha watching over the chanting monks within. I'd love to say I went there to join their meditation practice. In fact, it was the lure of mango and sticky rice, purchased from temple food stalls using funny plastic temple money, that drew me. That and the Thai Iced Tea, a divine beverage if ever there was one.

Barsotti had a different elixir in mind. I almost ran up his tailpipe when he braked suddenly and turned into a strip mall. I took a deep breath to slow my pulse, and sent a prayer of gratitude to the chubby Buddha next door. That would have been one pricey fender bender. Barsotti hurried into a Starbucks—or Fourbucks, as Bill likes to call it—phone glued to his ear. He emerged moments later with two 20-ounce Ventis nestled in a cardboard box.

Unless his car drank coffee, he was on his way to meet someone.

I sincerely hoped my gut wasn't leading me on a crazy chase for nothing.

Traffic again formed a thick clot, and I had no trouble keeping the sports car in sight as he turned right, toward the jumble of apartment complexes and houses that sprawl for miles out there, forming separate branches of the seemingly infinite grid known collectively as "The Valley." I found this part of town monotonous, flat, and downright depressing, but to each his own. I gave myself a mental attaboy for choosing to drive the Toyota today. A saffron Shelby Mustang would have made this part of the pursuit problematic. Happily, older Toyotas were a dime a dozen.

Coldwater quickly became Sheldon, condos became houses again, and I dropped back another two cars. His destination turned out to be a small but beautifully appointed cluster of stables and paddocks surrounding a riding ring, a jewel of a place in the East Valley. Several riders mounted on thoroughbreds trotted around the ring. A discreet sign revealed this to be the East Valley Equine Center. I knew about the enormous equestrian center in Griffith Park, but this was obviously the well-kept-secret alternative for wealthy horse-owners craving privacy. I parked across the street and watched as Barsotti maneuvered into a tight space between a Beemer and a Lexus. He carried both coffees to the riding ring, set them down, and leaned against the fence to watch the riders.

I now knew where we were, but I still hadn't a clue what either of us was doing there.

I left my car across the street, retrieving only my binoculars—they were getting quite a workout today. I found a secure vantage point and peered at the ring, trying to guess which rider, or horse for that matter, Barsotti was visiting. I swept my field glasses past an older man with a patrician nose and a young, fresh-faced teenage girl posting up and down in spotless jodhpurs, her braces glinting as she grinned.

Then my binoculars filled with the smooth, glowing face of a beautiful young woman in her 20s. Blond curls spilled out from under her black helmet. With mental apologies to my Tibetan teachers, I lowered the glasses slightly. Yup, the rest of her equipment was equally to Barsotti's taste, and I'm not talking about stirrups. She cantered past him, thighs gripping the sleek, chocolate-brown flanks of her horse. Barsotti's head followed her around the ring as if magnetically connected.

As Julie would say: All righty, then.

A freckled kid on a two-wheeler screeched to a halt near me.

"Whatcha doing?" he asked.

I wasn't going to lie. First of all, way back when, as a novice monk, I had vowed not to. Second of all, children get enough of that every day from the people they know; they don't need strangers running cons on them, too.

"I'm watching a man watching a woman ride a horse."

"Cool," he said, and pedaled off. Would that all human communication were so simple.

I decided to give the binoculars a rest before I drew less agreeable attention. I let them dangle and took a slow stroll around the perimeter of the equestrian center, keeping watch on Barsotti out of the corner of my eye. As I completed one full lap around the place, staying well out of Barsotti's line of vision, the blonde dismounted. She passed off her reins to a handler. He walked the horse toward the stables. She sashayed over to the fence and gave Barsotti a quick kiss. The giant rock on her left hand flashed and bounced light like a laser. Trophy wife, I thought. Explains the weight loss. Barsotti passed her a coffee and they shared a short conversation. As she left the riding ring, he escorted her over to, wonder of wonders, another brand-spanking-new Mercedes, this one a gleaming silver SUV. Same new plates. Same dealer. I took note of the name. One, or maybe both, of them went on a shopping spree recently, purchasing two new sets of wheels. I was betting on Barsotti, myself.

She got in her car and drove off. He got in his car and followed her. I got in my car and followed him following her. This is the exciting reality of detective work. A lot of waiting. A lot of watching. A lot of following.

They wound up parking several miles south, in an upscale condominium complex. I immediately deduced that the place had just opened—it had the freshly painted, newly planted exterior of a recently constructed building.

I heard Bill's voice: "Right, detective. And that huge banner hanging from the roof proclaiming 'Grand Opening, Now Leasing!' has nothing to do with your conclusion."

This is why my head will never get too swelled.

The two lovebirds, hand in hand, disappeared into one of the condos. I readjusted my thinking. Trophy mistress, maybe? They would be occupied for a while. I couldn't think of anything more I could learn from the lovers, not pertaining to my case, anyway.

Assuming any of this pertained to my case.

I pulled out my iPhone, fumbled around until I opened the little pad-icon, and typed in the dealer name, as well as the unit number and address of the complex. After a few false starts, I also located Bill in my cell phone's address book.

"Hey, partner," he answered.

"Oh, hooray. I'm still 'partner,'" I said.

"You must be about to ask me for a favor."

"Dang, you're good. Yes, I need you to run a couple of plates for me. Dealer plates. Can you do that?"

"Sure, unless they're brand-new, as in a day or two old."

I read him off the numbers.

"You're in luck," Bill said. "I'm at the office in front of the computer. Stay on the phone."

Bill hummed a tuneless song while the keyboard clacked in the background. I already missed that habit of his, that endearing, tone-deaf drone.

"Okay," he said. "Got something to write with?"

"I can use my phone."

"Well, aren't you the fancy one," Bill said. "So, the E550 belongs to the dealership, Golden State Mercedes-Benz over in Pasadena. The SUV is registered . . . let's see, uh, as of three weeks ago, to one Ramona C. Cunningham. Same dealership, though I'm guessing you already knew that."

"Got an address for Cunningham?"

He read off a Newport Beach address, a long way from a condo on Coldwater Canyon. My mind quickly revised the front-page lede: Prosperous middle-aged lothario lures someone else's trophy wife from her unhappy home in Newport Beach for trysts at a love nest in The Valley, with the help of a horse, a car, and a cappuccino. Catchy.

"Hey, Ten?"

"Yes, Bill?"

"Any money fall out of any tree yet?"

"Funny. Really funny." I hung up on the sound of his laughter.

Next stop, Pasadena. Golden State Mercedes-Benz, to be exact. Three freeways later I parked at the far end of their visitor's lot and started walking, praying to slip inside unnoticed. No such luck. Out of nowhere, a trim, eager young man in a suit and tie intercepted me. His eyes darted over my shoulder to my long-suffering Toyota, looking clunkier than ever. It slowed him down, but not for long.

"Good day, sir," he said, offering me his hand. "Chad Willoughby, sales consultant."

"Tom Smith," I said. I'm nothing if not original at times like these.

"Do you have an appointment, Mr. Smith? All showings are by appointment only."

What would Sherlock do?

"No," I said. "No appointment, but I spent some time with Mr. Barsotti this morning, and I really liked his new E550." This is called lying and telling the truth at the same time, a skill all detectives, Holmes included, learn early in their careers. It was the closest I could come to observing one of the five root vows, while still being remotely effective in my job.

His demeanor changed instantly after I dropped the Barsotti bomb.

"Of course," he said. "Please! Right this way."

He led me to a row of brand-new SLK and E-class coupes, laid out like metallic jewels on the tarmac.

"Beautiful, aren't they? Lease or purchase?"

"I haven't decided," I said.

"There are advantages to each," Chad said. "I can go over them with you."

I circled each car, squatting down to look at the tires and making other traditional auto-shopper-type moves.

Peering in a window, I kept my voice casual. "How long have you known Mr. Barsotti?"

"My boss? I've been working for him about a year over here. Before that I was at his Ferrari dealership on Pasadena Boulevard. When he sold it and moved here, so did I."

So he owned a car dealership as well as a hog farm. Busy little bee, this Barsotti.

"Ferrari to Mercedes? Bummer," I said. I was just making conversation, but Chad jumped on my comment with the intensity of the recently converted.

"Are you kidding me?" he said. "Ever know anybody with a Ferrari?"

I didn't.

"Well, here's everything you need to know about them: They suck. They're great to look at and fun to drive, but they're basically expensive pieces of c-r-a-p, crap. Buying a Ferrari is like finding out the blue blood you married is actually a stripper."

Chad Willoughby might be politically incorrect, but he was also unusually candid for a car salesman. That could prove useful.

"Vince Barsotti will tell you the same thing. That's why he unloaded the dealership." He sighed. "Selling them's a snap, mind you. They sell themselves. It's what happens later that's the problem."

"How so?" I asked, trying to keep him loose and in the mood to confide.

"Guy comes in; maybe he's just made his first big movie deal. He lays eyes on the Ferrari, it's like he's seeing his girlfriend naked for the first time. Practically drooling, you know? Twenty minutes later, you're out on a test run with him, he's listening to the snarl of that exhaust pipe, and he's hooked. An hour later he's taking his new baby home, I've got ten grand's worth of commission in my pocket, and everybody's happy."

"Sounds good to me."

"Yeah. Like Christmas, right? The problem is, two weeks later the guy calls and screams at you for an hour because his new quarter-million-dollar pile of doo-doo has stranded him and his girlfriend on the side of the road somewhere. Again. You get one thing fixed and something else breaks a month later. Welcome to the Ferrari lifestyle. A year of that and the guy learns the truth about owning a Ferrari: the two happiest days of your life are the day you buy it and the day you unload it on the next poor sucker."

He patted a bright red hood. "You can count on these," he said. "They ride like hell, run forever, and start every time."

"I'll bet you say that to all the girls," I said.

After that, Chad Willoughby was putty in my hands.

"Would you like a test drive?"

I pointed to the black hardtop in the showroom. "I'd like to see that one."

Once inside, I used the "Which way to the restroom?" excuse to check out several framed photographs of my new pal Vince Barsotti, posing with sports celebrities and famous actors. No prize-winning pigs that I could see, at least of the hoofed species.

When I got back, Chad was using a chamois to stroke and polish the Merc's hood.

"You're a little beauty, aren't you," he crooned. He turned to me. "Carbon copy of Mr. Barsotti's. You'll love it." He winked. "Shall I get the paperwork started?"

I pointed to an SUV nearby. "That's the same model Ramona has, isn't it?"

"Ramona?"

"Vince's friend, Ramona."

His body stiffened. I stayed relaxed. Said nothing.

"I think Mr. Barsotti handled that sale himself," he muttered. "I'm not really sure."

I reached into my pocket and pulled out my phone, as if I'd just felt it buzz. Raising one finger, I stepped away and engaged in a brief, intense conversation with nobody. I finished the phantom call and smiled an apology at my new buddy. "I'm needed back at the office—can I get your card?"

"Uh, okay." A scrim of disappointment dropped over Chad's face. I almost felt sorry for the guy. I pocketed his card and gave his hand a quick shake.

"Do you have a card?" he asked.

I slapped my pockets. "Fresh out," I said. "But here's a number you can call." I rattled off a series of random digits in the 310 area code. It was definitely a number—just not one that had anything to do with me.

"I'll let Mr. Barsotti know you stopped in," Chad said.

"Please do," I said. "I'm sure he'll be surprised, if not thrilled."

By now, I was starving, but out of time, and almost out of gas. I filled up at a local Arco station and grabbed a packet of peanut-butter crackers at the counter.

Made a mental note to remember wine for dinner.

Then I dashed back to Barsotti's love nest, "dash" being a relative term anywhere in Los Angeles any time after three o'clock in the afternoon. It was close to dusk when I pulled into the complex. I was glad to see both cars still in place.

I'd no sooner opened my crackers when Barsotti emerged and quick-walked over to his car. Here we go again. I stayed five cars back as he hacked his way through traffic, this time taking Coldwater south. It was a slow grind, climbing up and over Mulholland, dipping down into Beverly Hills. Night was closing in by the time we reached Beverly Drive. I checked my watch. I was cutting my dinner plans close. Barsotti hooked a left, onto a quiet street in the part of Beverly Hills known as "the flats."

I rolled past as he pulled into the circular driveway of a two-story English Tudor, centered on a large manicured lot. The garage door opened to admit his car. Well, what do you know? Another Mercedes SUV was parked in the his-and-hers garage. Silver, like the girlfriend's, but an older model. I glanced in the kitchen window. Barsotti was hugging a woman. Blond, like the girlfriend, but an older model. Mrs. Barsotti, I presume.

Two preteen Barsottis were already sitting at the kitchen table, set for four. So Vince was a family man who believed in good old-fashioned family values . . . with one small exception. I doubted the missus knew about that exception, especially the bit about the newer, shinier sheet metal. Beverly Hills wives can be touchy on that subject.

A security car pulled up next to me. Now my Toyota stuck out like a tutu at a wrestling match. What a difference a few miles makes. The patrol car's window slid down and a uniformed guard leaned his jaunty cap out the window.

"Help you, sir?"

I explained I thought someone I knew, a friend, lived on this street, but I was mistaken.

Lying while telling the truth. Easy as pie.

CHAPTER 14

In L.A., there's "fashionably" late, and then there's "just plain rude" late. I arrived at Julie's front door somewhere in between the two. I hate being late at all—monastic living trained me to be a stickler about keeping to a schedule, otherwise you never found any spare time for yourself. I also hated to show up for dinner empty-handed, but with no opportunity to pick up a bottle of wine, I just had to make do with what I had.

My choices were limited, but between an opened packet of peanut-butter crackers and a paper bag of raw almonds, the almonds won easily. At least they had a nice story to go with them.

I pushed the doorbell, suddenly aware of a swarm of winged creatures fluttering inside my rib cage like newly hatched termites.

The door opened. Julie stood smiling at me, framed by the soft light from inside. She was wearing jeans, a white cotton shirt, and a bright purple apron. Rolled-up sleeves showed off her toned muscles, and her apron was snug over her breasts. Fit, yet voluptuous, what a combination. We cheek-kissed. Her skin was slightly damp and her hair smelled of jasmine. I pulled away quickly. I didn't want to think about what I smelled like.

"Sorry I'm late," I said. "Crazy day. I'm a little worse for wear."

"To say nothing of your Mustang," Julie said, looking over my shoulder at the battered Toyota parked in her guest slot.

Oh, well.

I handed her the paper bag of almonds. "For you," I said. "A bag of nuts, straight from the grove. Don't let anyone tell you I'm not a romantic at heart."

She laughed, and ushered me inside.

"Welcome to the land of beige," she said. I looked around. Sure enough, the walls were beige. The wall-to-wall carpet was beige. Even the photograph of a mountain range hanging over the living room sofa was beige. "I bought the apron as an act of self-defense." She spread her purple apron and curtseyed.

I'd forgotten how quirky she was.

The smells coming from the small kitchen area were enough to make me weep. Sautéed garlic and onions. Balsamic vinegar. Something else, creamy and comforting. I honed in on a bottle of Pinot Noir breathing away on the counter. Soon I was perched on a stool by the kitchen island, sipping delicious wine and watching delicious Julie perform culinary magic.

She opened the oven and leaned in to poke at something. I spotted a cast iron pan loaded with bubbling, thinly sliced potatoes.

"You didn't," I said. "Potatoes Anna? Really? What are you, psychic?"

Not psychic, a voice inside me said. *Manipulative.* A drop of uneasiness tainted the pleasure, like ink in water. My chest constricted, though I kept my tone casual.

"Did you talk to Martha?"

Julie turned. The heat from the oven flushed her cheeks a becoming pink.

"Guilty as charged," she said. She pulled a basket of morels from the refrigerator and waved them at me.

"She also told me you loved these."

My jaw must have tightened.

"Hey," Julie said. "Give me a break. I never cooked for a monk before."

She had a point.

Soon we were tucking into heaping plates of crispy, buttery potatoes; big, juicy grilled mushrooms, and a tart, delicate salad of arugula, avocado, and crumbled blue cheese. Her silent concentration on the food blessedly matched my own, until our plates were clean.

I helped myself to more of everything.

"I thought morels weren't in season," I said, refilling our glasses. "Where did you find these?"

"The competition can be fierce, but we chefs have our own inside informants," she said. "They're called exotic food suppliers. I got the morels from one of our regulars, in Calabasas. Guess where they're flown in from?"

I had no idea.

"The Southern Himalayas," she said. "Not too far from where you grew up, right?"

Again, I felt that little kink of unease. She seemed to know a lot more about me than I did her. I took another bite of potatoes, and as the buttery mixture melted on my tongue, I let the feeling melt away along with it.

"So, how's the chef gig going?" I asked.

"Sous-chef," she said, "and it's a nightmare, thanks. I'm dealing with a maniac. When they interviewed me, I neglected to ask why the executive chef didn't bring his own sous-chef with him. Turns out she's in rehab for alcoholism."

She poured herself another glass of wine. "I may be headed that way myself."

She described her chef's latest tantrum, one of many. Broken dishes and a weeping waiter were involved. I told her I understood, and detailed several infamous outbursts by my own former boss, the king of homicidal rages.

"He's one of the reasons I left," I said. "What about you? Do you have to put up with it? Why not quit?"

"Oh, you know. The three P's: Prestige. Perfectionism. Pride. I want to have my own restaurant one day, and this job could be a great launching pad for me. If I get the offer—permanently, I mean—I'll probably take it. Send for my things. Actually move out of this homage to blandness."

She lifted her glass and toasted the walls. "To anything but beige," she said, and met my eyes. "Should I open another bottle?"

Her offer was like an unfurling red carpet. I knew exactly where a second bottle of wine would lead. My heart took a small step back.

"No more for me, thanks. I have to drive."

She looked down. Nodded. Message received. I couldn't tell how she felt about it, though.

I moved to the sofa and sat, patting the cushion next to me. After a moment, Julie joined me. Her upright back told me she wasn't as cool about my little rebuff as I'd thought. We perched side by side, awkward with each other for the first time all evening.

Suddenly Julie jumped up. She crossed to the kitchen area and pulled out a mortar and pestle. She poured some of my almonds into the pestle and began grinding, giving those lovely biceps an energetic workout.

"Shouldn't let these go to waste," she said. "I'm thinking marzipan might be nice for dessert."

My mind hopped back onto the red carpet and raced ahead to the main event, followed by all the future meals and desserts I might enjoy with this talented woman and her gorgeous musculature.

I felt my own muscles stirring, one in particular. I quickly trawled my brain for conversational topics, before I embarrassed myself.

John D seemed safe.

As I told her a little about my new friend, I again pictured John D's family photograph, set in the flowering grove.

"I never knew almond trees were so beautiful in bloom," I said. "They remind me of those Japanese paintings."

"Good call," Julie answered. "An almond is actually in the plum family, along with apricots and cherries."

"And the blossoms. Pink and cream. Like your skin."

Julie gave me a strange look.

"Is there a problem?" I said.

"Uh, don't bring me any more almonds from random groves, Ten, okay?" Then she added insult to injury by scraping the ground almonds into the garbage.

"I thought they tasted just fine." My voice was tight.

"You already ate some?"

"But if they don't meet your professional standards, just say so." I was acting like a deprived child, and I knew it.

"Ten, some raw almonds can make you sick. I'm sorry. I'm probably overly-careful, but when you said—"

"No, I'm sorry," I interrupted. "I'm an idiot. Can we just . . . reboot somehow?"

Julie took a minute. But then her eyes regained some of their twinkle.

"Our first food tiff." Her smile was a gentle invitation to let the tension go. "I'll make you a delicious dessert. Promise." She yawned. "But not tonight."

I matched her yawn with two eye-watering ones of my own. She plopped down next to me on the sofa, leaning closer this time. Everything was suddenly all better.

"Long day," she murmured.

"Long week," I said. I gave her a brief rundown. She turned to face me, wrapping her arms around raised knees. She was a good listener, and seemed genuinely interested in my transition from cop to detective. Soon we were swapping tales of academy training, hers culinary, mine with the police. The process of moving up the ladder was more similar than you might assume, though Julie's involved learning to work with pastry and poultry, mine with graffiti and gangs. On one point we agreed completely—negotiating with all the idiots out there provided the biggest challenge.

"Believe me," Julie insisted, "if you met some of the jerks I've cooked under, you'd probably think dealing with ex-cons was a day at the beach."

"At least chefs don't shoot you," I said.

She looked me straight in the eye.

"I've got one word for you," she said. "Cleavers."

I laughed out loud.

"Okay." I smiled. "I'll stick with detecting."

"It's a deal," she said. "You do the detecting and I'll do the cooking."

She slowly extended her hand. We shook. I looked down at our joined palms then up at her eyes. Her gaze was steady. I let go of her hand and leaned in, a little awkwardly. Our lips touched, and I felt hers curve into a smile under mine. A tingle of electricity vibrated through my body. She placed her hand over my heart, and the heat radiated into my core.

"Whoa," I said.

"Indeed," she said.

Next thing I knew, we had dispensed with the narrow sofa and were pressed tight together on the expansive beige ocean of carpet, my hands on the small of her back, hers around my neck, our mouths locked as we exchanged an extended series of hot, deep kisses.

When we came up for air, Julie leaned her forehead against mine. Her breath was warm and delicate.

"Morel mushrooms," she whispered. "Who knew?"

My heart gave a little flip. I was enchanted by this woman.

You always are, at first.

I leaned in and brushed her lips with mine, a sweet, short, until-next-time kiss. I stood up and held out my hand. She took it, and I levered her to my side. I tried to ignore the sprinkling of freckles across her collar bone, a constellation of promise.

"It's late," I said. "How about we do some more of this soon, when I'm not quite so exhausted?" I waited. A great evening could easily implode right about now.

But Julie was cool. She nodded and stretched. "Good idea. Lovemaking is so much better when both people are awake."

You're leaving now? Are you crazy?

I soothed my inner *Canis lupus* by suggesting Julie and I get together on her next night off. She promised that would be soon. I offered to wash the dishes, but she wouldn't hear of it. By then, my eyelids were starting to actually droop.

As I walked to my car, a corner of my mind nudged at me. I sensed I had forgotten to pursue something, something important, but my brain had thickened into one dense fog of fatigue, and nothing was going to penetrate until I gave it some sleep.

I got back to the house in record time and was greeted at the door by a grateful, if impatient, cat. Tank has access to dry food and a running-water cat-fountain when I'm gone all day, so he's never likely to starve or go thirsty. However, his two favorite foods require someone with opposable thumbs. How else to open cans? In our small family, that honor falls to me. Sometimes I think it's the main reason he loves me.

Late as it was, I popped open a can of Mixed Grill, and added a liberal squeeze of fragrant tuna water.

Even so, Tank gave me a long, suspicious look before he lowered his head to his dish. I wouldn't be surprised if he smelled Julie's jasmine kisses on me, and was trying to assess the extent of the disaster.

"Don't worry," I mumbled. "She's nothing like Charlotte."

I staggered into my bedroom and was asleep before my head hit the pillow.

CHAPTER 15

I'm lying face down on a concrete floor. I look around. A man watches me from the shadows in the corner. My father. His face is stern, judgmental. What does he want from me?

I step outside. The ocean is right at my doorstep. Waves roll in, one after the other, crashing into foam at my feet. A pair of white seabirds, pelicans, with broad wingspans and long, sword-shaped bills, fly low over the sea. I want to body-surf, but I don't know how to get out there, where the waves are breaking. Then I realize I can fly, like the birds. I open my arms and barely skim the water, then joyously ride a wave in. As I land, I see that the concrete building where my father still stands is shaped like an X. I turn to face the waves, and take off, flying low, when it dawns on me I cannot really fly. That I am dreaming. That this must be a lucid dream. I look at my hands, and they sprout green tendrils, which bud and blossom into pink blooms.

"Tell me what you want me to know," I say. And I am standing at the base of a tall watchtower. It is dark inside. I know all my enemies are within. I look at the winding staircase leading upward. It wants me to climb the stairs.

"I can't," I say. "It is too soon," and I am back laying on cold cement, my father scowling from the corner, my cheek pressed against the floor. A body lies down on top of mine, heavy but comforting. A low voice speaks into my ear. It is neutral, neither male nor female.

"Don't you know that you can find freedom, just with your heart?" it says.

I feel afraid. I look at my wrists, and see that they are in shackles.

"Is this prison?" I ask.

The room fills with the gentle arpeggios of a distant harp.

"No," the voice says. "This is paradise. . . ."

Harp notes invaded my brain, rolling up and down in relentless repetition.

I grabbed for my phone, knocking a full glass of water sideways onto the floor. The glass shattered, creating a dripping mess of broken shards.

"Shit!"

Tank leapt from the base of the bed, landed on the floor with a thump, and sped out the door, my dream slithering away behind him.

The harp sounded another round of dulcet notes, making me want to smash something else, this time on purpose.

"Hello," I croaked into the phone. I checked the time. I'd been asleep maybe five hours.

"Mr. Norbu?" The voice was high-pitched and panicky. "This is Wesley Harris, Freda's husband. She's in a coma. I didn't know who else to call."

I took the Mustang. Freda was in Glendale, at Providence Saint Joseph, and I didn't want to waste any time. As I sped along Pacific Coast Highway, the dawn sky scalloped with pinks and blues, I tried to retrieve my dream as best I could. Something about my father, and a tower.

A sentence floated up: *Don't you know that you can find freedom, just with your heart?* I glanced at the ocean, and more came drifting back. Pelicans. I was close to knowing something, but not close enough.

A chorus of crickets erupted in my pocket—I had changed my ringtone from celestial strumming to nature's jaunty fiddlers, much more my style—and I fumbled to attach the little white earbuds that would keep me legal. Mike's goofball grin beamed from my screen.

"You're up late," I said to Mike.

"You're up early," he replied.

Then I swear I heard soft laughter. Female laughter.

"Are you with a girl?" I said.

"Not 'a' girl, 'my' girl," he said. More giggles.

Well, that explained the ear-to-ear grin.

"I've got some answers for you, boss," he went on.

"First things first," I answered. "Your girl. I need some who, what, and when's, please."

"Tricia, a grad student studying cultural anthropology at UCLA, and we met at my rave the other night. She's practically moved in."

"To your house?" My voice was more of a bleat. Was he out of his mind? "Are you out of your mind?"

"Hey, it's cool, Ten. With our crazy schedules, it's the only way we'll see each other. Anyway, what's it to you?"

I felt like reaching through the phone and knocking Mike's block off, but he had a point. What was it to me? Apparently, I didn't like the ease, the warp-speed with which these two were moving ahead together. I filed that thought under "Later."

"So Ten, I called because I found a few more policies with TFJ."

"Go on."

"I'll send you the links, but basically I was able to find three more contracts, each one for two million bucks."

"All old-time musicians?"

"Two of them. The other was a retired character actor, Jeremiah Cook, did a lot of television back in the day. Best known for a recurring role on *Star Trek*, where he played some crazy Russian author or something. He made a second career for himself signing memorabilia at Trekkie conventions."

"Florio has no doubt got him believing he's owed a bunch of unpaid royalties on that stuff."

"Yeah, well you can put that in the past tense," Mike said.

"He's dead?"

"Yep."

"How?"

"Cancer, they say, though—get this—his wife, Camille, claimed he'd been in remission since he went to Mexico for some kind of hoodoo, new age treatments. Insisted his collapse came out of nowhere. Sound familiar?"

"How old?"

"Eighty-two."

"Let me guess. No autopsy."

"No autopsy."

It was looking more and more like Florio was either playing with marked cards or on intimate terms with the Grim Reaper. First Buster, then Jeremiah Star Trek, and now Freda was in a coma. He must be ahead $4 million, at least. That's a lot of ostrich loafers. I had no doubt Mike would dredge up even more payouts before he was finished.

"Okay," I said. "While we're on the subject of Florio, there's something else I want you to do."

"Shoot."

"This is probably a long shot, but could you see if there's any connection between Tommy Florio and a guy named Vince Barsotti?"

He whistled. "That's too fucking weird, man."

My attention pricked, like a hunting dog on point. Mike was about to flush something from the bushes.

"Here's what else I found. TFJ and Associates is a Nevada corporation, registered a few years ago by Thomas Florio Junior and two other dudes. Guess who one of them is?"

"Vincent Barsotti," I said.

"Bingo."

"Who's the third guy?"

"Dude called Liam O'Flaherty."

"Florio, Barsotti, and O'Flaherty. Sounds diverse," I said.

"Yeah, well, guess what career path O'Flaherty was on for a good thirty years?"

"I can't wait to find out."

"Same path as me, probably, if you hadn't turned my head around. He did a series of stretches in prison—Irish prison, to be exact. He could con beans out of a can, this guy. Then he took a little break before he became a legal crook over here. He's thought to be affiliated with the Irish Mob."

The Mob again.

"What about Florio and Barsotti? Have they done time as well?"

"Nothing on Florio yet. I'm just beginning to work on Barsotti. There's a big pile of Vincent Barsottis out there."

"Maybe I can help you with that." I ran down what I had learned in my two days of old-fashioned door-to-door snooping.

"Nice work." Mike said. "For someone who's technically challenged, you're a pretty good spy. I'll call you when I find out more. Oh, and Tricia thinks your name is cute." He hung up before I could respond.

The new pieces of information shifted and re-formed with what I already knew, but the kaleidoscope remained too abstract to decipher. What did Florio and Barsotti have in common, besides Italian last names? One of them was running a scam on older celebrities, and the other owned pigs and luxury cars. How did they end up in business together? And what was their connection to O'Flaherty? To the Mafia? To the Children of Paradise?

I pulled into the hospital parking lot none the wiser. As I headed for the ICU, I had a sinking feeling any answers it might hold were locked deep in Freda Wilson's comatose mind.

Freda lay still, a felled animal in a nest of tubes and fluids. Wesley sat by her, stroking one swollen hand. Their son stood at the foot of the bed. Gone was the swagger, the sullen, rebellious stance. He looked like what he was, a scared boy whose mother's survival was at the mercy of machinery, or maybe a miracle. My heart hurt as I took

in this tableau of family grief. Human life is so very fragile. My years of Buddhist training underscored an awareness that death can come at any moment, but the sight of
Freda made this awareness all too real, and painful.

The steady beeping of mechanical pumps and
dispensers told me Freda's body could no longer function
without technological help. How much inner life was
still there, I did not know. I bowed my head, closed
my eyes, and tried to reach her heart with mine. I felt
no corresponding warmth. I did the next best thing,
surrounding her with a peaceful light. If she was meant
to recover, I hoped it would speed her healing. If not,
maybe it would help create more ease for her passage to
the next realm.

I left her, and went to the visitor's lounge to wait.
Wesley soon joined me. He looked a decade older than the
last time I saw him.

"I'm so very sorry," I said. He nodded, and his eyes
filled. He sat down next to me, and hunched over. His raw
pain was palpable.

I reached back to my time in the monastery, all those
hours of sitting, practicing loving-kindness toward myself
and others. I closed my eyes, and located a powerful drop-
let of condensed compassion, lodged deep in my chest. I
invited the caring to expand, fill my body, spill over. *May
you enjoy happiness. . . .* It spread like bittersweet syrup.
May you be free from suffering. . . . I tried to direct it to the
source of Wesley's grief, coat it with comfort, or at least
leach away some of the soreness. *May you rejoice in the
well-being of others. . . . May you live in peace, free from anger,
hatred, and attachment. . .*

Wesley lifted his head from his hands.

"She didn't want to keep me up," he said. "She started
coughing, it was the middle of the night, and she didn't
want to keep me up."

He turned to me.

"Why didn't I tell her to stay in bed with me?"

The story spilled out of him now, how she'd been fighting the remnants of the flu for weeks. How last night she ran out of cough drops, couldn't stop coughing, and finally put on her robe and went to the kitchen, to make a hot toddy.

How he woke up with a start several hours later and stumbled out of the bedroom and found her lying on the living room floor. "I thought she was asleep," he said. "Her cheeks were so rosy and pink."

He turned to me, his eyes haggard. "They say her lungs are full of fluid. That her heart is failing. That her . . . her brain is . . . that she may never come back." His voice cracked. "Why didn't I tell her to stay in bed?"

"Wesley, listen to me," I said. "It's not your fault. It may not be anybody's, but it's definitely not yours."

He looked at me. "What do you mean by that?"

I decided to give him the truth.

"Look, I don't want to alarm you, but there's something odd going on, something related to Florio. At least two other people he signed contracts with have died under suspicious circumstances. This may be related."

Wesley shook his head, as if trying to wake himself up. "You saying this isn't the flu?"

"I'm not sure what I'm saying," I admitted, "but things aren't adding up here. Freda may have been the victim of foul play."

Wesley's face darkened as he absorbed this new information. He grabbed my wrist, his grip strong.

"You find out anything more, you tell me, understand? Bastards!"

"I will," I said.

He stood. "I've got to get back to Freda." His body swayed. I jumped up and took his arm to steady him.

"Mr. Norbu, thank you for telling me this," he said. "I was carrying more weight than I knew."

I walked him back to the ICU and left him there, holding Freda's hand. I couldn't undo what had happened, but

I was glad to at least bring him some small relief from his unfounded guilt.

I saw Bill had phoned. No message. I called him back from the parking lot.

"Yo," he answered. "I got something for you."

"You up for some lunch?"

"As long as pastrami's involved."

I arrived at Langer's a few minutes early and grabbed a booth by the window. My favorite waitress, Jean, came at me like a heat-seeking missile. She filled my coffee cup without asking.

"Ten-zing," she sang, in her distinctive Arizona drawl. "I've missed you!"

"Likewise," I said, bowing and kissing her hand. Jean is in her 60s, tall and thin, with a quirky, if careworn, beauty and a bobbed haircut straight out of the roaring '20s. She's been waiting on cops at Langer's for over two decades, with the brashness and bunions to prove it.

"I hear you quit the force," she said. "Good for you. I wish I could quit."

"What's stopping you?" I said.

"I still owe the Scientologists a hundred thousand dollars," she said.

We shared a laugh. Jean had, in fact, been a devoted member of the Church of Scientology for 16 years, signing up with them in her early 20s. She was one of the few people who quit and lived to tell the tale: "They told me I was totally clear. I told them, 'I'm not totally clear, I'm totally broke, thanks to you guys, so fuck you very much, and good-bye.'"

Jean gave me a stern glare over her coffeepot. "You look tired, Ten-zing. Are you all right?"

I admitted I was working pretty hard, for an unemployed person.

"And how's the bad news doing?"

"Ruling the household, as always."

Jean has called Tank "the bad news" ever since the time she harangued me about my lack of a love life. I told her she was wrong, I had all the intimacy a man could want.

"The good news is, I've been in a long-term, committed relationship for four years," I'd said.

"What's the bad news?"

"It's with a cat."

Bill slid into the booth across from me, and Jean jotted down our orders: pastrami and Swiss for him, a grilled cheese sandwich and a side of slaw for me.

I took in Bill's coat and tie, and shifted a little in my seat. I was still in the rumpled jeans and T-shirt I'd pulled on in the dark this morning.

"Hey," I said.

"Hey," Bill answered. He reached under his coat and pulled out a manila envelope.

"You wanted to know the autopsy results from the woman who got killed over your way."

"Barbara Maxey."

"Right, Maxey. Well." He pushed the envelope across the wood.

I slid out the report and found myself staring down at the photograph of Barbara's ashen cadaver. Her warm smile flashed in front of me, then was gone. I skimmed over the details: "petechial hemorrhaging" and "laryngeal abrasions," cold, clinical terms, belying the violence of her death.

Then my breath caught.

"Did you see this?" I asked, pointing to the bottom of the last page.

"I saw it," he said, his voice grim.

"Her voice box was crushed *after* she was strangled to death?"

"Yep. Looks like somebody was making a point."

Don't talk, I thought.

Jean delivered our plates. Bill leaned over and inhaled the aroma. "Mmm-mmm. I'm telling you, Ten, you have no idea what you're missing."

Jean, still hovering, snorted. "Shame on you, Bill. He can't eat cows on account of they're sacred to him. Right, Ten-zing?"

I didn't have the heart to tell her that would be the Hindus. As Jean zoomed off to another table, I slipped the autopsy report back in the envelope and set it aside.

Don't talk. But about what? What had Barbara known that demanded such a brutal message?

CHAPTER 16

Bill, being a working man, had to eat and run. I sat in the parking lot for a few moments, digesting, and testing my emotional insides. They were tender, sensitive to my mental prodding, like a canker sore. Reading the details of Barbara's autopsy had walloped me, delivered a brutal gut-blow matching the fist-smash to her own jugular. What was I doing to help her? I had no money coming in, and was no closer to figuring this stuff out than I was to earning a salary.

I looked at my clenched fists, resting on the steering wheel. Loosened them, finger by finger. Self-recrimination was going to get me absolutely nowhere. There were too many questions swirling like loose sediment in my psyche. I had to find a quiet zone to sit, let the silt settle. See what I actually knew.

I drove north on Alameda, turned right on Third, and again on San Pedro. I circled the block to look for street parking, and then thought better of it. A bright yellow Mustang might prove irresistible to gangbangers and car thieves. I grudgingly parked underground at Five Star and walked the two blocks to the Japanese American Cultural & Community Center. I tried to leave my resentment over public parking outside the gates of my secret downtown refuge, an authentic Japanese stroll garden.

I had stumbled onto the garden early on in my police training. I'd gone into Little Tokyo for takeout and was looking for a quiet place to eat. Something drew me to the Cultural Center, and I'd soon spotted a small side gate. I pushed it open, and was rewarded with my first glimpse of the Seiryu-en, the Garden of the Clear Stream. It turned out food wasn't allowed, but ever since, I'd visited this garden many times to partake of my other necessary sustenance, the spiritual kind.

I looked around. I was alone. Good. I stood still, letting the melodious sound of water cascading over rock soothe me. The azalea bushes were glossy green, with tight buds hinting at the spring bloom ahead. The delicate foliage of the heavenly bamboo still showed traces of the bright crimson it wore through the winter months, but I could picture the clusters of creamy white blossoms to come. The same with the Japanese wisteria—its green leaves held their secret close, but within a few months the vines would be draped with flowering lilac clusters, smelling of grape and possibility.

My eyes traced the tumbling waterfall as it forked into two streams near its head, splitting around a small island, then slowing and reuniting in a shallow, quiet pond.

I stepped onto the walking path, and let my attention rest on the sensation of my upright body, my arms hanging by my sides, my hands lightly clasping each other. I let my eyes rest on the ground, a few feet ahead of me. *Lift, move, press. Lift, move, press.* I paused, breathing in and out, feeling my lungs bellow and compress. *Lift, move, press.* Feet touching the ground, the space between each step, the feeling of stopping and starting. The mental silt began to settle, the inner chatter to fade away. *Lift, move, press.*

I paced the circular path, feeling the terrain change beneath me: hard granite . . . beaten earth . . . knobby, uneven stepping-stones. I traversed the three arched, wooden bridges, hanging like lanterns over the gurgling water. *Lift, move, press.*

Pieces of my dream tiptoed back to me, enticed by the clear, empty vessel that was now my consciousness. I let the images flow: my father standing guard . . . the X-shaped building . . . the pelicans . . . the watchtower.

A geometric tattoo, straddling a man's thick neck. Guards. Pelicans. Prison. Paradise.

Got it.

As I left, I stopped at a small fountain, cupping my hands under the cool stream of water flowing from a bamboo spout into a stone basin. My teachers taught me well. *Thank you.*

Bill met me in the lobby of the Police Headquarters.

"Two Tenzing sightings in one day," he said. "I like it."

We took the elevator to his fourth-floor office, where he closed the door. I told him about the insurance policies. The suspicions I had about Buster's death and Freda's illness. My visit to the Children of Paradise. Barsotti's pig farm. John D's almond grove. Then I ran the dream images by him, and what I thought they meant.

Bill nodded at once, like he got where I was going. He pulled up a page on the computer and tipped the screen my way. I found myself staring at an overhead view of the Pelican Bay State Prison. My eyes zeroed in on an X-shaped cluster of white concrete buildings set apart from the main facility.

"What is that?" I pointed.

"That's the Security Housing Unit," Bill said. "Pelican's supermax-type control unit for the superbad. Affectionately referred to by inmates as 'the Shu.'"

Is that what you want to go back to? The shoe?

"The Shu. Of course," I murmured.

"Those are some bad boys in there, Ten. Not to be messed with."

"Can you see if they had an inmate by the name of Monroe, Eldon Monroe?

Bill picked up the phone. Three re-routes later, he had an answer for me. No. It was what I expected, though not necessarily what I needed to make sense of anything else.

"You'll get there," Bill said.

On my way out the door, insects started chirping. The look on my partner's face was priceless.

"New phone," I told him. "Very green."

I glanced down. It was Zimmy.

"Hi, Zimmy," I said.

"My man. How're you doing on this fine day? I hope I'm not calling at a bad time."

"I'm doing great," I said. "I just finished an hour of walking meditation, so you are probably talking to the clearest version of me you're going to get."

Bill made a gagging motion from his desk.

"Good deal," Zimmy said. "I had an idea pop into my head clear as day myself—something I want you to do for me—and I'm not taking no for an answer."

"That's quite an introduction," I said. "I'm all ears."

"Jilly and I have been talking it over, and we want to hire you as a private detective to get to the bottom of all this stuff. Florio, Barbara's death, the whole thing."

I smiled. "Thanks, Zimmy, but I'm already investigating this on my own. You don't need to pay me for it."

"You don't understand, Ten. I do. See, when Barbara and I first got together, she had some money saved up, several thousand dollars. Me being me back then, it wasn't long before I'd put it up my nostrils, and hers."

I waited.

"I have to make this right somehow," he said. "It's eating away at me, you know? Jilly can always tell when I'm getting wound up, so last night we had a long talk. We've been real fortunate up here, Ten. We just found out we're gonna have the biggest crop of pears since we started growing them. We've got some extra money to spend. But even if we didn't, I'd be asking you. I owe this to Barbara. I'm telling you, my peace of mind, maybe even my sobriety, depends upon repaying this debt. You'd be doing me a big favor by letting me buy five grand's worth of your services. So, do we have a deal?"

I spot-checked my insides, and his, for any hidden agendas, and came up clear.

"We have a deal," I said.

"Fantastic. I'll get a check in the mail to you this afternoon. And Ten? I love you, brother."

"You're a good man, Zimmy. I'm proud to have you as my first official client."

I hung up, and beamed at Bill.

"What?" he said.

"Magic is what, Bill. Five thousand dollars, falling from a tree, is what."

"Zimmy hired you?"

"Zimmy hired me."

"Then I guess it's true, what they say. 'If you investigate it, they will come. . . .'"

"Who will come?"

"Forget it." Bill walked over and clapped me on the back. "My dad used to tell me the only difference between an amateur and a professional is one dollar. You are now a bona fide professional private investigator. Congratulations. Now get to work."

I drove home smiling. Tank met me at the door. I picked him up and gave his sturdy body a hug. His eyes blinked, like, "What's the big deal?" I was on a spiritual roll, so I beamed him a little mind-movie, a series of mental pictures of me happily working on the case, and a cupboard stacked high with cans of tuna fish.

Then, just in case he didn't pick up my vibes, I carried him into the kitchen and opened one, emptying the entire can in his bowl. Tank's eyes opened wide in appreciation as he vigorously chomped down the contents, and happiness reigned supreme in our little household of two.

The Buddha tells us our thoughts and emotions, good or bad, never stay put. Rather, they pass like weather systems, so long as we don't attempt to control them. As I watched Tank eat, I concentrated on just enjoying the feeling of abundance, without trying to staple it to my brain.

I made myself some green tea, and settled on my deck to make some calls. I scrolled through to find Julie's number, and as I did, sure enough, a wisp of cloud passed over my sunny mood. I was grateful Bill hadn't asked about us—I still didn't know where "us" was going.

On the one hand, I liked her a lot. Her humor. Her confidence. Her freckles. But I couldn't help but wonder if her self-assurance would soon prove to be a facade, as it had every time before with the women I dated. What if she turned around one day and was wearing another face, her real one, her warm, shining eyes replaced by two black holes of neediness?

Maybe it's your neediness, not theirs.

I pushed that idea away. If anything, I was too self-sufficient for most women.

Okay, then. Don't call Julie today. It's still too soon. Better yet, let her call you.

I turned my attention to the Children of Paradise. I decided to check in on John D and see if I could get any more information out of him about the cult. Fortunately, his number was listed.

"Hello!" John D sounded startled, as if he didn't get a lot of phone calls.

"John D," I said. "This is Ten Norbu."

"Oh, yeah," he said. "What can I do for you, young fella?"

"I'm wondering if you can tell me a little more about your next-door neighbors."

"You're welcome to whatever I know," he said.

"Besides Nehemiah, have you seen any other members? I'd like to know how many there are."

I heard his breath wheezing as he thought things over.

"Every now and then they'll gather in the field in a big circle, holding hands. I reckon there's maybe forty people, all told."

So they hadn't expanded.

"And do they ever leave the place?"

"A few of 'em go down Thursdays to buy groceries."

"Go down where?"

"There's a farmer's market in town every Thursday,

THE FIRST RULE OF TEN

down near the Vons. I see 'em there buying vegetables and fruit. I like to go myself—that's how come I know."

"Is it always the same people?"

He chuckled. "I'm sorry, son, I'm seventy-seven years old. One robe-wearing hippie looks just about like every other one to me." He paused, as if revisiting the question. "Come to think of it, though, there is this one woman, she's got long brown hair, she does the shopping most of the time. I remember her 'cause she'll smile at me sometimes."

"The rest of them don't smile?"

"Nah, they're a real serious bunch. She sticks in my mind 'cause when you're old like me, you don't get a lot of smiles from young women. Maybe I'll see her at the market tomorrow. You want me to call you?"

"How would you feel about taking your newly adopted son there in person?" I asked.

I heard his rumbling chuckle again. "Danged if my adopted son don't visit me more than my actual one! Sure, come on out. I'll show you all the best stalls."

"If you think of anything else important, just give me a call."

"If I think of anything else important, I'll write it down first, *then* give you a call. These days, by the time I get to the phone, I've already forgotten who I was calling."

CHAPTER 17

The next morning, I put myself through my paces, and was on the road, earning my keep, by nine. I took the Mustang. I wasn't planning on any off-road surveillance this trip, and truthfully, I wanted to see John D's reaction to my roadster.

Ninety minutes later, I was kicking dust up the hill into his driveway. He was ready and waiting, rocking on his front porch in a checked short-sleeved shirt and stiff new jeans. He pushed himself upright, and stared. Then he started fanning his face, like my car was giving off too much heat.

"Hoo, boy," he said. "Will you lookie there."

I grinned with pleasure.

Soon he was circling my car.

"You win the lottery or something? Pop the trunk, wouldja?"

I did, and stood beside him like a proud parent as he located the battery, lodged in the back. John D closed the trunk, ran his hand across the rear spoiler, and squatted to check the mufflers.

"Nice glasspacks," he said. "V-8?"

"V-8, three-oh-six horsepower."

He grunted and opened the driver's side door to peer inside, letting out a long, low whistle at the steering wheel. "Mahogany, and a horn button. Lordie me, this takes me back. Override traction bars, too, I see."

Then John D spotted the snake emblem on the glove box. He wheeled on me, his eyes glinting.

"Son, how on God's green earth did you get yourself a '65 Shelby Mustang?"

"Hop in and I'll tell you."

I spared him no detail as we drove to the market. I hadn't had such a rapt audience since the time I was stopped on the street by a guy driving a yellow Lotus. It was the same color as mine, but not nearly as rare, therefore sexy, and the poor guy's face told me he knew it.

"I was on patrol," I told John D. "Got called to the scene of a drag racing accident, a bad one. One fool was doing ninety blind drunk. He swerved into the other guy, they both flipped, and that was that. Both drivers were pronounced dead on the scene. Vehicular homicide, times two. The cars were pretty much totaled, but something about one of them, a white Mustang with black stripes, caught my eye. The chassis was smashed all to hell, but I pried open the trunk on a hunch, and spotted the telltale backyard battery. The fuel tank was another giveaway— thirty-two gallons instead of the usual sixteen. And of course there was no backseat, just a fiberglass ledge, or what was left of it, for the spare."

John D nodded. He knew cars.

"They impounded the car as evidence, until all the paperwork was in," I continued, "but I kept my eye on it. To this day I don't know why nobody else figured out that it was a Shelby, but when it went up for auction, I put in a quick early bid, and it was mine for just under five thousand."

John D chuckled. "Just about what it cost brand-new, way back when. What I want to know is, how'd you know what it was in the first place? You being a monk and all."

"Well, I'm not what you'd call a shining example of commitment to the Noble Eightfold Path. Tourists sometimes visited our monastery, and one of them left behind a classic auto magazine, which I salvaged from the recycling bin. A refurbished '65 Shelby was featured in one of the articles, and I fell for it, fell hard. I can't tell you how many meditations I spent trying to free myself from that obsession."

John D looked puzzled.

"As you can see, it worked really well," I said.

John D laughed. Then he leaned his head back, and closed his eyes.

"Darcy Forsting," he said, finally.

"Who?"

"Darcy Forsting. My first, and prolly best, roll in the hay, which wasn't in hay at all, but the front seat of a '56 Corvette Stingray Coupe. Tighter than a nun's you-know-what—the front seat I mean, not Darcy—but that didn't stop us. It was my uncle's, and a beaut. Painted shiny red, like one of them fireball candies. Lord, but I loved that car. Talk about muscle."

We shared a moment of silent appreciation for first loves.

As we entered downtown, John D directed me to a lot near the bustling farmer's market. He hitched up his pants, and off we went on our mission. Exactly what the mission was, wasn't very clear to me, except that I wanted to get close to some of the Children of Paradise, if possible, and observe them away from their native turf. As we entered the market, John D grunted, "Over there."

He steered my eyes down a narrow lane of vegetable stalls crowded with shoppers. At the far end, I spotted three people in robes, two men and a woman with a long rope of hair. They were bent over what looked like a stacked wall of leafy greens.

"That the woman you were telling me about?"

He nodded.

"Okay," I said. "Let's go see what we can stir up."

One young acolyte was filling a pushcart with bunches of green and purple kale. He had bug eyes and a weak chin. I dismissed him as the peon of the group.

The other man was a different story. He stood slightly to one side, his eyes sweeping the Thursday morning crowd. His robe could not hide the fact that he was muscled and very fit. His stance was not so much relaxed as coiled, but probably no one but a detective would notice that.

I saw his eyes narrow at something across the way. A rapid series of minute but distinct responses flashed across his face. It was like watching a slide show as he shuttered through a range of feelings, from suspicion, to anger, to—and this made no sense—what looked like a kind of . . . vulnerable pride?

I followed his gaze to a young couple. The guy had the flat-topped buzz cut and green camouflage pants of an army man on leave. He had his arm around a young, very pretty woman. She had a wide, lumpy cloth wrapped around her waist and chest, and I realized somewhere in there a baby was tucked. I looked back at the man in the robe. Interesting; something about this scene both angered and touched him.

Lookout Man shot his eyes in my direction, as if he felt my stare, and I quickly shifted my attention to the nubby avocados in front of me. I picked one up and studied its skin.

The threesome moved on. I observed from a distance. The woman appeared to be the produce scout. She'd reconnoiter each stall, poking and prodding, and then point to what she wanted. Peon and Lookout Man loaded up the scales, and she'd pay the vendor with bills peeled off a fat roll. Then she'd move to the next stall as they piled the pushcart with enough foodstuffs to feed a small army.

I ambled closer to the woman, careful to keep one eye on the bodyguard. As I neared her, I could see that, like Barbara Maxey, she was older than she first appeared. At least 50 in her case. She had a desert-weathered face, and her lank brown hair was banded into a ponytail that reached halfway down her back. John D drew next to me.

"Definitely her," he murmured.

She moved over to peruse a huge stall piled with root vegetables—russet potatoes, crimson and gold beets, bunched carrots, and a big pile of bulbous fennel.

We hadn't rehearsed anything, so John D's direct approach caught me by surprise.

"Hello there, young lady," he called out. "Remember me? I'm your next-door neighbor, John D."

She looked up. Sure enough, she smiled.

Her eyes cut over to me, then to her two robed companions. They were busy stacking their cart. She returned her attention to John D.

"Oh, yes," she said. "The Prophet speaks of you often."

John D slapped his thigh in delight. "He does? What's he say about ol' John D?"

"He says to be polite to you." She glanced at me again, and gnawed on a cuticle.

John D caught her eye-flick in my direction. "This is my son, Charlie. He just got outta the navy. He used to be friends with that blond lady, the other one who came down here sometimes. What was her name again, son?"

"Barbara," I said, watching the woman closely.

"Sister Barbara?" she whispered. Confusion rippled across her face, then panic, as if two worlds were about to collide and she had no tools for surviving the ensuing explosion.

I nodded. "She came to see me just before she died."

"Sister Barbara's dead?"

"We think she may have been murdered," John D added.

She wheeled, doubling over as if to stifle an upswell of grief. Her elbow knocked a stack of potatoes, sending them tumbling. Several people moved in to retrieve the spilled tubers, and the hubbub acted as a flare to Lookout Man and his sidekick. They quickly finished filling their cart and slalomed it through the crowd. As they rolled closer, the woman used her fists to scrub the tears from her creased cheeks. She took a deep breath and was suddenly, eerily calm.

"I'm sorry," she said. "I cared for Sister Barbara. We all did. Her fall from grace was tragic."

I said, "I wasn't in touch with her while she was in your group, so I never got the whole story of why she left."

"Sister Barbara is in God's hands, now," she said. "I have nothing more to say."

Her two companions were moments away.

"At least tell me your name," I said.

Her head-shake was almost imperceptible. Then Lookout Man was at her elbow.

"Sister Rose, we should go." He gave me a hard stare. I kept my expression mild.

"Yes, yes," she said, and she walked toward a stall of apples, the two men flanking her like guard dogs.

John D sighed. "My daddy always used to say, 'Dear Lord, protect us from Your followers.' I think he got that just about right."

"She knows something," I said. "But we may never know what it is."

"Well, Mr. Detective, what's our next move?"

"Good question," I said. "Let's do some shopping. I'm sure I'll think of something after that."

We split up, and I went straight back to the fennel. I had no idea what one did with fennel, but I knew someone who might. I bought a big bulb of it, topped with feathery fringe. I added purple kale, parsnips, shiny flat peppers the color of red lipstick, and a paper bag of chanterelles that resembled pale sea anemones. I pictured the chanterelles sautéing in olive oil.

Why hadn't Julie called me?

In a blink, self-sufficiency flipped into a sudden desire to hear Julie's voice. I pulled out my iPhone and called her. I got her message again, and felt the clean cut of disappointment. She was mighty unavailable, for a single gal.

"Hey, Julie, I'm at the Antelope Valley farmer's market, loading up on produce I have no idea how to cook. Little help, here?"

I was putting my purchases into my trunk when John D wheezed to my side. He dropped his shopping bag next to mine and leaned against the car to steady himself while he caught his breath. I noted the self-satisfied grin.

"What?" I said.

"You prolly think I was just getting supplies, Ten, but turns out I was doing a little detecting, too."

He rummaged in the front pocket of his jeans and pulled out a little scrap of paper.

"Sister Rose slipped this into my hand before she left."

She'd torn a corner off her shopping list. I read the girlish, looped handwriting: "Meet me on the hill tonight. 8 P.M."

It looked like I was going to spend more time in scenic Lancaster than I had planned. Fortunately, I had a local with me. My stomach growled; sampling the occasional strawberry and tangerine section had only succeeded in making me ravenous.

"I'm starving," I told John D.

"I got just the place," he said. I should have known from the glint in his eye I was in for it.

I parked my Mustang between a pickup and a Prius, outside "Josecita's Bar and Eats." Apparently Josecita had something for every pay grade. As I followed John D into the ramshackle eatery, a rooster bumped his way past my legs.

"That's Henry," John D said. "Don't mind him. He's blind." My eyes adjusted to the dark, saloonlike atmosphere, and I realized Henry wasn't the only oddity. A young goat was tethered to the jukebox, a tiny white pig was roaming free, and a couple of mangy dogs lay curled in the corner. I heard a weird chattering above my head. I looked up and blinked.

"John D," I said. "Is that a—"

"Yes, it is. A South American woolly monkey. He goes by the name of Bonaparte."

"Hunh." Monkeys were a dime a dozen in India, but this was my first Southern California sighting.

We found an empty table. I grabbed a seat, and John D crossed to where three coffeepots perched side by side on hot plates, like broody hens. He returned with one and filled our cups with thick sludge only a mother could love.

"House rules. You pour your own," he said.

"John D!" a thunderous voice bellowed from across the room. An enormous woman, part brawler, part lover, loomed in the kitchen entrance, encased in a psychedelic, multicolored muumuu. "Gimme some sugar!"

Three hundred pounds of quivering love made a bee-line for my friend. She wrapped him up like a burrito and squeezed. Then she caught sight of me over John D's shoulder and spring-loaded him free.

John D recognized the avid look on her face.

"Josecita, I don't think . . ."

She darted behind me, and for an instant I was enveloped by two billowing breasts, hanging like warm water balloons on either side of my head. Then Josecita cackled and was gone.

My cheeks burning, I grabbed John D's arm.

"What the hell was that?"

John D grinned. "She must like you, Ten. She just gave you the famous earmuff treatment."

Soon she was back with two greasy menus, like nothing had happened. John D waved his away.

"I'll have the burger, darlin'," he said.

I opened my menu, but Josecita snatched it back. She bored in on my Asian eyes and almond-toned skin. Read me like a tea leaf.

"You one of them vee-gans?" she asked. I saw John D shake his head at me slightly, warning me.

"Well, not exactly . . ." I hedged, when she clapped me on the back. It was a little like getting sideswiped by a bus. I braced myself for the mockery that was sure to follow, but her face split wide with a gap-toothed grin.

"Good for you. I love all God's creatures myself. Listen, honey, I'm no angel, and I do love my burgers, but I ain't never turned away an animal that didn't have a home, or a man who was hungry. I'll fix you up, don't you worry."

She disappeared again, and I slumped with relief.

"Welcome to the monkey house," John D said. He laughed, and his laughter turned into a hacking cough, which went on longer than it should have. He patted his lips with his napkin, and I saw his hand was shaking a little. A shadow swooped my heart like a barn swallow. I put my fingers on John D's forearm.

"How are you doing?"

"Doing just fine," he said.

"No. How are you doing, really?"

John D took a moment before answering. "You want to be careful posing that question to a person my age, 'less you're prepared for a full-on organ recital."

"Well, I'm asking anyway."

He met my eyes. "Okay, then. I got a tumor down in my belly growing like weeds in summertime. They wanted to stuff me full of chemo and radiation a few months ago, back when it was about the size of a grapefruit, but I turned 'em down. If I'm gonna die, I'm gonna do it my way, not theirs." His glare was a challenge.

I let his words settle. Probing what lay beneath, I found only certainty. "Sounds like the right decision to me."

"You think so? I do, too. The doctors are fighting me every step of the way, though."

"When it comes to dying, everybody gets to be their own boss."

"Yep, that's the way I look at it, but I can see the other side too, I guess. Doctors are trained to never give up. Besides, everyone involved can make a bundle keeping an old guy like me alive, even if it's only for a few more months."

"What about your son?"

"What about him? Fighting me on everything is just a habit he can't break. How I sired such an opinionated, uptight stick-in-the-mud is beyond me. I swear he was born blinkered."

Another father disappointed in his son. In this case, I was pretty sure I'd side with the father. Still, I noticed John D didn't exactly answer my question straight on.

"Norman believes I'm too stoned to know my own mind about anything," John D went on. "Wait until his body starts breaking into pieces of pain—he'll be begging for the evil weed."

John D was just full of surprises.

"You smoke pot?"

"Medical marijuana," he said.

"Really."

"Perfectly legal," he added, with noticeable satisfaction.

Josecita slammed a hamburger the size of a dessert plate in front of John D, and a steaming vat of vegetarian chili before me.

"Wow," I said. "That's a lot of chili."

"Eat it or wear it," she said, and sailed like a spinnaker back to the kitchen.

I ate it. I had no doubt she would make good on the threat.

CHAPTER 18

Back at the house, John D invited me to join him on the porch while he "rested his bones." After a few minutes of rocking, his chin slumped down on his chest. Soon he was snoring like a walrus.

I decided to do some exploring. I took a good long stroll around his property. As I weaved a path through the acres of dying almond trees, I came upon two groupings of young living ones planted side by side across the road and separated from each other by a low wire fence. The trees on one side were marked with neon-yellow plastic ties. Other than that, I couldn't see any difference between the two groves.

On my way back, I checked out a small patch of marijuana, maybe half a dozen healthy-looking plants, tucked in the corner of John D's backyard between the tomatoes and nasturtiums.

John D was still asleep. I tiptoed inside for a drink of water. I paused at the photograph on the mantel he'd showed me the other day. The blossoming branches and smiling faces made me a little melancholy.

I walked back outside and got my own rocking chair going, enjoying the shady coolness. I closed my eyes. Embracing the motto "Whatever works," I used the rhythmic snort and snuffle of John D's snoring to settle into a meditation.

Sometime later, his snores tapered off. I opened my eyes just as John D woke up. He looked around, confused for a moment before comprehension clicked in. He gave himself a back-cracking stretch and lumbered to his feet.

"Coffee?" he asked. I told him coffee was an excellent idea. I followed him inside to observe. He dumped several scoops of dark, oily beans into a cast-iron hand-grinder clamped to the counter. He cranked the beans into the consistency of cornmeal and loaded them into an old-fashioned percolator.

"Now, here's the secret to a good cup of coffee," he said. He broke off an inch-square piece of eggshell from a bucket by the sink and dropped it into the ground coffee. "Don't ask me why, but it mellows out the taste."

The coffee was strong and rich but without any acid bite or bitter aftertaste.

"Delicious."

"Toldja," John D said. "Now bring your brew and come sit with me while I take my medicine."

He opened a cupboard and removed a corncob pipe and a mason jar containing dried marijuana, the buds frosted white with THC, the active chemical component of the plant. He followed me outside and sat again, wincing with pain. He packed the stubby pipe, fired it up, and took a prodigious hit of smoke into his lungs. He held the pipe out to me. "Want some?" His voice had the strangled tone of an experienced stoner.

If there's a "Private Investigator's Rule Book" somewhere, I'm sure it says something about not partaking of cannabis on the job, but the opportunity to get high with a guy like John D didn't come along very often. Anyway, what was I going to do? Fire myself? I took the corncob and sucked in a mighty puff.

"I saw your backyard supply," I said, holding the smoke in.

"Yup. Been growing it for years. Legally, like I said. It's the only thing that helps with the pain, especially now that I got the cancer. I tried that stuff the doctors pass out like candy—Vicodin, Oxycontin, whatever—but it just makes me feel like I got a head full of mud. Pot's better."

He took another long inhale, trapped it tight, and then let the smoke stream from his nose. "Norman thinks

I'm turning into a dope fiend. I say bring it on. What do you say, Ten?"

I told him I had long ago forfeited my right to disapprove of anyone seeking relief from this world's pain. I told him about coming of age not far from the Kulu Valley in India, where the locals have been growing world-class pot for thousands of years. I confessed that as a teenager in the monastery, I would on occasion sneak out myself, late at night, for a little "herbal entertainment."

"No kidding." John D said. "Well, okay, then. I guess I don't have to worry about you warning me about the evils of smoking weed."

"How about this for a warning? John D, if you keep smoking that pot, eventually you are going to die!"

"What are you," he said. "Some kind of prophet?"

We got a pretty good snicker going over that, so good that we didn't hear the crunch of gravel on the driveway until it was too late. A white SUV rolled to a stop.

"Oh, shit!" John D gasped, and he shoved the mason jar and pipe under his rocking chair, looking so much like a kid with his hand in the cookie jar I let loose another round of laughter.

"Stop, stop!" John D gasped, waving his hands around. "He'll see!"

"Who'll see?"

"My son, the fun-buster."

I turned to look. The vehicle was marked with an L.A. County Department of Public Works insignia. A chunky middle-aged man in a white shirt and dark tie clambered out and huffed across the yard to the front steps.

"Hey, there, Norman," John D said.

"Hello, Dad." Norman looked back and forth between us.

I decided to introduce myself. I was afraid hearing John D's intoxicated butchering of my name would set me off again. I stood up and offered my hand.

"Tenzing Norbu. Most people call me Ten."

His handshake was unenthusiastic. "Norman Murphy."

John D giggled. "Most people call him Norman Murphy."

Norman looked at his father sharply. He was still standing at the bottom of the steps. I noticed John D hadn't asked him to sit and join us. I reclaimed my chair until further notice.

"What's his business here?" Norman asked his father. His tight little mouth barely moved when he spoke; I had the thought that he'd been weaned too early and was still pissed about it 50 years later. I stifled a snigger. Man. Marijuana was stronger than I'd remembered.

Then John D said, "What's your business what his business is with my business?" and I had to bite the inside of my cheek to quell the rising hysteria. My eyes watered from the effort.

Norman gave up on John D and turned to me. "I'm sorry, why are you here?"

I took a deep, steadying breath and prayed for self-control.

"I just met your father the other day," I said. "I had some business with the people next door and struck up a conversation with him. He invited me to his home. I've been hearing all about the almond business."

Norman's eyes narrowed. He opened his mouth as if to delve deeper, then seemed to think better of it.

"Right. The good old days," he said, his voice laced with bitterness. He turned back to his father. "So Dad, are you going to invite me to sit down?"

"Ain't nobody stopping you," John D answered.

I started to rise, but Norman parked his ample butt on the top step. Unfortunately, this put him directly opposite John D's rocking chair. It took Norman about two seconds to spot the pipe and jar of weed underneath.

Busted.

Norman's face reddened. "I knew it. Have you already been smoking that stuff today?"

"Yep," John D said, "and I plan to smoke plenty more before the day's done. Want a hit?"

Norman glared at me. "What about you? Are you doing drugs with this old man? Are you that pitiful?"

Heat suffused the muscles of my upper back and neck. Some people have a smarmy self-righteousness that begs for retaliation. Norman was one of those people.

"Maybe I should go," I said. "Let you both talk in private."

John D reached over and patted his son's knee. "Norman here hasn't been out to say hello to me for close to two months, so I'm pretty sure he don't have anything I want to hear now."

Norman stood and dusted off his pants. He directed his parting words at me. "I don't know what the hell you're doing here, but I want you to leave my father alone."

One part of me wanted to knock Norman sideways; another wished John D would tell him to piss off. Somewhere inside, a third part, the healthy part that wasn't attached to being right, frantically waved for my attention, telling me to just calm down. That part wanted to find out if there was anything more to be gleaned from the situation.

Without another word, I walked past Norman, crossed to his car, and leaned against it. He stared at me blankly, trying to guess at my motives. Finally he gave up and joined me.

"What's this business you've got with the people next door?" Norman asked. "I assume you're referring to that nutcase religious outfit."

I ignored his question. Instead, I tapped the official insignia. "How long have you been with the Public Works Department?"

"Uh, seventeen years. Why?"

I chose my verb tense carefully. "I started with the LAPD nine years ago. You've been with the Public Works Department even longer. Maybe we can help each other."

Narrow-minded people can't entertain paradoxes. Their minds are like one-lane roads—they work just fine until somebody approaches from the opposite direction. Then they experience an unsolvable dilemma, caused by the limited range of their thinking. Every situation has to be win-or-lose, dominate or be dominated. Giving ground so the other car can squeeze by is unacceptable. Better to crash head-on than let go of being right.

Norman's eyes flickered as he tried to squeeze the idea that I was a cop into the narrow alleyway of his brain. He was so busy trying to comprehend this new piece of information that he forgot to ask for my badge.

He relaxed, lowering his shoulders, and the body language told me he'd bought my story.

"So, what are you after them for?"

"You remember when they had that conflict over stealing power from the pig farm?"

"Yeah, but that got settled quite a while ago."

"They may be involved with something else now," I said.

"Like what?"

He seemed a little too interested to me.

"Sorry, I can't discuss it with you."

His leaned closer, man to man. "Come on," he pleaded. "We're both on the same side here—we're both concerned with enforcing the law." He offered me his hand. "Look, I want to apologize for the way I spoke to you up there. He's my father and, as you can imagine, I'm worried about him, out here on his own."

I went ahead and shook his hand, and I felt a little twinge of aversion.

"I've got to get back to the office," he said. "Here's my card. Call me if you need anything."

I pocketed his card. "Will do," I said. "I'll just say 'bye to your father."

Norman's SUV roared to life as I walked back toward the house. He gunned the engine, spitting gravel in his wake.

John D had nodded off again. Our date with Sister Rose was still a few hours away, so I decided to test my new phone out here in the boonies. I strolled to the far side of the yard and called to check on Freda.

Wesley answered on the first ring. He must have stepped outside the hospital for a smoke or something.

"How is she?"

"The same."

"How are you?"

"The same."

There wasn't much else to say after that.

Then I left a message for Mike. He'd be waking up soon. "Send me any contact information you have on that actor Jeremiah Star Trek, and his wife," I told him.

Finally, against my better judgment, I tried Julie again. This time, she answered.

"I was just about to call you," she said. "I'm off tomorrow. How does homemade minestrone and crème brûlée sound?"

"Dangerous," I said. "I have to warn you, minestrone is my favorite, but I am almost always disappointed by it. And as for crème brûlée, well, I grew up in Paris."

"Oh, goody. A challenge," she said.

I sat cross-legged with my back against a tree and recounted my day, starting with the fennel and ending with the forthcoming assignation with Sister Rose. Julie made me laugh with her culinary escapades. I made her laugh with my tale of Josecita's earmuff hazing. It felt nice to have someone to download my life with, besides Tank.

We talked until the sky grew dark. I looked across the yard. John D was up, moving around inside his lighted living room.

"Time to go," I said. "'Bye now." I waited for Julie to end the call. Her soft breath told me she was doing the same with me.

I smiled, letting the silence linger between us.

"On the count of ten, Ten," she finally said, but she hung up before I got to two.

Inside the house, John D was tipped back in his recliner, studying the photograph of himself with his two sons.

"Sorry about Norman," he said, without looking up.

"Hey, not to worry," I answered.

John D set the picture aside. "You still got your parents?"

"My father," I said. "My mother died a few years ago."

"You close to them?"

How to answer that question?

"Not really," I said. My mother's beautiful, haunted face flashed before me.

Valerie. Born and raised in Middle America, a free spirit trapped in a Midwestern, upper middle class world. She hated everything about her life, everything, that is, but the trust fund she inherited at 18. Bye-bye parents, hello India: she wanted to "find herself," like any self-respecting child of the '60s. Instead, after guru-jumping for two years, she found my father in Dharamshala, and found herself 20, pregnant, and too proud to return home. There was no question of her staying with my father; that became clear very quickly. So she moved to Paris to have me, still determined to live the bohemian life. Which in her case meant drinking herself to an early death.

A wave of sadness engulfed me. I had loved my mother desperately, but there was always a thick, hazy curtain of booze and pills hanging between us.

John D was watching me, his eyes kind.

"My mother was kind of a mess, and I don't think my father has known what to do with me since the day I was born. I spent my early years shuttling between her apartment in Paris and the Dorje Yidam Monastery in India, where Apa was an abbot. After Valerie died, I lived full time in the monastery. Sometimes I'd catch Father staring at me, from across the dining hall, or during group sits, and clear as a bell, I'd hear him wondering, *Who are you? Where did you come from?* And not in a good way, you know? When I left for California, I'm sure he was filled with relief."

John D looked at me, his eyes troubled. "Maybe. Or maybe he was filled with regret. It's not always what you think it is."

He moved to the kitchen and rinsed off two Fuji apples from the market. He tossed one to me.

"Okay, son, time to see what Sister Rose has to say."

We hiked to the fence separating John D's property from the Children of Paradise. Sister Rose kept her word; a few minutes later we saw her ghostly figure coming up the hill toward us.

We greeted her with smiles. Her face was expressionless. "I can't stay long," she said. "They know I like to go out for a walk in the evening, but they'll get suspicious if I'm gone long."

"Who's 'they'?" John D asked. She just shook her head.

"I appreciate what you're doing," I said.

"Sister Barbara would have done the same for me."

We stood another moment in the darkness. The silence was peppered with night sounds: rustling leaves . . . the scuttle of a small animal.

I got to the point. "Can you think of any reason somebody would want Barbara Maxey dead?"

Her eyes filled. "It's still so hard to believe . . ."

"I know, but we have to move fast if we want to find out who did this. After forty-eight hours, the statistics on solving a crime drop like a rock. It's over a week now, and I'm afraid we're going to miss our chance. If there's anything you know or may have heard that could help us, please tell us now."

She said, "Sister Barbara was stubborn. She was the only one who'd stand up to Brother Eldon. She came here long before he did, back when Master Paul was our teacher." She turned to John D, almost pleading. "Master Paul was different; he loved us, even when we were bad. We fear Brother Eldon and respect him, but there is no love."

I pictured Brother Eldon's thick menace and Nehemiah's querulous insistence that something needed to happen, and soon. "Has anything changed recently? Anything that would cause Barbara to want to escape?"

A branch snapped and Sister Rose startled, her eyes darting back and forth. I scanned the field. The air settled into stillness again.

"Nothing out there," I said. "I promise."

Sister Rose stepped close, her voice low. "Brother Eldon asked us all to get insurance. Barbara refused to sign up for it."

My heart beat against my rib cage, a rapid, tapping staccato.

"What kind of insurance?" I said, though I already knew the answer.

"Life insurance." Her words tumbled faster. "Barbara told Brother Eldon that Master Paul had always spoken against insurance, that if our faith was strong enough we wouldn't get sick. And once we died we'd be with God anyway, so there was no need for any of mankind's worldly inventions like insurance. Master Paul believed insurance was the path to greed, and the work of the devil."

"How did Brother Eldon react when she challenged him?"

"He berated her in front of the community. I wanted to speak up for her, but I was too afraid. Later that night, Sister Barbara defied our curfew. I think she must have been spying on Brother Eldon, because when she returned to our yurt, just before dawn, she was very angry—and Sister Barbara *never* indulged in the sin of anger. I asked her what was wrong, but she wouldn't tell me. Told me to go back to sleep. The next morning I woke up, and she was gone. Now she's dead and I'll never . . ." She trailed off into quiet sobs.

John D wrapped both arms tight around her. She leaned into him like a child, her shoulders shaking. I added my own form of comfort, surrounding her with a blanket of compassion. I hoped she could feel it.

Her sobs lessened after a time. She pulled away, wiping her nose on her sleeve.

"Do you want to leave, to get out?" I asked.

She looked over at me. "I don't think I can do that," she said. "My life was an awful mess before Master Paul. He helped me get straight. And I've been here so long. I don't know any other way to be."

"I could help you find another place, someplace where you wouldn't be scared all the time."

"And do what? I'd rather be scared in here than scared out there. At least I've got a place to sleep, people who know me, accept me."

"Did you sign up for the insurance policy?"

She nodded.

"Have you thought about what that means?"

She bit her trembling, lower lip. "It means I'm worth something if I die."

"But to whom?"

"To the others, to my family of sisters and brothers." Her voice rose. "Don't you see? Even if I didn't do anything with my life, I can do something good by dying. When it's time for me to go, I can help build the new Paradise. A better one."

"The new, improved Paradise, you say?" John D's voice was skeptical.

She bobbed her head. Her eyes gleamed in the darkness. "We're working toward the day when we can rebuild and restore our earthly home. Brother Eldon has a plan for a new city of God, right here on these hills."

A pig farm and a field of dead almond trees didn't seem like an ideal spot to erect this new Eden, but what do I know? Having grown up in a Buddhist monastery, I'm hardly qualified to judge someone else's attempt at terrestrial nirvana.

I said, "But what if Brother Eldon decides you should die before you want to?"

Sister Rose jutted her chin, showing a little more spunk. "We've talked about that in our community meeting," she said. "Don't think we haven't. If Brother Eldon does sound the Call to Paradise, he's insisting the community make the ultimate decision by a majority vote."

I said nothing.

John D cleared his throat. "Sister Rose, a majority vote inside a brainwashed cult ain't exactly democracy in action."

She wheeled on him. "Judge not, John D. Judge not, lest ye be judged!"

She started down the hill. Then she turned back, as if regretting her outburst.

"I'm really sorry about Barbara," she said. "I hope you find whoever did it."

We watched her pick her way across the field, until we lost sight of her among the yurts.

John D sighed. "Nobody can say you didn't try."

It wasn't much consolation. I think we both felt we were watching her descend into the Valley of Death.

"Life insurance policies for a cult. I never heard of anything like that in my life. Have you, Ten?"

Unfortunately, I had. A year or so ago, bored out of our gourds on an all-night stakeout, Bill and I had listened to a long Public Radio exposé on exactly this subject.

"'Dead Peasant' policies, at least I think that's what they're called." I dredged the memory to the surface.

"Dead Peasants?"

"Yes. From back in the feudal times, when greedy land-owners used the names of dead serfs—still conveniently registered as alive, mind you—to guarantee loans. As I recall, in the modern-day version, big companies secretly insure thousands of their low-level employees, naming themselves as beneficiaries. When their workers eventually die—even if they've long since left the company—the bosses rake in tax-free payouts."

"Sounds crooked as hell."

"Nope. Completely legal. Like reverse Robin Hoods, they steal from the poor to make themselves richer. No one seemed to even know or care about this massive tax loophole until recently, when companies like Walmart and Winn-Dixie got caught with their hands in their janitors' piggy banks. So, yes, I've heard of such a thing," I said grimly.

John D shook his head.

"Poor Sister Rose," he said.

I had to agree. Sister Rose's intentions were pure, but in reality she was just a dead peasant waiting to happen.

Meanwhile, I had a pretty good idea who the lords might be in this feudal system.

CHAPTER 19

I woke up at dawn with something pressing against my brain, like a splinter just beneath the skin. It continued to irritate me through two cups of tea, my morning stretches, and a 45-minute run. Suddenly, near the end of my meditation, the thought surfaced: if Norman hadn't been to see his father in two months, why did he decide to visit yesterday?

Detectives face situations all the time that strike them as odd, raising the question: Is this a coincidence or a conspiracy? After a while, most of us stop believing in coincidence. Most chance connections turn out to be anything but.

So while it was possible Norman's visit was coincidental with mine, I had trouble believing it, especially since he'd come and gone in such a hurry. If he was there to check on his father, why did he do nothing but harass him? And why all the hostile interest in me? It was much more likely that somebody tipped Norman off, and that I was the person he wanted to check on.

If that was the case, who was the "somebody" doing the tipping off?

Maybe John D would have an idea. I made myself a tofu scramble over a toasted English muffin and washed it down with a mug of fresh coffee. Then I gave John D a quick call from my landline, a number he'd recognize. I let it ring a long time, but he didn't pick up. I pictured him rocking outside on the porch, and I smiled as I made a note to try him later. I washed my dish and my pan, and put them both away. Fed an impatient Tank. Poured myself another coffee, and sat down at the kitchen table, facing the window.

My "office" was now open for business. I picked up my multitasking cell phone and got to work.

First things first. Sister Rose's mention of the saintly Master Paul, aka Paul Alan Scruggs, reminded me I'd never really looked into his death. I did a search, using his full name, to see what I could find out. Within moments I had everything I needed to know.

According to a short obituary in the *Antelope Valley Press*, Paul Alan Scruggs had died suddenly three years ago, after a brief illness. "Brief illness" could mean a lot of things. Buster died after a brief illness. So did Jeremiah Star Trek. And Freda, too, was comatose after just a brief illness. Coincidence or conspiracy?

Or murder, plain and simple.

I caught Bill on his cell driving down the 101 toward police headquarters.

"Administrative meeting downtown," he groused when I asked what he was up to.

"You don't sound too excited about it."

"Let me put it this way: if I could choose between going to a meeting on crime statistics and getting a prostate exam, I'd say 'Give me the finger, please.'"

"I understand. Let me give you an opportunity to do a good deed, then," I said.

"You haven't gotten yourself in trouble, have you?"

"Nothing like that," I said. "I just need some information about a guy who died out in Lancaster three years back. He was only in his fifties, so I'm guessing they did an autopsy."

"What's your interest?"

"The obit says he died after a short illness. I'm thinking there's more to it than that. I'd like you to talk to the medical examiner who did the autopsy and see if he found anything suspicious."

Bill said he'd see what he could do.

I took Tank outside and played "climb the tree" with him—a man can only sit cooped up in an office for so long.

Tank must have been an inside cat for the first few years of his life. While he can scoot up just about anything, including tree trunks, he never quite learned how to get *down* from a tree, so I give him lessons every once in a while. While I had him trapped on a high branch of the eucalyptus, I told him a little bit about Julie.

"You'll meet her tonight," I said. "I think you'll like her. She's a whiz at opening cans."

Then I gave the Mustang a bath and buff. As I ran a cloth over the steel wheel hubcaps, I rearranged information in my mind, looking for a pattern, any pattern at all, that made sense. Florio, Barsotti, and O'Flaherty. Key man and Dead Peasant policies. Pigs and Paradise. How did they all connect?

Two hours later, Bill called back.

"What's the prognosis?" I asked.

"The administration is full of crap, like always," he said. "But I did get hold of the ME on the other matter."

"And?"

"And I got nothing."

"Hmmm," I said.

I heard a horn honk, and Bill mutter "Asshole" under his breath. I waited. I knew he wasn't finished with me yet.

"Strangulations. Pig farms. Dead musicians. You going to tell me what this is about, partner?"

"I wish I knew," I said.

"Any chance we can meet for a beer later?"

"Maybe," I said. "I'm a busy man."

"Asshole," he said again, but this time his voice was smiling.

My phone beeped, indicating another call coming in. I had no idea how to put Bill on hold with this new phone, so I just left him stranded. He'd forgive me. What else are partners for?

A crisp, businesslike female voice said, "Is this Tenzing Norbu?"

I said it was.

"Nancy Myers, Nurse Supervisor at Mercy Hospital. We have an elderly gentleman here named John D. Murphy, and he put you down as both emergency contact and next of kin."

My stomach lurched. I walked out to my deck, pulling deep mouthfuls of air into my lungs. The brisk voice continued.

"Mr. Murphy has suffered three broken ribs and some facial contusions. He's doing fine, but we're going to keep him overnight to make sure things are stable."

"What happened?"

"Mr. Murphy was attacked by two men this morning, on his way to breakfast, he told me."

John D attacked? A narrow bolt of energy crackled from my brainpan to my coccyx, and back. Whoa. Down, boy.

"Can I talk to him?"

"He's champing at the bit. I'll put him on."

"Hey, Ten." John D's normally gruff voice sounded weak and constricted.

"John D, what the hell? Are you okay?"

"Fine as frog fuzz," he said. "It only hurts when I breathe."

I felt the muscles in my belly relax slightly. I told him I was glad he hadn't lost his sense of humor.

"If I ever lose that, just shoot me," he said.

"I'll have them put an addendum on your DNR," I said, which triggered a couple of wheeze-chuckles from the other end of the phone.

"I gotta get out of here before they get me hooked on drugs," he said. "I keep just saying no, but nobody's listening."

Classic John D.

"Do you need me there? Is there anything I can do to help?"

"Well . . . they say they're gonna let me go tomorrow, so long as I don't drive. If you got nothing better to do, how 'bout giving me a lift home?"

"You got it," I said. He put me back on with the nurse for the particulars.

After I hung up, the air whooshed out of my lungs, which told me how long and hard I'd been holding on to it. I did a body-check and soon located the high-pitched sizzle in my ears and clenched muscles in my upper back that signaled I was still really angry. I tried taking a few long, deep breaths to disseminate the rage. I had to think clearly. Fight or flight is fine, but not when I need the tool of reason.

I didn't waste a moment wondering whether the mugging of John D was another coincidence. Too many things were stacking up; something was going on, even if I didn't know what. Yet.

I paced around my deck, under the watchful eye of Tank, perched on the railing. *Fucking cowards, jumping an old man like that. I'm going to find you and kick your scrawny little . . .*

Okay, pacing wasn't doing it for me either; I needed to burn off the excess energy still sputtering in me, orphan sparks left over from the original bolt of lightning at the news.

I went out to the garage and fired up the Mustang. I pushed it hard, savoring its deep-throated roar on a high-speed run all the way to the ocean. As I took the curves, there was so much cornering force the idiot light came on and the gauge wavered, from oil surging in the sump.

I parked in the public lot and climbed over the dunes to the beach. I kicked off my shoes and executed a long series of 50-yard wind sprints up and down the beach. I ran until my lungs screamed and sweat poured off me in rivulets, and then I ran some more. Stripping to my boxers, I took my final sprint right into the waves, and swam through the frigid water, gasping at the cold. Then I stood under the hard spray of the open-air shower until my skin was fizzing. Better.

I spread out a towel and lay on my back. The afternoon sun flashed gold against my closed eyelids. As my skin warmed, I listened to the beach sounds all around me. The grunts and cheers from a nearby volleyball game. The happy squeals of children, mingled with the drone of an overhead airplane.

Another body-check. Physical exertion had blown most of the anger right out of me. Then I checked in with my mind: it still felt hardened, and in need of repair. My deep attachment to John D had taken me on a direct skid into violent thoughts of revenge on his attackers. Rage might make me feel temporarily powerful, but in the long run it weakened me, and clouded my thinking. I needed to find equanimity toward my enemies, as well as my friends, to be effective.

I breathed in and out. I let my connection, my concern for John D, soften this time, into compassion. I let the feeling of compassion grow, ripple outward from the personal to the universal. My heart opened a crack, and the bittersweet nectar of loving-kindness spilled out, spreading to include the playing children, the calling gulls, and, finally, the men who had harmed my friend out of their own ignorance. The last vestiges of hatred dispersed into emptiness, like a cloud dissolving into pure, unblemished sky. I felt peace.

For now, anyway.

Next thing I knew, the sun was low on the horizon, and I was about to be late for my date with Julie.

I tore back up the hill and hustled inside. I brushed my teeth. Ran a hairbrush over my thick black buzz cut, not that anyone but me would notice any difference. I changed into a white linen shirt and a clean pair of black jeans, and put a good bottle of Pinot Grigio into the fridge. I pictured her freckles, her warm lips and soft curves. Added a second bottle.

Julie's car pulled up at 7:30 on the dot. Good girl, a time-Nazi just like me. I added a mental check to the

"Pro" column. As the bell sounded, Tank arched his back and ambled to the door.

"You behave," I said as I opened it, and he ran off.

Julie was wearing tight black leggings, black leather boots, and a soft angora tunic the color of cream. She was carrying a cardboard box containing a blue enamel casserole, out of which wafted the rich scents of rosemary and stewed tomatoes. My saliva glands reminded me I had skipped lunch.

She set the box on the kitchen counter and held out her hand.

"Keys," she said. For a horrifying moment I thought she wanted her own set of keys to my place. But then, "You still owe me a spin in your Mustang."

She looked past me, and her eyes widened. Tank had deigned to poke his head around my bedroom door and check out the new visitor.

"Who's this handsome fellow?" she crooned. She hunkered down on the floor and made a come-hither motion with her right hand. To my shock, Tank hithered right over. She scratched behind his ears. "Oh, yes, you are quite the Romeo, aren't you?"

Tank rolled over and put all four limbs in the air.

"I couldn't agree more," Julie said. And then she did the same thing. I never knew a cat could actually look gobsmacked. He and I were both in big trouble.

Here's what I learned about Julie on our second date: Her minestrone was undeniable proof that divinity can exist in edible form; crème brûlée tasted even better when served by a curvaceous chef clad only in an apron; and holy shit, this woman was gifted handling a close-ratio, four-speed racing stick.

CHAPTER 20

I woke up calm and clear-headed. Any residual anger had been loved right out of me, and I savored the sense of spaciousness, the clarity of intent. Somehow, a plan had formed in my mind. I knew what I wanted to do, and I knew how I wanted to do it.

I glanced to my right. Julie faced away from me, asleep on her side. The dip from shoulder to hip was breathtaking, like the curved lines of a cello. I ran my palm along the slope and rise of her.

She rolled to face me. Her eyes were warm and direct, and clear as a bell I heard her thinking, "Who are you? Where did you come from?"—only from her, the questions were tinged with wonder. She snuggled closer, arranging my arm so it draped around her neck. She pressed her ear against my chest, and I could feel my heartbeat against her cheek.

"How did you end up in Los Angeles, Ten? It's so unlikely."

"A Lama sent me," I said.

She raised her head. "I'm serious."

"So am I," I said. "Lama Serje Rinpoche Neysrung. Rinpoche's a highly regarded spiritual leader, scholar, and teacher in my order. He traveled all over the United States in the 1980s, setting up dharma centers for His Holiness."

I explained how I was 17 and in a high state of rebellion when Serje Rinpoche paid a surprise visit to our monastery.

Julie's head rose and fell on my chest, as I breathed quietly, my heart remembering that day, the one that changed everything.

"I was a typical teenager, I guess, getting into one conflict after another with the three ruling lamas of the monastery." I felt my voice tighten, along with my jaw. "One of them was my father."

Julie shifted away, so she could see my eyes. I pulled her close again.

"Apa only ever had one goal for me: that I be the greatest Gelugpa scholar in all Tibetan monkdom. Just his luck, his only child seemed to have been born without the studious gene. He'd always tell me I was gifted with intelligence far beyond his, that if I only applied it I could be a great lama. That I was squandering my gifts with my childish rebellions. But I didn't know how else to be. The truth is, I just hated it. I hated being a monk."

I sat up, my stomach and chest tensing as long-buried resentments poked their heads out of my past.

"Tibetan monasteries are oppressive institutions, little fiefdoms, did you know that? Nothing is ever done by logic or reason or any kind of democratic process. It's all about following the rules. In my monastery alone, there were more than two hundred we were supposed to remember, and obey. Rules that had been made over a thousand years ago. Only a handful of them even make sense anymore. 'Extinguish candles before going to bed.' Okay, that one makes sense. 'Monks may only read sacred literature.' I broke that one every night, and got busted for it at least once a month. Oh, and how about 'A Monk must not jump, or swing his arms when walking'? Do you know how hard that is for a rambunctious eleven-year-old? My best friends, Yeshe and Lobsang, embraced their monastic life: the rules, the shaved heads, the red robes. I struggled at every turn."

Julie laughed softly. I stiffened. Was she mocking me? "What?"

"Nothing," she said. "It's just . . . people never think that, do they? That a monk might hate being a monk? We just assume it's all bliss and enlightenment and peaceful navel-gazing. Poor thing. You were only a kid. It's not like you could just quit your job."

I felt my heart give a little flip.

She understood.

Then, just as quickly, it flipped the other way, into a defensive stance.

"It wasn't that bad. I mean, I had two great friends, and all my needs were taken care of there. I had a roof over my head. Two meals a day."

Julie put her hand over my mouth.

"Stop, Ten. It was that bad. Let me feel for you a moment, will you?"

I tried to appreciate her empathy, but I was relieved when she said, "Okay, so this . . . Rinpoche?

I nodded.

"This Rinpoche came for a visit and . . ."

". . . and I think he spotted the tug-of-war going on inside me that day. In fact, I'm sure of it, because after he finished a long lecture on the importance of maintaining a disciplined practice, he pulled me aside. He told me he and my father had entered the Litang monastery in Tibet the same year. That they had been friends a long time. Then he asked if I had any questions for him. All I could think to ask was . . . was . . . whether he thought my father would ever be proud of me." I swallowed.

"What did he say?"

"He said, 'Your father is the way he is. Do not ask for mangoes in a shoe store.'"

"I like that."

"Well, at the time, it infuriated me. I thought it was just another glib aphorism, and I'd had my fill of them from my father. Rinpoche left soon after to spend time with His Holiness. But later that week, he came back. The whole monastery was abuzz with this second visit, coming as it did so close to the first. That night, my father sent for me. He told me Rinpoche had proposed a radical solution to the Tenzing Norbu dilemma: send me to the West to share the Dharma teachings with American teenagers. He'd contacted the Tibetan center he'd founded in Los Angeles, and they'd agreed to sponsor me—they had a special outreach program to introduce meditation to young people. I was to be a novice member of their team. I could continue my studies there, and postpone the decision to take my final vows. My father was quick to agree with this plan." My voice hardened. "Of course he was. I was nothing more than an embarrassment to him by that point."

Julie touched my cheek. I covered her hand with mine, and gently removed it. I didn't want her touching my face, for some reason.

"It all happened very quickly. With an American mother, I could bypass all the immigration issues. Within six months I was living in a small back room in the Dharma center, earning my room and board as a teacher, wondering if I'd ever belong anywhere again."

I fell silent, remembering how hard I tried to be a good teacher of the Dharma, and how hypocritical I felt. Young Los Angeles seekers took one look at my robe and shaved head and set me on a spiritual pedestal that bore no relation to my actual inner world.

I may have felt rebellious at the monastery, but here, I felt like a sham.

"I was adequate as a meditation teacher," I said. "But inside, I was dying. Still, I thought I was hiding it well, until one day one of the team leaders, a psychologist, took me aside and asked me an important question, one I had never dared to ask myself: what did my heart truly long to do?"

"Another guardian angel."

I smiled. "I guess you could say that. Anyway, the instant he asked, the answer flew out of my mouth: 'A detective. I want to be a police detective.'"

Julie nuzzled my neck. "I'm loving this, but can we take it into the kitchen? I'm starving."

"Almost done," I said. "I kept teaching meditation, but at the same time, I got my GED, and somehow landed a part-time summer job as an administrative aide at the Parker Center—that's the old police headquarters downtown. It was a revelation, you know?"

Julie pushed up on her elbow to watch my face.

"In the monastery, elders would regularly throw major tantrums if we didn't wear our robes just so. At the Parker Center, I watched uniformed cops meet terrible, sometimes even life-threatening, situations on a daily basis with grace, patience, and gritty humor. I learned more about practical spirituality in the real world during one summer in law enforcement than I ever had in the monastery. The week I turned twenty-one, I turned in my robe and entered the police academy."

"And here you are," Julie smiled.

"And here I am." I felt a little tug of discomfort.

"What are you thinking?" she said, picking up on it.

"I was just wondering if Rinpoche knew I'd end up here." I took in her naked curves. "Well, not here, here, but you know, that I'd end up in law enforcement."

"You never asked him?'

"Not really. A few years ago I found out he was coming to Los Angeles to give a public lecture in a big church in Pasadena on 'Buddhism and Democracy.' I worked up the courage to go. The church was packed, but he spotted me in the audience, I know he did. Whether he recognized me is another thing. I was six years older, in uniform, and my hair was grown out."

I smiled, remembering Rinpoche's quick, knowing grin before he continued with his lecture.

"So, what about your father?"

My smile died. "What about him?"

"What does he have to say about your new life?" Her words lanced my good feeling with shocking speed. I felt betrayed by the question. My voice hardened into flint.

"My new life is none of his business. And my father is none of yours."

Julie's cheeks reddened. She got out of bed and started pulling on her clothes, avoiding my eyes. I reached for my own jeans and shirt.

"Sorry," I muttered. "Sore subject."

"That's okay," she said, but I could hear in her voice that it wasn't.

"Do you want some coffee?"

"No, thank you," she said. "I need to get home. I'm working again tonight."

I followed her to the front door.

"I'll call you, okay?" I said.

"Okay," she said.

I hugged her. Her body was rigid. She left without another word. As she drove off, Tank stiff-walked past me, into the kitchen. Even his tail was indignant.

"I messed up," I told him, but he'd already ascertained that. It wasn't the first time, and it probably wouldn't be the last.

Chapter 21

I had invested in a new pair of binoculars, Barska Gladiators with a built-in zoom, and I could see individual droplets of sweat dripping off the forehead of the farmworker I had in my sights. I'd taken up position on a hilltop across from both the pig farm and the cult. For the past 20 minutes, the worker had been engaged in the highly challenging task of washing Barsotti's car.

His green one-piece coveralls were tucked into steel-toed rubber boots the color of caramel, or brown muck. The tips were pale yellow, like they'd been dunked in clotted cream. I took out my digital camera and clicked as the worker scrubbed at the globules of mud under the wheels.

It must have rained here last night, and the road up to the farm was full of muddy potholes. Under today's blazing sun, steam rose visibly off the ground. I didn't want to think about how bad that steam must smell—the only thing worse than working on a pig farm on a hot day must be working on a pig farm on a hot, humid day.

I closed my eyes, willing my mind to stop dancing around the subject I so wanted to avoid. I had hurt Julie's feelings this morning, and if I wanted to see her again, I probably needed to figure out why.

But, but, but she had no business . . .

No, Tenzing. No buts. This is an old pattern, my friend, and you need to take responsibility for it.

I snapped off a few more shots of the farm from different angles. Then I turned and did the same with the Children of Paradise yurts.

I swapped back to the binoculars. The Mercedes gleamed like polished onyx, once again spotless. It must be nice to have people wash your cars for you. I watched as the worker dumped his cleaning materials into the back of a dusty green Chevy pickup. Back to the camera: *Click. Click. Click.*

I should cook for Julie next time. Maybe dumplings are the way back into her heart.

Vince Barsotti bustled out of the building and circled his car, inspecting it. He must have liked what he saw, because he handed over several bills. The worker bowed and scraped, so I was guessing they were tens, maybe even twenties. Then Barsotti started talking, windmilling his arms for emphasis. He wagged his jaw for several minutes, and his employee kept nodding, mouthing *Sí, sí, sí.* Finally, like a Roman emperor deciding a gladiator's fate, Barsotti bestowed a definitive thumbs-up gesture on his employee, and climbed into his gleaming chariot.

Barsotti kept it pretty slow leaving the parking lot, carefully avoiding the muddy potholes on the pitted lane that led to the main road. I expected him to turn left, toward the freeway. He turned right, taking the narrow dirt road up the hill to the Children of Paradise.

Well, well, well.

Barsotti parked at the fence and tapped his horn a couple of times. Brother Eldon came out of his yurt and lumbered down the hill to the car, only today's Brother Eldon had ditched the robe. His T-shirt was tight across the chest and loose over his jeans. I focused my sights on his exposed linebacker neck, with its distinctive tat. *There was an old ex-con who lived in a shoe.* Thanks to Mike, I'd been brushing up on my nursery rhymes. I moved to the ink on Brother Eldon's arm, the crude sword with its swirling, leafy scrollwork.

Barsotti suddenly opened the car door and got nose to nose with Brother Eldon. Both appeared spitting mad. I tried to read their lips, but they were too far away. After a few moments, things cooled down. Barsotti got back in the car, leaned across the seat, and opened the passenger door. Brother Eldon climbed in next to him.

This was not good. I stuffed my gear in my backpack, ready to make a mad dash to my car. But they didn't go anywhere. My expensive new binoculars were useless. I cursed the hot sun, tinted windows, and Barsotti's air-conditioning.

After ten minutes, it was over. Brother Eldon jumped out and stomped up the hill. Barsotti drove back to the pig farm. I stayed where I was, squinting under the hot sun, completely in the dark.

So they knew each other. Big deal. For all I knew, Barsotti was just relaying my own interest in the cult, like any good neighbor might. Beyond nothing, I now had zip.

I pulled into the hospital's patient pickup area just as a large male nurse wheeled John D down the walkway to the curb. The attendant eased him into the front seat. He grunted a thank you to the nurse and a good morning to me.

"No muscle car today?" he commented.

"Not today." I flashed on Julie's glowing face last night as she shifted gears smoothly in the empty beach parking lot. It was her idea to practice driving the Mustang there first, before taking it into traffic.

She might just be one in a million.

"Well, I appreciate you coming all the way out here," John D said.

"No problem. I stopped off on the way and spied on your neighbors for a little while."

I described the heated conversation between Barsotti and Brother Eldon.

"Any idea what those two might be fighting about?"

He shook his head.

"How about yesterday? Any idea who might be behind that?"

He shook his head again, and yawned.

"So what actually happened?"

He sat back and closed his eyes.

"John D," I warned, "if you don't tell me exactly what happened, I'm making you hitchhike home."

He chuckled, and opened his eyes.

"I'm just messing with you, Ten," he said. "I'll tell you what I can. I was out of cash, so I stopped to get some from my bank's ATM, across the street from Dot's Double Good Diner—that's where I always get breakfast. I was about to cross the street when these two guys ran out of the alley and jumped me so quick I didn't know what hit me. Or who. One of 'em grabbed my money right out of my hand, and the other one knocked me down and started boot-kicking me in the ribs. I heard someone yell from across the street. Good thing. I think the plan was to finish me off. I guess I passed out. Next thing I know, some para-medic is strapping an oxygen mask over my face."

I asked him a few more questions, but he had nothing more to add, and I could see he really was getting sleepy. When we got to his house, I helped him into his bedroom and got him stretched out on the bed. He was sound asleep before I got his work boots unlaced.

As I left his house, something snagged the corner of my vision. I crossed the yard to his little patch of medicinal weed. The marijuana plants had all been uprooted, the earth around them trampled. At first I thought maybe it was raccoons, but if so they were fairly selective. They had left the flowerbeds and nearby tomato plants untouched. Unless there was a gang of dope-smoking voles around here, this was caused by a human. A human filled with spite or greed, who neither knew nor cared about John D's pain.

Back came the rage, in a hot surge. This was becoming a regular habit of mine.

I walked inside and took a look around for the mason jar of buds, but I couldn't find it, either. This was looking more and more like the work of that steadfast upholder of family morals, Norman the conservative Fun-Cop. I left a sticky note next to a full glass of water on John D's bedside table. I included my cell phone number, in large numerals, and the words CALL TEN.

I was just pulling up to the bank when John D called, sounding a lot more chipper.

"Listen," I told him. "I'm here at the ATM where you got jumped. I need to look at yesterday morning's surveillance footage. I'll have better luck if you hire me as your private investigator. I'll even give you a special rate—you can pay me with a bag of almonds."

"You're hired," he said.

"Thanks. Anything you need from town?"

"Nope. I'm gonna take my meds and maybe sleep a little more."

I broke the news to him about his garden raid and the missing mason jar. He took it better than I expected.

"It's irritating, but it ain't the end of the world. I got a backup stash from last season's crop. Every farmer knows you gotta plan ahead for the lean times."

I decided to do a reality check on something. "I need to ask you a question, John D. Does Norman know about your tumor?"

There was a pause. When John D answered, his voice was noticeably cooler.

"Nope, and I don't have any plans to tell him, either. He and I have been butting heads our whole lives, and lately it's gotten out of hand. So the way I see it, my cancer is none of his business."

His words echoed my own from this morning's meltdown. If the subject was as sore for him as it was for me, I'd better tread carefully. I didn't want to lose John D's trust.

"Do you mind telling me what's been going on?" I said.

"Give me half a minute."

I heard shuffling, and the scrape of a struck match.

John D inhaled deeply. In the ensuing gap of silence, I pictured him holding the perfumed smoke in his lungs. He answered on an exhale.

"Three or four years back, I asked my son to look into something for me, a professional favor, you might say, having to do with the family land, and he blew me off. Then he started pestering me about selling my acreage to those pig farmers. They offered four hundred thousand for the whole parcel, but I told them they could go straight to hell. I didn't work this land for thirty years to have it turned into a pig farm. I'm not selling, and I'm not moving."

"How many acres?"

"Eighty."

That was curious. From my observations of the pig farm, the last thing they needed to do was expand.

A few dots began dancing and circling each other in the back of my mind.

"Do you have any life insurance, John D?"

"Nope. Never saw a need."

"How about your estate? Is Norman your beneficiary?"

"He was, but I just changed my will." John D's voice rose. "Do you know I've never even met his wife? Four years married, and he's too ashamed of his own father to introduce me to her. Well, I say screw him and the horse he rode in on. I'm leaving it all to the Nature Conservancy—maybe they can turn my crops around. Norman don't know that yet, but I can't wait to see the look on his face when I tell him." John D was practically panting with anger.

I backed off. I'd find out more later. Right now, John D needed to rest, and I needed to go. I said good-bye and asked him to stand by in case I required him to run interference with the bank manager.

He went me one better. By the time I was ushered into the manager's office, John D had already paved the way. According to the elderly Mr. Acheson, they'd been doing business together since the early '70s, when the population of Lancaster barely tipped 30,000. He was "outraged, simply outraged," at the attack. Half an hour later, I was holding my own personal DVD of the ATM surveillance footage from yesterday morning.

I made a quick stop at a grocery store for some hummus and chips. I figured John D and I could watch the footage on his flat-screen together, and with any luck, he'd recognize one or both of the men who jumped him.

At this point, my Toyota practically drove itself to John D's. Halfway there, I spotted flashing lights in my rear-view mirror. A patrol car was closing in fast. The siren emitted one short blast, and I put on my turn signal. I was well under the speed limit, so I knew it wasn't that, but my heart jumped to my throat anyway, and I was flooded with a kind of shame.

Welcome to the other side of the law.

I pulled over and started fumbling for my license and registration. Then I glanced back and realized it wasn't California Highway Patrol after all—the car was marked with the seal of the Los Angeles Sheriff's Department.

A heavyset man looked in at me. His khaki uniform was spotless, and the crease in his pants could slice a baguette. His pocked nose was beaded with sweat, his eyes a striking color of blue. I put his age at just one side or the other of 50.

"License and registration," he said. No "sir" or "please" attached.

I handed him both, keeping my voice mild. "Can you tell me what this is about?"

He glanced at the documents, and passed them back.

"You the fellow that's out there all the time smoking dope with John D. Murphy?"

So Norman already had a good friend in law enforcement. And here I thought I was special.

"Well, 'all the time' might be overstating. But yes, I'm that fellow. And you are?"

"Jack Dardon," he said. "Deputy Sheriff, District One." He didn't offer his hand. Nor I mine.

I waited him out, which he didn't like much.

"You running some kind of hustle on that old man?"

"No hustle, sir. I work for him. I'm a private detective; before that I was with LAPD Robbery/Homicide for nine years. I'm trying to find out who beat him up."

He nodded at that.

"Where're you based out of?"

"My office is in Topanga Canyon."

His voice was skeptical.

"And John D hired you to come way the hell out here just to find out who beat him up?"

I chose to tell the truth, figuring a man that meticulous with his uniform probably cared about correctness in other matters.

"I came out here on another case, Deputy Dardon, something involving one of John D's neighbors, and I happened to meet up with him in the course of my investigation. We connected. I like the man."

Dardon removed his hat and ran his fingers through his gray-brown curls. "What kind of case would that be?"

"I can't give you many details, because to tell you the truth, I don't have many yet, but it has to do with the religious group that lives next door."

He stared at me for a long moment. Just then his cell phone rang; he fished it out of his pocket and glanced at the screen. He stepped back a few paces to answer.

"Yeah?" I heard. Then, "Right now?" Dardon shot a look in my direction. "I'm talking to him this very moment." He mumbled a few final words to his caller. Then he walked over to my car again, his eyes sparking with some new mischief.

"You headed for John D's?"

I nodded.

"You strike me as a stand-up guy. Norman wants me to help him declare his father mentally incapable. What say you follow me up there, see how well that flies?"

Norman was waiting on the front steps of his father's house. He glanced at me, then barked at Dardon. "What the fuck?"

Dardon's jaw tightened. "Norman, watch your mouth."

So Norman and the deputy were not as tight as I had thought. Good. Even better, Norman chose to ignore Dardon's warning. Face darkening to a dull maroon, Norman actually started to sputter. "Goddamn it to hell, I'm a taxpaying citizen and a county official. You're supposed to be helping me here."

Dardon said, "Norman, I'm not supposed to be doing anything but finding out what the heck is going on with your daddy. Which I am now going to do. You can just stay outside until you get your head straightened out."

Norman huffed at that, but didn't move as the deputy sheriff left us both and walked straight into the house. Norman glared at me, but somehow managed to hold his tongue until the officer returned. Dardon hooked a finger at me. "John D wants to talk to you."

Norman exploded. "—the fuck d'you mean? This guy is a total—"

"Shut it, Norman," Dardon said, and we walked inside. John D was enthroned in his recliner, chuckling at an old caper movie. He paused it and turned to look at us. His eyes appeared suspiciously red to me.

"Hey, Ten. How're you doin'?" His gaze latched onto the bag of chips poking out of my grocery bag.

"Doing great," I said. "In fact, I found a copy of that DVD I told you about. Maybe we can watch it later."

The Chief canted a curious eye in my direction.

"John D and I are big movie fans," I explained.

"Movie fans. Right," Dardon said.

"So Ten," John D drawled, "seeing as how we been spending quite a bit of time together lately, why don't you tell Jack here whether or not you think I'm okay, that my mentus is, you know, compus."

"I think you are," I said.

"How about you, Jack? Based on what you've seen so far, you think I can handle my own affairs? Or am I a nut job, like Norman out there claims?"

Dardon stretched it out a bit, but the corners of his mouth were twitching, so I knew it was all in fun. He said, "No, John D, I think you're the same stubborn, ornery SOB you've been as long as I can remember."

John D gave us both a beatific grin, which froze at Dardon's next words.

"And I also think Norman's a chip off the old block."

Perfectly timed, Norman bellowed from outside, "You guys having a fucking party in there?"

Dardon shook his head. "You two don't need a sheriff. You need a therapist."

"Tell Norman that," John D growled. "He's the one causing all the trouble."

Dardon opened his mouth as if to say more, then closed it again.

Halfway out the door, he paused. "I assume you have a prescription for your marijuana, John D."

"I do, but I wish I didn't," John D grumbled. "If something's legal, it ain't half the fun."

CHAPTER 22

The sequence of black-and-white surveillance images jittered forward in a repetitive, déjà vu kind of way. The sizes, shapes, genders, and ages changed, but the actions were almost identical: fish out a card, squint at the screen, feed the machine its slice of plastic, tap in a code, remove tongue-thrust of cash, more squinting, count cash, remove card, remove receipt, walk away while pocketing all of the above.

"When was it?" I asked, keeping one eye on the time code.

"Around eight-thirty," John D said.

"Okay. We're getting close."

"There," he said.

I used slo-mo. John D shuffled up to the ATM, digging out his wallet. Fished, squinted, fed, tapped. The ATM spat out five bills. He counted the cash twice and turned away from the camera as he started to place the bills in his wallet. Still in slow motion, a smallish man materialized from somewhere left of the frame, his arm extended outward, moving as if he had all the time in the world.

Frame by painful frame, we watched him pinch the bills from John D's hand, shove him hard, then move off to the right, crossing paths with a second, taller man, who rolled in with his head lowered like a bull's. He body-blocked John D, who slow-tumbled to the ground, his mouth opening into a perfect circle of surprise. It would have been comical if it weren't so awful.

The man drew back a cowboy boot, the sharp toe sleeved in metal. One, two, three kicks to the ribs. I flinched with each pointed thrust. His mouth stretched into a sneer at the crumpled body below him. Then he executed a slow half-pirouette and followed his partner off screen. I checked the time code. Less than 30 seconds from start to finish. It had felt like a lifetime.

Then I checked John D. He was hunched forward in the recliner. His arms were crossed high and tight over his chest, and his breath was shallow. Well, mine was, too. My body had gone bulletproof, tightening into an armored state of readiness, as if to ward off the blows on the screen. I ran the segment again, and freeze-framed the first assailant.

I leaned closer. I knew him, only last time he had a sponge in his hand and was lathering up the muddy underside of a luxury coupe.

The second guy, the one with the boots, took longer to identify. He had the requisite black hoodie pulled low over his face. I guess some assaults don't count unless you wear a hoodie. I rewound and froze the image of him sneering at John D's crumpled body. The garment hid his face, but it couldn't hide the small bowling ball of a paunch.

"Nehemiah," I said. "Why, I'd know your paunch anywhere."

My first verifiable link between Barsotti and Brother Eldon.

John D pushed himself off his chair and peered at the grainy image.

"Yep, that's him," he said. He scratched his grizzled chin.

"I guess he didn't get the memo from Brother Eldon," I said. "The one about being polite to you."

That got a laugh out of John D, then a wince. "You got any idea what these two are up to?"

I thought about that. "Not exactly, but my partner Bill always says that most crimes can be found hunkered behind one of two motives: love or money. Since I truly doubt you're Nehemiah's type, I'm choosing money."

"Okay," John D said, "but what's the payoff? Setting aside the hundred bucks I withdrew."

"Eighty acres," I said. "The payoff is eighty acres of land. John D, who besides you knows about your plan to donate the land to the Conservancy?"

John D shook his head. "Nobody. I mean, one of their lawyers is helping me set up the trust, but nobody else . . ." An odd look crossed his face.

"What?"

"Well, the Conservancy sent out a young man, one of them notaries, a few weeks ago, with some preliminary papers for me to sign. He told me I needed a witness, and could I think of anybody to ask, a neighbor or someone. Only one handy was Brother Nehemiah."

"God will provide."

John D put his head in his hands.

So now we had a ticking clock, and a hog farm and cult looking to expand their operations at the expense of the Conservancy. Not to mention John D's sole surviving heir, though I had a hard time believing that Norman would resort to violence against his father. He struck me as just a basic run-of-the-mill loser: more grown-up brat than criminal mastermind. Still, I couldn't completely rule him out.

"Well, at least we know the how of it," I said. "And maybe some of the who."

John D's face had gone a little gray. He protested, but I sent him to bed. I'm sure watching those two men beat the living daylights out of him in slow motion didn't help his mood much.

As for me, I needed to review my options. I sat on the porch and rocked and thought, and rocked some more. The obvious move was to hand over the surveillance DVD to Dardon, along with my suspicions as regards the perps. But I didn't want to do that, for two reasons. One: this was my case, and two: this was my case.

My eyes drifted to the torn-up pot patch. I walked over and squatted to inspect the ruins. One corner of roiled earth offered up the clear impression of a partial sole-print, a distinctive series of diagonal chevrons. I snapped a picture of it. Then, researching rubber work boots, I quickly matched the print to that of a neoprene Servus steel-toe—the same muck-brown color, same toes dipped in cream, as the boots Barsotti's lackey was wearing in the hog yard.

I felt a prickle across the nape of my neck. I urged my Toyota to the top of the hill where I'd begun this long day. First I scanned my photographs and zoomed in on the car washer's pickup. I pulled up my little notepad and added the license plate number to my growing laundry list of clues.

I felt like a modern gunslinger, camera in one hand, phone in the other. I stashed the camera, and picked up my binoculars, sweeping them from one corner of the lot to the other. No pickup. No Mercedes either.

Barsotti was probably back in Condo Heaven, happy as a pig in slop. Given his place of work, he would know.

As for Neoprene Boot Man, my immediate guess was he'd successfully completed his extracurricular activities—rolling John D, then ripping off his weed—and been given the rest of the week off. I suspected he was lying low and enjoying the plunder.

I caught Bill on his way out the door, leaving work a little early. He grumbled, but he ran the plates for me anyway. I sweetened the deal with the promise of a six-pack when I got back into the city. He was back with an answer quickly.

"José Gutierrez, ex-felon, and don't say I never did anything for you."

"I never have and I never will."

"I suppose you want the address as well."

A minute later, José Gutierrez's name, address, and phone number were in my digital directory.

Maybe I should friend him, as well.

With the aid of my phone's GPS, I was at his street in under ten minutes. I had a brief flash of guilt over trumping Sherlock's meticulous tracking methods, then I thought, screw it, he'd be thrilled to have a toy like this. Dr. Watson could be a real downer sometimes.

I heard the cavernous *thump thump* of a massive sub-woofer before I even turned onto José's block. I would have parked, but for the motley assortment of cars and pickups jammed every which way in his driveway, and up and down both sides of the street. My ears adapted slightly, and I was able to separate the bass-thump of sound into the brass, wind, percussion, and high-pitched acoustic guitar of Jalisco mariachi.

The front door opened and a man staggered out, propelled by a chorus of ululating falsetto yells from his compatriots. He reeled to the side of the house and puked into a potted succulent. Swells of raucous laughter ebbed and flowed inside. A major celebration was under way, and I had a pretty good idea what was fueling it.

I was undermanned for a commando raid; the first significant disadvantage I could see to partnering with a phone. Plus, stealing *mota* from a mariachi party wasn't my idea of a worthy goal. So I did the next best thing: I called Deputy Sheriff Dardon.

"Am I catching you at an okay time?"

"Make it quick. I'm just about to turn into my driveway, where I got a bowl of my wife's chili waiting for me."

I told him about the missing mason jar and home-grown plants, the telltale neoprene boot print, and the all-points bulletin bash going on at José's place.

"You're a regular one-man neighborhood watch, aren't you?" Dardon said.

"I just think it would be good for José's karma if he got busted."

"Karma, eh?" Dardon sounded amused. "That's rich. I'll be sure to tell José when I send the party car over to collar him that what's bad for his police record is good for his karma."

"Just trying to be a good citizen," I said.

"Right. Well, I'd better go in and explain to the wife why I'm missing dinner again. See how that works out for me, karma-wise."

He had a point there. I called Bill to tell him I was on my way, and stopped by a minimart for beer. I had Mexico on my mind, but there was no Noche Buena to be found. Where was the Cerveza Fairy when you needed her? I settled for a six-pack of Corona and a couple of rock-hard limes.

I pushed the Toyota to a bone-rattling 55 all the way back to Los Angeles.

Two hours later, matching redheads, bounded by plumped-up pillows, contemplated me across a king-size bed like two baby Buddhas. My pulse was racing. This was the first time I'd ever been left completely alone with one infant, much less two. Give me a dangerous stakeout anytime.

Bill and I had only managed one Corona each before the bedtime clock started ticking and Martha corralled me into their bedroom, a baby balanced on each hip, and set the three of us up.

"They won't break, I promise. Just try not to let them roll off the bed," Martha tossed over her shoulder. "Thanks." Then she and Bill drove off to pick up the Thai takeout she'd ordered for their dinner. Parking's a nightmare on Larchmont Boulevard, and this way they could halve the time between ordering and actually eating—when you have twins, every minute counts. I'd of course offered to get the food for them, but Martha admitted they loved any opportunity to finish a sentence with each other before exhaustion took over.

Lola/Maude stared. Maude/Lola stared. Now what?

"How's it going, girls?" I said.

Lola's mouth was an immovable line.

"That good, hunh," I said. "I can relate." I switched my attention to Maude and her eyes met mine. Then the bottom half of her jaw opened like a drawbridge, and she flashed a gaping, gummy smile that took up most of her face.

Up until recently, Lola was the grinner and Maude the baby with the unblinking stare. Now they appeared to have switched personalities.

"So what happened? You swap souls or something?" Lola lifted one dimpled starfish hand and started to suck

on the middle two fingers. Her eyes glazed over with pleasure. Maude chortled and reached in my direction, causing her to tip onto the mattress in a perfect face-plant.

"Whoa!" I jacked her upright, no worse for wear. She
was dense and warm, and she smelled like muffins. "Uncle
Ten's not so good at this baby stuff, ladies." Lola uncorked
her fingers at that, and leveled me with a look that said,
"Stating the obvious, Uncle Ten." Then she plugged in
again, definitively. I laughed, and her mouth bowed up
around her fingers. It was better than winning the lottery.

"Bah, bah, bah," Maude said.

"Bah, bah," I echoed.

"Bah," Maude said again, and squealed with delight. I
started to relax. I heaved them closer together and pulled
out my phone. "Say cheese."

I snapped off several shots. Two pairs of marble-blue
eyes fastened on the clicking sound and rose in unison
to find my face behind my phone. They gawked at me in
awe, like I was a magician.

An unfamiliar euphoria swept over me. I was alone
with two delicate, untrammeled baby psyches, and they
trusted me absolutely. Their parents did, as well. Maybe I
could do this baby thing after all.

Full of apologies, I begged off dinner with Martha
and Bill when they got home. I'd decided to make an
impromptu visit, to take care of some unfinished business. Once I told them where I was headed, Martha practically shoved me out the door.

Julie opened hers in her purple apron. I checked for
clothes. Yup. A tight spandex top and loose drawstring
pants. Did I mention how much I love her body? She's
strong, but with a lot of interesting curves. Now that I
knew those curves somewhat, I felt an instant stirring
down in my jeans at the mere sight of her.

I wanted her. But her unsmiling face told me what I
already knew. I had some repair work to do. She stepped
back silently, and I made my way into the lair.

I perched on a bar stool at the island as Julie returned to stirring and sampling a bubbling pot.

"Smells amazing," I said.

"Butternut squash soup," her back replied. "I'm testing out a recipe for work. And compliments will get you nowhere."

"Julie, I . . ."

Julie spun around to face me, her eyes flashing.

"I recently broke off a four-year relationship, Ten. I'm sure Martha and Bill must have told you that. But did they tell you why? Because," and Julie enunciated each word with crisp precision, "I. Do. Not. Have. Time. For. Games." She glared at me. I knew enough to nod but stay silent. She was just getting started.

"I don't want to expend one more ounce of the precious energy it takes to create real intimacy, with one more man who is terrified by it. My life is very full right now, and very challenging, and my free time very limited. If I am going to share that free time with someone, it will only be because that someone else wants to walk toward me. Freely and fully. A good relationship adds to the Fulfillment column, for both partners. If I feel it subtracting instead, honestly? I'll take a pass. Sorry, but I just can't go there again." She turned away.

I moved to her side. "I'm a fool," I said. "A fool who's walking toward you as best I can."

She looked at me. I waited.

She seemed to make a decision.

"Good. Consider yourself warned. Now, eat my soup and take me to bed."

So I did, and I did.

But I drove home afterward. I told Julie I needed to feed Tank. It was half-true. The other half? Hungry pets provide one of the few remaining acceptable excuses for escaping to one's own burrow after making love.

I lay awake in the dark for over an hour, trying to understand the small kink pinching my chest. Julie was perfect. Sexy, warm, smart, and honest. Generous without being cloying. Funny without being mean. Independent yet vulnerable. Perfect.

So why did my upper torso contract and my breath grow shallow every time I imagined fully committing my heart to this woman?

CHAPTER 23

I sat at the kitchen table, pen in hand.

"Venerable Brothers," I wrote, but I couldn't concentrate. Instead I found myself doodling, filling the margin of my notepaper with a leafy, scrolling pattern, wrapped around a blocky sword.

I was mimicking the design inked onto Brother Eldon's forearms. I stared at it. Got nothing back. I closed my eyes, groaning in frustration.

Venerable Brothers, I am two weeks into my new job, and my ideas are nothing but a load of crap.

Lobsang's familiar voice was faint inside me, but unmistakable: *Maybe that's because you're facing in the wrong direction.* My bark of laughter startled Tank, who lifted a disapproving head from his windowsill perch. Leave it to Lobsang.

I set my letter aside and moved to my meditation room for a different kind of linking up with my two best friends.

Sometimes, when I'm too distracted to count breaths, I find that attending to the hum of distant traffic, punctuated by an occasional honking horn, works as a kind of urban channel into serenity. I closed my eyes and invited the outside sounds to guide me into a place of calm.

The far-off drone entered me, lulled me. *Allow.* I expanded my auditory awareness to include the subtle rustle of leaves outside and the almost imperceptible tick-ticking of the clock on my kitchen wall. *Allow. Allow.*

My breath became slow, even. My thoughts mere wisps, drifting across a spacious mental sky. *Allow.* I went even deeper, and wider, letting each sound merge into all sound, and all sound into no sound, until the channel was clear and my heart and mind fully opened, still, and ready to receive a clear connection with my two soul-brothers.

Venerable brothers, I began again. *I send you greetings. Are you there?*

This time, I was facing the right direction. Seconds later, like entering a clear body of water, I slipped into the current of subtle energy I've shared with Yeshe and Lobsang since we were children. For a moment, I just basked in the familiarity of the link between the three of us.

Yeshe has a simple, instinctive acceptance of others that is as strong as it is pure. Unlike blind naiveté, which can be self-deluding and an excuse for inaction, his tolerance is grounded in a deep understanding of humanity, with all its flaws. He loves me absolutely, unconditionally, and with no strings attached.

Lobsang's personality, while magnanimous, is more particular: his love for me tempered by a fierce expectation of excellence. Without imposing his own goals, he has nevertheless always pushed me to be my very best. Between the two of them, I feel both adored and motivated. They are like the good parents I never had.

I sat with my eyes closed, barely breathing, sensing my two friends bobbing side by side like buoys, far away but tethered in the same ocean.

I am happy to have you in my life. Is there anything I can do for you, my friends?

They let me know they were fine, each in his own way.

I need your help. I have many uncertainties. They cloud my judgment and prevent me from finding solutions.

The silent field became charged with curiosity and anticipation. They like it when I include them in my work, though Lobsang also enjoys needling me when I'm stuck. I let the disparate events of the past two weeks play across our shared screen like a movie, albeit with a very confusing plot. Then I posed my questions:

How can I discern what lies beneath the murky mysteries of the pig farm, the cult, and the dead insurance-policy owners, so that justice can prevail?

What are Barsotti, Florio, Brother Eldon, and the others really up to?

How can I use my skills and presence to ensure that the highest good is accomplished?

I ended with an all-purpose benediction I apply whenever I ask for assistance from unseen forces, even when they're my best friends: *May answers come to me by easeful attraction rather than stressful pursuit, and may all beings benefit from these inquiries.*

I set the questions adrift on the ocean of resonance linking me with my friends, tucked away in their monastery 8,000 miles away.

I sat for a few more minutes, basking in tranquil clarity. Opportunities to go deep like this are rare for me, and therefore precious. I slowly resurfaced, rotating my neck and shoulders, coaxing my consciousness back into my little body in my little room in my little house in my little canyon.

I rubbed my hands together briskly and pressed the heated palm-skin to my eyes. *What the—?* A bitter metallic flavor spread across the back of my tongue, sudden and noxious.

I gagged, a tight convulsion of throat muscle, and swallowed sour saliva. The sharp toxicity immediately seeped back into my mouth. I tried to stay with it this time, probe its source. I sampled the bitterness, tried to explore with awareness. It was unfamiliar, a completely foreign taste. My heart constricted: it was the taste of death.

I opened my eyes, and the harsh tang disappeared as quickly as it had come. The whole experience had lasted ten seconds at most, but it left me wondering: whose death was I tasting?

I made breakfast without incident, thankfully, and took my second cup of coffee onto the deck. I sat and sipped. The morning air was crystal-clear; tiny boats floated like miniature toys on the horizon. But Lobsang hadn't quite rung off, apparently, because his insistent voice kept nattering at me. *Come on, come on, come on. Get to work, Tenzing.*

"Good-bye, Lobsang," I said out loud, but I went inside and got to work. I started by pulling up unopened e-mails on my phone. I quickly found one from Mike labeled "The Three Stooges." It was a pretty good guess his cyber-chase of Florio, Barsotti, and O'Flaherty had brought results. Maybe the answer to everything was one message away. I felt a fluttering, a tremor down in my belly, signaling fear. But as my teachers used to say, fear is just excitement without the breath. I threw a couple of inhales at the dread, and it transformed into a happy caper of anticipation.

Staying in touch with my feelings can be a lot of work sometimes.

Before I had a chance to actually open the e-mail, Mike himself buzzed up my drive, balanced on his motorbike like an awkward insect. I watched from the window as he dismounted, popped off his helmet, and gave me a jaunty wave. I'd never seen him look so relaxed. He was clearly spending a lot of quality time, most of it between the sheets, I was guessing, with what's-her-name.

Tricia.

He walked inside, helped himself to the last of my coffee, and plopped down at the kitchen table. He continued to grin, and his grin continued to irritate me, though I couldn't say exactly why. Well, maybe I could.

Mike raised his mug to me.

"Ain't love grand?" he said.

He set his mug down next to my aborted letter to Yeshe and Lobsang. Mike has no compunction about reading whatever's around. He picked up the notepaper and examined my scrolled doodle.

"Feelin' lucky are we, O'Ten?" he said, in a bad Irish brogue.

"Sorry?"

"Your doodle, boss. All these four-leaf clovers, otherwise known as shamrocks."

"Shamrocks?" Mike always made me feel like I needed to spend a month-long retreat glued to an encyclopedia, a thesaurus, and a year's subscription to *Science* magazine.

"Shamrocks. Irish clovers. Don't play dumb. You're the one who wrapped them around a Celtic cross."

I snatched the paper, staring at what I had always assumed was a vine-wrapped sword.

"You're saying this illustration is Irish?"

"As corned beef and cabbage," Mike said.

My mind whirled.

"Mike, did you find anything more on O'Flaherty's activities here in the States?"

"Not much. Like I said before, he kind of disappeared for a while, after he did his time in the motherland."

My growing excitement consolidated into fierce certainty.

"Let me guess. You lost track of him for five years, right? Ending last year?"

"Right, but how did you—"

"Because that's the same five years Eldon Monroe was serving time at Pelican Bay."

Mike whistled. "You're saying Liam O'Flaherty knows Eldon Monroe."

I smiled. "No, Mike. I'm saying Liam O'Flaherty *is* Eldon Monroe."

Mike opened his laptop. One click and a lot of things snapped into focus. He had collected more data on O'Flaherty's activities, criminal and otherwise. He had also managed to collect images of Liam through the years, mostly mug shots, as it turns out.

Mike tipped the screen in my direction, and together we watched a slide show of Liam O'Flaherty's steady descent from choirboy to felon. First, a pink-cheeked cherub, dressed in white.

"Catholic. First communion," Mike muttered. There he was again, a few years on, holding a soccer ball high. There was the clean-shaven, unlined face of the petty thief, getting booked into adolescent detention. And booked again, this time with a smirk, and a small but nasty red goatee.

We watched as Liam grew meaner and scarier with each mug shot, like a nightmarish version of computer-generated age simulation. It culminated in a grizzled, 40-year-old Liam, beefy and bald, smiling defiantly into the camera, booked in Dublin for some felony or other. I sat back, as at least one jigsaw piece snapped into place with a satisfying *click*. My guess was correct. Young or old, Liam O'Flaherty was most definitely Brother Eldon Monroe.

I fished my checkbook out of my jumbled office supply drawer, directly beneath the silverware holder. I made out a check to cash, for $4,000, and handed it to Mike.

He studied the handwritten check as if it were a fossil. "Haven't seen one of these in a while. You are so very old-school." He looked at the amount and smiled. "Home office time?"

"Home office time. Keep the change, buddy. That's all there is left."

I sent Mike off to research home office equipment, and got to work.

First I called Zimmy.

"Ten, what's the news?"

"I think I may be onto Barbara's killer."

"No kidding."

"He's a bad man, Zimmy." I filled him in on Liam's past, and the connection to TFJ & Associates.

"Can you prove this?"

"Not yet, but I'm getting closer, I can feel it."

"You be careful, Ten."

"Don't worry," I said. "I'm well protected, thanks to Bill Wilson."

There was a long pause.

"I didn't know you were a friend of Bill W's," Zimmy said.

"Well, not a friend exactly," I said. "But he did custom-build me a fine thirty-eight-caliber Supergrade."

Another pause.

"I think we got our Bill Wilsons confused," Zimmy said.

I promised to keep him informed, and set myself the task of finding out more about Thomas Florio, the one Stooge I hadn't yet laid eyes on. I made a few notes but felt a little hamstrung with only my phone as a search engine. This lack of proper equipment was getting old fast.

Tank batted his bowl with his paw.

Right. Lunch first, then Florio.

I slapped together an avocado and Swiss on rye for myself, and a can of mixed grill for my man. As I lifted the sandwich to my mouth, I heard the crunch of tires on gravel. Darn.

Then my gut twanged. I stepped out of sight just as a pewter-colored Maserati snaked up the drive like a sleek and shiny eel. The owner stepped out. He was equally sleek and shiny, a sharp-dressed guy in his 30s, slim and compact, with wavy black hair and gold-rimmed aviator shades. I disliked him on sight.

He minced his way to the house, taking care where he stepped. I was unsurprised to note that his shoes were made from the tanned and bumpy hide of some unfortunate two-toed African bird. So that's what thousand-dollar ostrich leather loafers looked like.

I smiled. Talk about answers arriving by easeful attraction as opposed to stressful pursuit—this was the ultimate in effortlessness: the very guy I wanted to meet was making an actual house call.

I opened the door, and he stepped inside. Then he spotted Tank, and he backpedaled out.

"Allergies," he said, pursing his mouth and sniffing, as if the word itself triggered a reaction.

I glanced at Tank. His whiskers were laid back and starchy, a sure indication of extreme dislike. I couldn't argue with him. This guy was a weasel of the first order.

I joined the varmint outside, and he handed over a business card, pinkie curled in the air like a little flag.

"Thomas Florio," he said, his nasal voice a high-pitched whine. I looked at the embossed card.

Thomas Florio, Jr., it read. Junior. That meant there was a Senior out there somewhere, responsible for this creep.

He didn't waste any time coming to the point.

"I called your friend Zimmy Backus," he said.

"How is Zimmy?" I asked.

"He's fine, but he refused any further discussion of the business deal I was proposing. He said I should speak to you from here on out."

"Okay. But he's already turned you down once. Why did you call him again?"

Florio nodded. "Things have changed since we last talked. My company stumbled across some unpaid royalties. I wanted to let him know this is no longer speculation—there's a guaranteed payoff involved."

A guaranteed payoff, or someone deciding to sweeten the deal, someone maybe growing a little more desperate to get Zimmy to sign?

"How much would Zimmy get, after your fees and other expenses?"

"About seventeen thousand." He spread his hands apologetically. "I know it doesn't sound like a lot, but it suggests there's plenty more out there."

As long as I had Florio standing in my doorway, I might as well trawl for as much information as I could. I decided to pull the pin on a little grenade and toss it his way. See where it landed.

"I've been talking to Buster Redman's widow, Beulah," I said. "Nice lady. And your other client? Poor Freda Wilson? I'm sure you know she's taken ill."

I had to hand it to Florio. He barely blinked. He did appear to reappraise me, though.

"You're quite the sleuth, aren't you, Mr. Norbu?"

I kept my voice bland. "Time will tell," I said. "I do find myself curious about what you guys are up to."

"Us guys? Which guys are you referring to?"

"You. Barsotti. O'Flaherty."

Florio's smile was tight. "Looks like your curiosity has been working overtime."

"It's certainly working all the time, if that's what you mean."

"And what have you learned from this curiosity? Have you met Barsotti, met O'Flaherty yet?" His voice was rising in pitch. Pretty soon he'd be silently whistling for dogs.

I was still feeling remarkably relaxed, myself. "I haven't met Barsotti, but I've had binoculars on him a few times."

"Where?"

"Oh, you know, the usual. Pig farm, car dealership, his house in Beverly Hills." I observed Florio closely. "Visiting his girlfriend out in The Valley."

He stiffened almost imperceptibly at the word *girlfriend*, so I elaborated.

"She's quite the little equestrian, isn't she? Very impressive in the saddle."

But Junior had his own agenda, and he was sticking to it. "I wouldn't know. So, what about Zimmy? Will you talk to him about the contract?"

Impatience climbed my spine. I was tired of his pursed mouth and one-track mind.

"I've got things to do," I said. "So if you'll excuse me."

Florio was glaring at something over my shoulder. I glanced back. Tank had moved to the sliding glass door and was fixated on Florio, his tail flicking from side to side like a windshield wiper.

"Big cat," he said.

"He is indeed," I said.

"I'm not much of a cat person, myself."

"That's fine," I said. "He's equally picky about people."

"I'll keep that in mind," Florio said. "And while we're handing out warnings, remember what curiosity did to the cat."

"Get the fuck off my property." I said.

I went back in the house and got my Wilson out of the safe. I jacked a round into the chamber and joined Tank at the glass door. Together, we watched Florio get in his car and head back down the driveway.

"Weasel," I said. Tank ambled away. A few moments later I heard the *crunch-crunch* of cat teeth nibbling on dry food. Tank's appetite is a sensitive barometer of his feelings, and I was happy to see that Florio's visit hadn't put him off. I considered this a challenge, so I ate my sandwich as well, but I didn't taste a bite.

Fucking pinkie finger in the air. Who does he think he is, Queen Fucking Elizabeth?

Dial it down, Tenzing. Way down.

I huffed around the house, until I realized I was just looking for something else to resent, kind of like a cranky hat looking for a hook. I decided to make tea for myself. Proper Tibetan milk tea. I poured some milk in a saucepan, and added loose black tea, and a healthy dose of sugar. As it came to a boil, I checked my e-mails. I had one from Mike, with a home address for Jeremiah Star Trek Cook's surviving spouse, Camille.

Good. Taking action would help me calm down.

I poured the fragrant tea through a strainer, into a cup, and lifted it to my lips, happily anticipating the aromatic brew.

My hand froze. The metallic taste had returned, an astringent sharpness in the back of my throat. This time it lodged in my taste buds. I drank my tea anyway, but the chemical flavor lingered, like a hint of menace at the base of my tongue. Talk about disappointing.

I may occasionally confer with cats and old friends using unconventional techniques, but that doesn't mean I'm automatically woolly-brained. I ran through every rational explanation I could think of that might cause this particular taste to arise. Had I started taking some different vitamin and mineral combinations? No. I'm a creature of habit, and I'd swallowed the same handful of supplements for years. Was my body having difficulty with something I'd eaten? I couldn't think of anything unusual I'd ingested, except for Julie's sautéed morels and Potatoes Anna. No way they were the cause—too delicious, and, more to the point, too digested by now.

I filed the experience under "Cause Unknown" for the time being.

The cricket choir trilled from my pocket.

I checked the screen. I didn't know the number, but the prefix was 310, the moneyed code of lawyers, agents, and other persons of swank. I decided to answer. Who knows? Maybe easeful attraction was still at work.

CHAPTER 24

The voice was rich and smooth, like good coffee. "Mr. Norbu?"

I agreed I was.

"Mr. Norbu, my name is Thomas Florio."

My mind froze up for a moment, trying to reconcile this soothing timbre with the nasal whine of the Thomas Florio who'd paid me a visit. Then I realized, of course, this must be Thomas Sr.

"What can I do for you?"

"Apparently my son just paid you a visit—without my knowledge, I assure you. He called me to relay details of your conversation together. He was quite agitated. I wish to apologize to you for his behavior. Tommy has often proved challenging for Mrs. Florio and myself. The trials have not lessened in adulthood."

"I can imagine," I said. "He did strike me as having too much accelerator and too few brakes."

Florio chuckled. "Well put, Mr. Norbu, well put. Professionals have labeled it 'poor impulse control,' but I like your description better. I have enjoyed many blessings, but my desire for a serene family life continues to elude me."

"I wish you success in attaining that goal," I said. "Thank you for calling, but there's no need to apologize." I glanced at the time. Much as I was enjoying our little love fest, I needed to get back to work. "Is there anything else I can do for you?"

"Yes, yes there is, Mr. Norbu. I'd like to discuss some information that emerged from your conversation with Tommy."

"Go ahead," I said.

He cleared his throat. "If you don't mind, I'd prefer to discuss this matter in person, rather than over the phone. I suppose I might be considered very old-fashioned these days, but I much prefer to meet face to face."

There was something very likable about this man. With his mellow voice and courtly manner, he was hard to refuse. "Okay," I said. "How can we make that happen?"

"I propose that we meet at the Jonathan Club. Do you know it, Mr. Norbu?"

I did, the same way I "knew" a lot of icons: by reputation only, and from a distance. I'd driven past their blue awning downtown many a time, but I'd never made it inside. The Jonathan Club was elite and expensive, a favorite haunt of L.A.'s well-to-do aristocracy. Not too many boys and girls in blue on their membership list.

"I'm familiar with the club. When would you like to meet, sir?" Florio's graciousness was contagious.

"I'm here now, Mr. Norbu. I come here almost every day. Would you consider joining me for a drink?"

"I can be there in two hours," I said. "I have to make another stop first."

"Excellent. I'll let them know you're coming."

I don't go out much to begin with, and since I got laid off, I had moved my formal wear, so to speak, to the far end of the closet. There was no way my jeans and T-shirt would make it through the front door of the Jonathan Club. I riffled through my hangers and came up with gray slacks, a halfway decent striped button-down shirt, a black wool sport coat, and a relatively clean blue tie with yellow stripes. I rolled the lint-remover over my pants and jacket, hopefully sticky-taping off any stray Tank-hairs. After I'd gotten dressed, I modeled the new me for Tank.

Not bad, he seemed to say, for an ex-cop.

I was never more grateful for the Shelby. Driving into the parking structure in my Toyota would have resulted in banishment to the hinterlands. I felt sure my brash

Mustang would be a welcome addition to the luxury sedans stabled in front.

But first, a trip to Pacific Palisades. I had just enough time to follow up on Mike's information, and pay a quick visit to Jeremiah Star Trek's widow. I pulled into the driveway of a spectacular two-story Spanish home, way up in the Highlands off Sunset. A fountain trickled merrily from behind a wooden gate to one side, and the front door's knocker was a cast-iron lion's head, clasping a ring in its jaws. I lifted the heavy ring and let it drop with a loud *clang*. Then I pushed the electric buzzer, for good measure.

After a few minutes, the massive door swung open. A handsome woman in her 70s, her blue eyes framed with white wavy hair, met me with a smile that would melt snow. Mrs. Cook seemed to approve of my jacket and tie.

I introduced myself and told her why I was there. Her eyes darkened, and she ushered me inside.

I stepped into a California version of a medieval castle, complete with stained-glass windows, thick velvet curtains, and a pair of hand-carved gargoyles, sculpted out of what looked like animal bone.

She caught me staring.

"Jerry liked to sculpt between acting jobs," she said. "He hated to be idle." She gave me a quick tour of the house. Our first stop was a small room packed full of *Star Trek* memorabilia, from cookie jars to bobble heads. I never knew a spaceship, much less pointy ears, could fit on so many household goods. Following that, she ushered me in and out of two bedrooms, and a large study. She pointed out several more of his sculptures, lovingly describing them in detail—a garish, grinning *commedia dell'arte* mask of flat cow bone; a mobile of two twirling dancers, teased out of antelope ribs; a magnificent eagle, wings spread, carved from a camel's femur. The house was a mausoleum of abandoned bone, reconfigured as art.

If I were a camel femur, I could think of a lot worse ways to be reincarnated.

We soon sat facing each other on high-backed velvet chairs, in front of a fireplace big enough to roast one of Barsotti's pigs. A small, beautifully carved treasure chest sat on the mantel, another of Jerry's works, I was quite sure.

"Now," Mrs. Cook said. "What do you need to know?"

I hesitated. "This could be painful to talk about."

"Mr. Norbu, what's painful is knowing something's very suspicious about your husband's death, and having no one else believe you. I know he had prostate cancer, but he was in remission. The laetrile was working. His father and mother both lived well into their nineties, for goodness' sake!"

"Can you describe to me exactly what happened?"

The events were so familiar. The visit from Florio. The signed contract. The promise of money.

"Mr. Florio seemed so certain about the royalties." Mrs. Cook sighed. "And then, when he came back with the check . . ."

"He came back?"

"Yes, a few months later, with a check for two thousand dollars, and a dear little gift basket of local wines and cheeses. Jerry and I celebrated our good fortune that night." Her voice grew bitter. "The next day, my husband was dead."

I glanced at my watch. I did not want to be late for Florio Sr.

Then I caught myself. This woman was in pain. Florio could wait. I reached over and touched the back of her hand.

"I lost my mother very suddenly. The death of a loved one is never easy," I said. "But when it's sudden, the pain is that much more acute, isn't it?"

She squeezed my hand. We sat together in silence for a few minutes.

"What am I thinking," Mrs. Cook exclaimed. "I never even offered you something to drink!"

"Thank you, but I should get going," I smiled. We both stood. "I am curious, though. Have you received any more money from TFJ?"

She shook her head. "Not one penny."

I met her eyes.

"One last question and I apologize for this one. Would you consider making your husband's body available for an autopsy?"

Her eyes filled. She walked over to the mantel. She reached for the carved wooden chest and turned, hugging it close.

"I'm sorry," she said, "but it's too late. This is what Jerry wanted. To be here at home, with me."

I took Sunset south, hopped on the Pacific Coast Highway, then jumped onto the 10 to the 110 South. I kept one eye on the road and the other in my rear-view mirror for traffic cops. The traffic was pretty light, for once. I put in my little white earbuds and called Julie.

"Guess where I'm going," I said.

"Dharamshala, to visit your father."

"Very funny. I'm invited for drinks at the Jonathan Club."

"Is that good?"

"That's very good. The drinks are free, and the club, I'll have you know, is extremely exclusive."

"All righty then. I was going to offer to cook at your place tonight, but I guess you just vaulted out of my league."

I laughed. "Please come. The keys are under the front mat, and Tank will be thrilled to have you to himself for as long as possible. I'll be back around seven."

"Good," she said. "As you must have figured out, Detective, I'm hoping to seduce you."

Actually I hadn't figured out any such thing. This particular detective was notoriously poor at detecting the obvious, when it came to women.

"Sounds perfect," I said. "What are we having for dessert?"

"Don't push your luck, Norbu."

I exited at 6th, hung a left, and drove past the front entrance to the club. I took a moment to glance up at the elegant brick facade. Part Italian Renaissance, part Parisian folly, the building managed to feel opulent without being decadent. The navy blue awning, cupped over the entrance, was marked with a discreet shield bearing the initials JC in angular white. It reminded me of a cattle-brand.

I turned into the underground garage. A parking valet was at my side in an instant.

"Beautiful 'Stang," he said. "I've always wanted to drive one of these."

'Stang? I handed him the keys, and hoped that the Jonathan Club was as meticulous vetting its parking attendants as it was its membership. As I suspected, high-end Beemers, Mercedes, and Cadillacs were strategically placed in the prime front slots. I was gratified to see the attendant slide my Mustang right in the middle of them.

I walked through a glass door, down a short hallway, and through a second set of doors, glass and wood this time. A concierge sat at a table to my right.

His suit put my outfit to shame.

He gave me a covert once-over. I stood up straighter. I might not have the bone structure, coat, and teeth of a pure-bred, but I at least hoped to meet the minimum standards.

"Good afternoon, sir. Can I help you?" he sniffed.

"Tenzing Norbu, here to meet Mr. Thomas Florio," I said. "Senior."

"Of course. Mr. Florio is expecting you." He ushered me through the foyer and into the lobby, which was spectacular. Muted rugs covered highly polished pink marble flooring, and the hand-painted ceiling was a work of art in itself. I felt like I had stepped into my own private Taj Mahal, Greco-Roman style.

"Mr. Florio is in the Library," the concierge murmured. Gliding silently, he led me past display cases of antique porcelain and landscapes by artists I was sure I'd seen in one of my art books, to a wide marble staircase covered in red and gold carpeting. We ascended, crossed a second foyer, and climbed a few steps to a small mezzanine. I barely had time to register the artwork when up we went again, to a beautifully appointed hallway, lined with still more landscapes. We stopped midway, at a huge pair of ornate wooden doors.

"The Town Club Library," my guide announced. He opened the heavy wooden doors, and I stepped into a secret world of hushed opulence. Wall-to-wall flooring echoed the downstairs in a repeating pattern of rose and gold florets. A row of columns marked smaller private sitting areas. A painting of a man in a scarlet robe and cap pinned me with stern eyes, pegging me as an interloper of uncertain beliefs.

My guide turned left, but I paused to scan the spacious room. I might never get this close to a museum-quality world again. Lots of columns, sculptures, busts, and ornamental vases. Lots of portraits of hoary men staring into the distance, calculating their net worth. I felt completely intimidated, which was probably the point.

"He's in the stacks," the concierge said, and led me between two enormous cloisonné urns, one black, one red: possibly the final resting place of expired associates who couldn't bear to give up their membership.

This was the "book" part of the Library. The shelves were full of them, floor to ceiling. Maybe six or seven thousand print volumes, and not a Kindle or iPad in sight.

Directly across from us was a large fireplace under a magnificent carved wooden mantel. Two leather wingbacks flanked the hearth. A distinguished gray-haired man sat in one, reading a leather-bound book. He gave a little wave. The concierge left us, melting into the background and out the door.

My chest was reminding me I needed to breathe. I was strangely nervous as I made my way to Thomas Florio, Sr., stepping around an Old World globe set in a four-legged wooden frame. It was tipped on its axis, just like me.

Florio was compact, very fit for a man in his 70s, with a full head of wavy hair combed back on both sides and crested over the top. His black suit and pearl-gray tie were somber, but a vivid red pocket square added a waggish dash of color. An old-fashioned leather briefcase rested on the floor next to him. He set his book aside and slowly climbed to his feet. He reached out a slim hand.

"Mr. Norbu. I'm Thomas Florio. Good of you to come."

"Please call me Ten. It's short for Tenzing."

"Thank you, Tenzing. Ten. No doubt you're of Tibetan heritage?"

"More of a hybrid, actually. My father is Tibetan, my mother was born in America, but moved to Paris before I was born." I changed course. "Beautiful place," I said, gesturing to the elegant decor.

"Yes, I find it very pleasant. So pleasant, in fact, that I've come here almost every afternoon for twenty years."

He moved to the globe and set it spinning with one slender finger. "As I'm sure you know, most of the world first heard the name Tenzing when Sir Edmund Hilary and his Sherpa climbing partner, Tenzing Norgay, summited Mount Everest back in 1953."

I told him my father had the good fortune of actually meeting Tenzing Norgay once, when I was just a child.

"Good for him," he said. "So, then. Tibetan-American-Parisian—you come from unusual stock."

I could feel him waiting for me to reciprocate. Normally I'm not one for prolonged small talk, but I was on his turf. I also sensed this was some sort of an audition, and if I was to pass, I needed to adapt to the social rituals of this select tribe.

"And you, sir? What is your background?"

Florio smiled. He took his seat and gestured to the matching leather chair across from him. "Sit, please, Ten!"

I sat, glancing at the spine of the book Florio was reading. I smiled to myself. It was *The Prince*, by Machiavelli, the famous Renaissance guide to attaining political power. Perfect.

He laced his fingers and settled back in his chair. "My grandfather emigrated from Italy almost a century ago. He established himself in the banking business, inspired by the great success of a distant cousin, A. P. Giannini."

Florio's eyes lasered in on mine, assessing my reaction. Giannini. Oh, man, I knew that name. Mike's face popped in my head. I took my best shot.

"He founded . . . Bank of America?"

Florio nodded, pleased. "That's right. Amadeo Giannini was in fact a revolutionary, the first man to create a bank for the masses. Before him, banks were only for the wealthy. My grandfather and father followed his lead, although on a much more modest scale. But times have changed, and banking is no longer what it was. In my era, I have found it necessary to diversify into other areas."

I was dying to ask what other areas, but we were getting along so swimmingly, I decided to wait. "Sounds like quite an immigrant success story. I'm trying to be one of those myself."

"And from what I hear, doing a fine job of it. A stellar member of law enforcement, and now an entrepreneur of sorts."

Okay. Enough. I was starting to go into sugar shock with all this sweet talk.

"What can I do for you, Mr. Florio?"

"Thomas, please."

"Thomas."

"Let's repair to the Tap Room, shall we?"

Fine by me.

The Tap Room was a pedigreed drinker's dream. The polished bar, lined with studded black leather barstools, was 50 feet long. The authentic assortment of colossal Old World beer steins displayed above it made my ale-swigging soul swell with anticipation. The walls here were lined with black-and-white photographs of past luminaries, interspersed with the only bow to modernity I had seen, several flat-screen televisions. They were tuned to different channels, broadcasting the breaking news of politics, finance, and sports to people who moved money accordingly.

We sat in leather club chairs at a table in the corner, under leaded glass windows. A waiter materialized to take our orders: for me, locally brewed India pale ale on tap, for Thomas Sr., something with a fancy Italian name I didn't quite catch.

Thomas Sr. exchanged nods with a few businessmen across the room. A pair of women in power suits glanced our way before returning to their conversation.

The waiter set a tall stein of straw-colored ale in front of me, and two small snifters of thick amber liquid before Mr. Florio. He raised one glass to mine.

"Amaretto," he said. "A custom I inherited from my grandfather." We clinked glasses, and I took a long, happy draw. The icy-cold ale cut through the road dust on my tongue. I sighed with pleasure. Nothing like good beer, on tap, for free.

Florio drained his liqueur, and set his first glass down. "Here is my concern," he said. "During your conversation with my son, you mentioned something about Mr. Barsotti. Specifically, that Mr. Barsotti had a girlfriend. Did my son hear that correctly?"

"Yes, he heard it correctly."

He frowned. "I'm very sorry to hear that," he said.

"If you don't mind my asking, why is this of any interest to you?"

"Do you have any children, Mr. Norbu?"

I shook my head.

Florio took a small sip from his second glass. He stared off into the middle distance, then returned his gaze to me. His voice was firm. "Mr. Barsotti is married to my daughter. He is my son-in-law."

Looks like I stepped right into the middle of an old-school family muddle. I could almost feel the quicksand sucking at my feet.

Florio's mouth flattened into a horizontal crease of distaste. "Can you give me the details, please?"

I described the horse-riding blonde, the SUV, and the subsequent stakeout at the condo—everything but the girl's name. Florio's eyes held mine throughout, without flinching.

"Permit me a few moments to digest this information," he said. He closed his eyes and sank back in his chair. Suddenly he seemed frail and diminished; the worry lines on his forehead and around his mouth deepened, bathed in the ocher light of an antique lamp on the table.

He firmed up his shoulders and the lines smoothed. When he opened his eyes, they were steely, and for the first time I sensed iron beneath the velvet voice.

"This presents me with a dilemma," he said. "Vincent Barsotti is the father of my grandchildren. What is best for the grandchildren? Is it better to be raised by a cheating father or to have no father in the house at all?"

I knew which one I'd pick, but I wasn't standing in the Barsotti children's shoes. I pictured the two youngsters as I'd last seen them, waiting at the kitchen table for their parents to join them for a family dinner. With that in mind, I tried on both scenarios, and they both felt awful. "I don't know. I don't know which is best."

"Welcome to the complicated world of parenting," he said. "My daughter is married to a man who cheats, and my son has been known to cheat me. You're from the East, Ten. Perhaps you can explain to me how bad karma works. I think I am getting my nose rubbed in it."

How to answer? Every situation comes with myriad karmic influences and conditions. The Buddha himself said that karma is so complex a person could go crazy trying to figure it out: the only way to simplify, he suggests, is to follow the basic principle that it is our *intention* that determines our karma. Good intentions produce good karma; bad intentions produce bad karma. When conditions are right, in this or a future life, effect follows cause, and the seeds of your good and bad actions ripen into the fruits that are your karma. Or something like that. Anyway, Mr. Florio wasn't asking for a treatise on karma. He was asking for help.

"I'm not sure karma has anything to do with it," I said. "But I will say this. It seems to me a skillful parent is like a skillful teacher. Such a person is mindful of their charge's well-being, taking note of their actions and intentions, and steering them straight when they veer off course. Closing our eyes to their wrong actions, choosing to avoid or withdraw from them, can cause the wrong to boomerang back, more often than not, in a harsher form."

Florio's chuckle was rueful. "Well put, well put. I guess I'd better find out what I closed my eyes to with both my son and daughter, because the boomerangs seem to be coming faster and faster."

"May I ask you a couple of questions?"

"Anything," he said.

"Did your son tell you why he came to see me?"

"He told me you represented a former client of his. He didn't elaborate."

No, I'll bet he didn't.

"You say he has cheated you. In what way?"

He grimaced. "It's painful to discuss."

"As you wish," I said. I waited.

He went on, "It's a pattern he's played out several times, and unfortunately I have been a willing participant. I hire him to work for me. He behaves irresponsibly, creating a mess that someone then has to . . . no, that *I* then have to clean up. I enable. I grow frustrated. I withdraw all support. Time passes. His mother weeps. He begs, and comes crawling back to me. I am convinced by both him and his mother that he is no longer irresponsible. I hire him again. And so it continues."

"And now?"

He nodded. "Ah yes. Now. Now I have him working on a real estate deal. Up to this point, everything seems to be progressing smoothly."

I watched him closely. Did he believe this? "I'm glad for you," I said.

His eyes bored into mine. "What do you really think, Tenzing? You've just spent time with my son. Can I trust him this time?"

I held his gaze, letting my lack of reassurance speak volumes. Mr. Florio gave a short nod, as if I had confirmed something.

"A father knows, you see," Florio said. "My son grows secretive, yet also agitated. Unlike you just now, he does not meet my eyes. He avoids my calls for days. I know the signs, Tenzing. It is like an addiction, only the drug for Tommy is breaking the law. Thus far, he has never been formally charged with a crime, but only thanks to my timely interventions. I'm afraid he is going to run afoul again."

Florio picked up his second glass and took a small sip. His voice grew firm. "This time, should it happen, I have taken a vow not to protect him. And I always keep my vows. Always."

"That sounds painful, but in this case wise," I said. "Maybe it will break the pattern you describe."

"I hope it's wise. I know it's long overdue."

I stood up. I felt sad for Thomas Florio, Sr., but there wasn't much I could do besides send him good thoughts; he would have to do the rest. Life demands that we face the consequences of our actions, and sometimes it boils down to a series of sweaty ten-minute conversations that you're either willing to have or you're not. Florio had a few such conversations looming over his future, and I hoped for his sake he wouldn't put them off for too much longer.

I thought about me and my father. Who was I to talk?

I held out my hand to take my leave, but Florio was unclasping his leather briefcase. He withdrew an envelope, and clicked it shut.

"Still, one prefers to know such things ahead of time, doesn't one," he said, as if continuing a conversation in his head. "I'd like to engage your services for the next week, Ten, to keep an eye on my son's activities."

This was getting interesting. And tricky. "I'm already conducting an investigation for another client," I said.

"Please. There's no reason you can't report to two people. Unless you're aware of a conflict of interest?"

I thought it over. Zimmy could only gain by anything I learned on Florio's dime. And Florio Sr. didn't know it, but I was already onto some of Junior's extracurricular shenanigans, thanks to Zimmy.

"We need to be clear on something, right up front," I said.

"What's that?"

"If it comes down to a choice—discovering the truth or concealing it to save your son—you need to know that I'm after the truth. Period. I have zero interest in protecting Tommy Junior, or anybody else for that matter, from the consequences of their actions. Are you absolutely sure we're on the same page there?"

He nodded. "We're both after the same information, Tenzing."

I took the envelope, peeked inside, and sealed the deal with a firm handshake.

Immobilized in bumper-to-bumper traffic on the way home, I opened the envelope and took a second look. I rolled down my window and stuck my head outside.

"Woo-hoo," I yelled to the startled driver to my left.

I called Mike and gave him the good news. With ten thousand more in my account, I could finally pay him for his time.

"So, Mike, can you do a detailed, due-diligence report on Thomas Florio Senior, please?"

"Planning to bite the hand that feeds you?"

"More like quietly run its prints. It's always good to be cautious," I said, thinking of Florio's reading material. "Also, I need an in-depth background check on Norman Murphy, John D's son."

"Will do. When do you want me to install your new equipment?"

"Now, baby. Now."

I made a quick side trip to the bank and got there just before closing time. I deposited Florio's check, less $600 in cash. I liked the feel of the folded Franklins in my back pocket.

I'd just doubled my fee as a private investigator, not to mention tripled my monthly pay at the LAPD, in under two weeks. Everything is impermanent, subject to change, and guess what? That goes for poverty, too. The pleasurable tickle in my belly migrated lower. Apparently, earning big bucks was an aphrodisiac. I pictured Julie, probably hip-chopping something astonishing in my kitchen. I called Mike back.

"Uh, Mike? About installing the office? Let's make that a job for tomorrow."

I pressed hard on the accelerator and rode my magic carpet home.

CHAPTER 25

My turn to cook for the chef. I had made a quick early-morning run to the local market and now was sawing off thick slabs of freshly baked sourdough *boule*. The frittata was in the oven, the coffee was brewing, and Julie was sitting across from me in my button-down shirt, and nothing else.

Her tousled hair spilled over one shoulder in a tangle of rich brunette curls. To me, even sleepy, she looked like a movie star. In Los Angeles, that's saying a lot.

"So how does a gentleman like Florio end up with a son like Tommy?" Julie said. "It doesn't compute."

"I know," I said. "This is why the notion of having children scares me. I feel like I'm surrounded by sons disappointing fathers, and vice versa."

Julie opened her mouth then shut it again.

"Listen, I get it," I said. "I'm probably hyper-aware of this stuff because of my father and me."

"Like when Martha couldn't get pregnant," Julie said. "She'd call me in tears, swearing the entire city was made up of expectant women about to pop."

I served Julie a wedge of frittata and two pieces of hot buttered toast. My eye happened to catch a shadowed womanly curve, just inside the unbuttoned part of the button-down shirt.

Julie stood. Our mouths met.

We backed into the bedroom, stumbling and laughing and kissing and never once detaching. We fell onto the bed, and the air exploded around me, and inside me, and Julie was right there beside me, with me all the way.

We lay entangled in the sheets and each other.

"Okay," I said. "Okay. That was pretty amazing."

Julie rolled on top of me, pinning my arms to my sides.

"Pretty amazing? Pretty amazing? I'll give you pretty amazing," and she tickled me until I promised to reveal my deepest, darkest secret.

So I told her about Apa and Valerie. How I was a mistake, the accidental result of a Tibetan Buddhist monk's midlife folly with an ethereal American girl trekking around India in search of enlightenment.

"Well, it *is* kind of romantic," Julie said.

"Not really. He was almost forty," I said, "and she was twenty, going on fifteen. For reasons that were never clear to me, they ended up falling in love. Or falling in something, anyway. Whatever it was, they fell out of it just as quickly."

"Hate when that happens," Julie said.

"He insisted on a quick marriage. She insisted on a quicker divorce."

Julie had moved closer to me, and her freckled skin glowed in the morning light. Her hair had devolved from tangled to totally disheveled. Irresistible.

I reached over for a curl. I tugged it into a long, straight lock, then released. It bounced back to a tight spiral. Change is hard.

"Valerie used to say, after a few too many glasses of Bordeaux, that she knew they were going to break up before they'd even gotten together."

"You called your mother Valerie?"

"She was adamant. She said 'Mom' made her feel too old. She shrugged off motherhood instantly, just like she shrugged off my father."

Pulled another curl straight. Released it.

"Ten?"

I looked up. Julie's eyes were serious.

"It doesn't always have to be like that."

"I know," I said. "I know it doesn't." But I didn't know any such thing.

Mike showed up in a small U-Haul at noon, with dark circles under his eyes, and an ergonomically correct office chair, a laptop, a computer table, a combination printer-fax-scanner, an external hard drive, a wireless mouse, a docking station, an extra monitor, a work lamp with an adjustable arm, a surge protector, and enough cables to choke a small city.

I'm handy with guns and cars, but digital electronics make me weep with frustration, so I made über-strong coffee and stayed out of the way. After everything was unpacked, Mike downed one last swallow of caffeine, planted his empty mug on the kitchen table, and surveyed my designated office space.

"Southeast corner. Very feng-shui, boss,"

"Very only-spot-available-that-works," I replied.

He placed the computer table catty-corner facing the front door, and got busy with the transformation.

Mike is a mutterer—he talks nonstop under his breath while he works. I decided to go for a run. I needed to clear my head, and I needed not to stuff a sock in Mike's mouth.

By the time I got back, the office was up and running, and Mike had news.

"So. Norman Murphy. I got something." Mike pushed away from the computer table, stepped aside, and offered me a seat with a bow and a flourish.

I sat in my new chair and wheeled up to my new monitor. It felt good, almost official. I scanned the short article on the screen in front of me. It was from the *Antelope Valley Press* again: Lancaster's go-to place for news, but this time dated four years ago. The item stated that an employee of the Department of Public Works, Norman Murphy, had been disciplined by the County, suspended for one month without pay, and ordered to pay $500 restitution, for using department resources on an off-hours personal project. The story concluded with a brief but recognizably self-pitying statement from Norman, who said he was unfairly targeted, outraged by the accusations, and totally innocent of all charges.

"Good work, Mike," I said. "And my office is fantastic." I dug my checkbook out of the kitchen junk-drawer, wrote him a check, and put the checkbook in my new, empty office drawer. Life was good.

"Thanks," Mike said. "Can I go now? I have a brilliant hottie waiting for me to get home. Living together is awesome. You should try it sometime." Great. Madly in love for ten days, and now he's an expert in relationships.

I made a few calls, and finally tracked down Deputy Sheriff Dardon on his cell phone. He didn't sound too thrilled to hear from me.

"What is it, Detective? You sending more bad news my way?"

"Not exactly. Norman Murphy got in some trouble a while back, got suspended without pay from the DPW. I'm wondering what you know about it."

Dardon made an unhappy rumbling sound in his throat. "You're like a dog with a bone, aren't you, Norbu?"

"I'm very engaged with this case, Deputy Dardon."

"What makes you think I can add anything?"

"Because it takes a good investigator to know one."

He sighed, and I knew I had him. "Most of what I know comes from bits and pieces out of the guys at Waterworks. Seems that Norman took home a computer and some other equipment over the weekend, for personal use."

"What kind of equipment?"

"I'm trying to remember. Some sort of sonar thing, I think, for surveying and such. Anyway, it was expensive—Public Works said it cost the county over twenty thousand, new. That's why they got their knickers in such a twist when he borrowed it."

"What happened?"

"Norman messed up the machine somehow while he was out there prospecting. Then he put it back broke."

"How'd they connect it to Norman?"

Dardon permitted himself a small laugh. "You're going to love this. Come Monday morning, he let it slip he knew the thing was busted. When his boss confronted him, Norman broke down, cried real tears. Of course he denied everything when they suspended him."

"Any guess what he was looking for?"

"Hell if I know. Nobody ever said, but I haven't heard rumors of any buried treasure in these parts. If there was, I'd be out there digging for it myself."

I spent an hour playing with my new toys, organizing, rearranging, and testing the equipment. Everything worked. Mike had spent a quick morning executing what would have, one, taken me at least a week of frustrated finagling; two, included many more four-letter words than Tank was accustomed to hearing; and three, culminated in an emergency call to Mike to come out and save me from tearing out my already-too-short hair.

I've learned the hard way it's better to just skip directly to three.

Time to make it mine.

I took a scavenging stroll outside and returned with a sprig of hummingbird sage, a coffee scoop's worth of sandy soil, and five very small stones of varying shapes and colors. My best find was a polished gray oval, narrow and flat like a guitar pick.

I placed the sage by my new laptop, where it could remind me that a world of hawk and deer and wildflowers waited right outside my office door.

I scoured my cabinets and came up with a shallow ceramic dish for olive oil dipping. Sorry, friend, you've got a new job. I filled it with the sand. Using the polished oval stone like a tiny hoe, I smoothed the surface. Then I positioned all five stones in the sand, choosing spots that felt just right for that moment. *Et voilà.* Instant Zen garden.

I called John D and let him know I was headed his way.

"I need your help with something," I told him. I didn't tell him I probably could have gotten my answers over the phone, but I wanted to check on how he was healing.

"You're coming out here so often, you oughta consider running for mayor," he said.

Ninety minutes later I arrived with a quart of fresh fruit salad, a loaf of cracked wheat bread, a wedge of sharp cheddar cheese, and my growing affection.

He seemed delighted with all four.

"Are you sure you're up for this tour?" I asked.

"I'm a farmer," he said. "We're tough."

He did look amazingly spry for a man with a tumor who was recently mugged.

As we hiked slowly around his property, I gave him a rundown on what I'd learned from Dardon.

"Norman never said one word to me about any of that," John D said. He scraped at the earth with one work boot. "What you gotta know about Norman is, he's always got some kind of scheme going. Always has, prolly always will." A small smile crossed John D's face. "One summer, when he was just a kid, he set up a farm stand selling fruit, only the fruit came from our own kitchen bowl."

"Does Norman have kids?"

"Not that I know of. No, Norman is all that's left of the Murphy gene pool." John D shrugged. "Maybe that's a good thing."

I said nothing as we reached the end of a row of dying almond trees. John D parted the branches of one, and plucked a bruised black leaf from a smattering of green ones.

"Look here, Ten. This is what's been happening." His forefinger traced the bright yellow streaks striating the blackened surface. "Within a year, this tree will have only black leaves. Then it won't have any. It'll be dead, just like all the others."

"And nobody could ever tell you why?"

He shook his head. "They said maybe acid rain, but nobody seemed to care much, one way or the other. Eighty acres is small potatoes."

He pointed. "Over there, that's what you'll be wanting to see." John D led me over to an old wooden well. He drew up a bucket of water.

He dipped in a forefinger and touched it to his tongue. "Tastes okay to me." He offered me the bucket.

I did the same. And spat reflexively. There was no mistaking the faint but familiar residue left on my tongue: bitterness, metal, and death.

John D was peering at me. "Boy, that's some look came over your face right then. You okay?"

I told him about the taste that had paid a visit two days earlier, a foreshadowing of this moment with him.

John D squinted. "Hunh. Seems like your inner dowser's been working overtime."

Something was niggling at me.

"John D, didn't you say you asked Norman to look into something for you, having to do with your land?"

John D nodded. "Yeah. I told Norman about the trees dying when I first noticed it. Asked if his department could do what they do, you know, analyze the well water I use for irrigation. He came out and took some samples, but then, who knows, I prolly made him mad about some dang thing or other, because he never got back to me."

I said nothing. John D took a moment, but he put it together.

"Oh, Norman," he said.

Norman's house was at the end of a cul-de-sac, one of the worst places for any kind of covert surveillance, so I had little choice but to go overt. I had come equipped, in the form of a direct-mail postcard of a hollow-eyed missing child.

I made my way down the street toward Norman's place, ringing doorbells, flashing my postcard, and getting blank looks and head-shakes in return. Too bad. I could have addressed two wrongs with one right action.

Norman's driveway was like a play yard for a giant toddler. A gleaming new speedboat, hitched to a trailer, sat next to a bright red motorcycle with three fat wheels, just an oversized kid's trike.

I didn't see any SUV, though, official or otherwise, so I rang Norman's doorbell. A few moments later the door opened and I had my first look at Mrs. Norman Murphy, wiping her hands on a dishtowel. I blinked. Her shoulder-length auburn hair was pulled off her face with two clips. Pink cheeks. Hazel eyes, a little watery. A nice figure, kind of regular, not too skinny, not too plump. She wore stretchy pants and one of those short-sleeved shirts with a tiny embroidered alligator on it. She looked . . . nice.

"Yes?" she said.

I showed her my postcard and asked if she'd seen the little boy. She glanced at it, then back at me.

"I'm sorry. I haven't seen him. Poor little thing."

I was astonished to see her eyes brimmed over with tears.

"Ma'am?"

"I'm sorry," she repeated. "I'm . . . really emotional these days." She started to close the door, so I blurted out the first thing that came to mind. "You're Mrs. Murphy, aren't you? Norman's wife?"

"Yes. I'm Becky Murphy," she nodded, her forehead furrowing.

"I used to work for the city," I explained. "I've met Norman. He's quite a character."

"He is, isn't he?" Her smile was amused, yet slightly apologetic, like that of an indulgent parent. It occurred to me she might actually love Norman, which meant some part of Norman was actually lovable.

"I notice Norman's a boater," I said.

Mrs. Murphy's eyes widened as tiny beads of sweat formed on her upper lip. She swallowed twice, and shuddered.

"Unh," she said, and all the pink drained out of her face, leaving it the color of putty. "I have to go. I'm going to be ill," she whispered. She covered her mouth and closed the door.

Maybe just the thought of Norman's boat made her seasick.

CHAPTER 26

I reached Mike just as I hit the 170. I told him what I needed. New office equipment or not, this particular piece of research was way beyond my skill set.

He called back as I was chugging up the hill to my house.

"You hacked into Public Works already?"

"Didn't have to. I found a pdf of their annual report on employee suspensions, which gave me the personnel codes I needed. From there, it was a hop, skip, and a jump into Norman's office computer. It took a few minutes to break into his files, but once I got inside, it was like driving a go-cart, boss."

"Were the reports there?"

"Yeah. John D's place, the pig farm. The whole area tests clean as a whistle. Maybe I should move out there."

"Hunh."

"Then again, maybe not. Ever heard of neptunium-237? . . . Me neither. It's a by-product of uranium tailings. Also comes from spent nuclear rods. Norman had a bunch of encrypted information on it."

Acid started to pool in the back of my throat and I almost gagged. "Toxic?"

"Highly. And it's got a half-life of two million years. They just found some buried in Utah."

"What does that mean exactly?"

"It means if you visit Utah four million years from now, some of the neptunium-237 might be gone."

"But everything tested clean?"

"That's what Norman wrote."

I was inside my house, opening a can of tuna for Tank, when I got a follow-up text message: NM BOUGHT BOAT ON EBAY 2 MO AGO 88K CASH.

As a public servant, Norman took home about $5,000 a month, if he was lucky. Now he had the cash to buy new boats? Love or money: I picked door two. Norman was into some dirty money, and he didn't seem too concerned about flaunting it. I thought about Mrs. Murphy, and wondered if she knew about Norman's latest scam, or if his secret lay buried deep inside their marriage, slowly but surely poisoning the well.

My landline rang, and I recoiled a little inside. I was tired. My mind was starting to spin. I needed to sit on my meditation cushion with my eyes closed for at least half an hour. But I worked out of home now, so I had to check.

It was Julie. I pinged and I ponged, should I, shouldn't I, but guilt won out and I answered.

"Hey," she said.

"Hey."

"How are you doing?"

"Great," I fibbed. Instead of making me feel better, it irritated the hell out of me. I started over.

"Actually, kind of tired. I've been beating the bushes out in Lancaster. How about you?"

She sighed.

"I'm rotten, Ten. I begged off work early today. The chef reamed out another busboy, just for breathing the same air as far as I could figure out, and I couldn't take it. I may never go back."

She paused. I knew she was waiting for me to invite her over. I ran through my options, and none of them felt good. But she was sounding needy, and I was sleeping with her, and I knew what that added up to. I suggested she come over in a few hours.

"Are you sure you're not too tired?"

"I'm sure," I fibbed for the second time. The pressure behind my eyes started to re-form into a headache.

"Okay. If you're absolutely sure. What would you like to eat?"

"Julie," I snapped, "my brain's fogged over at the moment. Just food, okay?"

The line went silent.

Then, "You know what, Ten? Forget it."

"Julie . . ."

"No, I mean it. This is called three strikes and you're out. I'll see you around, okay?"

I spent my entire meditation defending myself to myself, which did little to relieve the tiredness or the guilt. So I took a long, hot shower and changed into my last clean pair of jeans. Tank and I moved outside to the deck. A flat, gray bank of fog hung like a pall on the horizon. The sun was sinking behind the wall of vapor. Fingers of orange-yellow light reached downward, as if in supplication. Then the mist swallowed up the last of the sun, snuffing out the flames.

It doesn't always have to be like that.

Yes, it does.

I shivered and walked inside, shutting the door hard on the dank night.

I couldn't shake the heavy feeling of dread, nor could I identify its source, beyond disappointing yet another woman, that is. I opened a bottle of Pinot Noir and set it aside to breathe. My cell phone chirruped from the bedroom, and I ran for it. Maybe Julie was calling me back.

It was a Lancaster number, one I didn't know. I answered.

"Mr. Norbu? This is Norman Murphy." His voice was strained and tense.

"Norman," I said. The silence stretched out a while. I wasn't going to make this easy.

"Listen, I happen to be in your neck of the woods this evening. I wonder if we could meet for a cup of coffee?"

"A friend was planning to meet me here in an hour, so it needs to be quick," I semi-lied. This was becoming a regular habit. "What's this about?"

"It's about my father."

I didn't much care for the tightness in Norman's voice. I grabbed my Wilson to stash in the Mustang's glove compartment.

I was halfway down the hill, hugging a steep curve, when my windshield was flooded with light. A black Cadillac Escalade had gobbled the turn just below me, and was charging like a bull. I yanked the Mustang hard to the right, skidding to a halt. The canyon dropped into darkness somewhere just beyond the shoulder. The Escalade slowed to a crawl, drew alongside me, and stopped. It loomed over me, a beast of chrome and metal. I craned my neck, but I couldn't see inside the tinted windows. Every nerve jumped to the surface of my skin. *Okay. Okay. Keep breathing. It may not be what you think.*

I started to squeeze past, maybe two inches of space between cars, when the back door of the Escalade opened and a man stepped out. I couldn't proceed without running him over, and I couldn't reverse without driving blind. I was wedged in so tight I couldn't even open my door.

I lunged across the seat for the glove compartment, but the door blew open, and I was face to face with the ruddy menace of Liam O'Flaherty—Brother Eldon, to his faithful flock.

"Hello, Ten m'boy," he said.

He raised a .38 snubnose and aimed it at my sternum. A Smith & Wesson Airlite. He cocked it and smiled.

It looked like a cap gun in his big paw, but I knew better. A high-velocity .38 Special cartridge will drive a 110-grain bullet into its target at 1,000 feet per second. And it doesn't have a safety.

Liam knew better, too.

"It's a modest little weapon," he said, "but it can make a right mess of you. Now get out."

I slid across the front seat and ducked outside. Liam kept the gun trained on me until I was standing in front of him.

"We can do this hard, or real hard. Your choice," he said.

Roach, aka Brother Nehemiah, stepped next to Liam, his expression feral. I glanced down. He was wearing the silver-tipped cowboy boots he'd used to kick John D.

"What's the matter, boys," I said, "Run out of old men to rumble?"

The blow whipped my head back. A streak of pain seared my jaw.

"Shut yer gob hole!" Liam thundered.

I did a quick risk-assessment. Three of them: Liam, Roach, plus the driver. All three were locked and loaded, I was sure. One of me: armed with a phone and a set of car keys. This was not going to be a fair fight, if in fact I got to fight at all.

Liam snapped his thick fingers at me.

"Cell phone," he said.

As I reached into my pocket for it, my fingers felt the two-pronged cork opener, right where I'd left it. Now we're talking. I maneuvered the opener so it lay fairly flat along the waistband of my jeans. I prayed it would stay put. I handed my phone to Liam, and Liam tossed it to Roach.

"Burn it," he told Roach. Then he patted me down, and I could smell the sour sweat coming off him in waves. He must have been out of practice, because he found the keys, but nothing else.

He snapped his meaty fingers again, this time at the driver still inside the Escalade. "Brother Jacob!" he called.

The man who climbed out of the driver's seat and opened the rear door was lean and muscled, and instantly recognizable as Sister Rose's Lookout Man from the farmer's market. I stared at Jacob, but he wouldn't meet my eyes.

Liam herded me into the backseat, gun prodding the small of my back. I climbed in and settled next to public enemy number four, Norman Murphy. He was pale as a ghost, and pretty much scared to death.

"Hello, Norman," I said. "I'll take mine with cream and two sugars, please."

"Shut up," he whispered.

"Not in the mood for chit-chat?"

"You think I want to be doing this?" he hissed. "Just shut the fuck up!"

Roach slid in next to Norman, and Liam and Jacob got in front. One U-turn later, we were gunning it down Topanga. We turned onto Entrada, and I knew where we were headed. What goes around comes around, and all that.

Liam directed Jacob onto a rutted dirt road that angled toward the back boundary of Topanga Canyon Park.

"Pull over here," Liam said. We bounced off road, and Jacob parked by a motley cluster of trees. I mentally recited their names, to calm me down: *scrub oak, blue gum, California sycamore.*

All four of us climbed out. I could hear the faint rush of moving water somewhere behind me. Maybe running water was the last sound Barbara Maxey ever heard. Maybe it would be mine as well.

Liam prodded me deeper into the woods, and backed me against the slender, peeling trunk of a young eucalyptus. The others filed after, meek as schoolchildren.

Roach was fiddling with my phone, yanking at it, as if trying to pry it apart. Liam reached one hand inside his coat and pulled out two coiled cotton ropes. Norman and Jacob stood aside, silent, as Liam wrapped the clotheslines tight. Legs first, then my chest, pinning my arms to my sides. Blood pounded at my temples and against my ribs. I felt sure my skin was visibly jumping. *Breathe. Focus.*

I concentrated on stemming the flow of adrenaline, while expanding the presence of *prana* in each cell. *Breathe. Focus.* I flexed my biceps, triceps, and extensors, and curled my fingers under slightly, not enough for Liam to notice, but enough to create a slight expansion of muscle mass. I visualized a cellular swell of subtle body matter, creating the potential for give. I hoped it was enough.

Now lock it down.

"Fucking piece of cell phone fucking shit," Roach snarled. "How do you get it open?" He threw my phone on the ground and stomped spider cracks into its face. Then he lofted it into the shrubbery with his silver-tipped boot.

There went my partner.

Liam stepped close. "So, young fellow, this is your big opportunity. We're going to leave here in a little while, and you won't be coming with us. The question you need to answer is, 'Do I want to be alive and tied to a tree or dead and tied to a tree?'"

When there are only two choices, one of them involving pie-in-the-sky thinking, the other including one's inevitable death, it's time to change the subject.

"What are we all doing here, Liam?"

Liam turned to Roach, and I exhaled, letting my arms slacken and chest relax.

"You see what we're dealin' with here, Brother Nehemiah?"

I had maybe a quarter inch of give to work with. I shifted my arms back and forth.

"Mr. Ten is that most dangerous of all God's creatures, the inquisitive human being. No wonder he and Sister Barbara got along."

I again pressed hard against the rope, keeping one eye on Liam, the other on his friends. Roach's reptilian smile made my skin crawl. Norman and Jacob stared fixedly at the ground.

Liam turned to face me. I stopped moving.

"I want to have a wee heart-to-heart with ya, my boy. Are ya feeling chatty?"

A faint chorus of crickets chirped from deep in the shrubbery. I got chatty in a hurry, raising my voice to cover the other sound. "I'm not going anywhere that I can see," I said. "So I guess the correct answer is yes, I am feeling chatty. Let's talk."

Liam laughed out loud. "Listen to him, boys. This fellow here has right spunk!"

He moved in closer, so close I could smell the blood-lust seeping from his skin like musk.

"You ever done jail time?" he whispered.

Come on, Liam. One more inch, one more inch.

He stepped back.

"Jail time? Sort of," I said. "I did a dime in a Buddhist monastery."

The forewings started sawing away again, and Liam's eyes jagged to the right, toward the cluster of scrub oaks.

"It wasn't so bad," I said quickly. "At least I didn't have to take it up the ass like all you altar boys—" The hook caught me square in the mouth. My lip swelled into tight-skinned sausage, and I tasted blood. I ran my tongue over my teeth, to see if they were all accounted for.

"Listen up, boyo," Liam snarled. "You've managed to get your yellow nose right in the middle of my business, and that's no place to be, is it?"

"Up yours, Liam O'Flaherty."

The next stinging blow jerked my head sideways.

Breathe. Just breathe.

"You got a mouth on you. A blasphemer, that's what you are. A blasphemer, and a sinner," Liam called over his shoulder. "What do we do with sinners, Brother Nehemiah?"

"We smite them," Roach said.

"That's right," Liam crooned. "We smite them."

"Me? I prefer to be choked," I said, and braced for the next blow.

But Liam laughed, holding up his hands like two raw-boned steaks. "I could do that," he said. "I've choked the devil out of more than one person in my time."

I stared into his eyes, and it was like looking into a pair of cesspools.

"Why? Why did you strangle Barbara Maxey?" I asked.

Jacob shifted, took a half-step back. I shot a glance his way. He looked shocked.

Liam shrugged. "Most junkies have a little streak of rebel in them, but Barbara was one of the worst. What she

couldn't get through her head is you're not really committed to the church unless you're willing to die for the
church." He jerked his thumb at Roach, Jacob, and Norman. "See these three? They're committed."

Norman started shaking his head. "Hey, leave me out
of this! I told you, I'm not a member of your church, and
I'm certainly not going to die for it."

Liam licked his lips. He gave me a broad wink, pulled
the snubnose from his pocket, and turned.

"Yes, you are, Norman," he said.

"Norman, down!" I cried out. The air erupted and
Norman jerked as a small hole bloomed ragged in his
chest. He blinked once. Then he crumpled.

"Norman!" I called again.

He found my eyes, and I held his gaze. Blood was leaking out of him. Life was leaking out of him, too.

"Ten," he said, his voice already thready.

I nodded, keeping my eyes locked in on his.

"Tell Dad I'm sorry. Tell him—"

A second shot cut short Norman's apology—permanently.

Liam crossed to Norman's body and poked at it with
the toe of one boot.

I wrenched hard at the ropes. They gave another half
inch, and I was able to move my right hand just enough to
slide the forefinger into the waistband of my jeans.

"Drag him back a ways and hide him in the brush,"
Liam told Roach and Jacob. "Then wait for me at the car."

I pushed against the opener. I almost had it hooked
when my finger slipped. It fell halfway down my pant leg,
blocked by the tight rope. I was screwed. He was going to
kill me, and soon.

Liam turned and smiled a smile of pure evil. He
cocked the hammer as he walked.

"There's a lot of money at stake here, boyo. The hour
is upon us. Life everlasting for they that believe. I cannot afford to have a crazy Chink mucking things up.
Understand?"

"Tibetan," I said.

"What's that?"

"I'm Tibetan, dumbass."

He stepped close, pressing his gun against my chest.

"I'm going to enjoy this," he said.

I need a miracle.

The insects chirped in the brush. Liam hesitated.

"Crickets, Liam," I said. "Guess what? Crickets bring good luck," and I head-butted his fat Irish nose into pulp.

He dropped his revolver and grabbed at his face. Blood spurted between his knuckles.

Footsteps pounded up the trail, mixed with the faint wail of sirens.

"Liam, someone's coming! We gotta split!" Roach yelled.

"Shoot this bastard," Liam screamed. He blindly reached for the .38 and hurled it at Roach, who ducked instinctively as the loaded weapon arced over his head and landed behind him somewhere in the dark. The night lit up with a thunder-crack as the gun discharged on impact. The siren wails strengthened, and Roach took off again back down the trail.

If I weren't lashed to a tree, with Norman gone and Liam wanting me dead next, I'd have maybe even enjoyed this three-ring circus.

Liam lurched up to me and wrapped his meaty hands around my neck. He started to squeeze, each finger an individual steel rod, conducting hurt. Looked like I was going to get my death wish. My eyes bulged. I squirmed and pushed at the ropes, burning and shredding skin. The cords gave maybe another half inch.

In one crazed motion I jammed my right hand down my pant leg, hooked the opener, wrenched it free, and jailhouse-jabbed six quick pops straight into Liam's neck. The short deep cuts welled with blood, fang bites from my makeshift shank—a two-pronged knuckle-duster.

He howled and now we both heard the *thumpa-thumpa* of an approaching police chopper, and both saw the searchlight sweeping the area, and finally, finally Liam lumbered off. I waved my free arm and rasped out a yell and the helicopter executed a few turns before it found me and hovered, fixing me in a pool of light.

"Ten? Ten!"

"Over here!" I croaked as I flapped and struggled like a pinned moth.

Bill thrashed his way through the brush, followed by a swarm of uniformed cops and firefighters and ambulance attendants.

"Black Cadillac Escalade!" I called, as best I could. "License MV7XL2P."

One of the cops spoke into his handheld, and the chopper rose vertically and banked off toward the park entrance.

"There's a body in the scrub, Bill, maybe twenty feet due north, his name's Murphy, Norman Murphy, homicide victim, the weapon's a snubnose, S and W, he tossed it right around here, the shooter, he's Liam O'Flaherty, and Bill, my phone, can you get it, my new phone is—"

Bill pulled my top half into a fierce hug to shut me up. I gasped, one quick sob, and it was done. He pushed away and busied himself unwinding the cords.

I stomped feeling back into my legs and breathed deep, in and out, in and out, as Bill hit the bushes with his flashlight. He returned with my phone. He raised an eyebrow at its smashed face before handing it over.

"You should have seen the other guy's phone," I said.

I pocketed it. Met Bill's eyes. "Thanks."

"Thank Julie. Whatever you did to piss her off this time, and I don't even want to know, she called Martha to vent, and Martha said to just go over and have it out with you in person. That's why Julie passed your Mustang lying all cockeyed to hell on the side of the road, and you nowhere to be seen. She knew enough to know something was very wrong, so she called me. And I called your phone, with its GPS locator, and here we all are. Smart girl, that Julie."

An ambulance attendant started swabbing my face. As he butterfly-taped my split lip, one of the cops got off his handheld and waved Bill to his side. They talked quietly for a minute. Bill rejoined me.

"They found the Escalade," Bill said. "It went off road, about two miles north of here. Did a nose dive into the canyon."

"Good."

"Not good. The Escalade didn't skid off the shoulder, Ten. It was pushed. No sign of any driver, or passengers. Not there. Not anywhere."

"But how did they . . ."

Bill just looked at me, with something like compassion.

"Don't tell me," I said. "They took the Mustang."

Chapter 27

I caught a ride home from one of the cops. As I let myself in, all my nerve cells clicked off, like a SWAT team standing down. The adrenaline and cortisol drained from my limbs, taking with them any ability to function. I was too tired to eat, too tired to shower, too tired to call John D with the bad news. I fell into bed like the dead man I very nearly had been two hours earlier.

And came wide-awake two hours later. It was three in the morning. The witching hour.

The hour is upon us. Life everlasting for they that believe.

I slipped out of bed, pulled on a sweatshirt and a pair of running pants, and stepped onto the deck.

The neighborhood was dead quiet. An owl hooted, a mournful call from another hillside. Through scattered shreds of cloud, the waning moon cast a faint, oily sheen on the ocean. I pressed three fingers to my neck. The skin was sore to the touch. Liam's flushed face swam before me, eyes flat with hate.

There's a lot of money at stake here, boyo.

My landline rang inside the house. *The hour is upon us.* I hurried inside to answer.

"Ten? It's John D."

Of course it was.

"John D," I said. "So you know."

"I hate to trouble you this time of night," John D said, as if he didn't hear me. "But there's something doing next door."

An icy finger wormed up my back. "Go on."

"I woke up a few hours ago, felt like I'd been punched in the gut or something, and I couldn't fall back asleep.

I was just laying in bed, worrying about nothing, and that's when I heard it. A chopper, Ten, seemed like right on top of me. 'Course I went outside for a look-see. Turns out it was landing in them hippies' field."

"Police raid?"

"That's what I was thinking, but fifteen minutes later it took off again, and I got a good look at it. It was an old Huey, a big one. And then, 'bout thirty-five minutes later, it came back."

A muffled pounding, like a massive drumbeat, swelled in volume through the phone line.

"There she goes," John D yelled. "I'm going over to take a look." And he hung up.

I ran to unlock the safe. And stared at the empty canvas Wilson kit. My prized gun was in the glove box of my prized Shelby, and my prized Shelby was gone. There was no time to even process my feelings, attached or otherwise.

I grabbed the Glock and an extra clip. Then I called Mike.

"Yo," Mike said.

"I hope you're good at geometry," I said. "Point A is the Children of Paradise. Point B is however far a transport helicopter can fly in fifteen minutes, twenty max. It's a Huey, and probably loaded down, so take that into consideration when you calculate radius and circumference. Oh, yeah, and it has to be somewhere remote. Mike, I need to know where that chopper is landing."

"Is this going to be on the final?"

"Do it now, Mike!" I said. "People are going to die."

I ran to the Toyota and prayed it would hold together one more time. As I careened down Topanga, I pushed away the image of my Mustang, smashed at the bottom of some cliff, my beautiful custom Wilson locked inside. At least I still had . . .

And realized I couldn't remember the last time I saw Tank. I had no idea where he was. I was three for three.

This was turning into a bad, bad night.

I left a message on Julie's machine. I had to.

"Julie, I can't talk now, but will you please go back to the house and look for Tank? If he's gone underground, he won't come out for just anybody. Use tuna water."

I covered the 70 miles in just over an hour. Don't ask me how. As I smoked past Paradise, sure enough, a big transport helicopter lifted off the field and banked south. I floored it to John D's farmhouse and jumped out just as he limped his way across the field to me.

"I think that was the last load," he panted. "The place is quiet as a tomb. What the hell happened to your face?"

"Never mind that. How many trips did it make?"

"Three. Looks like at least a dozen got on every time."

I pulled out my phone, with its splintered screen, to call Mike.

"What the hell happened to your phone?" John D said. I waved him off.

"Mike. What's due south of Paradise?"

"I wish you wouldn't do that," Mike said. "I was just about to call you. Best guess, they're heading due south, to the San Bernardino Mountains, specifically. I'm guessing Mount San Gorgonio. It's tricky, but a skilled pilot could land on the easternmost escarpments."

"Give me the exact coordinates," I said. I spun John D around and used his back as a surface to jot down the information. I ended the call and scrolled to Dardon's number, about to ruin another good man's night of sleep, when John D grabbed my arm. His grip was strong for a man his age.

"Tenzing Norbu, are you going to tell me what in the Sam Hill is going on?"

My brain felt too big for my skull. Dozens of strangers were about to make a fatal mistake if I didn't act fast; a man I called my friend deserved my undivided attention for as long as it took. I had no idea what to do.

Yes, you do. Speak from the deepest level of truth you can muster.

I met John D's eyes. "Something really bad has happened, and something even worse may be about to, and I'm right in the middle of both of them."

"Okay," John D said.

I gripped John D's shoulders.

"Norman is dead. He was killed earlier tonight. Shot. I was right there, but I couldn't stop it from happening. I'm so sorry."

John D let out a deep grunt, like he'd been slugged in the gut, and sat heavily on his front stoop. He put his head in his hands. Wheezing sobs racked his body.

I rested my hand on his shuddering back and tried to absorb some of the pain. I told him that Norman had gotten in way over his head. That he loved his father. That he was sorry. After a time, the sobs subsided. John D straightened up, shaking off his grief like a wet dog. His grizzled face met mine.

"What else," he said.

So I told him what else. What I knew, and what I feared.

"You were about to call Dardon?"

"Yes."

"Do it."

I gave a sleepy Dardon the one-minute version. He woke up fast, and called me back even faster.

"Meet me at Palmdale Regional, Plant forty-two."

I touched John D's hand.

"Are you going to be okay?"

John D's eyes were steady.

"Whether he was in over his head or not, my son had a hand in this mess. Which means I do, too. Go. Make it right, Ten."

I took the 14 south and turned east on Avenue P. There was no one on the road, so I covered the 11 miles to the Palmdale Regional Airport in ten minutes. I parked at the private terminal at the far end, next to an LASD patrol car in an otherwise empty lot. I ran onto the small airfield, where Dardon was talking to a deputy pilot from the Aero Bureau. Dardon waved me over.

"Ten Norbu, former LAPD," he told the pilot. "He's coming with. He knows the shot."

The pilot nodded, and the three of us headed for a small single-engine six-seater perched on the tarmac, a metal dragonfly of turquoise and green. SHERIFF was stenciled across its tail in white block letters.

"Eurocopter A-Star," Dardon said. "She'll do just fine for our patrol. Air-5 is also deploying a second chopper, a twin turbine Sikorsky H-3 out of Los Angeles. Big mother, loaded up with Tactical Response and paramedics, just in case. You carrying?"

I opened my windbreaker to reveal the Glock under my arm. His nod was curt.

"Okay. But no hot-dogging, Ten, understand? We're just going to take a look."

We climbed in, and buckled up behind the pilot. He handed us headsets and did a safety check. The engine bup-bup-bupped to life, and I was inside the drum this time. We lifted off, banking sharply to the south. We were over the San Bernardino range in 15 minutes, and aiming for the tallest peak.

"There's San Gorgonio. If you know any Buddhist prayers, now's the time." Dardon's deep voice resonated through the headphones. "In '53, a Dakota C-137 heading for Riverside Air Base hit this baby head on. Thirteen dead. A month later, the Marine Corps sent a chopper to recover the bodies, and it crash-landed in the same place."

"Thanks for sharing," I said. *May we be safe and protected.*

The top of San Gorgonio was sere and rubble-covered, like the surface of the moon.

"The Indians call it Old Grayback," Dardon said. "You can see why."

We circled once, scanning the rocky surface. Second time around, we found them—several dozen shivering acolytes clustered close together under an outcropping of rock. The pilot hit them with the searchlight and hovered while we looked for any sign of weapons. They made it easy for us. White robes flapping, they were holding their empty hands aloft, their faces frozen in what looked like ecstatic bliss.

"Maybe they think we're delivering more cult members," I said into the headset.

"Maybe they're just fucking nuts," Dardon shot back. "Deputy, can you set her down?"

The pilot shook his head. "Too tight," he shouted. "The Huey must have dumped those people using a pinnacle maneuver. I can go down on one skid if you want to jump out."

Dardon scowled. "Forget it," he said. "I got a wife and kids, and anyway I'm too old for this crap."

I grabbed Dardon's arm.

"Let me," I said. "Please. If it's just potluck and prayers, no harm done. But if it's what I suspect, I can try to distract and delay until you move in."

Dardon studied my face. Then he held out his hand.

"Give it up, Cowboy."

I passed over my Glock.

"We'll be back soon, with troops. Good luck," he said.

The pilot dropped the bird slowly, and sure enough was able to touch down, aslant on one strut. I unbuckled, Dardon hauled open the glass door, and I tumbled onto the churning surface, the flying grit peppering my face and neck. I ducked my head and ran for the white robes fluttering, as if in surrender.

When I reached the outcropping, I slowed to a walk. I approached with my hands up, just like them, but minus the ecstasy. They lowered their arms and stared. I offered a smile, as I scanned the group. I paused at a familiar young man. Our eyes met. Brother Jacob wrapped his arm around the shoulders of a sweet-faced woman and pulled her close, his expression unreadable.

I did a quick head count. I came up with 37, but the Children had started milling around anxiously, and with all those billowing white robes it was like trying to count a flock of restless doves. I tried again and got 37 again. Mike had said there were 42 members. With Barbara dead, that left 2 unaccounted for, plus Roach and Liam.

The helicopter circled back around, and I gave Dardon a little "I'm okay" wave. It sailed off.

"It says 'Sheriff'!" someone yelled out. "He's a cop!"

"Do it, before it's too late," called another member.

An older man began distributing small paper cups out of a canvas carryall. One by one, the Children raised them high, like chalices. A second man followed close behind, muttering something as he poured viscous amber liquid into each cup.

It was mass suicide—Heaven's Gate, all over again.

I stepped close.

"I'm not a cop," I said. "I'm a Tibetan lama. And I'm interested in the same thing you are. Liberation."

They shifted in confusion. The thing about cult members is they really are children, children in a big family that functions smoothly as long as Daddy's around. Take the father away and they're quickly lost. I needed to become their replacement-Daddy, and fast.

Have I mentioned I've never had kids?

Work with what you've got, Ten.

I felt the rubbled ground through the soles of my shoes. Settled into an awareness of my body . . . my rib cage opening and closing . . . my heart pumping blood. I sucked oxygen in and released carbon dioxide out, in and out, deep, cleansing breaths. Possibly because of the thin air, or lack of sleep, or simply the intense weirdness of my situation, my awareness tilted into hyper-alert. I'd shifted into an altered state of consciousness. Yes, I was standing on this outcropping facing an anxious crowd, but another part of me was parked outside myself, watching everything unfold.

I asked that part for help.

Like a guardian deity, a low voice spoke into my ear. I recognized the tone. It was the voice of my lucid dream—neutral, neither male nor female. I opened my mouth and the words poured out:

"You want liberation more than life itself." I saw a number of heads nodding. "And now you're here, on this mountaintop, and Brother Eldon has promised you that if you do what he asks, you will find liberation. Total freedom. Right?" They nodded.

"Wrong," I said, raising my voice. "You are wrong to believe this. Brother Eldon is wrong to teach it. You think liberation is a destination, a place to get to. That it lies somewhere else, anywhere else but right where you are. You think you have to leave your bodies to find freedom." I found Jacob's eyes. My voice trembled with conviction. "Don't you know you can find freedom right here, right now, just with your heart?"

I heard the distant *whup-whup* of an approaching chopper. Search and Rescue, I thought. They had found us.

Then: "Brother Eldon! Brother Eldon is back!" a woman cried. "Praise God," a man shouted. "Praise God," others echoed.

The transport Huey closed in on us from the north, like a giant pterodactyl. It started its descent, then froze in midair, at a height of about 100 feet. I could see Liam's bandaged face staring down at his flock from the copilot's seat. Roach was leaning out of the opened side door, an assault rifle close to his side. I guess Liam wasn't taking any chances with last-minute abstentions.

The chopper moved laterally and slipped behind the cult members. They turned away from me, necks craning upward. The pilot dropped the bird ten feet, illuminated the searchlight, and tilted the Huey slightly, so Liam was smiling directly down at his children, bathed in a circle of bright light.

Big Daddy was back.

Liam disappeared, and reappeared at the opening next to Roach. He mouthed something to his followers, but the noise of the rotaries drowned out the words. Liam held out his hands, as if in supplication, clasped them together, and mimed drinking from a cup.

"No!" I screamed. "Don't!" A couple of the cult members downed their drinks and sank to their knees, praying. I ran to the front of the crowd.

"Don't do it!" I yelled again. "Please!"

That's when Liam caught sight of me.

The ground boiled with flying grit and dust, as the hovering chopper descended another 15 feet. A second helicopter materialized on the horizon, the turquoise A-Star this time, Dardon's small white face peering wide-eyed through the glass. Right behind loomed the whirling twin turbines of the Sikorsky, a big white bird, its nose and tail dipped in red.

Liam's mouth opened in a silent scream of rage. He grabbed Roach's assault rifle and aimed for my forehead.

Where was my guardian deity now? I dropped.

And Liam's chest was tattooed with bullets—a four-inch grouping at 25 yards. He looked down in astonishment, then tumbled out of the chopper and bounced like a rag doll on the harsh terrain, his graveled grave.

I spun around. Jacob stood behind me, face grim. He lowered his arm. He was holding a Wilson Combat .38 Supergrade, and I was pretty sure it was mine.

The Huey banked hard and executed a lateral lurch, clipping a steep rock face. Suddenly it turned on its side and dropped like a stone into the canyon, sending up a cloud of dust and snow. A moment of utter silence was followed by an erupting ball of flame.

The air reverberated from the explosion, overlaying a welcome sound—that of approaching rescue helicopters.

Jacob handed me my Wilson. It felt just as good in my hand as I remembered. "Nice shot." I said. "Iraq?"

"Afghanistan. Two tours," he answered.

"Mind if I take credit for your aim?"

He nodded in relief and hugged his young companion close. She started sobbing uncontrollably.

"This is my wife, Cassie," he said. His smile was both proud and vulnerable, and I remembered the same mix of emotions he displayed watching that young couple at the farmer's market. "Cassie's pregnant. We couldn't go through with this. There's been enough death."

"Congratulations. And I'm very pleased to meet you, Cassie." She pulled away from Jacob's chest and gave me a watery smile.

"Your husband is a very brave man," I said.

This provoked a fresh bout of wails.

"I'm sorry," she blubbed. "I'm just so emotional these days."

Even in the midst of all this craziness, another penny dropped.

The air shook with the deafening roar of the descending Sikorsky. Its belly opened and a paramedic was lowered to the ground, holding a canvas duffle. He ran up, unzipped the bag, and started pulling out individual white plastic antidote kits, packed like little lunchboxes.

"There's only the two," I said, pointing to the unlucky pair of swallowers. They were doubled over. One was starting to retch. The paramedic ran over with two kits.

More paramedics and emergency personnel dangled from the copter like wasp stingers and dropped to the ground.

"Norbu! Let's go!"

I looked over my shoulder. Somehow the A-Star had managed to perch on the one strut again, and Dardon was bellowing at me from the opened door. I ran over and leapt on board. I finally had some answers, and maybe a solution. I was happy to go.

We lifted, and banked north. The clustered Children of Paradise watched us float away, their faces tipped to the sky.

CHAPTER 28

I pulled into John D's place at dawn. The sizzle of adrenaline in my body had dimmed to a background hum; I could feel the dull ache of fatigue in my shoulders and arms, but otherwise I felt pretty good.

I opened the front door and called his name softly through the screen. A slow scuff of footsteps announced he was up. He pulled the screen door open, turned, and shuffled back into the living room without a word. He looked crumpled, inside and out.

I followed him. Dozens of photographs lay scattered in small heaps around his recliner, like autumn leaves after a windstorm. He picked one up and sank heavily into his chair, tears tracing the deep lines in his cheeks.

I walked to his side. He was clutching the photograph of himself and the boys.

"They were like chalk and cheese, those two," John D said. "But they loved each other something fierce. I gave them their own acre, on the far end of the property, and they dug every dang hole themselves. Charlie wanted to plant sweet almonds, and Norman, well, he was drawn to the bitter ones, of course. They're still growing out there, two groves, side by side—the only trees that didn't get struck by the blight. Ain't that a kick?"

John D honked into a damp bandanna and cleared his throat. He raised his swollen eyes to mine.

"Norman begged Charlie not to enlist," he said. "Not me. I was all for it. I told my wife the military was Charlie's ticket to a better life. But the truth is, I needed someone to blame for those towers falling. I thought we needed to go over there and kick Saddam's butt."

"You and most of America," I said.

"I urged him on, Ten, told him to make me proud." The tears were falling freely now. "When we lost Charlie, it damn near destroyed us." He slugged the arm of the chair with his fist. "What am I saying? It did destroy us. Norman fell apart. He and his mother both blamed me, and they were right to, you understand? Then my wife died of hypertension, and Norman . . . Norman just lost his way."

"You were suffering. You'd lost your son, and then your wife."

"And then my other son. Only that was on me most of all. Norman reached out a couple times right after his mother died, but when I looked in his face, all I could see was my own failure, and when I turned away, all he could feel was denied."

John D let go of the photograph, and it fluttered to the floor.

"Ten, I got nothing left. And all I can think is Norman's out there in the dark somewhere, full of fear and shame, and with no one to lead him into the light."

"Send him love, John D. He's sure to feel it."

"It's too late for love," John D said.

I went to the kitchen and filled a glass with cold juice from the fridge. I brought it to John D.

"Drink," I said.

He drank.

"It's too late for love," he said again.

I pulled up an address on my phone and wrote it down for him.

He read the name and address, then looked up at me, bewildered.

"Norman's wife," I said. "Her name is Becky. You need to pay her a visit. She needs you in her life, now more than ever. It's never too late, John D."

He nodded, and I could see a faint shaft of hope push from behind the pain.

"What about you? What are you going to do now?"
he asked.

"I'm going to find my Mustang and two missing cult
members. Not necessarily in that order."

John D reached down for the discarded photo and
handed it to me.

"Take us with you," he said. "For luck."

As I crossed the yard, my phone went off. I saw it was
Wesley, Freda's husband, and my heart clenched.

"Wesley?"

"She's gone. They said there wasn't any Freda left in
there anyway, so we stopped all the machines. I thought
you'd want to know."

"I'm so sorry."

"You any closer to finding out what happened?"

"Maybe a little."

"Well, they're cutting her up right now. I talked to
her doctors about what you'd said, and they agreed with
me that under the circumstances it made sense to do an
autopsy, so . . ." His voice caught, and he hung up.

I felt a swelling sensation, building hot behind my eyes.
Shame, this time. Another death. Another loss. Maybe not
my fault, but I was in too deep not to feel responsible.

I sprinted across John D's field, vaulted the fence, and
raced down the hill into Paradise. I ran hard. It helped.

I stopped and listened. The faint *thrum-thrum-thrum*
of some kind of industrial equipment echoed across the
predawn sky. I pegged it as originating at the pig farm.

I jogged from yurt to yurt, beaming my flashlight
into the dim curves. The cots were made. The floors were
swept. The yurts were totally empty. I ducked into Liam's
headquarters and played my light across the floor. A couple of wooden cases with Italian lettering had been pried
open and emptied—looked like they'd held some sort of
liquor or wine.

I swung my light to the far side of the yurt and illuminated two still bodies. I ran over and knelt by the first, a

young man, and checked for a pulse. The open-eyed stare belonged to the third cult member I'd seen at the farmer's market. Up close, he was more child than man, and he was very dead. Sister Rose lay next to him, gray and still as a slab of granite.

I punched 911 and fired information at the operator: exact location, number of victims, extent of injuries, and cause of death.

"Strangulation," I said, noting the necklace of raw bruising around the young man's throat. *Om mani padme hum.* The violent hands of Brother Liam had been hard at work, choking life out of two more sinners. I was sure in this case their sin was a last-minute reluctance to get on a helicopter.

A ragged moan caused my skin to shrink-wrap with dread.

I looked around, then down. Sister Rose was working her mouth. I leaned my ear close to her mouth.

"Help me," she rasped.

I took her hand, careful not to jostle her until help came. "I'm here, Sister Rose," I said. "You're safe now. I'm here."

I sat with her. I would sit with her forever, if necessary.

Forever turned out to be five interminable minutes. The Emergency Responders found us first. They said the cops were right behind them. Sister Rose's breath was rough and labored, but an EMT checked her vitals, and said she'd live.

I waited until they had loaded her safely into the ambulance.

I ran to the far side of the Paradise property. Sure enough, my Shelby was right where Jacob had told me she was, parked under a tree, covered by a blue plastic tarp. From here, the thrumming sound was even louder. I jumped the fence and dashed across the far boundary of the pig farm, and up the steep hill, to my favorite vantage point.

Barsotti's Mercedes was already in his designated spot. I checked my watch. Barely four in the morning. Barsotti was keeping monastery hours, though I doubted he was meditating in there. A familiar battered green pickup was also in the lot. Off to my left, a bright halo of light spotlighted the source of the thrumming. I started downhill in the direction of the light, but skidded to a stop when a pair of black-and-whites screamed by.

A door slammed. Barsotti burst out of the office building and ran into the lot just as a car squealed off the main road and up the farm's driveway.

Florio's silver Maserati, in a big, big hurry.

He fishtailed the curves, spewing gravel, and slewed to a stop. Tommy got out, mouth already wagging at Barsotti. He jabbed a finger to the south, then up in the air, then south again.

I had a pretty good notion of the subject matter.

Barsotti jumped in the pickup. Headlights off, he crept out of the parking lot and headed up the dirt road toward the back of the property, with Tommy following right behind. I was tempted to go back for my car, but the problem with that was literally easy to see: a bright yellow sports car was going to be hard to miss out here. I decided to leg it.

Two pairs of brake lights flickered and bumped to a stop a half mile away. I motored after them by foot, digging deep for my best pace given the uncertain terrain. I used one arm to press the Wilson tight against my rib cage.

It was a hard, four-minute slog. I stopped just outside the circle of light to catch my breath and reconnoiter. Two vehicles: one green pickup, one silver Maserati, both lit up by a bank of temporary lights. Two sounds: the throb of a gas-powered generator, and the *whunk-whunk-whunk* of a drill biting into the ground.

Three men.

I moved closer, taking cover behind an ancient, gnarly almond tree. Tommy Jr. stood leaning against his car with his arms crossed as Barsotti talked and gestured and talked some more to his favorite multitasking employee, man number three: José Guttierez—washer of cars, stealer of weed, basher of friends, and who-knows-what-of-what this particular morning.

Barsotti clapped José on the back in a hearty, good-job kind of way. He dug out his wallet and gave José a bill. Then he climbed into the Maserati beside Tommy and drove away.

José loaded the back of his pickup with tools, and killed the drill and gas generator. The dawn air was suddenly, inconveniently silent.

I ran for my car.

Ten minutes later, José's pickup bumped its way down the hill, through the lot, and onto the main road toward town. I followed, hanging back as far as I could without losing him.

Streaks of light brightened the sky like luminous ribbons. José turned into a strip mall and parked under a blinking neon sign shaped like a sombrero. "Los Caballeros," it flashed, promising an all-night refuge for bad boys and insomniacs. I parked on the street and followed José inside.

It was a dismal place, a virtual monument to loneliness. A jowly man in a dirty shirt stood guard behind the bar. I counted three customers, including me. José was already staring down a draft beer. A blowsy middle-aged woman, raucous and bleached blond, swigged straight from a bottle at the other end of the bar. The jukebox was playing a sad country song about liquor and losers.

I sat near Blondie and ordered a draft. Normally beer wouldn't be my top choice for a breakfast beverage, but I was looking to fit in with the crowd, and it might help soften the edge of desperation in here. I paid with one of my Ben Franklins. The bartender had to go out back for change.

"Hey, Big Bucks. I'll bet you're even bigger where it counts. Name's Olivia." Olivia slipped onto the stool next to me and scissored her arms together so her cleavage pushed up under her tonsils.

I signaled the bartender to give her a refill. He gave me a look I interpreted as "You have got to be kidding, dude" and grabbed a cold one out of the refrigerator.

I was treated to the full radiance of Olivia's smile, marred slightly by a missing eyetooth.

"What're you doing out and about this time of night?"

"Sightseeing," I said.

Her cackle was backwashed in phlegm. "You stay in this hole awhile, you're gonna see some real sights."

"How about you, Olivia? What brings you here?"

"Oh, this and that. I met with a couple clients earlier, if you catch my drift, and I'll probably meet with a couple more when the breakfast crowd comes in."

All I could think to say was, "I didn't know they served breakfast here."

I saw some movement to my right. José had moved a few stools closer. Olivia stood and waved her arm, her bingo-wing jiggling like Jell-O.

"Git on over here, sweet cheeks," she yelled.

José pulled up a stool on the other side of Olivia, and I got my first close look at the man. He had dull eyes and a built-in sneer. His upper lip was so short as to be nonexistent.

Olivia didn't seem to mind. She told him he was "lookin' fine." José just stole my chick. Oh, well, they come and they go.

José was working on his third beer, which told me he was drinking for a purpose. This made me glad; drunk people will tell you damn near anything. The trick is to figure out how much of the "damn near anything" is true.

I said to him, "You look like you've had a long night."

"Sí. Long."

Olivia jumped in. "That's why I quit Burger King. Why take home fifty bucks for an eight-hour shift from hell when I can make two hundred in the parking lot easy, four clients, in and out?"

I could think of several reasons why I'd pick Burger King over In-N-Out, but that's just me.

José fished a bill out of his pocket and gave it a glum stare. "He is terrible, my boss. I am working my *cojones* off all night making him rich, and he give me a fifty. That's just wrong, man, you know?"

Olivia eyed the bill and moved her stool a little closer to José's.

José kept going. "That cheap *hijo de puta*, he be making millions." He stuffed the money back in his pocket.

I shook my head in brotherly solidarity. "He's making millions and giving you fifty? What a jerk!"

"*Verdaderamente*," he said, draining his beer.

I called for another round, though my first draft sat untouched. "What's your boss got going that'll make him millions?"

José cast bleary eyes up at me, suspicion forming somewhere deep in his anesthetized brain.

"You a cop?" he asked.

I laughed. "No way. I'm a private investigator." I reached into my wallet and counted out five $100 bills. Olivia let out a little moan. I fanned them across the bar like a deck of cards. "I buy information," I said. I watched José carefully to see if he was going to bite.

He bit. "What you want to know?"

I was too tired to be bothered with a preamble.

"How's Barsotti going to make his millions?"

The bartender set down two more drafts, and a bottle for Olivia. I gave him two twenties.

"Good-bye" I said.

He grunted and moved off.

José took a swig and licked the foam off his upper lip. "He ask me to drill his land, until I make the water flow again."

"How's that going to make him millions?"

"The water, she is no good."

I pushed a hundred over to him. He blinked at it: Really? Free beer and a hundred bucks for that? The bill disappeared into his pocket.

Welcome to the Information Economy, José.

"That's interesting," I said. "Why does he want to pump toxic water?"

"He suing the government. *Por mucho dinero.* For a lot of money."

"Why would the government care?"

He went silent on me. Quick learner.

I slid two more bills over. "Holy Mother of God," Olivia said. José's pocket fattened.

"Why, José?"

"The government, they bury some kind of nuclear pipes in the land. Long time ago. Never told nobody about it. My boss, he think he can get a million an acre for they do this. He say the same thing happen in Utah."

"How many acres does he own?"

"Maybe twenty, but he thinking he have more very soon. I hear my boss talking with his friends. They say they getting maybe five hundred acres."

And five hundred million dollars.

My son is working on a real estate deal for me.

The stakes were finally high enough to justify Florio Sr.'s presence.

I had to think this through. But first things first.

"I want to talk to you in private, José. Can we go outside?"

He watched me pick up the remaining two hundreds. *"Por que no?"*

I walked him away from the flashing sombrero, into the shadowy corner of the parking lot. I kept my voice light.

"How much did you get paid for mugging the old guy at the bank?"

His eyes blinked rapidly at this new twist in the conversation. "Barsotti gave me a hundred bucks," he mumbled.

"A hundred dollars, huh? That's your price for hurting an old man who never hurt you or anyone else?"

He started backing away from me. "Guess what?" I said. "I'm going to do it to you for free." I drove my right fist deep in his groin.

He doubled over and projectile-vomited five and a half beers across the asphalt. He stayed down, clutching his belly and moaning.

I said, "That old man is a friend of mine, and he had just gotten, guess what, a hundred dollars out of the ATM when you rolled him. So you got his hundred, plus a hundred-dollar tip. You need to make reparations."

He looked up at me, confused.

"Give me two hundred back and we'll call it even."

He dipped into his pocket and fished out two of the three bills I'd just given him.

"You crazy, man," he said.

I tucked the money away. I'd give it to John D later.

"Hey, what's going on?" Olivia had followed us into the shadows.

"Karma," I said. I gave Olivia my last two hundreds. "Take the rest of the night off."

Olivia smiled. "I like karma. I'm going home. Get me some sleep."

It sounded like a good idea all around.

CHAPTER 29

I dragged my limping carcass out of the Mustang and up to the house. It was eight in the morning, and I hadn't really slept for 36 hours. Julie's car was parked in the driveway.

Tank.

I ran inside. She had left a note on the kitchen table.

I read "Eucalyptus tree" and knew exactly what had happened. I grabbed my stepladder from the garage and lugged it down to the tree, where Julie stood, looking up. I followed her gaze. A fuzzy blue tail flicked back and forth, from a very high branch.

"How did you find him?" I said.

"I looked and looked. Finally I just gave up, and sat on the deck. He must have spotted me from his perch, because he meowed."

"Tank *meowed* at you?"

I felt an actual stab of jealousy. I really needed to get some shut-eye. I was losing it.

I climbed up the ladder and reached across for Tank. He gave me the eye, but I was just able to grab some loose neck skin and tug him toward me until he gave up and walked over. I clasped him close, and he let me, all the way down the ladder and back into the house.

Once inside, Tank executed a high-wire leap from my arms to his food dish. He buried his face in the awaiting feast of sautéed liver and tuna, compliments of Chef Julie.

I watched him eat, my own throat suspiciously thick.

"Ten?"

I turned. Julie walked up to me. She touched my split lip, and traced the bruises on my throat.

"Bill told me everything. I'm so glad you're okay."

"Julie." I started to take her in my arms, but she pressed her finger on my lips. She moved away a few steps.

"Let me finish. I thought I wanted a fling, Ten. Turns out I'm not so good at flings." Her eyes brimmed over, and she swiped at the tears with the back of one hand. "Anyway, I quit my job. It just wasn't for me, you know? I'm going back home to regroup. I just . . . I wanted to thank you. Because after the last guy, I didn't know if I could ever open up my heart again. But I could. I mean, I did. Spending this time with you reminded me I have this huge heart, and the willingness to give it to someone else absolutely. I just picked a guy who wasn't ready."

She gave me a quavering smile. "I'm sorry."

I stared at her. A rush of hot panic flooded my body. Old. Familiar. *How can you do this to me? After everything I've done for you, how can you leave me? Please don't leave me.*

"Anyway, I baked you some almond cookies," Julie said. "Nontoxic, I promise."

"Is that supposed to be funny? A cute little joke?" I shot back, my voice still hoarse, only this time with feeling. "Is that supposed to make everything okay?"

I couldn't look at her.

Julie's reply was calm.

"No, not funny, Ten. True. Bitter almonds can kill you if you don't process them properly."

She touched my shoulder. I met her eyes. "As pissed off as you've made me, I don't wish you dead."

She kissed me once, lightly on the lips.

"'Bye."

And then she left.

I moved to the window and watched her drive away. Tank lifted his head from his dish and gave maybe the second meow of his life.

The agitation slowly drained out of me, leaving bone-deep exhaustion in its place. I staggered to the kitchen and sat for some time, flattened by the sudden, total absence of her.

Finally, I ate one cookie, washing it down with hot tea. It was delicious, and it made me very sad.

I crawled into bed.

Warm sun, bathing my eyelids, woke me up. It was just after one o'clock in the afternoon. I stretched my sore limbs, testing my muscles here and there. For a moment, I felt pretty good. Then the loss-of-Julie pain hit. I felt it start to drag me into its undertow, too deep and familiar to only be about Julie.

Valerie.

I took several deep breaths. *In, out. In, out.*

I had felt this before. Survived it before. I would survive it again. I had to. I had a lot left to do.

My phone chirped. *Julie.*

Mike's skewed face grinned at me from the cracked screen.

I answered.

"Ten, I found the mother lode. I had to hack into thirty-eight different systems, but I finally found all the policies. What a nightmare. Forty-two cult members insured by dozens of companies. Plus that other guy, Norman Murphy—there's a policy on him, too."

"You're kidding."

"And guess who's the beneficiary of every policy?"

"TFJ & Associates," I said.

"Elementary, my dear Watson. I'm talking about the silent partner. The one no one else will ever find, because I'm just that good."

The King.

"Thomas Florio Senior."

The line went very quiet.

"Boss, you really know how to take the wind out of a person's sails, you know that?"

The kaleidoscope re-formed into a picture, a spider web of sorts.

A father knows, you see. This time, I have taken a vow not to protect him.

I made a big pot of coffee while I ran through what I knew. There were still some pieces missing. I took a steaming mug over to my office area and sat down. My eyes lit on the little makeshift Zen garden.

I started rearranging the stones. I set down a round stone representing Florio Sr., first. To his right, I aligned Barsotti, Tommy Jr., and O'Flaherty, with Tommy centered next to his father. Norman, the land surveyor, was centered on their other side. What connected them all? I went in the kitchen and returned with a few whole beans of coffee.

In went José, between Barsotti and O'Flaherty. In went Roach, between O'Flaherty and Florio Sr. In went Zimmy, between Florio Sr. and O'Flaherty. And in went me, between Florio Sr. and Tommy Jr. I stared.

I was looking at a shamrock . . . or maybe a prison structure.

Well, somebody else's luck was running out.

I went back to the kitchen and poured myself a second mug of coffee. I had the motives. I still needed the means.

I reached for an almond cookie to dunk.

Nontoxic.

I ran back to my computer and spent another 45 minutes writing up and printing out my report, based on what I knew. I slid it into my canvas carryall and put in a call to Florio Sr.

I got his voice mail, as I knew I would. No cell phone use in the Jonathan Club. I told him I had some things to report, but I was feeling old-fashioned and preferred to do it in person. This afternoon, in fact. Then I left Barsotti and Tommy Jr. their own messages, each one tailor-made to suit my plans.

I pulled on my going-to-the-Club outfit, still flung over the back of a chair in the bedroom. The striped shirt was a little wrinkled, but I wore it anyway. It still smelled faintly of Julie. Finally, I called Bill and told him to meet me in his office.

I fired up the Mustang and pushed it hard all the way downtown. I could have used the valet parking at the Jonathan Club and walked the mile between Figueroa and North Los Angeles Street, but the 4-minute drive takes 20 to walk, given the lack of sidewalks in this fine city.

I parked at the Five Star and jogged to the Death Star, forgoing the slow elevator to take the stairs two at a time to the ninth floor.

Bill was ready and waiting. We gave each other everything we needed, and I was handing my keys to the Jonathan Club parking lot attendant at 4:00 on the button.

I did one last gut-check. My gut said *Go*. Either I'd be right, or I'd be done.

A different concierge led me inside and upstairs. As we crossed the hallway to the Library, he reminded me cell phone usage was not allowed.

He didn't say a thing about Wilson Combat .38 Supergrades.

Inside the Library, he motioned me left again, past the urns. This time, however, he closed the tall sliding wooden doors that separated the stacks from the main Library behind me. I stood for a moment, scanning the empty room.

"Hello, Tenzing," Florio said from my left. "I got your message."

He was seated in one of four red brocade chairs, set around an antique table of polished oak. His leather briefcase lay at his feet. He was studying a beautifully appointed chessboard of dark and light wood. The heavy chess pieces were of carved marble, black and white, some of them as tall as eight inches. The two armies were locked in battle. Thomas Florio, Sr., appeared to be at war with himself.

"Do you play?" Florio asked, gesturing at the game.

"No."

"Pity," he said. "I find chess a wonderful way to focus my mind. Perhaps a bit like your meditation. Do you mind if I continue to play while we talk? I'm almost done."

"Please. Go ahead."

He picked up a white piece and used it to replace a taller black one.

"Check," he said.

He turned to me. "You've been a busy young man since we last spoke, haven't you?"

I acknowledged that I had.

"I want to thank you," he said. "You did me a big favor, albeit inadvertently."

"Which was?"

He picked up the biggest black piece on the board, and knocked over the white piece.

"Checkmate," he said, smiling to himself. "You eliminated a business partner with whom I no longer wished to be in business. I refer of course to Mr. O'Flaherty. In my life I've found it necessary to work with the occasional unsavory associate. I wish that all of them could be disposed of so efficiently."

"Glad I could be of help," I said. I placed my carryall on the table and sat in the chair across from Florio. "Before I give you my report, I have a quick question, Mr. Florio. Why did you hire me, me in particular, to investigate Tommy?"

"I would have thought that was obvious," he said. "I take it you haven't read any Machiavelli?"

I had, but I played dumb for the time being.

"He is much maligned these days." Florio sighed. "*The Prince* is possibly the best book on business tactics ever written. Machiavelli is most famous for a brilliant piece of advice: Keep your friends close, and your enemies even closer." Florio's smile was utterly smug.

"Most attribute that quotation to Sun Tzu," I said. "But I believe the honor actually belongs to Mario Puzo. *The Godfather, Part Two*."

Florio's smile hardened.

I kept going. "I prefer Kautilya's *Arthashastra* for my strategies," I said. "Kautilya was the chief adviser to

Chandragupta Maurya, the king who united the Indian subcontinent around 300 B.C. Kautilya had a lot to say about power. Powerful fathers, and how they should handle their sons. Powerful princes, and how they should handle their kings. What a corrupting influence power can be. Quite the political realist, Kautilya."

Florio watched me, wary as a cobra.

"I'm curious about something, Mr. Florio. You're a very wealthy man. Yet the drive to accumulate, I might even say compulsion, remains. At what point do you realize you have enough?"

His mouth twisted. "It's obvious you've never been exposed to privilege."

"Please. Enlighten me."

He brought a finger to his lips. A secret. He was enjoying himself. "The great truth of money and influence, Ten, of power, is that there's no such thing as enough."

I heard low voices from the main Library. "Right on time," I said.

The wooden doors slid open. Tommy Jr. and Barsotti stepped inside the stacks. The doors slid closed behind them.

Tommy was empty-handed. I felt my stomach clench. Had I read him wrong after all? If so, I was screwed.

"Hi, Dad," Tommy said. "Fancy meeting you here. And with the monk, no less."

Florio hid his surprise well.

"Hello, son. Vince." His voice was smooth. "Your timing is impeccable. Ten and I were just discussing how to deal with one's enemies."

Florio picked up a large carved stone turret from the chessboard and rolled the heavy piece between his hands. He smiled pleasantly. "Vincent, would you mind putting your foot up on this chair?"

Barsotti said, "What?"

I thought: *What?*

"Just put the sole of your shoe up on the edge of the seat, so your knee is bent like this." Florio demonstrated.

The mystified Barsotti did as he was told. Florio raised the stone chess piece above his head with both hands and lowered it sharply, like an ax, onto Barsotti's kneecap. The bone cracked audibly.

Barsotti howled and dropped to the floor, rolling in pain. Florio stood over him. Behind the mask of the gentleman patriarch was a brute.

"You dishonored my daughter," he spat. "You're lucky I didn't kill you."

Barsotti opened and closed his mouth a few times, like a gaffed fish, before he thought better of responding. Anesthetic shock must have set in, because he was able to push himself upright and hobble back to the table.

Florio composed himself. He shrugged. "How many times have I said it? Betrayal begets pain."

He motioned to me. "Now, Tenzing. Shall we conclude our business?" His turned to his son with a wintry smile. "Tenzing's prepared a report for me, though I doubt there's anything in it I don't already know."

The wooden doors slid open.

A waiter came in with a tray. Four short snifters on it, and a cut-glass decanter glowing with amber liquid.

Yes.

The waiter placed the tray on the table and left.

Tommy's voice was jovial. "I ordered up a little surprise for you, Dad. With O'Flaherty and that other deadbeat gone, I thought we should toast to our future."

Thomas Sr. opened the decanter and sniffed.

"Why, Tommy. Amaretto. How thoughtful."

He doesn't know.

Tommy filled all four glasses.

"To the future," Tommy said.

"To the future," we repeated, and tapped our glasses together.

Thomas Sr. drained his glass. I pretended to drink. Barsotti was in too much shock to do much of anything— broken kneecaps can have that effect. Tommy Jr. just watched his father. His expression was that of a hungry coyote, finally about to get his fill.

There's no such thing as enough.

Thomas Sr. held out his snifter for a refill. Tommy Jr. removed the glass from his father's hand.

"No more for you, Pops," he said.

Florio's mouth knotted tightly at the insolence.

Tommy swiftly collected the other three glasses and set them on the tray. Barsotti gimped over to the doors and slid them open. Tommy picked up the tray.

"You coming, Ten?"

"Not yet," I said.

"Fine. I'll let them know you're not to be disturbed."

Florio rose to his feet.

"Tommy!" Florio's imperious tone filled the space, brooking no disobedience.

The doors closed behind them.

Thomas Sr. wheeled on me. "Do you mind explaining what that was about?"

"That was about a prince betraying his king," I answered, and pulled out my gun.

CHAPTER 30

I trained my Wilson on Florio.

"You paid for a report," I said. "You're going to get one. Sit."

Florio sat.

I sat across from him.

"Let me run a little scenario by you," I said. "About four years ago an old man asks his son to find out why his almond trees are dying. The son finds something in the water, something bad. So he tests the aquifer on an adjacent piece of property just to be sure. A pig farm. The water there is also bad.

"This guy, let's call him Norman, knows how the government works; he knows whoever owns this contaminated land can make a lot of money. There's even a precedent, and judges love precedents. But Norman's thinking small, he's not a natural-born criminal like your son Tommy and his brother-in-law, Vince. It took them to figure out there's another 400 toxic acres to be had for the taking. A piece of Paradise, right next door."

Florio's skin was beading with sweat. "I don't know why you're telling me this," he said. He started to rise in his chair, but I waved him back down.

"You know, when we met, you told me Tommy always came crawling back to you, begging for a job. Not this time. This time he came strutting, with a five-hundred-million-dollar tiger by the tail. And that's when you took over."

"I'm not feeling very well," Florio said. "I think I need a doctor."

"Don't worry. It will get worse."

Florio let out a low groan.

"So a plan is hatched. Your plan. Tommy didn't like being elbowed to the side, mind you. Who would? But that wasn't your problem. Barsotti's pig farm was already in the family. So far, so good. And keeping Norman's father, John D, in the dark was easy. Norman could handle that, or so everyone assumed. The Children of Paradise were the real challenge. Thanks to Brother Paul, they had an iron-clad deed of ownership, each and every one of them. Equal shares. Communism, your worst nightmare, I'd imagine. What to do? How to get those people off your four hundred acres. Enter Liam O'Flaherty, con man, felon, sociopath. How did you put it? Unsavory associate."

Florio's breathing was becoming a little more labored.

"And that was the first murder, wasn't it? O'Flaherty poisoned Brother Paul and took his place. Everything was proceeding like clockwork. But when are humans ever as reliable as clocks, Thomas? John D got stubborn. Tommy got greedy. Barbara got nosy. O'Flaherty got ugly. And me? I got paid money—by you, in fact—to figure it all out."

"What is happening to me?" Florio was drenched with sweat.

"You know, it's a shame you left all the hands-on work to your minions. Your three—stooges, is it?" I said. "Otherwise you would have known not to go near Amaretto, at least Amaretto served by your son."

"Tenzing, for the love of God . . ."

"At first, I thought the poison must have been a solution of neptunium-237. But it didn't make sense, because no one in their right mind would try to handle it, much less get anyone to swallow it."

I reached into my pocket and retrieved the faded photograph of John D and his two smiling sons, surrounded by almond trees bursting with frothy pink and white blossoms.

"Amaretto. There is already that hint of bitter almond, properly processed, of course, to remove the toxin. It's genius, really. So easy to add more of what's already there, enough to ensure that the level of cyanide is fatal."

Florio was shaking his head back and forth slowly.

"By the way, you were right about Tommy. He did get greedy. He started a little side business, skimming a few thousand here and there from the company pot to lure struggling artists into thinking he could make them rich. You sowed the notion of Dead Peasant policies in him, and he decided to reap his own extra benefits, so to speak. He delivered contracts and false hope and gift baskets with bottles of poisoned liqueur tucked among the other goodies like deadly scorpions. Especially deadly to an elderly man with heart problems, a chronic smoker suffering from the flu, and a gentleman actor with laetrile, another form of cyanide, already in his system."

I slid the photograph toward him, face up.

"Bitter almonds. Such pretty pink blooms. So toxic when ingested in concentrated form, unlike the sweet variety. And normally so hard to come by, unless there is a private supply growing right next door."

I glanced at my watch.

"You know, it's too bad about that 'no such thing as enough' issue, Thomas. You could have simply bought the acreage from the cult members at the going rate, and sued the government for your millions. Shady, though not necessarily illegal. But no. That would have required spending your own cash. How much better to steal their land and benefit from their deaths? I've met some genuinely bad people. But trading forty innocent lives for a cash payout? That puts you in a class by yourself."

Florio's face was getting very rosy.

I checked my watch again.

"It's been fifteen minutes. Your symptoms should be pretty painful right about now."

"Please," he said.

I pulled a white plastic box out of my carryall.

"You'll be interested to know this antidote kit contains everything you need to get better."

"Please," Florio said again. "I'll make you rich."

"I'm a monk. You've already paid me for my work. Anything more would be, well, greedy. Don't you think?"

He winced, grabbing his stomach.

"But I didn't do anything!"

"That's the problem, Thomas. You're too clean. Too smart. There's never anything to tie you to anything else, is there? Your son and Barsotti are probably being booked right now. They're filthy. They'll go down for murder one, at least. But you don't have any chips to bargain with. And then there's the question of your intentions."

Florio's eyes darted back and forth, looking for a way out.

"You wanted to know how karma works? It's a bitch."

Florio clawed open the leather briefcase at his feet.

"In here," he gasped.

He held up a manila envelope, stamped with the official L.A. County Department of Public Works insignia. His hand shook uncontrollably, but his eyes begged me to take it. I flipped through the contents. It was Norman Murphy's neptunium-237 report. The original one.

The one that made Thomas Florio, Sr., an accessory to a whole lot of crimes.

I opened the kit and administered the ampule of amyl nitrite inhalant. Then I motored past dignified urns and columns and masterworks of art to the top of the sweeping marble staircase and called out for help in a most undignified way. In minutes ambulance attendants had strapped Florio onto a gurney, loaded him inside, and whisked him off to Cedars-Sinai, an IV of sodium nitrite and thiosulfate already binding and removing the cyanide from his veins.

Bill was waiting outside with his own report: Barsotti was cuffed and on his way to the hospital. Tommy Jr. was cuffed and on his way downtown for booking in the back of a black-and-white. And as promised, the evidence of at least one attempted murder had been served up to my partner on a tray. In this case, literally.

Bill's eyes bored into mine.

"So," he said.

"So."

"Run your phone convo with Tommy Florio by me again? You weren't making a whole lot of sense in my office."

I shrugged. "I told him that his father had hired me to check up on him, and that I was on my way to the club with proof of Tommy's shenanigans. That unless Tommy had a better idea, he was about to lose everything, because Mr. Florio had vowed that Tommy would get no more chances, and Mr. Florio struck me as a man who kept his word. That like it or not, his father still owned him. I said it would be a shame if nobody but Mr. Florio benefited from all Tommy's hard work."

"That's all you said?"

"I might have reminded Tommy how much his father enjoyed his daily dose of Amaretto."

Bill shook his head.

"You took a hell of a chance, Ten. How did you know he wouldn't just run to his father?"

I smiled.

"Call it a hunch," I said.

After Bill drove away, I stood outside the Jonathan Club a few minutes longer. The sky was a deep blue, scattered with puffy clouds. I breathed in deeply and felt the pavement firm beneath my feet.

I would have administered the antidote to Thomas Sr., either way. But this way was better. It meant a few less karmic boomerangs, for both of us.

CHAPTER 31

My house was spotless—I had spent hours going over every corner of it until it gleamed from the attention.

I poured myself a large glass of beer. I located Tank, lying in the sun on the windowsill.

"Happy Losar, Tank," I toasted. "Happy Year of the Iron Rabbit."

It was March 5th. Another new year, which meant another opportunity to reflect on things. I sipped, and I sighed with pleasure.

This morning I used my *thangka* as a focus for my meditation. I let my attention rest on the rich colors and abundant images of light and dark comprising the Eternal Circle of Life. *Samsara*. Illusion. And yet it feels so real. As I sat, I absorbed the harsh contradictions, painted on silk: compassionate deities and ignorant, but inspiring life forms, equally gripped in the talons of a ferocious Mara. Mara seems bent on their destruction, but shift the eyes a little, and it looks a lot like protection. It's not always easy to tell which is which, you know?

It's a paradox, a contradiction in terms, just like me.

I've been reflecting a lot on the concept of richness. Not Thomas Florio richness, but the richness of thoughts, flowing through the mind. Think about it: Our thoughts emerge unbidden, seemingly out of nowhere, and then they're gone. This process happens thousands of times an hour, and the abundance never stops, even when we're asleep. To know this is to be rich. Lobsang loves to point out that each thought is an exact replica of life, and to open fully to the free flow of thoughts is to open fully to life itself. Yeshe insists that the opposite is true—that meditation has the effect of quieting the flow of thoughts, enabling us to experience a still point, where all thoughts cease for a time, and true wealth lies. But really, it's both. Like I said: paradox. To be in touch simultaneously with absolute stillness and the flowing river of thoughts is the exquisite paradoxical backdrop of every Buddhist's moment-to-moment experience.

I raised my glass again.

Happy Losar, dear friends. Blessings, abundance, and good health to you both. May your lives be filled with richness. I think of you every day, and today most of all.

I moved to my deck, Tank on my lap, waiting for everyone to arrive. The evening air was cool and damp, redolent with scents released by yesterday's heavy rain.

I remembered sitting with my father in the monastery garden one afternoon, when I was eight or nine. A hawk was tracing lazy circles above us. Suddenly it dived, and reappeared with some small creature wriggling in its beak.

"Apa, why do we have to die?"

"It is a paradox, son. Life's rich pageant. Paradox is everywhere we look, because we, the ones who are looking, are living paradoxes ourselves. We are wired for bliss, but we choose to make ourselves miserable. We are capable of speaking the truth, yet we choose to spin webs of lies. We are here to learn the greatest wisdom of mankind, yet we choose to gossip and rebel."

I remember squirming. My father couldn't help but turn every question of mine into an opportunity to lecture me.

"But why do we have to die?" I asked again.

"I don't know. But I suspect we have to die, so that we may learn to live."

An approaching vehicle snapped me back to the present, to my own rich pageant of life, about to become even richer.

John D and his daughter-in-law Becky, her bump of a baby now visible, climbed out of his truck and walked up the drive. Becky carried an apple pie.

I took the pie.

"Looking better, John D," I said.

"Yeah, well, the treatment's going pretty good," he said. "I know it'll get harder soon, but they say I could get maybe three more years this way. You have any idea how long that is in grandbaby years?"

I gave him two $100 bills and told him it was compliments of his mugger. With interest.

More cars arrived—Bill and Martha's family van, two little redheads in back, strapped in their car seats and wearing matching Dodger caps. Julie followed, her car loaded up for the long drive back to Chicago. Casseroles and salads and fresh-baked bread collected in my kitchen. Deputy Sheriff Dardon and his wife pulled up with a big batch of meatless chili, and Mike and his spiky but sweet live-in Tricia carted inside a cardboard container of hot coffee and a dozen glazed crullers.

Everyone crowded onto my deck as the sun spilled red in the distance, where land and ocean met. I leaned the photograph of Norman with his brother and father, surrounded by almond blossoms, both sweet and bitter, against the potted impatiens, front and center on the table. I added his business card, the one he gave me way back when. I laid out three bowls of rice, and three homemade *torma* cakes magically conjured into being by Chef Julie. My Buddha statue was there, as was the feather and mangled bullet.

I asked Becky to light the candle.

I looked at Norman's smiling face. I felt his hope. I felt his sorrow. He had lost his hero, and his faith. He had lost the love of his mother, and the respect of his father. And then he had lost his way.

I understood.

I couldn't change the past. But I could address the present. Norman didn't have to remain alone and without friends. I dipped the hawk feather in water, sprinkled it over his smiling image, and began to chant him home.

ACKNOWLEDGMENTS

GRATITUDE FROM
GAY HENDRICKS

First, I'd like to express my deep gratitude for all the mystery writers who have inspired me throughout my reading life: John D. MacDonald, T. Jefferson Parker, Michael Connelly, Sue Grafton, Robert Ferrigno, Don Winslow, Stieg Larsson, Georges Simenon, and Leslie Charteris. At the peak of this Everest of talent, of course, is the inimitable Arthur Conan Doyle, whose life I admire and whose talents I salute for giving me 50-plus years of pleasure.

I'm very grateful to have Tinker Lindsay as a co-author. Tinker writes like an angel, laughs like a pirate, and dispenses good vibes to all who are privileged to know her. Working on this book with Tinker has been one of the great pleasures of my literary life.

Louise Hay, Reid Tracy, Patty Gift, Laura Koch, and other members of the Hay House staff are a writer's dream team. I'm very grateful for the warmth, professionalism, and enthusiasm they've gifted us.

I owe a debt of gratitude to the many Buddhists from different lineages with whom I spoke in my background research. My travels have taken me to monasteries in Tibet, India, Nepal, and Thailand, as well as to places closer to home such as Tassajara in Big Sur. I am grateful to have known the remarkable lama Kalu Rinpoche and to have been initiated by him in 1973.

Felipe Correa, executive director of the Hendricks Institute, is an ever-pleasant beacon of efficiency in my busy and multivaried life. Katie and I both give thanks regularly for his presence in our lives.

Like our hero, Ten, I am graced with a remarkable feline companion, our 16-year-old Persian princess, Lucy. Most of my writing is done to the accompaniment of Lucy's purrs; no better background music for inspiration has ever been composed.

For 32 years I've been blessed with the mate of my dreams, Kathlyn Hendricks, who is the ideal partner for a quirky writer. A passionate poet and dancer as well as nonfiction writer, Katie understands the creative process in her bones and knows how to nurture it in others. Everything I write comes out of living in the sphere of her love, and it is to her that I give my ultimate bow of gratitude.

GRATITUDE FROM
TINKER LINDSAY

First, I'd like to thank my parents, Nancy and Rod Lindsay, for proving that avid readers raise avid readers. My late mother was never without a book in her hand, and I inherited her lifelong passion for detective novels. To this day, my father continues to pass along to me his own favorites. Literally. In taped cardboard boxes with stamps.

Thanks to my beloved sister, Cammy, who has had my back since before I could crawl, and my brother, Bob, whose talent is only superseded by his generosity.

It's almost impossible to express my gratitude to my co-author Gay Hendricks. He swooped into my life like a comet and invited me to join him in a space where there's no such thing as can't, won't, or shouldn't. I thank him for giving me the opportunity to riff with unfettered abandon on his themes, for encouraging me to embrace and embellish the world of Ten, and for telling me I can do no wrong. Writing with him is a joy and an honor, not to mention a total hoot.

To my wonderful ones: Jon, Blossom, Thomas, and Dorothy; and their wonderful ones, Courtney, Brian, Rebecca, and James; and to Daisy and Addie, my hilarious and most remarkable granddaughters. Heartfelt thanks to them all for understanding my need to hole up in my cave and write, and giving me the best incentive anyone could have for stepping outside for fresh air. They are the reason any of this matters.

My gratitude to Patty Gift, Laura Koch, Sally Mason, and the entire creative and editorial team at Hay House, both for their enthusiastic support of our novel and for their brilliant, seemingly effortless ability to adapt and flow with any new idea or challenge that arises.

Thanks to Irene Webb, for saying yes to me first; to Jerome Lewis, for giving me, well, me; and to Peter Chelsom, my dear friend and co-writer—a man who makes work feel like play, understands my obsessive relationship with semicolons, and inspires me every day with his original humor, unique imagination, and loyal heart.

A special shout-out to my writers group: Monique de Varennes, Barbara Sweeney, Emilie Small, Bev Baz, Kathryn Hagen, and Pat Stiles. I am beyond grateful to these talented and amazing women for their friendship, care as readers, and inspiration as writers.

Thanks to John Burridge for introducing me to Wilson Combat Supergrades; to Arjuna Ardagh for recommending me to Gay; and to Kendra Crossen, for her meticulous attention to Tenzing's Buddhist roots.

And finally, to Cameron Keys: my best friend, my partner, and my muse. You are my magnetic field, surrounding me with love, drawing out the finest from me. You believe in me, and my writing, unconditionally. All I can say is: back at you, my love.

ABOUT THE AUTHORS

ABOUT
GAY HENDRICKS

Gay Hendricks, Ph.D., has served for more than 35 years as one of the major contributors to the fields of relationship transformation and body-mind therapies. Along with his wife, Dr. Kathlyn Hendricks, Gay is the co-author of many bestsellers, including *Conscious Loving* and *Five Wishes*. He is the author of 33 books, including *The Corporate Mystic, Conscious Living,* and *The Big Leap*. Dr. Hendricks received his Ph.D. in counseling psychology from Stanford in 1974. After a 21-year career as a professor of Counseling Psychology at the University of Colorado, he and Kathlyn founded the Hendricks Institute, which is based in Ojai, California, and offers seminars worldwide.

In recent years he has also been active in creating new forms of conscious entertainment. In 2003, along with movie producer Stephen Simon, Dr. Hendricks founded the Spiritual Cinema Circle, which distributes inspirational movies to subscribers in 70+ countries around the world (www.spiritualcinemacircle.com). He has appeared on more than 500 radio and television shows, including *The Oprah Winfrey Show,* CNN, CNBC, *48 Hours,* and others.

ABOUT
TINKER LINDSAY

Tinker Lindsay is an accomplished screenwriter, author, and conceptual editor. A member of the Writers Guild of America (WGA), Independent Writers of Southern California (IWOSC), and Women in Film (WIF), she's worked in the Hollywood entertainment industry for over three decades. Lindsay has written screenplays for major studios such as Disney and Warner Bros., collaborating with award-winning film director Peter Chelsom. Their current screenplay, *Hector and the Search for Happiness*, is in development with Egoli Tossell Film. She also co-wrote the spiritual epic *Buddha: The Inner Warrior* with acclaimed Indian director Pan Nalin, as well as the sci-fi remake of *The Crawling Eye* with Cameron Keys.

Lindsay has authored two books—*The Last Great Place* and *My Hollywood Ending*—and worked with several noted transformational authors, including Peter Russell, Arjuna Ardagh, and Dara Marks.

Lindsay graduated with high honors from Harvard University in English and American Language and Literature, where she was an editor for *The Harvard Crimson*. She studied and taught meditation for several years before moving to Los Angeles to live and work. She can usually be found writing in her home office situated directly under the Hollywood sign.

AN EXCERPT FROM . . .

THE SECOND RULE OF

TEN

Topanga Canyon, Calif.
Aug. 2, Year of the Iron Rabbit

Lama Yeshe and Lama Lobsang
Dorje Yidam Monastery
Dharamshala, India

Dear Brothers in Spirit,

I find myself reaching out to you because
my own spirit lies heavy in my chest this
evening. A few weeks ago a pair of cops
in a city just south of here answered a
call about a homeless vandal breaking into
parked cars. They arrived on the scene and
found the culprit at a bus depot nearby.
He resisted arrest. They threw him to the
ground, shocking him multiple times with
their stun guns. Backup cops arrived, mob
instinct took over, and soon six cops had
tasered and clubbed him into a coma as he
cried out for his father. . .
. . . who was at home, mere miles away,
oblivious to the unfolding catastrophe.

. . . who was, it turns out, a retired member of the police force.

Three days later, this heartbroken retired cop took his son off life-support, finishing what his brethren had started. And today's paper tells me the perpetrators are themselves under investigation by the FBI.

Multiple tragedies built on false assumptions. A homeless young man with a mental disorder, beaten to death by my other brothers, the ones in blue who carry badges. And all because they couldn't see what was actually in front of them—a suffering human being gripped by paranoia, in need of medical attention. They saw the ground-in grime and ragged filth of the chronic vagrant, and assumed "homeless" meant abandoned and disposable, like trash. Maybe even dangerous. Their preconceived prejudices stripped the victim of all humanity.

His confused brain told him these officers were monsters. They obliged by responding monstrously.

Here's the thing. As I sit here on my deck, watching the sky darken, I understand. I understand how those officers got caught up in the moment. How the flood of adrenaline swept aside reason and fellow-feeling. How the twitch of an outstretched limb could seem as threatening as a cocked trigger. I want to believe that I am incapable of that kind of delusion, but I know better. As do you, my dear Yeshe and Lobsang, who know the deceptive capabilities, the hidden mines, of the mind better than most.

Lately I've been seeing more clearly how I use my false beliefs to deceive myself. I'll notice self-critical thoughts running through my mind, labeling me as incapable, of discipline, when suddenly I'll realize it was my father who'd always labeled me lazy. Or I'll look at a beautiful woman and assume she is needy, then suddenly realize it's my mother's neediness I'm seeing. It happens in my work, too: I found a missing 16-year-old I was searching for—found her pushed against a wall by a man twice her age, and assumed she was being raped. Nothing could have been further from the truth, but my unconscious assumptions kept me from seeing reality as it was.

So, I'm making a new rule for myself—a reminder, really, of a truth I tend to forget: From now on, I'm going to be on the lookout for unconscious beliefs, the kind I hold so closely I mistake them for reality. As familiar as they are, as safe as they make me feel, too often these convictions serve as blinders. They prevent me from understanding what is actually happening in my life. I'm taking a new vow, to challenge my old, limited models of thinking. To be willing to release them. Their job may be to protect, but more often than not they mislead, and in some cases even endanger. In the split second it takes you to figure out the difference between your perception of reality and reality itself, a lot of bad things can happen. In my chosen line of work, that split second can mean the difference between living and dying.

The lost-and-found teenager, Harper Rudolph, was my latest such lesson in humility. I'm not complaining. The job paid well enough to see me through several

lunar months, and I can now report that
I am more than holding my own as a private
investigator. I'm grateful for that. And
I guess you could say I closed the case
successfully, though Harper didn't see it
that way. She may have been missing in her
father's eyes, but the last thing she wanted
was to be found.

   After maybe three minutes of face time
with Marv Rudolph, I felt like heading for
the hills myself.

   But that's another story for another
day. The air grows cool and moist against
my skin. An eyelash of moon has just
materialized, low on the horizon. Can you
see it as well? I like to think so.

   I miss you, my friends, even as I hold
you close in my heart. Not a limiting
assumption. Reality.

90

   Ten

CHAPTER 1

I flipped the envelope over, rechecking the address in Dharamshala, making sure I had it right. But of course I did. How many letters, over how many weeks and months and years, had I mailed to my friends in just this way?

The original postmark was still there, stamped and dated months earlier. Yeshe's and Lobsang's names were x–ed out. *Return to sender!* blared across the envelope in black ink, with a slash of arrow pointing to my Topanga Canyon address.

I recognized the handwriting. I had grown up with it, the jagged letters gouged into small index cards summoning me to the monastery headquarters once or twice a week, so that my father, or should I say my father the Senior Abbot, could chastise me for yet another infraction. His stiff, angry scrawl was permanently etched in my brain. I would know it anywhere.

I refolded the letter and slipped it back inside its paper pocket. A low sigh escaped, originating deep in my chest. Now that I knew Yeshe and Lobsang hadn't received my latest letter, I felt a little lonelier than before. Nothing had changed, yet everything felt different. The sweet feeling of clarity I had been savoring, the one that often lingers after a deep afternoon meditation, was clouded now by a sense of loss.

I allowed it in.

In the distance, the ocean was quiet and majestic, the lights of distant boats just beginning to twinkle in the fading dusk. I took a sip of green tea. It had cooled in its cup as I sifted through my mail, turning tepid as I mulled over this unexpectedly returned letter. I cast my mind back.

Marvin Rudolph and his daughter Harper. What a pair.

I felt my lips purse with taut disapproval, and I forced myself to relax into a half-smile. Whenever my mouth tightens in judgment like that, I look a lot like my father. That tells me I'm thinking like him, too.

I tried to recall the case, which had turned equally tepid in my mind after all this time. I closed my eyes and opened my other senses. Sometimes I have to let them do the remembering for me.

An acrid scent filled my nostrils.

Bad breath and potholes, that's how it started. . . .

"Find her. She's just a kid." Marvin Rudolph leaned close, wheezing from the effort of walking the ten yards from his car to my living room. I wanted to recoil from the fetid combination of sushi and cigar smoke. My feline housemate, Tank, darted under the couch, probably for the same reason.

"Don't you mean, find her again?"

"Whatever."

Marv had already filled me in on his elusive daughter Harper—at 16, a newly converted connoisseur of the seedy and the derelict. Six months earlier she'd made her first escape, bolting the family mansion to savor the dark side, in this case Adams Boulevard, near Skid Row. He'd discovered his daughter hunkered in a downtown loft with a drug dealer named Bronco Portreras.

Marv handed over a photograph. I studied it. Harper must have gotten her looks from her mother. Dark wavy hair framed a heart-shaped face dominated by huge gray eyes.

"How did you know where to find her?"

Marv settled back in his chair. His belly billowed over his jeans, encased in a black linen shirt one size too small.

"Good story. We were open-casting for a dope dealer when in saunters Portreras. Think early Banderas meets Robert Pattinson, plus tats, minus the fangs."

I must have looked as baffled as I felt.

"Hot," he clarified. "I'm just sayin'. He nailed the reading, too. Anyway, the insurance company balked, because it turns out it wasn't an act. He really was dealing dope. Everybody wants to be a star, know what I mean? A week later, when Harper didn't come home from school, I logged on to her Facebook page. Bingo. She'd put a link to Bronco's audition on her wall, posted it on YouTube, too. He'd already gotten like twenty thousand hits. . . ." Marv's voice grew wistful, probably envisioning yet another gilded statuette that got away.

"So you tracked her down?" I prompted. It was almost ten o'clock at night. Way past Tank's bedtime.

"Yeah. He'd given his contact information to the casting agent. A crack dealer, leaving his digits on file. Dumber than a stick, right? I found Harper and him in his loft downtown, high as kites on weed, coke, maybe a little E. I threw a coupla grand at Bronco to shut him up, dragged her sorry ass home, and cut off her allowance until further notice."

It seemed to me that Marv was better equipped to deal with his daughter than I was, and I told him so.

"Not anymore," he said. "She's blocked me. Fuckin' privacy settings. My wife and I can't get on her page. And she won't answer her phone."

Marv's mouth twisted, and for a flash I saw the ruthless producer whose reputation for intimidation, especially when crossed, was legendary, even in an industry known for bullies. Then it was gone. His face sagged. With his grizzled day-old beard and loose jowls, he looked like a disappointed mastiff.

"Please," he said. "She needs to come home."

"Why not go to the cops?"

"Are you on crack? This whole thing would go viral before the cops even left the building."

I had one last question.

"How did you get my name?"

"I talked to one of your buddies down at police headquarters."

I immediately thought of my ex-partner, Bill. He was always worrying about my finances.

"Bill Bohannon?"

"Who? Nah," Marv said. "The Captain. Told him I needed a private detective, someone discreet. He told me you're more than discreet. You're some kind of Buddhist monk. Tight with the Dalai Lama and all. That right?"

"Something like that," I said.

"So, you into poverty, then?" Marv's expression grew shrewd.

"Five grand a day, three day minimum," I said. "Plus expenses."

He wrote me a check then and there. Three days, prepaid.

With that kind of discretionary income, you'd think he could afford mouthwash.

Whump! Tank—all 18 Persian pounds of him—thudded onto my lap, startling me out of my reverie. He draped his chunky body across my lap. I scratched under his chin, and he made a deep, gentle *prrrttt* sound. He tilted his head and eyed me, lids half closed, as if to say, "Don't let me stop you."

"Where was I?" I asked Tank. He flicked his tail like a whip.

"Right. Potholes."

Devouring contraband mysteries every night, hiding under the covers of my monastic pallet in Dharamshala, I tended to romanticize the life of a detective. I'd open Raymond Chandler, read "Down these mean streets a man must go," and picture dark, smoky alleys with music drifting out of open windows, and beautiful women leaning in doorways, their long legs toned, their eyes glinting at me. I say "me," but in my mind I wasn't a skinny Tibetan teenager living in a Buddhist monastery, with a shaved head, maroon robe, and sandals. I wasn't Lama Tenzing Norbu. In this fantasy version of me, I lived in a big city. I solved crimes. I was armed, and I was dangerously good at what I did. Fedoras were involved, as well as a sexy car and sexier gun. My street handle was "Ten."

A lot like my current life, come to think of it, though I don't own a fedora.

Yet.

Anyway, the mean streets in my imagination didn't have potholes the size of garbage cans threatening to break my Toyota's axle and hijack one of my kidneys, like the ones en route to finding Harper Rudolph that night.

After Marv left, my first and only call had been to Mike Koenigs. It was late, close to midnight, so he'd be having breakfast right about then. Mike is my personal "information security contractor"—according to Mike the word "hacker" is now considered passé, if not slightly insulting. I helped him out some years back, keeping him out of federal prison for dabbling with someone else's data. In return, he was my go-to man for digital matters, big and small.

"Can you get past Facebook blockades?" I asked.

"Boss, where's the love? Where's the respect?" he replied. "Name?"

I gave him Harper's name.

Pause.

"Okay, I'm on."

I waited.

"Hunh. She's posting as we speak. Whoa. Some serious partying pictures." Mike let out a long, low whistle. "Is that Keith Connor?"

"Keith who?"

"Ten, even you must have heard of the guy. Ex-rocker-turned-actor? Bad-boy heartthrob? Daily fodder for TMZ?"

Oh.

"She says, and I quote, 'Keith's place is off the hook.'"

I heard light tapping.

"Yeah, and guess what? He's about to start work on a film produced by Harper's daddy, Marvin. Seven-digit salary. No wonder he's gigging it up."

Half the time I have no idea what Mike is actually saying.

"Can you give me his address?"

"Give me a mo'. Celebrity cribs are tricky."

In Mike-time, a mo' usually equals two breaths in and out. Sure enough . . .

"Okay, here it is. Hartley Crest. One-five-five-two. Beverly Hills. I'm also sending you a link to Keith's IMDB page."

In another moment, my iPhone screen was filled with a Caucasian male, late 20s, light brown hair, hazel eyes, and a reddish sexy demi-beard that looked like he'd "forgotten" to shave for exactly the right number of days. He was gazing to his left, scowling slightly. He may have been going for a bad-boy heartthrob effect, but to me he just looked silly.

I sent Marv a text: LOCATED HARPER AT PARTY IN BEVERLY HILLS. ON MY WAY THERE. STAY PUT.

I grabbed my Wilson Supergrade from the gun safe in my closet and headed out.

First decision: which set of wheels to use? I quickly settled on my faithful workhorse, the Toyota-that-would-not-die, but not without regret. I hated leaving my real car, the thoroughbred, stabled at home, but a bright yellow '65 Shelby Mustang lends itself to surveillance about as well as a maroon monk's robe would.

There wasn't much traffic at that hour. Soon I was lurching along Wilshire Boulevard, traversing my way into Beverly Hills. I would be at Keith's soon, if the drive didn't put me in traction first.

I know. Beverly Hills and cracked pavements don't seem to mix. And in fact, if you take Sunset Boulevard, the minute you enter Beverly Hills proper, the pavement magically loses its pockmarks as a thick profusion of multicolored flowers suddenly bursts into bloom along the medians. Like an A-list actress, that area of Beverly Hills wouldn't be caught dead in public without makeup and blond streaks. But drop south of there and it's one big bad hair and acne day.

According to the latest city infrastructure assessment, there are over half a million unfilled potholes in Los Angeles at any given time, and maybe a dozen patch trucks to deal with them. Once a year the Mayor announces Operation Pothole, and maintenance crews fan out across the city to patch and plug. They usually manage to repair 30,000 holes over a single weekend. That's 30,000 down, 470,000 to go. It's like doing battle with a wrathful Tibetan deity, the kind with never-ending multiple arms waving thunderbolts and skulls. When I was still a rookie, on traffic detail, one jaded city official put it this way: "Potholes, like diamonds, are forever, son. So you tell me, how do you stop forever?"

Welcome to my brain when I'm driving around, dodging troughs, working a case.

I checked the map on my phone, zig-zagging my way north and west, and eventually turning onto the bumpy byway known as Hartley Crest, set in the wooded hills off Benedict Canyon, where the houses are in the $4 million range. As my beater car and I labored up the steep, winding street, a dim drizzle of wet fog slimed my windshield. The Toyota had a bum wiper on the driver's side, which I kept forgetting to replace.

I started passing high-end coupes and SUVs parked nose-to-tail along the narrow road. Maybe I should have taken the Shelby after all. I squeezed into a space between a dark blue Mercedes and a silver Infiniti. I considered grabbing the .38 out of the locked glove compartment, just in case, but thought better of it. Guns and teenagers don't mix. I climbed out of my car and took a moment to collect myself.

A bottom-heavy hip-hop beat shook the night. *Boom Boom THUD, Boom Boom THUD, Boom Boom THUD.* Raucous laughter. A girl's high-pitched bray. I had found the party.

I passed between a pair of tall wrought iron security gates, wide open and inviting any and all to enter, and picked my way up a driveway paved with antique cobble stones. Sherlock would have felt right at home. The house was a large two-story Mediterranean, stucco and red tile, with a second story turret. It looked like it had been built in the '20s, and renovated this morning.

First things first. I tested the door to the attached garage. Unlocked. I peeked in. I was curious what an ex-rocker-turned-actor drove. I saw a gleaming black sedan I couldn't immediately identify. I slipped inside. I had to take a look. Well, well, well. A Maybach 57 S. Maybe the most expensive car in the world. You don't see that every day. I gave its flawless German features a respectful bow and continued on to the heavy, ornately carved front door.

The sound inside was deafening. I changed course— no one in the middle of that was about to hear the ring of a doorbell. I moved around to the manicured pool area in the back. Light spilled out of a large kitchen window. I took a closer look.

A young couple was engaged in a prolonged mouth-to-mouth exchange of oxygen and saliva. He had her pinned against a marble kitchen island, and she had her legs gripped around his waist like a monkey. Neither one paid me any attention as I slid open a glass door and slipped inside. I passed a gleaming row of never-been-touched, top-of-the-line appliances, and moved into a large, arched entryway. To my right, a gigantic flat screen television loomed over an oak-paneled den that was bigger than my house. Several young people, glassy eyed and still, were fixated by the flickering images on the screen. To my left was a step-down living room, where more kids sprawled on leather chairs and sofas, passing around an elaborate bong. If good looks were illegal, they'd all be locked up. I caught the eye of one young temptress and she gave me a glazed once-over, followed by a dismissive smirk. I was barely 30, but already a fossilized life form to her, a curious leftover from the late Paleolithic. Ouch.

I scanned all the faces. No Harper. No Keith, for that matter. I mentally stepped into his shoes. If I were a rising hot actor about to hook up with my producer's daughter, I'd want to do my hooking up in private. In the master bedroom, for example.

I bounded up the curved and carpeted marble staircase and was faced with three doors. Two of them were ajar. I headed for the closed double doors at the end of the hallway. I pressed my ear to the wood. Animated voices, one low, one high. Arguing? I cracked the doors open and spotted a muscular, naked man groping at a slight young woman, tearing her clothes off as she gasped and cried out. My mind screamed, "Two-six-one! Two-six-one in progress! Sexual assault!"

Adrenaline coursing, I threw open the doors and flung myself across the room. I peeled off the brute—Keith—and tossed him to the floor.

I turned to the victim—Harper—expecting to see relief and gratitude.

With a high-pitched scream, Harper launched herself at me, arms flailing. I had to hold her wrists aloft to prevent her from gouging out my eyes.

"Who are you? What do you think you are doing," Harper shrieked. "I was about to fuck Keith Connor! KEITH CONNOR! Are you COMPLETELY INSANE?!"

I moved to a window seat, well out of reach of Harper's talons. Keith watched me from the floor with a kind of stoned curiosity. He was stark naked, and seemingly too high, or uninhibited, to care. I turned my attention to Harper.

"My name is Tenzing Norbu. I'm a private investigator," I told her. "Your father hired me to find you and bring you home."

"I hate you," she said.

"Dude," Keith's voice piped up. "For real? Like Charlie Chan?"

I met Keith's reddened eyes. "For real. Dude. And you should be ashamed of yourself," I added. "She's sixteen."

His eyelids drooped. His facial expressions flickered as several fuzzy concepts formed their way into an unpleasant pattern:

Marv.

Movie.

Underage Daughter.

Detective.

He sat up.

"Shit, man," he said. "You really know how to mess with a guy's buzz."

Irritation made the back of my neck itch. *Entitled jerk.* I glared at him, daring him to make a move.

Keith remained unfazed. He looked at me with interest. "So, what, you're like Chan? Chinese or something?"

"Tibetan," I snapped.

"Awesome. Yaks, right? Some guy asked me to sponsor one last year. So, tell me, what's it like in the Land of Snows?"

"I wouldn't know," I replied icily. "I was raised in a monastery in India." *Moron.*

He blinked in confusion.

I opened my mouth to continue. Then I closed it again. There was no point giving him a history lesson about China's brutal takeover of Tibet. One: the systematic destruction of Tibetans' culture, and the exile of thousands of monks and nuns, happened more than 30 years before I was born. And two: China's war with Tibet was not to blame for my current state of mind.

Simply put, something about this guy was getting me way too riled up. I used my intuition like a metal detector . . . and found the cause of my unease.

Right. I was jealous. Keith Connor might be much closer to my age than Harper's, but young lovelies were lining up for the privilege of throwing themselves at him. And not at me.

Harper jumped in. "Hey, I've got an idea. How about if we just pay you some money and you go away?"

"Babe, he's not going to do that. He works for your dad, okay?" Keith's voice was patient.

He stood up, closed the doors, and scooped a rumpled pair of gray cashmere sweatpants from the floor. As he stepped into them, I snuck a closer peek at Harper. Her minuscule panties and featherweight tank top left little—no, make that nothing—to the imagination. With her slim hips and small, firm breasts, she was beautiful, in a waifish orphan kind of way. My taste in women tends toward the voluptuous, not to mention legally aged, but there was no denying it. The girl was hot.

I'm an ex-monk. I never said I was a saint.

I quickly turned my attention back to Keith. He gave me a half-wink, as if to say, "See what I have to deal with?"

"So, detective," he drawled, "what's Marv paying you, anyway?"

I saw no reason to stonewall him. "I get five grand a day for jobs like this, three-day minimum."

His eyes widened, as if he was impressed. I guess he momentarily forgot his own day rate. He gave me a friendly nod. He'd decided to have a little chat, man to man.

"Okay, so now, let me see if I've got this straight. You're pretty much obligated to go back to Marv and tell him you found Harper here, and me about to bone her, right?"

"Pretty much," I said.

In actual fact, I wasn't sure about getting into the details. Fathers like Marv with sexually precocious daughters like Harper have enough to worry about. The fact that Keith was on Marv's payroll further complicated things. I wasn't exactly sure what my next move needed to be.

"Dude," Keith said, "I've got twenty thousand in cash in the top drawer of my dresser. I'll hire you for four more days to forget all about this, and you can refund Marv's money. Or you can keep his money, and take my twenty as a little bonus. I don't care. I just don't want to fuck up the movie. I don't want any bad vibes between me and Marvin."

He must have remembered his day rate after all.

Before I could respond, loud bellows erupted down in the foyer. Heavy footsteps thudded up the stairs.

The double doors burst open for the second time, and there stood all three hundred quivering pounds of Marv Rudolph, cigar in hand, face clotted with rage.

As he swayed in the doorway, I was fascinated to see how wrath transformed him. His left eyelid twitched, and a vein on his forehead swelled into a caterpillar of pulsing anger. Hot fury rippled from him, like poisonous waves. Behind me, Harper whimpered.

Very unskillful. I countered with a few deep breaths. One. Two.

Before I could get to three, the room exploded. Marv, screeching like a wounded pig, broke for Keith, who desperately tried to scoot backward. Harper threw herself between her father and Keith. In the resulting collision, she and Marv tumbled to the floor. Keith leapt nimbly over them and trotted out of the bedroom, holding his sweatpants up with one hand.

I stepped outside after him. He was at the stairs when Marv hurtled past me and made a diving tackle. No contest. Now Harper was screaming "DADDY DADDY DADDY" at the top of her lungs as Daddy and Keith bumped and slid down the stairs locked in a mutual choke hold. Finally they rolled to a halt on the landing. Both collapsed onto their backs.

"Fuck," said Keith.

Marv was too winded to do much more than groan

I was feeling pretty calm, calmer than they were, anyway. I took a seat on the bottom step and waited for Marvin's panting to subside. Time for a little family mediation.

"You shouldn't be here," I told Marv, "but now that you are, you need to cool it. You're going to hurt somebody, and the somebody I'm worried about is you."

Marvin twisted his stubbled face toward me, then glanced away. "I can take care of myself," he muttered.

Keith sat up, wincing.

"Does this mean I'm fired?" he asked Marv. I found the question absurd. Of course he was fired. Marv mulled it over, longer than I would have.

"You do her?" Marv finally said.

"No!" Keith answered. "Swear to God, no. Ask the monk."

Marv grunted. Keith's eyes entreated. Some wordless understanding passed between the film producer and his lead actor. Then:

"Thanks, man," Keith said. "I won't let you down."

Marv grunted again.

When it comes to the movie business, I know nothing.

I surveyed the scene: Marvin still flat on his back like a concrete slab, Keith clutching his ribs. A sullen, sniffling Harper, her cheeks striped with mascara, leaned against the banister, seemingly unconcerned with her father's well-being, or with the fact that she was the half-naked cause of all of this.

Weariness fell over me like a heavy blanket. I wanted to go home. The sooner I took charge, the sooner I could leave. I stood up.

"Harper, go get dressed, please, then come right back."

She flinched at my sharp tone.

As she started up the stairs, she shot me a look I couldn't quite read—half-resigned, half-pleading.

"Marv, take Harper home and put her to bed. Then get some sleep yourself." Marv grunted and pushed himself up to a sitting position.

"Keith, go into the kitchen and make yourself a cup of hot beverage, if you know how. Sip it, and count your blessings." He shuffled into the kitchen, the too-long legs of his sweats dragging behind like flippers.

"How did you figure out Harper was here?" I asked Marv.

"Two plus two equals Keith," Marv said. "She's a starfucker, just like everyone else in this town."

I was sorry I'd asked.

I marshaled the remaining revelers into the foyer. They were scattered throughout the downstairs like so many discarded empties.

"Party's over," I said. "And if I see one word of this on the Internet, I will not only track you down and have you arrested, I will serve your name to Marv Rudolph on a platter. And you don't want Marv Rudolph as an enemy."

They hustled out the door.

That was worth at least $5,000 in P.R. repair and maintenance right there. Operation Pothole, at your service.

It took me a few more minutes to shepherd the Rudolphs into Marv's smoky gray Lexus, parked askew in the driveway. Touching. He drove an LS Hybrid. For over $100,000 he could be comfortable, as well as politically correct.

Father and daughter drove off together in stony silence. I went back inside for one last sweep. Everyone but Keith was gone. The house felt very hollow.

"Hey," Keith called from the kitchen. "Want a cup of Darjeeling?"

"I'm good," I said. He re-joined me with his steaming mug.

With a sheepish smile, Keith offered, "I still want to pay you."

"What for?"

"I owe you, man."

I thought it over for one, maybe two seconds. "Send it to the Tibet Foundation," I said. "Twenty grand sponsors a lot of yaks."

My cell phone vibrated in my pocket, buzzing me back to the present. Tank leapt off my lap. I rotated my neck and shoulders. I was a little stunned at the almost total recall I had just experienced, especially after so much time had passed since I closed the case.

I grabbed my phone and glanced at the screen.

"Hello, Detective," I said.

"Hey, Ten. How goes it?"

"It goes, Bill. It goes. I'm just out here on the deck, enjoying a spectacular sunset."

"Rub it in."

Bill Bohannon, LAPD Detective III, Robbery/Homicide, is my former partner and one of my oldest friends in

Los Angeles. He and I have weathered a lot of weirdness together, including the ultimate male-bonding experience: shooting back at thugs who were trying to kill us. He'd recently moved to a desk job. Me? I'd just moved on.

"We're working a homicide, Ten. Messy one. Came in late last night. Some big Hollywood producer."

My skin began to tingle.

"The Captain thought I should give you a call."

Of course he did.

"The victim is a guy by the name of Rudolph. Marvin Rudolph."

Of course he is.

We hope you enjoyed this Hay House Visions book. If you'd like to receive our online catalog featuring additional information on Hay House books and products, or if you'd like to find out more about the Hay Foundation, please contact:

VISIONS

Hay House, Inc., P.O. Box 5100, Carlsbad, CA 92018-5100
(760) 431-7695 or (800) 654-5126
(760) 431-6948 (fax) or (800) 650-5115 (fax)
www.hayhouse.com® • **www.hayfoundation.org**

Published and distributed in Australia by: Hay House Australia Pty. Ltd., 18/36 Ralph St., Alexandria NSW 2015 • *Phone:* 612-9669-4299 *Fax:* 612-9669-4144 • www.hayhouse.com.au

Published and distributed in the United Kingdom by: Hay House UK, Ltd., 292B Kensal Rd., London W10 5BE *Phone:* 44-20-8962-1230 • *Fax:* 44-20-8962-1239 www.hayhouse.co.uk

Published and distributed in the Republic of South Africa by: Hay House SA (Pty), Ltd., P.O. Box 990, Witkoppen 2068 *Phone/Fax:* 27-11-467-8904 • www.hayhouse.co.za

Published in India by: Hay House Publishers India, Muskaan Complex, Plot No. 3, B-2, Vasant Kunj, New Delhi 110 070 *Phone:* 91-11-4176-1620 • *Fax:* 91-11-4176-1630 www.hayhouse.co.in

Distributed in Canada by: Raincoast, 9050 Shaughnessy St., Vancouver, B.C. V6P 6E5 • *Phone:* (604) 323-7100 *Fax:* (604) 323-2600 • www.raincoast.com

Take Your Soul on a Vacation

Visit **www.HealYourLife.com®** to regroup, recharge, and reconnect with your own magnificence. Featuring blogs, mind-body-spirit news, and life-changing wisdom from Louise Hay and friends.

Visit **www.HealYourLife.com** today!